### The pri

*I'm getting good at bli*
*giving me the practice.* S
slit, jerked quickly bac
through it. *Good eyes,*
beam melted gouges in the ceiling, brought down spatters of melted stone which were too far back to touch
her. She shut her eyes, felt about for him, lifted the
stunner and touched the sensor. The beam dancing up
and down the slit blinked out and the lifefire dimmed,
so she knew she'd got another. *Trouble is, there's too
many of them....*

She heard the pellet gun from the room on the
other side of the tower, the sound coming oddly doubled through the window and the room's open door.
For a moment she wished she could split in three.
Getting inside here had saved them for the moment,
but they were two defenders facing an attacking force
of at least twenty. She thought about the price the
Chav spy had put on her head and fought down a
surge of anger that blanked out the mindtouch for
a moment.

She knelt with eyes closed, brow pressed against the
cold stone, calming herself, transmuting the anger into
resolve. It wasn't just the spy, he was only a tool, it
was the Chave sitting in their enclave across the sea
decreeing her death, stealing the last few years left to
her. For an instant the thought amused her, after
twenty thousand, getting so het up about a hundred
or so. Then she sobered. Well, it was the reason she'd
begged Aleytys to find her a body. Now that her ending was always before her, the days, even the hours,
were jewels beyond price. Brighter and more glowing.
Or they were supposed to be. She considered this moment, sighed. "I'm only alive when I'm about to be
dead. Gods, what a ... Digby, it looks like you've got
yourself an agent. If I live through this."

# FIRE IN THE SKY

## THE SHADOWSONG TRILOGY #1

## Jo Clayton

**DAW BOOKS, INC.**

DONALD A. WOLLHEIM, FOUNDER

375 Hudson Street, New York, NY 10014

ELIZABETH R. WOLLHEIM
SHEILA E. GILBERT
PUBLISHERS

First Printing, May 1995
1  2  3  4  5  6  7  8  9

DAW TRADEMARK REGISTERED
U.S. PAT. OFF. AND FOREIGN COUNTRIES
—MARCA REGISTRADA
HECHO EN U.S.A.

PRINTED IN THE U.S.A.

# FIRE IN THE SKY

# 1. Off to See the Wizard

Shadith rubbed herself dry, then dropped the towel and inspected herself in the bathroom mirror. It wasn't a child's body any longer. The breasts had grown large enough to yield to gravity's pull, the muscles were more defined, though that probably came as much from her fight training as from maturation. She was even a little taller, having grown an inch and a half in the past two years. Her face was thinner, the hawk etched on her cheek distorted by the change. She leaned closer to the mirror, turned her head, and laughed because the line drawing had acquired a bad-tempered sneer she hadn't noticed before.

She'd cut her hair into a cap that fit close to her head and indulged in extravagant earrings to please the taste she'd discovered in herself for strong colors and wild designs, a reaction to the drab shipsuits she'd spent so much of her lives wearing, whether it was her body or another's.

She left the bathroom and dressed slowly, thinking about Aslan's dinner invitation. More than dinner involved, she was sure enough of that to speculate about the offer she thought was coming. She'd enjoyed the past two years here, she was fond of her teachers, Quale had dropped by a time or two to pay her grinning compliments before he went off with Aslan, and she was gaining respect for her compositions as well as her performances. This was a very pleasant life, but. . . . *Always that but,* she thought. The last several months she'd found herself getting restless, as if this peaceful existence were a waste of a precious and limited resource—the hours of her mortal life.

It wasn't that she needed more meaning in her life.

Breathing. Moving. The various modes of sensuality. Those were all the meaning she needed.

What she wanted was passion. She felt dimmed, cool. Even music had stopped reaching deep.

She thrust her feet into soft black slippers, smoothed the silky black dress over her hips, spun in a circle so the long skirt would bell out from her ankles. "While the body prowls howls growls, the soul revels and bedevils," she sang.

Dizzy, she wheeled to a stop, laughed, then danced to the dressing table and chose earrings that were a complex dangle of diamond-shaped silver pieces attached to fine silver chains of various lengths. She ran a comb through the cap of tiny curls and smiled at her image in the mirror. "You can't wait, can you. You'd leave tonight if you could."

It was one of Citystate Rhapsody's more splendid spring nights, the twilight lingering longer than usual, the air cool and soft against the skin. University's single moon was a hairline crescent passing through iceclouds flung like horsetails across its path as it neared zenith. She stood a moment outside the housing unit, thinking she might walk a while, then sighed and went to push the button that summoned a chainchair. The streets after dark in most of the Citystates of University were not for the fainthearted or those who wanted to keep appointments in reasonably clean and unmussed clothing.

Shadith stalked into Nik t' Pharo's Fishhouse swearing under her breath; she stopped just inside the door and tried to push the post of one of her earrings back in the bloodied hole.

Aslan came from the alcove where she'd been waiting. "Let me do that. You have the pinchclip?"

"Here." Shadith clicked her tongue at the smears on her hands. "I'll need a wash and a terminal. I'd better get my report in before the medic's."

Aslan snapped the clip onto the post of the earring, stepped back. "That should do it. What happened?"

"Scholars' brats out on a tear, drunk and high, thought they were going to play some games with me."

"Right. Let's go get you cleaned up."

Aslan looked up from the menu as Shadith reached the table. "Get through?"

"I go under the Verifier tomorrow. Assault complaint." Shadith pulled out a chair, threw herself into it, her dark eyes sparking with anger. "Louseridden little stinkards said I jumped them. Seems I broke a couple arms, cracked some ribs, and took out a spleen. Didn't do anything to their brains because they don't have any. Want to bet the complaint is pulled soon as someone with sense shows up?"

"Not me, Shadow. Still, when Scholars are involved, it can get tricky. Looks like a year or so offworld might be a good idea. Let things cool down."

Shadith leaned forward. "What's up?"

"Later. Let's order first. Anything special you want to drink? I'm on expenses." Aslan grinned. "Recruiting."

With a sigh of pleasant repletion, Aslan moved her plate aside and drew the glass of pale green wine in front of her. "Nik never fails. I make Quale bring me here at least once each of his visits. It's the only way I can afford it even with Voting Stock."

Shadith smiled; her enjoyment of the evening had returned with the food and the company. "Recruiting. For what, Lan?"

"There's a project I've been offered. If you'll do it, Shadow, I want you with me."

"Why me?"

"Let's say it's a mix of a few things. What I know about you. What my mother told me. Quale. Rumor. Scholar Burya Moy from the Music School who's drooling over something you did for him." Aslan lifted her fork and tapped it against her plate, drawing a musical chime from the fine porcelain. "The Yaraka Rep said music is important to the Béluchar. Especially harp music." She tapped the plate twice more. "And there's another thing. I've a feeling this business could turn awkward. Which I'll admit may just be leftover paranoia from what happened on Styernna. On the other hand, it could be real. Whatever, you're a lot better than I am at dancing round traps in strange places." She looked at the fork, set it down. "I am scared of going out again, Shadow. But I know if I don't. . . ." She wrinkled her longish nose. "I want backup."

Shadith ran her finger round the rim of her glass. "I don't work cheap, Lan." *That's a laugh, if she knew . . . ah gods, just the thought of getting away from here has set my feet to itching.*

"Don't have to. The funding's sweet." Aslan smiled, tilted the bottle over her glass, refilling it and then Shadith's. "Sweet as evenbriar wine. A thousand Helvetian gelders and a Voting Share of University Stock."

"It'll do." Shadith sipped at the wine, set her glass down. "So tell me about it."

"Duncan Shears will be managing the project."

"Wasn't he the manager when. . . ?"

"Yes. No fault of his what happened. With the local Powers running the frame, wasn't much he could do but get the rest of the team off planet and the word back here about what was happening." The green wine shivered as her hand shook. She set the glass down with finicking care. "I don't think I've ever been closer to dead."

"I've been dead. I don't recommend it."

Aslan's mouth twitched, but it wasn't much of a smile and soon gone as the memory of the fake trial on Styernna and her year as a slave deepened the lines in her face.

Finally, with an impatient tssah!, she lifted the glass, drained it, set it down. "Seriously, Shadow, no pressure. It's up to you if you want to go or not, but University wouldn't make a bad base for you. And there's that Voting Share. That's one of the concessions I got from the Governors. Yaraka must be making a very nice contribution to the Fund."

"That's the sweet. What's the bitter?"

"Lecture time. I'll try to keep it short. Any questions, break in. Don't worry about detail, though; I've got the set of flakes that the Yaraka Rep left with Tamarralda. Ah! She's Xenoeth's Chair this cycle. Since you're Music, you wouldn't know that. I'll send them round in the morning. Hm. Nik does a mocha that's wonderful," she sighed, "if you don't need to sleep much. Like me. I've a double dozen reports I have to finish before I can even think of leaving. Want some?"

"Reports?"

"Mocha, idiot."

"Why not."

After the waiter left, Aslan started talking, her eyes vague, her hands busy preparing the mocha. "The Callidara Pseudo-Cluster. Busy place. Round a thousand systems less than a light-year apart, two hundred of them inhabited, mostly colonized from other worlds. You might remember something about it, Shadow. That's where you and the Dyslaera flattened that bunch of Omphalites. Up until last year everyone thought that only ten of the systems had indigenes."

"Up till last year?" Shadith dropped a dollop of whipped cream into the rich chocolaty kava, swirled a spoon through it, watching the white lines turn ivory then pale brown. "What happened last year?" She scooped up a spoonful, rolled it on her tongue, smiled with pleasure.

"A little rat caught his tail in a trap. Good, isn't it. I love Nik's mocha. As the Yaraka Rep told it, a Lommertoerken smuggler called Cassecul found himself in difficulties both financial and criminal. The Rep was a handsome twerp. Nice fur and a mouthful of major words." She wiped whipped cream from her upper lip. "Our hero scratched about for something to buy himself a bolt-hole and came up with the location of an unlisted world. Béluchad. The local name.

"In the Callidara? I do remember the place. So much traffic round there the insplit shakes with it."

"Even the Callidara's got places nobody looks at. This one was in the upper right quadrant, tucked away in a nest of multiple stars some of which do have planets, but they're basically sterile rocks, the orbits are eccentric and the radiation's fairly lethal, so the usual scouts didn't bother nosing about there."

"Yesss, teacher."

"Snip. If you were in my class, I'd smudge your record. So listen. Up till Cassecul's hm indiscretion, maybe half a dozen free traders and a handful of smugglers worked Béluchad. Knowing Quale, you'll have a fair idea how much they weren't talking about the place."

"What's there for a smuggler to fool with?"

"Don't know. I expect it's one of the things we'll find out when we get there. Now comes the kicker. He sold it twice, our Cassecul. First to Yaraka Pharmaceuticals, then to Chandava Minerals, guaranteed exclusive each time."

"Enterprising, maybe. Stupid, definitely."

Aslan nodded. "From what the Rep said, he had to

12

duck and run real fast, with Chave, Yaraks, free traders and smugglers all out for a piece of his hide."

Finger following the brown lines burned into her cheek, Shadith frowned. "You said Yaraka Rep. Yaraka's financing this?"

"Yes."

"Lan. . . ."

"I'm not happy about that, but I can live with it. Shadow, even if you set aside what happened the last time I went out, it wasn't easy for me to decide to do this, but somebody is going to exploit that world; the word is out and it can't be erased no matter what we may wish. Lesser of two evils is the best description of the choice I had."

"Convince me."

"Right. According to the data I pulled from the files, the Yaraka have a history of co-opting and corrupting the locals rather than making them slaves or simply wiping them out. In other words, there's something left when they get through with a place."

"And the Chave?"

"Not so nice. They're Minerals, Shadow. They use satellite mapping to locate likely areas, their mines are automated, locals just get in the way. And Chandava is a closed society. They're from Cousin stock. From is the right word. Long way from. Stratified, custom-ridden, xenophobic. Outsiders are considered the moral equivalent of trained beasts, even other Cousins. They don't recognize the relationship as 'twere. You can see where that would lead."

Shadith nodded.

"At the moment, an advance force of Yaraks and another of Chave are hunkered down on separate continents, while the homeworld Reps sit on Helvetia and press their claims, snarling and threatening and each trying to get the other to back off."

The cold mocha was bitter on Shadith's tongue, so

she didn't finish it. "How much of a war did your Rep say they had going?"

Aslan sighed. "Mostly sniping and nasty tricks. Anything too overt would get recorded and used as ammunition in the Claims Trial. Naturally the Rep said we wouldn't be involved in that side of things. I believed that as much as I believed his high and noble speech about Yaraka's respect for the lives and culture of the indigenes."

Shadith pleated her napkin, running her fingers slowly along the smooth white linen. "And just what are we supposed to be doing there?"

"Recording the cultures, you know, my usual thing. Facilitating the interchanges between the Yaraks and the Béluchars so the Chave will have less of a chance of causing trouble by stirring up the locals. Persuading a local to allow a template for the Translator. That sort of thing."

"Glorified shills, sounds like. What are limitations on me?"

"Ah. You'll be listed as musical and linguistic consultant, but you're not a Scholar and not bound by the University Canon of Professional Conduct. If you manage to embarrass the Governors, they'll rescind the offer of the Voting Share, but I can arrange to bank your fee on Helvetia and I doubt they'll fight me over it. Basically, it's be discreet, do what you want."

"Registered Contract?"

"Right. With what I said spelled out in much more decorous prose."

Shadith stretched across the table, clicked her cup against Aslan's. "Here's to friendly sabotage and noble savages. When do we leave?"

# 2. Harp to Harp

## 1

Maorgan lay along the branch of the Solitary Oilnut, trying to focus the ocular on the fenced enclosure being built by the mesuchs infesting the Land. He was having trouble because the enclosure was a long way below the mesa where the Oilnut grew, between the arms of the Sea Marish, next the inlet from the Bakuhl Sea where the Denchok Smokehouse used to stand and because he still wasn't easy with the device which that imp Glois and his confederates among the Meloach stole from them down there, Chel Dé peel their tender hides. Which the mesuchs might do all too soon without divine help.

"Hhhhh." The image had finally come clear; he could count the nagals chewing at the wood of a building, so many of them the wall looked plated in black iron. He smiled. Another day and all they'd leave would be rotten shards.

His smile vanished before it had fully bloomed.

A nagal whose shell was big as his thumbnail shuddered and fell away from the wall, then another and another; an instant later the wall was clear. He shifted the field of the ocular, fought down the dizziness and nausea the disorienting motion produced. "Interesting. Wonder if they'll sell that effect." The nagal were lying belly up, the black threads of their legs pressed against their pale pink underbellies.

He clicked his tongue, slid the viewpoint over the house bubbles, slowly this time so he wouldn't trigger the vertigo, and scanned the dealing tables on the paved flat area outside the enclosure's main gate.

"Ihoi!"

The mesuch were doing a brisk trade. Maorgan saw three barge Kabits he knew, half a dozen merchants from Dumel Alsekum, and a handful of farmers. The chaffering was intense, though all in sign, the mesuch taking produce from the farms, vials of perfume, bottles of distilled liqueurs, lengths of embroidery—in fact, all the things Béluchars were accustomed to using in their barter with the occasional smuggler or free traders who set down on Béluchad. What they accepted in return were mostly small devices and the batteries to keep them running.

He shifted focus again and slid the viewfield of the ocular across to the bridge the mesuch had thrown across the river in a careless gesture of power that turned him sick with anger and envy. And swore again when he saw half a dozen swampies hovering in the shadow under the trees of the Sea Marish, still tied to the Marish by shyness and fear, though it wouldn't be long before the bolder ones trotted across the bridge and joined the traders. What better measure of how accustomed people were getting to this invasion.

Its translucent flesh taking on the varied greens of the leaves, a tentacle dropped through the leaves and touched his shoulder. From where xe floated above Maorgan, the Eolt Melech sang and the simplified words came to the man through the touch. *What is it, sioll Maorgan?*

*The trade's getting brisker. Word's out, I suppose. Look at the swampies. How much longer before they're caught too? I doubt we'll ever get rid of the mesuch now.*

Melech sang. *I see them, my sioll. It is a season of change and who knows the end of it.* Sadness flowed through the flesh link. *Do you see the children?*

*Not yet, let me. . . .* His voice trailed off as he increased magnification and began sliding the viewfield over the enclosure.

The mesuchs were quick men covered with fur that was more like plush, shades of brown from dark amber to almost black. The fur was darker about their eyes and some of them had white markings under the masks. The four at the trade tables wore long robes, but those inside the enclosure were mostly stripped to leather aprons and a few straps. How the steamy heat down there felt to all that fur wasn't something Maorgan liked to think about, not when they held younglings hostage to their tempers.

He counted them again. Four traders, six or seven who tended machines and supervised the work that their metal slaves did on the buildings inside the fence, two, maybe three, who looked like guards, three, four, maybe as many as seven who moved about as if they had tasks to complete, though he couldn't imagine what they were. Most of these last ones had the white markings under their eyes, but otherwise were hard to tell apart so he was never sure whether he was counting two as one or seeing the same one in several different places.

The buildings were stone bubbles, some single, some multiple. Singles were set in a neat row near the southern side of the enclosure, with small patches of growing things by the round sliding doors. There was a line half a dozen bubbles long near the eastern side, and in the middle, two taller structures. One was a pyramid with six or so bubbles—at the angle he was viewing from he couldn't be sure of the count—at the base, tapering to a single bubble at the top that seemed to be made of dark glass; it glittered like glass whatever it was. The second was a tower two bubbles wide, two deep and four high with round thick windows at every level.

In one of the windows on the tower's third level,

he caught a glimpse of a pale face and a shock of red hair; he steadied the ocular, fiddled with the focus again. "Ihoi!" *I see Glois. Looking out a window. Ah! Utelel just came up to him, put a hand on his shoulder. And I can see more movement behind xe. Looks like they're all there.*

He let the ocular drop to swing at the end of the neck strap, rubbed at his eyes then squinted at the distant enclave. The buildings were toys now, the mesuchs like chetor busy about their hills, so it took him a while to locate the building where the boys and the Meloach were confined.

*Are they in health?*

*From the little I could see. Glois was angry. That's nothing new. Utelel was dark and xe's chesisil flowers were closed to bud, but that was probably because xe was shut away from the sun. They don't look afraid.*

Melech sang satisfaction and the tentacle withdrew. A moment later xe was drifting free of the tree, a shimmering glass gas bell with trailing cords that glittered diamond bright where the suction disks dotted them.

Maorgan watched his sioll a moment with affection and appreciation, then lifted the ocular and began searching for a way to reach the young captives.

That fence looked absurdly flimsy, long thin rods planted at intervals slightly over a manlength with something that flickered between them. Not so insubstantial as they looked, though. He'd seen a young faolt spooked by one of the humming carts that traveled between the landing ground and the enclosure; the cub tried to run between two of those poles. It was fried in seconds.

The enclosure was a long rectangle with a tower at each of the four corners, metal chambers set on sticks that seemed as insubstantial as the fences and had as dangerous a bite. In the second week after the flying ships had settled onto the landing ground, the Denchok budline who claimed this ground and ran the Smokehouse in season had assembled and marched out, intending to remove the intruders as they would any other nuisance interfering with their property.

Lines of light had snapped at them from the towers. They dropped and knew nothing for about two hours, some waking a few minutes later than others, while the Denchok who was closest to the Change took the longest to come awake. It was like a big stick, they said, hitting them on the head and knocking them silly.

There looked to be no way in except floating over the fence and that was not a good idea. Unless this lot of mesuchs was even more unlike the lot across the Bakuhl Sea than rumor suggested. They weren't so tender over there. It was a killing light they used on anyone who got close. The story had come to Melech that Eolt Chelokl was caught in the backwash of a flying sled and swept toward one of the towers; the fire of his dying leaped a hundred manlengths into the air.

Maorgan shivered, lowered the ocular, and rubbed his sleeve across his face, wondering—even as he tried not to think about it—how Chelokl's sioll was handling that sudden rupture of the sioll-bond, the cutting away of half of himself.

He blinked. Melech's bell form was swelling and changing, getting ready to lift into the steering current layers.

He dropped the ocular, cried, "No!" Then shifted the word into a protesting whistle.

Melech sang.

| | | |
|---|---|---|
| not-same | necessity | simplicity is best |
| power/habit/restraint | | imperative/rescue |
| danger seen | curiosity | care will be taken |
| affection/amusement | anger/frustration | |

> light as beating stick          not light as killing fire
>                bond not broken as joy

Even after the years of sioll-bond, translating the complex harmonies of Eolt speech was difficult without the touch and Maorgan was never entirely sure he got even half the meaning clear in his head, yet everything he read into what he heard turned him cold with fear.

In the combination whistle and scatsong Fior Ards had evolved for nontouch speech as the sioll bond developed between the Ard and the Eolt, he went through all the reasons why Melech should wait, should take time and care before acting—knowing all along how stubborn and passionate his sioll was, how little likely to listen once xe's mind was set on a line of movement. But all he could see was a flame leaping a hundred manlengths high and a sudden amputation of all joy.

Melech sang.

Maorgan whistle/sang.

After several arias on both sides, the Eolt returned to xe's usual configuration while Maorgan swung from limb to limb and finally dropped to the ground. He lifted the harpcase he'd left at the base of the tree, slid the strap over his shoulder, and settled the case in its most comfortable position against his back.

Melech dropped a tentacle to touch his shoulder. *May words suffice, sioll Maorgan.*

*May the few words I have of the starspeech, suffice, sioll Melech.*

Mid-morning on the next day which was Chel Dé's day, so there was no one to come to trade. Ard Maorgan and Eolt Melech placed themselves before the Gate of the enclave. Maorgan swept a desilmerr on his harp. When he saw he had their attention, he sang to them in tradespeak. "Peace," he sang. "Trade for children. Let us talk."

"Hm, there is a slight problem that the good Sageen possibly didn't mention. Our surveyors chose this location because there were sufficient freshwater springs, bedrock close to the surface, easy access to the sea— and it seemed ... mmm ... unclaimed. There were two structures of a sort in place, but they were looked so ancient and ... mmm ... unsteady a breath would blow them over. Obviously long abandoned. So we simply removed them. Unfortunately, abandoned was not the correct description. We shall probably have to pay compensation to maintain passable relations with the locals." The Goës twitched his nose and flattened round ears against his skull. "Very annoying."

The Goës Koraka hoeh Dexios was a tall Yarak with lively brown eyes and fur like golden-bronze plush; he wore a light workrobe that covered him from chin to ankle, but from the way he moved as he paced about the tower room, his body was limber and very fit. The mask markings on his face were sharply outlined, the white band beneath the black narrow and crisp. He had the assurance of one who knew he was handsome and didn't need to wonder how people would react to him.

"We have been fairly successful at establishing trade. Contact with smugglers and such has prepared the way for us. To a degree. There is still some ... mmm ... hostility because we've obviously come to stay, though we have been overcoming that little by little. It would be easier if we could speak local, but we haven't attempted ... mmm ... to solicit language donors, though we have been collecting sound samples with EYEs, entering them into the Trans-Am for analysis. It's a slower process and prone to odd inaccuracies, but has less chance of ... mmm ... annoying the locals. With that unfortunate business with those hov-

els and with the Chave interfering like they are. . . ."
He flung his arms out, flattened his ears against his
head. "Ssssah! Killing a couple of locals with a cutter
and leaving their mutilated bodies lying on the road.
With tooth marks yet!"

They were in the office of the Goës, the glass bubble
at the top of the pyramid in the center of the Enclosure. It was a mostly empty room with pretensions to
elegance, lots of polished wood veneer, a Menaviddan
carpet, a Clovel polymorph cycling through at least
ten major mutations, and a scatter of small rarities laid
about with careful casualness. Half a dozen pulochairs
floated about the only indication that this was an office, a desk with its operating sensors discreetly covered except for a small screen in a privacy hood that
the Goës glanced at each time he passed it.

Aslan was in the seat of honor, a large pulochair
with a pseudo-moss surface whose dark green was a
pleasant complement to her coloring. In her own pulo
which was cycled to dark amber, Shadith was briefly
amused by this small sample of the Goës' cleverness,
though he was perhaps not as clever as he thought or
it wouldn't show so much.

Her amusement faded as he continued his attempts
to overwhelm Aslan with his abundant charm. Shadith
dropped her hand on the harpcase and gazed out
through the smoky glass wall, the flow of his words
passing over her head. In the distance she could see
a localized glimmer floating near the top of a tree.
She couldn't make out the details, but she thought
it was one of those aerial intelligences she'd seen in
the flakes.

*Come on, Yarak, finish this. I want to see those crea-
tures with my own eyes. Gods, they don't look real.
Like something Sarmaylen sculpted out of golden glass.*
The bits of local music included on those flakes
haunted her; she wanted to hear it, not recorded, not

inside where nuance was lost. Her impatience to get out set small itches to crawling along her skin.

"... thing which Rep Sageen would not have mentioned. We captured a band of local children on a thieving raid. We've treated them as well as we could and plan to release them eventually. One of the local adults has approached us. Apparently he knows a few words of tradespeak. Which isn't all that helpful, but we have managed to make clear to him that we expect some recompense for this intrusion before we return the young thieves. We have suggested using the Trans-Am for a language exchange, but haven't pushed it. Our contact was emphatic in his refusal." He made an angry spitting sound. "The k'tar't Chave have acted like the fornicating swine they are and have poisoned the well for us. Communication between the continents is better than we expected," a quick wry smile, a graceful flip of narrow hands, "or appreciate. The only advantage we have is that we look nothing like those heavy-world 'k'trin." He spread his arms in a gesture that swept the loose robe into dramatic folds. "I must warn you, Scholar. The Chave are irritated by our presence because it limits their actions; they like to have exclusive control of a world, so detailed reports of their activities don't get out. They have some sensitivity to public censure. As do we all," he added with a quick smile and a twinkle of his dark russet eyes. "So far, they've been ... mmm ... annoying nuisances with their sabotage and their attempts to stir up our locals. Musni gnawing at the walls. Since you'll be a part of our operation, in their eyes, at least, you should be on guard against treachery among suborned locals and vandalism, both subtle and unsubtle, once the Chave turn their attention to you."

Aslan shifted impatiently in her pulo; it flowed into a new conformation and changed color slightly. "I've done my homework, Goës Koraka. University's records are quite extensive. And Manager Shears and I have run missions in delicate situations before this. We understand the need for security."

Shadith suppressed a smile. It wasn't only the Chave who'd have a rough time getting into Aslan's files as Goës Koraka hoeh Dexios would discover soon enough.

The Goës glanced at the screen and came round the desk to perch on the edge. "Of course, of course. I spoke from concern, not from lack of confidence, Scholar. It worries me that you won't take residence in the enclosure. However, I must defer to your experience with such things. We have extracted a few concessions from the locals. If they approve you as intermediary, they will arrange housing as you've requested in the nearest ... mmm ... dumel, I think the word is. Communication has been difficult. Signing is ... mmm ... limited. As I'm sure you know, Scholar. And our contact has only the few words of interlingue he's learned from free traders and smugglers. He is more sophisticated in interspecies contact than one would have expected from the isolation of this world. Probably because of the interaction the two sapient species have been forced into over the past three millennia, if my memory of dates is accurate. We've done some testing on hair and skin cells from the Cousins among our young captives. My techs tell me it's almost certain their presence here is a result of the first Diaspora, probably due to a massive system failure on their colony ship. It's not a sector one would choose to explore, if the choice were available."

Aslan shifted again. When she spoke, her voice was sharp with displeasure. "I have to convince your contact to accept us? That's another thing your Rep didn't bother to mention."

The Goës shrugged, spread his hands. "It didn't seem important. In any case, I've arranged a meeting tomorrow noon with our contact, a Cousin by name

Maorgan and his ... mmm ... companion whose name I don't know. If it even has a name. My aides tell me your gear has been off-loaded and put in secure storage until you need it and your temporary quarters are ready. Your Manager and young associates are there, waiting for you. Is there anything else I can do?"

"Yes. I'd like to see your captives, if I may."

"Mmm ... that will take some arranging. They are ... mmm ... difficult to control without danger of injury." He twisted his mobile face into a clown's grimace. "There is no dealing with them except by sign, which they ignore when they feel like it. Are you sure you want this?"

"Yes. Flakes, however fine, cannot substitute for actual experience. What I could learn would greatly help with tomorrow's contact."

He glanced at Shadith for the first time, raised his eyes to the ceiling in a fine imitation of thought, then nodded. "I'll see to it." He went back behind the desk and reached under the edge for a sensor. "In two hours. That should give you plenty of time before we feed them." He nodded to the young Yarak who came in, stood beside the door. "The phora Galeyn here will take you to your quarters and fetch you again when the visit has been arranged. How many?"

"Myself and the harpist."

"T't't'." He came back around the desk, took Aslan's hand, and helped her from the chair. He had a slight musky smell that was pleasant if a little strange and he was half a meter taller than she was, his physical presence intimidating despite his pleasant demeanor. Aslan lifted her head and fixed her eyes on him, waiting for him to step back into more comfortable range. Again Shadith swallowed a grin. By the time she'd made rank, a University Scholar had faced far more intimidating individuals than Goës Koraka would ever be.

### 3

The fenced and patrolled enclosure beside the tower where young locals were being kept was filled with the pounding of feet, the slap of flesh against flesh from the energetic play, shouts, shrill screams, and snatches of song. Despite the amount of noise, there were only six of them, two Cousins and four Others.

One of the Cousins was a skinny red-haired boy with pale skin and a noseful of freckles, ten or eleven years old; the second was smaller, slighter, a dark-haired child a year or two younger; both wore dark brown shorts and white sleeveless shirts. The Others were all shorter and stockier than the redhead, bipeds with five-fingered hands and four toes on the feet. Their faces were triangular with the chin as vertex and the straight line of the moss across the brow as base. Their eyes were large and dark, shades of brown mostly, though one had lighter eyes than the others, amber, almost yellow. Their noses were hardly raised from the curved plane of the face, thin as knifeblades with long, fringed nostrils. Their mouths were wide, flexible, and produced an astonishing volume of sound.

A mossy growth more vegetable than fur covered torso and limbs out to the elbows and knees. Beyond that the skin was smooth, a pale greenish white like the inner layer of new bark. The moss also grew on the small round heads, much like hair, though it also resembled the plush fur of the Yaraka. There were buds among the head moss and here and there a small flower, narrow, arcing petals laid close to the curve of the head. The flowers were mostly white though Shadith could see one or two pink blooms and a bright yellow one.

They rushed the gate when they saw Aslan and Shadith coming, speech turning into whistles that seemed to be a combination of mutual support and preparation for attack. Shadith's head started hurting as the Translator she'd acquired from Aleytys began sorting through the noises.

The phora Galeyn waved at the guards, then turned to face his charges. "If you'll wait here, despines, we'll clear the children from the gateway first. They always rush us, trying to get away."

Shadith knelt, began undoing the catches on the harpcase. She glanced up to see the guards using tinglers, shuddered as she felt the waves of pain coming from the moss-children. They fled across the field, huddling near the far fence, but two of the guards kept tinglers turned on them as the third manipulated the gate lock.

She collapsed the memory plast of the case into a stool, then, pale with the pain from the Translator and the distress from the children, she slipped the harp's strap over her shoulder, picked up the stool, and got to her feet. She hesitated; what she wanted to say could be used against the locals, but the Yaraka had so many other weapons, perhaps it wouldn't matter. "If you keep that up, you're going to have problems," she said quietly. "It hurts them."

The phora frowned at her. "Why do you say that? How do you know?" There was an edge to his voice. He didn't like her or her comments; he'd had a sour look on his face and kept his distance from the moment he'd left the Director's office. One of those who didn't like outsiders.

"I can feel their pain," she said quietly. "The tingler doesn't bother the Cousins, it's the others who show distress."

"Feel!" He didn't bother to conceal his disdain, turned his shoulder to her, and spoke to Aslan. "If you'll go in now, Scholar. Quickly please. They're treacherous little nothi."

Smiling at the profound disapproval of the phora, Shadith followed Aslan in. The Goës was clever enough to cover any problems he had with having them on planet and, unless there was a lot of complicated dancing involved here between him and the homeworld, he'd asked for them. The phora was too young (or perhaps too well connected) to bother hiding his annoyance. He had white tips to his ears and the white lines under his mask were broader than Koraka's. From the data Aslan had passed around during the journey here, that meant he was a highborn cub, probably a second son doing his Mission-year before he settled down to one of the jobs created for his kind.

She glanced at Aslan. The Xenoeth had one of the Ridaar pickups pasted to her throat and was busily subvocalizing into it. It was the first time she'd seen Aslan at work and was surprised by the intensity of the woman, the sudden sharp focus which excluded everything except what she was observing.

The red-haired boy saw the harp and whistled something that Shadith almost caught. Along with one of the Others, he moved cautiously toward her.

He nodded at the harp, made a gesture of playing.

Shadith smiled. She dropped the stool, settled herself, contemplated him a moment, then drew her fingers across the strings. She played a lilting dance tune, brought to mind by the whistle talk since it had the same quick, sprightly movement.

The red-haired boy glanced from Shadith to Aslan. He grinned, pursed his lips in a whistle that was silent until he'd figured out intervals and tones, then he snapped his fingers and wove a sweet liquid line around her playing. His companion joined him.

The rest of the captives listened a moment longer, then they began whistling and dancing round and round the two women.

"Amazing."

Shadith glanced around but kept her fingers busy.

The Goës was talking to Aslan. She sighed and listened to them.

Aslan clicked off the Ridaar. "Oh?"

"How simple it is and how profound to bring a harpist to a world soaked in music." He sighed. "The Yaraka are many things, but musical we're not."

"Credit your report, Goës Koraka."

"Do you have enough from this meeting? The sun is nearly down and I'd prefer to button up here before long."

"I've enough to think about. There is one thing you might change. The harpist is also an empath; she says the tinglers cause real pain in the moss-children. If you could decrease the settings to minimum. . . ."

Shadith played a last chord, stilled the strings, and looked up. "Let me try something, will you?"

The Goës mobile ears went up as a Cousin might lift a brow, then he nodded. "As long as it doesn't mean trouble. You understand me, I think."

"It may prevent trouble." She stood, shifted the harp, closed her eyes, and rubbed at her temple; her head was throbbing still from the Translator's activity. When she looked up, the Béluchar children were moving restlessly, getting ready to rush the gate. She thought a moment, then whistled a warning phrase. For the first time she heard ordinary speech from them, fragmentary whispers, but words nonetheless. The pain stabbed inward more strongly than ever. She ignored it, whistled again, a complex trill that said something like: *wait, danger, help comes, wait, Maorgan comes.*

The whistle form of the name had them buzzing more loudly. The boy called out a few words she didn't understand. She whistled again: *wait, this is a friend, wait, help comes.*

The boy and his companion rested head against head, talking in low hums with descanted trills. They didn't try speaking to her again, but after a moment, the six Béluchar retreated to the far fence and sat down, legs crossed, hands resting on their knees.

Shadith drew in a long breath, let it trickle out; head throbbing, she trudged to the gate and waited impatiently for it to open.

"Amazing."

Shadith blinked away pain-tears, looked up at the tall Yarak. "You repeat yourself, Goës Koraka. And overstate. Whistle calls are generally simple and much alike from culture to culture. Like many musicians, I have a gift for the patterning of sounds." She had little patience now for his complicated strokings; it was all surface, in any case. Should he decide to have her probed, it would be done with the most elegant suavity, and if she died under that probe, he would mark her passing with a trope or two and none of that would touch the steel beneath. She glanced at Aslan, sighed, remembering the lectures about keeping the Director sweet. "By your favor, Goës, pardon my abruptness. I'm very tired."

"As we all are, Shadith." Aslan set her hand on Shadith's arm. "We appreciate your interest, Goës Koraka, but we do need to confer and organize our-selves for tomorrow's meeting."

4

The sun was brilliant, vaguely greenish in a sky whitened by heat haze when Shadith walked through the enclosure gate with Aslan, her Aide Marrin Ola, and Duncan Shears, the University folk a ragged knot with a pair of guards marching ahead of them, another pair behind. Beyond the paved trade ground, the land turned into a field of low ground cover plants, not grass but something like it, pale gray-green spears with ocher strips; it felt crunchy when Shadith walked on it and there were small gray green scuttlings with every step as if each spear had its own miniature ecosystem.

Strewn through the ground cover, small woody plants grew in pentagons, some complete, some partial, always at least three bushes, always the same distance apart no matter what the age of the plant; the ground cover plant didn't extend to the area within the pentagons, instead there was a scabby growth something like a lichen, pale yellow and grainy. Scattered more irregularly, there were taller plants, clumps with brown fuzzy growths at the end of long stems thick as Shadith's forefinger, plants that looked like the bulrushes on a world that no longer existed. Shayalin, blown to atoms before the life on this world was more than one bacterium contemplating another with speculation in its nonglance. Shadith sighed. Nostalgia was a disease she didn't seem to recover from even when she shifted bodies.

On both sides of the river, trees were dark masses set in shallow curves that bent with the brilliant blue of the water.

Half obscured by the haze above the trees, a number of the aerial folk floated like exquisite golden dreams above the forest, the sucking disks on their tendrils glittering diamond bright in the sun. They were singing/speaking. Like an organ miles wide, chords of splendid complexity, cadenzas, single notes as emphasis. She listened, shivering with pleasure. And with an ache growing in her head that told her it wasn't merely this world's equivalent to birdsong but speech.

The Goës Koraka hoeh Dexios and his angry young phora walked ahead of them, Koraka with his hands clasped behind his back, head turning as he scanned the line of trees, watching the fliers. Shadith wrinkled her nose at his back. *At it again, oh dear Goës. Making us markers in your games.* Despite his graceful assurances of free inquiry, he was there to set his seal on

31

them in the eyes of the Béluchar; he didn't want the locals getting ideas about playing University against Yarakan.

A man moved from the shadow of the trees, a golden flier hovering above him, pulsing and glowing in the sunlight. Maorgan, if Koraka had it right.

## 4

"Glois and the Meloach aren't there," Maorgan growled. He inspected the guards, then snorted with disgust. "Careful of his hide, our mesuch." He looked past the Director at the straggling group of strangers. "Those are the ones he wants to foist on us. Which one do you think is teseach?"

Simple-speech came through the tentacle touching his shoulder. *The Yellow-hair. It is to her the mesuch looks when he looks back. I am cast low, sioll, Utelel sang that the harper promised they would be free.*

"Utelel is Meloach. Xe may turn sioll one day, but xe hasn't seen much more'n a decade of sun-returns. Xe trusts us single-lives too much."

Rippling laughter from the Eolt. *Sioll Maorgan, you remember the harp and are jealous.*

"T'ck. I'm remembering xe said the harper learned the whistle talk as easy as a rebekii gulps bait."

*But you know how clever harpers are.*

"And how sarcastic Eolt can be. Shall we go to meet them?"

*As before, sioll Maorgan, and keep your temper tight, good friend.*

Maorgan left the shadow of the trees and walked the five kaels into the choa and stopped in the center of an oim korroi pentad with two points dead, the living bushes between him and the others; should flesh guards try laying hands on him, they'd discover the defenses of the oim, it was only the steel ones that made him worry. He swung the harpcase around and set it before him on the scab, wondering as he did so if he'd have a chance to play for the offworld harper and hear what she could do.

The yellow-hair watched him quietly from eyes blue as bits of storm-dark sea—clever eyes, calm eyes, eyes measuring him, lifting to Melech, returning to Maorgan. And the yellow of her hair was more a brown with amber lights. And when she smiled at him, the light spread over her face and leaped out from her and heated him.

He looked away before he fell too deeply into her web, and found himself meeting the eyes of the harper. She was strange in a way he couldn't comprehend; he touched his finger to Melech's tentacle. "What is it about her, sioll?" he murmured, keeping his voice low so the mesuchs wouldn't hear him.

*This xe can't find her song, sioll Maorgan. The yellow-hair is simple beside her. The others are servants, of no importance.*

"Sfais, despois," the mesuch with the fur face boomed at him. That was a man sure of his importance, pushing it off on everyone around him.

"Fes," Maorgan said. It was something the traders said to each other, some kind of greeting; he didn't care. Made things go easier when you followed the other party's rules. If you wanted them to go easier.

The Eolt Melech withdrew his tentacle and glided higher, rising and falling, using the layered currents of the air to oscillate in place above Maorgan, song speech flowing through the interstices of the word-exchange between Maorgan and the mesuch.

Telk a telk a telk, the time ticked past as they went over the same ground they'd gone over day after day. Yellow-hair listened, impatience glinting in her sea-storm eyes. The Harper watched Melech except when her eyes glazed over and she shut them tight. And when that happened, the air around her wrinkled with pain and implication.

From the corner of his eyes, while he tried to find a way to shut off the mesuch so he could deal with Yellow-hair, he watched the harper.

She knelt beside the case, opened the catches, and took out an instrument both like and unlike his own. Though it was made and not grown, it had the beauty of its essence and the track of loving hands along its wood. She played a tune on the case with her fingertips and he saw the thing he hadn't believed when Melech relayed Glois' tale.

The stuff of the case flowed and folded and in moments was a three-legged stool. She shifted to the stool and began to tune the harp, a pleasant distraction that worked into the mesuch's notice and brought an instant's irritation to his fur-masked face.

She plucked a string, and the sound with its brother tones was an insistence.

She sang, her voice rich and true, the words infused with all the fringes that only a near-term Eolt could manage, the silences filled with as much to think on as the sound phrases had, the strangeness of her, age and youth combined, present so powerfully she drew the drifting Eolt like a whirling wind-trap.

She sang:

> value     fleeting moment     understand
> necessity/insistence     no escape
> emptiness will be filled   no way to avoid   understand
> we/sympathy/sorrow     we/pride/completeness
> knowledge/trade   value for value/we/you   strength/wisdom
> friendship/limited     opening of doors
> let there be hearing/a coming to touch.

The Chorus of Eolts sang their astonishment and pleasure. The chords grew and blended as they discussed the phrases and intervals, as they debated what to do about the strong warning of complications and pain from the outsiders, a warning that what was done could not be undone, that they were found and must make a choice, that the choice should be grounded on knowledge, a warning that knowledge opened many doors they might want to stay closed, that change was inevitable, that there were ways to mitigate the damage as well as exploit the opening. The combinations and permutations of that short burst of song from the harper held a promise of endless play with meaning and possibility. There was fear and excitement in the chords of the Eolt, yearning and revulsion—and finally decision.

They sang:

> It must be done     let it be done.

# 3. The Sorrows of Ard Ilaörn

## 1

In the small bare room where he slept when he could sleep, a work shed built in a corner of the Ykkuval Hunnar's Dushanne Garden, Ilaörn, no longer Ard, fed his harp her oil and wax, slid his hand along the curve of her neck, feeling the live wood arch under his hand, responding like a cat to the caress. He didn't know why he kept her when he couldn't bear to play her. His Dushanne perhaps, if he had the concept right, his contemplation of the twists of the life-thread. He'd sworn not to play again when his sioll ... he stumbled to the cot and sat holding his head in his hands, acid tears dripping through his fingers.

"Cho!"

The shout brought his head up, his mouth spasming to match the twist in his stomach. *Boy.* He brushed at his mouth, looked at his hand; it was shaking—and wet. He scrubbed at his face with a corner of a blanket. *I was a man when he wasn't a thought. I've learned a new thing from these Chandavasi. To keep your power, diminish those who are ruled in your eyes and their own.* He got to his feet, smoothed strands of lank white hair from his face, settled his hands in their required position, the left flattened on his diaphragm, right flattened on top of left, used his shoulder to nudge the door open, and walked out, head down and humble.

The Chandavasi Ykkuval Hunnar ni Jilet soyad Koroumak stood by the curve of the small stream he'd had his techs run through the garden for him, its water an enclosed system that never left the garden, continually monitored for foreign, potentially lethal substances. In the past year the Ykkuval had rambled on about poisonings, challenges, sabotage, and other maneuverings that would have shocked Ilaörn if he'd had much feeling left.

Hunnar was as broad as he was tall, with a massive torso and legs that seemed too short for his body. His movements were not without grace, but tightly controlled. The first time Ilaörn had seen these mesuchs moving about Chetioll's Patch with their metal slaves, they bounced in a peculiar way when they walked, as if good earth were feathers in a pillow, but now only the newcomers moved like that, the rest were like Hunnar.

His hands were broad with short fingers and shiny black claws instead of nails, hooks that he kept retracted except when anger took him. In the same way, anger brought transparent membranes dropping over his copper-colored eyes, making them shine as if they were wet. They were shining now.

"That!" The Ykkuval jabbed a thumb at a small patch of gray among the greens, maroons, and ambers of the vines growing tight against the stream bank. "It's dead. I told you. Leave nothing dead in this garden. How do I possibly achieve dushanne with death in my face?"

Ilaörn touched his tongue to dry lips. "O Ykkuval, this one hesitates to contradict the exalted, but that is melidai in its dormant phase; it sleeps, it is not dead. A spore must have come in on your clothes or mine or those of a visitor."

Hunnar dropped his hand, the black hooks retracting; his inner lids pulled back as he squatted, peering at the tiny gray blotch. "It looks dead. Is it good for anything or is it just a weed?"

The garden turned to haze for a moment as the tension drained out of Ilaörn. Then he was angry again, though he didn't dare show it. He didn't know how, but the Ykkuval had somehow managed to plant an obsessive fear of death in him, a fear that took hold of him whenever the impulse to resist strengthened to a certain level. *His own fear,* Ilaörn thought. *I've got his fear in me. Even a pinch of sleepy melidai terrifies him.*

He steadied his voice, said, "O Ykkuval, it is a vesicant with several applications. The leaves are macerated and made into a paste. Weavers use the paste to draw moisture from c'hau bark so it can be pounded into fiber and spun into thread. That is woven into c'hau cloth which we find useful though ugly because when it is painted with boiled sap from a komonok tree, it is waterproof. Your procurers secured a number of bolts from the stoang ... um ... market room of the Kabeduch weavers."

Hunnar got to his feet with the bouncy quickness that always disconcerted Ilaörn. "Vesicant? Hmp. Dig it out, bag it, and give it to one of the techs. And make sure no more got in. I don't want it spoiling my peace."

Ilaörn bowed. When he straightened, the Ykkuval was walking away, heading for the waterhouse among the flowering trees. *These bloody-handed death givers with their stupid pretensions ... dushanne dreaming ... peace ... meditation on ... Chel Dé curse him....* He started trembling and couldn't finish the thought, too much pain, too much ... everything. Silently blessing the stray spoor that germinated so opportunely, he plodded to the lean-to with the garden tools. Hunting the melidai was something to focus on, to shut out thought and memory. To push away the acid bath of loneliness.

## 2

Ilaörn dreamed.

*He sat in the sunshine, tuning-in a new harp as Eolt Imuë drifted over him singing the pleasures of the late summer day. The songs of other Eolt came distantly into the small meadow, mixing with the rustle of leaves and the whistles of the angies fluttering from nest to ground to scratch among the spores and budlings under the kerre trees. Drawn by the plucking of the harpstrings, an angi whirred over to him, settled on an oim bush, its shimmering wings folded against a green and gold carapace, its soft charcoal eyes fixed on his hands as he set the intervals of the strings in the bul mode he preferred. The angi's broad blunt beak quivered as it sang to him.*

*Then it stopped singing, lifted its head; with a harsh scream of alarm it darted into the trees.*

*Ilaörn stilled his hands, listened. A buzzing . . . no . . . a whine . . . both . . . a strange sound, not one he'd heard before. "Sioll Imuë, what is that? Can you see it?"*

*\*I see a strange thing, sioll Ilaörn. It is dark and hard like a nagal the size of a rebou, but it flies without wings. And very fast. I think we should leave here, sioll. Quickly.\**

*The Eolt expanded and began xe's rise, searching the tiers for a layer that would blow xe quickly away. Ilaörn slung the harp's carry strap over his shoulder and moved into the shadow under the trees. Curiosity kept him close, though. He wanted to see this strange thing for himself. Besides, his joints were stiff from sitting and he was reluctant to go running off if there was no need.*

*Eolt Imuë's membranes had also grown stiff with age and xe's climb was labored and slow. Ilaörn watched and winced with his sioll. We are old, he*

*thought. Could be we should return to the Sleeping
Ground. He sighed. We'll have to talk when this thing
has passed.*

*The strange nagal whipped past Imuë, circled back.
It was a wagon that rode air instead of wheels and
there was glass across the front. He saw figures behind that glass, misshapen, trollish figures, and he
thought he heard them laugh as the wash of their
airwagon sent Eolt Imuë tumbling, though that was
probably a trick of his mind. The airwagon turned
again, a spear of light sprang from beneath it. The
light touched Imuë and xe was a column of fire flar-
ing to meet the sun....*

Ilaörn woke sweating and shaking. He swung his
feet over the edge of the cot and sat with his hands
dangling between his knees. Light from the security
beams atop the garden wall filtered through the c'hau
cloth curtains pulled across the window and the cracks
in the wall where the green boards had split and
pulled apart.

He was exhausted, but he wasn't going to sleep any
more, not tonight. If he tried, the dream would replay.
Over and over. He should have died when Imuë
burned, but the mesuch caught him before he had a
chance to follow his sioll. Nor could he escape into
madness, the Chave measured his blood, all his fluids,
and played their games with his flesh. No madness for
him. He was the Ykkuval Hunnar's pet native, his
source for truth and trouble.

They put a crown on his head and tore his language
from him, force-fed him theirs, then they changed
crowns and stole his memories.

He thrust his hand in his mouth and bit down hard
as he thought of those sessions with the probe. The
pain, the helplessness ... the pleasure ... the horrible
pleasure that brought a spending that went on and on

until he was a sack of skin that held only the ashes of orgasm.

It was another chain on him, and Ykkuval Hunnar ni Jilet soyad Kroumak held the free end. These days when he went under the probe, it was usually just the two of them there—no techs, no guards, just them. A kind of sex though neither touched the other nor spoke of what was happening.

Ilaörn rose with painful stiffness, his knees complaining, his stomach knotting, acid in his mouth. He pulled on his shirt; it was long enough to cover him so he didn't bother with pants. He lifted the hook from its eye, pushed the door open, and went out.

The sygyas were flying, tiny points of pulsing white light darting from the stream to the flowering trees. Squatting by the door, he watched them, their random patterns soothing, restful. He hummed, no sound, just a vibration of the throat, as his mind spun a melody from the intervals. His fingers twitched, responding to the cues; he'd not made music with his hands since Imuë burned, but two centuries was a long habit to break.

How much time passed he was never sure, but sometime after he'd left his room, Hunnar came from the Keep and trotted across the garden, sliding into the bush plantings along the high stone wall his iron slaves had built for him. Ilaörn drew his hand across his eyes, frowning at the place where the Chav had vanished.

He'd never tried holding back under the probe, he'd never tried answering the letter of the question and betraying the spirit. He'd been afraid to try because if that failed, there was nothing left. He started shaking; his eyes blurred as tears gathered in them, spilled over, and dripped down his face. If he discovered too much that he wasn't supposed to know, Hunnar would have him killed; the terror laid into his mind told him to go inside, pull the blankets over his head and forget what he'd seen. And yet. . . .

He forced himself to his feet.

Blood roaring in his ears, his legs shaking so badly he could only shuffle, he edged away from the workshed and pushed through the bushes until his hand was flat against the stones. Despite his struggle with his body, he moved silently through the darkness until he came to an opening where he knew there'd been solid stone yesterday. He slipped through, moved along the wall in the pool of shadow at the base, and stopped when he reached a corner in the eight-sided Kushayt wall and heard a low whistle just ahead.

He flattened himself on the ground and crawled forward to peer around the corner.

The watchtower was lit, the landing area bright with light tubes. The brightness dazzled his eyes; he rubbed at them and when they cleared, saw a flier down on the white porcelain surface of the pad, a strange flier, delicate and angular, poised like an angi on a pebble. He crawled a bit closer, keeping behind some bushy stinkweeds that had grown up since the wall was finished.

Unlike the heavy dark things the Chave flew, this airwagon was a two seater that looked fast as thought even when it sat without moving. A cloaked form swung down from it as Ilaörn watched, trotted to a jag in the Kushayt wall where the shadow was conveniently dense, starting to talk when he came close enough to see Hunnar waiting. ". . . pay me more, I was as near getting nipped this time . . . or give me a window."

"Kirg! You take me for a fool? Nothing written, nothing in the air. That was the bargain. You want Koraka humiliated and yourself off this world, you play the game my way."

Hunnar and his visitor kept their voices low, but the light breeze blowing into Ilaörn's face carried their

words farther than they knew. The visitor pushed back
the cowl to his cloak as he moved into the shadow,
the movement hasty, abrupt, echoing the irritation in
his high, light voice. His voice had youth in it, petu-
lance and a lilt to the words that Ilaörn did not recognize. He was taller and wispier than a Chav, round
ears set high on a furry head, a short sleek pelt like
one of the stambs that swam in the Bakuhl Sea.

*Has to be one of the mesuch on Banikoëh. Yaraka.
A spy! Bribed to work against his own.* Ilaörn shuddered, his eyes blurring, blood pounding in his ears—
dangerous knowledge, death in it. Or worse. . . .

When he could see and hear again, he found himself
facedown in the dirt, one hand dug knuckle-deep into
the dry earth, the other cramped around the stem of
a bush, the stink of its crushed membrane nauseating.
He freed his hands, moving so cautiously his arms
were shaking and his knees on fire by the time he'd
gotten himself together again.

The spy was still talking.

". . . the bitch from University has rolled him over
like he was some 'k'trin gynnis with his tongue out.
Turned the stinking little brats loose without so much
as a stick laid across their backsides. She and her lot
are out in the local village sucking up to the locals,
getting a house set up. He's sent 'bots out to set locks
and work security like he doesn't care a scorp about
expense. That harp player she has along, she's really
got to the jellies, give the bitch that. You let those
Xenos keep working and no way you're going to pull
hoeh Dexios loose."

Hunnar made an impatient sound deep in his throat;
Ilaörn could imagine the inner lids coming down and
his eyes starting to shine with anger.

"Let it go. That isn't what I'm paying you for. Do
you have the enclave plans and the lockwords?"

"On this flake." The spy's voice was muffled. Ilaörn
thought he sounded disappointed, almost cheated—as

if he'd expected more from Hunnar . . . appreciation, some sense of shared anger . . . something like that.

Hunnar had heard it, too; his voice turned mellow, his impatience vanished. "Good work. We'll deal with the Xenos when the time's right. I tell you what. We'll make things safer for you. One of my agents brought back some locals from near your place. One's a young woman. Juicy young thing, tender and pliant; you might find she has her attractions and she'll be willing enough once we've finished with her. Even if she doesn't suit you as playmate—you wouldn't be the first to have a taste for local beasts—you can use her as a drop. Leave your reports, pick up the registered receipts of the cash deposits on Helvetia. Which you will, of course, check over and burn immediately. You know what we want."

"Yes. Shipments, the Goës' deployment plans, reports from the University team, notations as to their movements. How long will this drag out?"

"We have to be sure to cut all links to the outside and erase the team; that takes some maneuvering, but I'd say we'll have you a hero before the year's out." Hunnar's voice went honey sweet again. "Look at this."

The spy took a small thing like a game chip, looked down at it, and sucked in his breath. "This is. . . ."

"A bonus. Yours if you agree to one more small thing. It has its dangers, but I'm sure you're clever enough you can contrive to lay suspicion on someone else."

The mesuch's hand closed round the chip. Ilaörn could almost smell the greed and spite in the creature.

Hunnar held out another small dark object. "There's a virus on this. If you can get it introduced into the com system, it will shut it down and your enclave with be completely isolated. When our arrangements are complete, we'll arrange a story of your fortunate escape from a vicious native attack and see that a free trader picks you up. You'll be a very rich man and there'll be no suspicion."

"Good." The spy turned his head. Ilaörn could see the flow of light over the golden fur, the darkness of the fur mask over the mesuch's eyes. "That tower, the guard. You're sure of him?"

"Of course. Goës Koraka may have found cracks in my security as we have in his, but Pismek in the Tower is my man to the bottom of his warty soul."

The spy pulled the cloak's cowl up over his head and ran for the flier.

Hunnar stepped out of the shadow and stood watching it dart away with the whippiness its shape had promised. "What a cinser. Not enough there to be worth wringing his neck," he said, contempt icing the words. "Taner bless all younger sons with greedy fists and empty heads."

### 3

Tech Girs snorted, slapped at a sensor. "Cinsing 'bots. If there's a way to chich up, they'll find it." He hunched over his board, eyes on the readouts, fingers busy on the touch plaques.

Yadak leaned back in his chair, patted a yawn. "Bet it's number five. What'd it get up to this time?"

The younger tech finished what he was doing, watched a moment, then said, "Ol' five's scratching along like it knew what it's for. It's nine this time. Messy eater and it's in a finicky fold area, chunk got past the shields, don't ask me how, sent the pichin son of a poxed deve straight at seven. Hoo, that'd been a thing to watch, hadn't I caught it, each of 'm trying to chew up the other."

"Ayyunh. And t' Ykkuval he'd take cost out your hide the next fifty years."

"Mp. Shift's nearly up. You hear what Nemlen said?"

"About spotting that herd of jellies?"

"That's it. Want to jog over on the way back and do some jelly burns?"

"Why not. Nothing else to do in this cinsing hole."

Girs swung down from the cabin of the tracker, stretched, and strolled toward the patch of pulverized scree they used for a pad as the flier from base settled with a quickly corrected sideways lurch. His replacement punched the door open, swung his feet out, and jumped down. Rubbing his fist against his coverall and swearing at sticking locks and cranky lifters, he trudged toward Girs.

"M'rab, Choban. How's a guy?"

"M'rr, Girs. You wanna watch this junkheap, think there's a hairline in one of the lifters."

"Ayyunh? Thought it was you hung over so bad you can't see straight." He wrinkled an eyeridge. "You on your lonesome?"

"Nah. Herm's in there working up nerve to move his head. He won himself some bonus time in Farkli's backroom and he spent it hard." He shrugged, started walking for the tracker, boots crunching on the gravel. "Me, I'd leave him lay, he has to move, he's gonna be wanting to kill something." He slapped at one of the small black flies that kept trying to bite them. "Kirg! I hate these things. Be glad when I earn enough time-tickets to transfer to a decent world with cities on it. Any problems?"

"I set a watchlink on nine. Went off program about an hour ago, charged number seven like a twi-horn in must. I reconfigured, but it's only a patch, not a fix."

"And five?"

"Chewing away, not a glitch in eight solid hours. Hear any more about those cinsing Yarks?"

"Rumor says Ykkuval's spy come over last night. Ol' Pismek was in tower like always when there's something going the Big Man he don't want stripped to heartstone."

"Chich! Might's well be blind in both eyes and deaf besides for all the talking Pisk does. So?"

"I heard that them from University got here, dossed down with a bunch of locals, and the Big Man, he's having fits at the thought. Buzz is, you volunteer for agitation over there, you can pick up extra time in s'rag, and if you manage some real hurt to the fuzz-heads, maybe even a bonus time-ticket or two. Ta'ma', it's only buzz, I believe it when I see it posted and certified."

"Hoy, Chob, you pulling a single?" Yadak tossed his yamsac from the door of the sleeping cabin at the back end of the tracker, followed it with Girs'. "This lot of mudworms will keep you crazy."

"Nah. Herm's along. He just not moving well right now."

"His luck's still running with the vagnag, hunh?"

"Ayyunh." Choban grinned, his eyes almost vanishing in a web of wrinkles. "Zorl was the big loser this time. He was really pissed."

"Ta'ma', Chob, alarms are set, any problems you get bonged. Girs, got a back on you? Flip you for who rousts Herm."

4

As they flew across the rolling savannah, Girs listened to the uncertain whine from the lifters and fiddled with the conter pad, trying to get a better balance. After half an hour of it, he said, "Don't know, Yad. Maybe we should go straight back. 'S a light world but I never much liked walking."

Yadak slapped his arm. "Naymind, look there, there's a clutch of 'em. Kick in high, it's not big enough jag to worry about."

\* \* \*

"Look at 'em scatter. Take it right through the middle, Giro." Yadak triggered the beam, sent it cutting through a large lumbering jelly, shouted as it burned. "Two miles if it's an inch. Look at that 'un, going down 'stead of up. Trying to be sly, hunh ol' havva? Gotcha. What you think those things there on the ground are? Those brown lumps, one of 'em's burning, ol' jelly fell on it. Hoosh, what a stink. M'ra, you feel that? Go through that smoke again, Giro. Haaaggghhh, that's good, you feel that, that's goo' tha' ssss goooo...."

## 5

The Ykkuval looked down at the charred bits that had been two of his techs, then at his chief of security, the Memur Tryben who was also one of his cousins, and at the two medics hovering behind him. "Ta'ma', what am I supposed tell their families?"

Tryben grunted. "Not the truth, that's sagg. I'll give you the witness' tale later; for now, Med First Muhaseb, tell him what you found."

Hunnar's eyeridges wrinkled, the inner lids slid forward until they were just visible.

His shoulders coming up in submission, Med Muhaseb fixed his eyes on the floor and spoke to the tiles in front of Hunnar's feet. "We found certain ... ahhh ... certain residues in the bodies of both techs. To put an ordinary name on it, we suspect they were drugging themselves with something local. It's not a substance on the List, that's why I say local." His shoulders hunched higher and he began choosing his words with extreme care. "It is ... ahhh ... difficult to determine the precise effects of the substance ... we're only beginning to test it ... but I would hazard a guess that it's both powerful and dangerous. The locals we've ... ahhh ... studied are not greatly divergent from the general run of Cousins and there are sufficient ... ahhh ... resonances with Chav ... ahhh

... physiology to ... ahhh ... make it reasonably certain that the locals will be aware of such a substance and its effects." He stopped talking but kept his eyes fixed on the floor.

Hunnar flexed his fingers, retracted his claws. "Right. Get on with your analysis. I don't expect miracles, we're not equipped for those, but I want a report on my desk by the end of the month, you hear me?"

"We hear, Ykkuval."

Memur Tryben slid a flake into the player but didn't touch the sensor. "Fayl Skambil—he's a good, reliable tech who knows how to keep his mouth shut. He belongs to a minor house, one of our affiliates, so he knows where his loyalties lie. Skambil was out scouting the foothills for locals, spotting the infestations so we can shift them once the factories are in place. Doing his own piloting, marking the grid and flaking the settlements."

Hunnar clicked a claw on the desktop; but Tryben didn't hurry himself. He was a methodical Chav; it didn't matter what his listener knew, he was going to say what he had to say and keep on till he was finished.

"He happened to be in the area when the two techs came by. They had deviated from the straight flight back to base and were having themselves some fun burning jellies. He was busy mapping possible habitations in the trees beneath him and paid little attention until he noticed the techs whipping their flier back and forth through thick gray-white smoke, windows dialed open, the inside so white with the smoke he couldn't make out the form of the pilot. He said he thought it might be a good idea to record what he was seeing, so he slipped in a new flake. And he said he thought it would be best that none of it go on public record. He saw the possibilities in that smoke. Could be profit for the family."

Tryben touched the sensor then and stepped back.

The sky was a brilliant blue, cloudless, the forested hills a dark nubbly green. The flier was a black bug diving through and through and through that column of smoke, each swing wilder and wobblier than the one before—until, finally, the flier looped completely over and went racing down down down—this time not turning, apparently no attempt to bring the nose up—down and down until it smacked into the earth.

He stopped the movement, left the image pinned in that moment. "When he saw that, Skambil slapped his intakes shut and went on bottle and scrub. The flier was on fire and the smoke got so thick he thought for a while the whole forest was going to go. He hung about until the worst of the burn was finished, then went closer to inspect the scene." He ticked his claw against the plaque and the play moved forward again.

The techs' flier was a heap of twisted, blackened metal in the center of a large meadow filled with interconnected pergolas, the lattices thick with ancient vines whose leaves for the most part concealed the ground beneath them. Where it'd crashed, the columns and horizontal latticework were broken; Hunnar could see large fibrous brown lumps in grassy nests—near the wreck they were almost completely burned to ash, but deep in the shadows they were only charred and smoking.

Tryben tapped at the sensor plaques with the tips of his claws. The image of one of the more intact lumps enlarged, filled the frame. "You can see those things are tended with considerable effort and care. Look how the grass is woven around the base there, not just grown but trained into place. The vines on the pergola have a combination of flowers and ornamental fruits, but there is no debris on the ground. There are possibly several hundred of the lumps there and each one is like this one. We don't know what they are, but they seem to be important to the locals."

He switched the scene to the worst of the burned areas. Wisps of greasy smoke were still rising from the lumps. "You will recall how the techs took their flier repeatedly through that smoke. It seems reasonable to me that the smoke is the vector for those ... mmm ... substances the medics found. As to their source, I'd say it was either those lumps or the vines. I suggest you haul in your pet and ask him some questions. I'll get back to the med techs and make sure they keep their mouths shut."

## 6

Shaking so uncontrollably he could barely walk, Ilaörn shuffled into the room. Without being told, he seated himself in the probe chair and waited passively as Hunnar locked down his arms and legs. When the crown was lowered about his head and he felt the faint tickle as the fields began their mapping, he shuddered, licking his lips.

"Open your eyes. Tell me about that."

When Ilaörn realized what the image was, he moaned and for the first time in months tried to fight the probe. He knew well enough it was futile, but he tried.

"What is that place? Answer in words, cho."

"Sleeping Ground." Ilaörn was shivering and sobbing as he spoke; the urge to babble was almost irresistible, but he shut his teeth on the words that wanted to come pouring out.

All of it was there where Hunnar could see it, he knew that, he'd seen flakes of earlier sessions. Hunnar made him watch them to grind the lesson in that there was nothing Ilaörn could hide from the Chave. The Ykkuval didn't need the questions, but they focused

Ilaörn's attention and made him form his thoughts in the Chandavasi tongue; more than that, they were another twist of the knife and Hunnar enjoyed that.

"Tell me the meaning."

"When Denchok feel their time pressing on them, they go to the Sleeping Grounds."

"To die?"

Ilaörn writhed in the chair, fighting the restraints; blood oozed from his scalp and trickled past his ears, his eyes shut tight, tears squeezing out and mixing with the blood. His mouth spoke, and he couldn't stop it. "To change. They eat the melodach and grow the husk around themselves, and when it is finished, they sleep until the change is complete and the Eolt is born."

"You mean those things that walk around like mobile gardens, they turn into the jellies?" There was a tension in Hunnar's voice that Ilaörn felt even through his distress.

"Yu ... yuh ... YES."

"Open your eyes, look at the image."

Again the dark flier dived at the smoke column, passed through it and through it, looped up and crashed.

"Why? What got to them?"

"S sss smoke. Hu HUSK!" The pressure was too strong. He babbled, betraying his sioll, betraying his harp, his people. "They must have been ripe, nearly ripe, ready to wake and fly, when the husk is green the dreams are few, when it cracks and the Eolt fly free you can fly with them, the sioll bond is set then, the pairing is complete, the music blends, burn the husk and breathe the smoke and fly...." He started to sing, his voice cracking with the pain that racked him.

"Be quiet."

The flood cut off. Hunnar didn't need the pain circuits any longer to control Ilaörn, though sometimes he played with them for the pleasure of it. He didn't do that today. *More important things on his mind,* Ilaörn thought wretchedly. *He's angry. Why? And worried. Why? And greedy. Chel Dé, the husk....* He'd seen enough of the Chave to understand dimly what was going on in Hunnar's mind. *They murder us for their games, what will they do when there's profit in it?*

# 4. Warnings

## 1

Maorgan sat on the roof with his harp between his knees and watched the strangers enter Dumel Alsekum.

It was a noisy entrance.

The tracktruck clanked along, its trailer bumping and sashaying along the road. It was a house on treads, a huge box with tinted glass in the windows. Inside he could see the driver, the Scholar and her company, and blocky forms of crates packed in with them.

Glois sat proud as a teseach atop the canvas covering the baggage in the trailer, Utelel kneeling beside him, leaning on his shoulder whispering at him. The rest of their band were scattered over the canvas behind them, waving and shouting at the young Fiors and Meloach who came running from the fields and lanes, the lot of them talking loud and long enough as they welcomed their friends and cousins home to make the two Eolts drifting above the tracktruck pulse darker with irritation.

Around the Meeting House the Denchok and the older Fior came to doors and windows or out into the street to stand watching, others stayed in shadow, uncertain how to take this invasion.

Melech's speaking tentacle brushed Maorgan's cheek, settled against his neck. *Change is on us, sioll.

We've drifted in a dream for a thousand and a thousand years and now it's time to wake.*

Maorgan grunted. "And about as welcome as any other waking time. It's sweeter to stay warm and drowsy under the covers."

Laughter came along the tentacle and filled Maorgan with Melech's warmth.

"It's too pleasant a day for listening to glagairh, but I suppose we have to go." He wrinkled his nose, crossed his hands on the top of the harpcase and leaned over them, watching the Fior Teseach and the Keteng Metau come from the Meeting House and walk toward the tracktruck. "That pair. Guarantee it's going to be a boring session knotting knots and pricking ayids. Omudh! Tes Ruaim is a pris with pleats in his soul."

*And Metau Chachil is a match to him.*
A sigh tickled down with the words. *The Meruu of the Eolts want word for word, so you are right, go we must and listen.*

"Is that what Mer-Eolt Lebesair came to say? Or has more news come across from Melitöh?"

*Both, sioll. Xe didn't say—but from xe's comport, I do think more song has been brought and it is something evil*
Another sigh and Melech sank lower until xe's grasping cilia brushed Maorgan's hair. *Xe came to tell me there will be a Klobach. The ingathering has begun. T' Meruu want the mesuch harper there if you and I agree it's wise.*

"I wondered when you didn't say anything, sioll."

*I was considering Lebesair's song and how temeroum it was.*

"What size are the holes and how many?"

*Large enough to float through and many indeed.*

"Sounds like secrets to me and that's a bad omen. Chel Dé grant the Meruus don't start down that road." He touched thumb to ring finger in the avert sign, then got to his feet and walked along the Harper's Way that circled the roof of the Meeting House, heading for the stairs that led down to the Center, the inner court where the meeting was set.

The Eolt Melech dropped xe's graspers to the roof holds and pulled xeself after xe's sioll.

## 2

The main part of Dumel Alsekum was laid out as an infinity sign with the Meeting House at the twist point. In one node the houses were low and rounded with an organic look as if they were grown rather than built and roofs that glittered in the sunlight, panels of translucent material that could be slid aside to let in the full force of the sun. In the other the style of building was more angular, walls built with a mellow ocher brick and wood with the gleam of pale bronze; the roofs were rough shakes with a crannied thready texture as if they were cut from bark rather than the wood itself. Moss grew in patches across these roofs, the dark rich green starred with small yellow blooms. Ketengs lived in the first node, Fior in the second. Despite this separation in the living quarters, Shadith saw children of both species playing together, the adults working together in the fields, standing together in the streets. She was pleased to see this, but couldn't help wondering where the catch was; the history of Cousin interactions with intelligent non-Cousins was on the whole bloody and depressing.

The Yarak driver stopped at the edge of the village. *No*, Shadith thought, *Dumel*. That was what the Béluchar called a village. *Dumel was the settlement, ordumel the manufactories and farms attached to it.* She touched her fingers lightly to her temple; the translator had settled down, the blinding ache was gone, all she had now was a twinge or two when she ran into a spate of slang like the shouts of those children outside.

The driver twisted around to speak to Aslan.

"Scholar, if you want me to take you to the Hostel, I'll have to go round outside this place. The streets are too narrow for the track."

"Wait here a moment. We're supposed to be met by local officials. Once we're out, you make your way round and wait. There's maneuvering to do before that's settled. I hope you brought something to pass the time since we probably won't get in till sundown, if then."

He flashed his pointed teeth at her in a broad, dangerous grin, his orange-brown eyes shutting to furry slits. His mask was a sketch of mahogany fur only a few shades darker than the rest of a pelt that was shaggier than the neat plush on Goës Koraka and the other highborn and there was no white on his face. "How it goes," he said. "Rush till you're rubbed down to hide, then sit around and listen to your fur grow while the big chods talk."

Aslan chuckled, clicked her tongue. "Hush now. Two of those chods are coming toward us." She pushed her chair around so she was facing the others. "Dunc, Shadow and I will see if we can light a fire under them and clear the way for you to start getting settled in."

Duncan Shears was a small wiry man with droopy eyelids that lent a mild and sleepy look to his round face, a man given to hoarding words. Now he simply nodded, settled down in his seat, and turned slightly so he could look through the offside window of the track's cabin and watch the maneuvering of the locals as they moved in staring circles about the tracktruck.

Shadith swung down and followed Aslan to meet the Béluchar, a Denchok and a Fior walking side by side, looking curiously alike though they were from different species.

Denchok. In Bélucharis it meant *settled* and *caretaker* and *middle term*, the three meanings blended in a way she didn't know enough yet to understand. Meloach were the children. That term was easier, it meant *beginning* and *herd* and *opening bud*. Eolt seemed to have only one meaning, being the generic name given to the intelligent floaters.

This Denchok had broad plump shoulders and grey-green skin like the bark of a willow tree. Unlike the Meloach, xe had no symbiote moss, rather a weaving of thready lichen that spread about the middle of xe's stocky sexless body and looked like brittle gray-green spiderwebs. Watching xe move brought to mind the march of a dead tree trunk weathered and old. Xe wore no clothing, merely a bronze chain about xe's short thick neck, a medallion dangling from the lowest link with worn symbols engraved on its oval.

The Fior was a plumpish man with a neatly trimmed white beard and mustache that framed thick red lips. He wore tight trousers and a tunic of deeply textured cloth that was a stylized echo of the Denchok's lichen web. He, too, had a bronze chain and medallion.

The Denchok stopped a few steps from Aslan. Fingering xe's medal with broad stumpy fingers, xe said, "I am the Metau Chachil. I speak for the Denchok."

(Shadith murmured a translation into Aslan's ear, added, "Local pol. Context fringes—xe's elected to the post, not born into it.")

"And I am the Teseach Ruaim. I speak for the Fior." The Teseach's voice was a silver tenor that might have been crafted to charm birds from the sky.

("Different word, same connotation," she whispered.)

Turn and turn about, dancing their voices through the phrases of the welcome speech with a practiced ease, the Teseach and the Metau welcomed their visitors to Dumel Alsekum.

When they finished, Aslan said, "May our interaction be pleasant and fruitful." She paused for Shadith to translate, then went on briskly, "If my associates

could be guided to the living quarters that were promised us, I would be most grateful."

The Teseach snapped thumb against forefinger,
dropped the hand on the shoulder of the youth who
ran over to him. "Diroch will show you how to go.
That contraption can't come inside the Dumel, it'll
have to go round."

("Nose out of joint," Shadith murmured. "No one's
moving into his town till he and the Metau approve.
You're going to have to keep this pair sweet or they'll
make trouble every chance they see.")

Aslan bowed as she'd been instructed, arms crossed,
the tips of her fingers resting against her shoulders.
"Teach your grandmother," she said, tucking the corners of her mouth in to keep from grinning. "Tell our
friends there how profoundly appreciative we are and
how we shall strive to be worthy of the honor and
keep your face straight while you're doing it, hm?"

The Meeting Room wasn't a room at all, but a pen-
tagonal court at the heart of the building with grasping
rods extending from the roof on the five sides, leaving
the center completely open to the sky. Three Eolt
floated above the court, their tentacles anchoring them
to the rods; below them a collection of Fior adults and
Denchok sat in witness on benches pushed against
four of the sides. Near a low dais that ran across the
fifth side, the Dumel scribe perched at a small desk
with a tablet, stylus and inkpad. Xe was a Denchok
who seemed older than the rest, xe's crust coarser,
grayer, xe's lichen web a thick matting of closely inter-
woven, crinkled threads.

The Metau and the Teseach climbed onto the dais,
stood waiting beside massive chairs carved over every
inch of their surface, chairs that looked extraordinarily
uncomfortable. Shadith and Aslan were left standing
at the foot of the steps.

A lanky Fior with a shock of gray hair brought out

folding backless chairs whose seats were pieces of heavy cloth stretched between wooden dowels. He clicked the chairs open, snapped home the cross struts, slapped at the cloth to make sure they were secure, then went to take his place on one of the benches.

Metau Chachil and Teseach Ruaim bowed to each other then seated themselves in the chairs. Ruaim closed his hands over worn finials and leaned forward. "Sit if you please," he said, his voice making a song of the words.

They sat. Shadith positioned the harpcase beside her knee, wondering if she should open it, decided not yet and straightened. From the corner of one eye she could see the Fior who'd served as the Goës' contact. Maorgan. His harpcase, like hers, was leaning against his knee. She wondered what his harp looked like. Would it be carved like those ugly chairs? What would that do to the sound?

There was whispering in the benches, creaks and scuffs as heavy bodies shifted position. Brushing sounds and soft exhalations came from the lattices as the Eolt shifted their holds on the horizontal rods.

The Metau leaned forward and spoke (Shadith translating in a murmur just loud enough to reach Aslan's ear), "We have listened to the Eolt and the Ard and have given you rooms in our Hostel, Scholar."

("Given is not exactly the word," Aslan muttered to Shadith, "seeing the size of the rent they twisted from us.")

Shadith smiled; she spoke to the Metau and the Teseach as if she were translating what Aslan had said, "For which we give thanks."

"What we wish to know is why you want it. What is your purpose here? The traders who came before the mesuch descended on us say University is subject to no one's will, but we know this, who pays for the song can name what they want to hear."

Aslan nodded as she listened to Shadith's recapitulation, then spoke slowly so the phrases could be translated into something like a coherent statement. "My purpose is knowledge, Metau, Teseach. My life-study is gathering the chronicles, songs and lifeways of different peoples, especially those on the verge of great change. All things change. A sage once said you cannot step twice in the same river. But the form of the river can be preserved and the memory of it even though it dries and dies. This is what I do. I document what might soon be erased by the press of time so that when the Wheel turns once more there will be a record of that heritage for those who wish to recapture something of what they were."

Ruaim leaned forward again. "If we could rid ourselves of those mesuch over there, we wouldn't need the record; things would go back to the way they were. Can you tell us how we can do that?"

"No. It is the short answer and a simple one, but it is the truth. The long answer is this: The word of your existence has spread too widely and will attract too many who want to wring profit from you and your world for you to be as you were. You could do worse—much worse—than the Yaraka. If you deal with them wisely, they will protect you from the...." Aslan said *wolves* and Shadith hesitated as she searched for an equivalent, then hurried to catch up. "The tukeol. And right now you need protection. What I can do is teach you about the Yaraka while I learn from you how your lives go. Knowledge brings power; ignorance, death."

"You speak with eloquence, Scholar, but you don't say much."

"What can I say? What I know about you is what I see. I speak with the Harper's tongue and listen with the Harper's ears because I haven't had time to learn your speech. I know even less of who you are and how you live. When one wishes to explain something, one needs to understand at least a little of what the listener knows and does not know, otherwise two people will only speak past each other and much misunderstanding will arise."

"That is true. But we do not know this Harper. How does she know us?"

"It is her Gift to understand strange speech. I can't explain, only be pleased to use it."

"Why do the mesuch want you here?"

"The Chave are testing them, trying to drive them away. The Yaraka don't have the time or resources to do what I'll be doing for them, they'll be too busy defending themselves and conducting their side-glance secret war. You do know about the Chave?"

"The mesuchs across the sea? We have heard. They are different?"

"Different worlds, different interests. Rivals. Enemies. You can use that, you know—if you learn how to play the Yaraka. You can't get rid of them, but you can control to some extent the change they bring to your lives."

The talk went on and on, the scribe stamping the wedge-shaped end of xe's stylo in complicated patterns down row after row of the pages of the tablet. Shadith stopped thinking about what she was hearing, giving the words only the attention needed to translate them.

Aslan explained over and over what her purpose and intent was, what University was, the kind of things she was going to record, what would happen to the record, what was her exact relationship to the Yaraka, what did she know about the Chave, why did they act that way, who would be able to read what she recorded.

"Anyone?" The Metau's heavy features drew together.

"Anyone who has the money to purchase a readout. As long as the data is not flagged for limited access, which this would probably not be." Aslan thought a moment (Shadith moved her shoulders, grateful for the momentary pause; she considered asking for a glass of water, but her need wasn't urgent and she didn't want to break the flow). "The Yaraka might consider it proprietary information and therefore privileged, but our Meruu of Scholars have strong feelings about unrestricted access to information, as long as the seeker can pay for it. They would probably deny such a request."

On and on.

The Alsekumers on the benches shifted position, whispered in hisses, went out, and others came in; Shadith could hear the faint rustles of their movements and envied them. She was getting stiff from sitting and her throat was beginning to burn.

A basso note of considerable power broke through a question; there was a sharp edge of impatience to the sound and a demand implicit in it. Shadith looked up.

An Eolt had moved out over the open center, holding position with a single tentacle. A long slit pursed open and snapped closed among the cilia in xe's base and more sounds poured out of xe, a wordless music that was at the same time an announcement that the Eolt had something to say and was tired of waiting xe's chance.

Ruaim and Chachil exchanged grimaces, then the Teseach sang, "Mer-Eolt Lebesair, be welcome to Alsekum Meet. Is there word you bring us from the Meruu of the Eolt?" He put frills on the words, made a fine production of the question.

("What's that about?" Aslan murmured.

"The Meruu is some kind of council, this Eolt is a rep from that council, here to look us over, I suppose."

"Wish xe'd opened xe's mouth earlier. Saved my ears and your throat. Have you picked up any idea what the relationship is between our floating friend up there and the walkers?"

"I've a few notions but they're too vague to talk about right now. Ah! Xe's warming up for a speech. I need to concentrate for this. When the floaters talk, it's complicated.")

### 3

Maorgan watched the two women as they answered the tedious and silly questions from that phrata pair preening on the dais. The Harper amazed him. After years of dealing with offworld traders and now these invading mesuch, he'd only acquired a few hard won words of tradespeech. To reach out and absorb a whole language well enough to make songs in it—that was a gift of gifts. He couldn't tell how much she really understood of what she was saying, but she set word against word in a proper way.

It made him think.

For the first time he wondered about Béluchad. Eolt drifted here and there, sioll-bonded Ard moved with them, back and forth from continent to continent. Sometimes places made new words and if they were good words, Eolt and Ard put them in their songs— like stirring soup so the flavors blended. There was one speech everywhere and no need to learn how to learn another.

The mesuch were different. The ones over here spoke their own langue, as well as tradespeak, and probably others. He had no doubt the mesuch on Mel-itoëh were much the same.

He stroked his hand along the harpcase, remembering the made-look of the woman's harp. Someone had put knife and plane to that wood, hadn't lived with the growing matrix and shaped it with song and caress into a companion and complement. Some of the strings were metal with a harsher tone than his sweet singer but also one that was more precise, steadier. He wanted to hear it again, to learn its song. He wanted to tell Teseach Ruaim and Metau Chachil to shut their yammering mouths and listen to the song he could make with her and Melech.

He didn't, of course. The relationship between Ard and Dumel was a prickly one, oversweet reverence with a backtaste of resentment. If it weren't for the sweet bouncy flesh of Fior girls, he'd stop at a Dumel only when he needed to shelter from a storm. He caught here and there furtive glances from ordu girls on the benches and some that boldly challenged him. An Ard baby brought honor to a family and there seemed several here who'd like to try for one.

He looked up as Lebesair lost patience and stabbed a call for attention into the babble below xe, then he waited for an announcement that would match the imperious demand for hearing.

Into the silence that followed Ruaim's song, Mer-Eolt Lebesair launched a great mourning bellow that battered at the court. Concentrated sorrow. Keening for the dead.

FIRE          leaping to the sun          an Eolt dies
      sport for mesuch      killing with light
FIRE          dropping like rain          death DEATH
      CURSE the killers      SOULless MONSTERS
FIRE      mourn for the dead      Mourn MOURN!

After the echoes of the final word had died, the Eolt shifted mode to simple-speech.

"Every day on Melitoëh Eolt and Denchok die, hunted like beasts by the mesuch. Others are driven from their Dumels and their fields. Fior males are killed or made slaves, Fior women are killed in terrible ways or live as slaves. A Sleeping Ground was burned a week ago and news has come that mesuch have gone

back and ripped the husks from the few Sleepers still
in life. This I leave for you to think on. Remember
the Shape Wars. Remember the sorrows a thousand
and a thousand years ago."

Maorgan shuddered. The old songs had been
leached of their anger and pain by the passing of centuries, but if that time was coming again, there were
horrors waiting that put a chill in his soul. He thought
about what the Scholar said—you can do worse than
the Yaraka. He didn't like these mesuch thieves—
what else were they but thieves, taking what didn't
belong to them—but the contrast between the reports
from Melitoëh and the way the Yaraka had treated
Glois and Utelel and the rest told him she was right.

"The Meruus of Eolt and Fior are called to a Special
Meeting. Tomorrow is Chel Dé's day. The Meruus cry
out to you to make it a day of meditation and prayer.
Especially pray for the success of this meeting."

## 4

Aslan listened to Shadith's translation with fascina-
tion, distress and anger. She tucked away the name
*Shape Wars* as something to investigate and steamed
as she thought of all the omissions in the Yaraka
Rep's report. She was also angry at the Goës; though
he did try to persuade her to live inside the Fence, he
hadn't given her any reasons or said word one about
these killings. Sniping between two Companies was
one thing, this other business could lead to . . . well,
she didn't want to think where it would lead. *If I'd
known*, she thought, *would I even be here? Is this
going to turn into another Styernna?*

Waves of chill ran through her.

Shadith's hand closed round hers, warm and
reassuring.

Her breathing steadied. *I need to think about this.
It changes things.*

The Chave were killing sentients for sport. If they didn't know that now, they would soon enough—maybe as soon as she sent out her first reports since the Ykkuval probably had bought out one or more of the Goës staff. Once University heard about this, they'd work to get Chandava Minerals blacklisted on Helvetia. The Ykkuval responsible would likely be called home and stripped of his standing and the minute he realized that, this side-glance war would go real. *Have to talk to the Goës as soon as I get loose. Do I call this off now? Have to talk to Shadow and Duncan, see what they say.*

She kept her listening mask firmly in place, but slipped in a quick glance or two at the benches. She didn't know Keteng expressions yet, but the Fior were still Cousins enough that she could feel their fear and a rising anger.

"Ignorance is death, the Scholar said, and that is true. Sioll Maorgan has reported that the mesuch have a way of transferring understanding of strange speech. Strange and frightening as those devices are, the Meruus ask that some among you who are closest to the mesuch show the courage to undergo this transfer. The Béluchar must know what the Scholar knows and hear what the mesuch say."

5

Shadith sighed as she passed on that last bit. Having to do all this translating made her feel caged, as if she were a machine bolted to the floor. *I'm not a Scholar*, she thought. *Won't ever be. I haven't got that kind of patience. The body has some age on it now and I can look even older if I have to. Hm. Digby keeps after me to work for him. Maybe when this is over. . . .*

She glanced at Aslan. A muscle jumped at the corner of the Scholar's eye; sweat beaded on her forehead and her mouth had a stiff look as if her lips were trying to tremble and she willed them quiet. *She's been scared half to death since that Eolt starting speaking.*

"This is important because the Meruus think of calling the Scholar's Harper to the Klobach so that she may contribute to the deliberations. They have asked this Mer to discover if such a notion would be wise. Harper, heed me. Sing for us. Not our songs, but yours. Show us your heart. Teach us who you are.

Shadith looked up, startled, then reached for the harpcase. "Happy to," she said. "And if you have a wish to join in at any time, honored Eolt, feel free." She smiled at Maorgan. "And you, Ard Maorgan."

She bent over the small harp Swardheld had made for her, touching the strings lightly as she considered what she should play. Play your heart, the Eolt said. Which heart? She smiled as she thought that.

Something stirred in her—a need she hadn't fed since she took Kikun home. *I wonder . . . no, can't think of him now.* She closed her eyes. *Dance for me, sisters. Let me have Shayalin again. You have to come alone this time, no Kikun to power you, no dream pollen to make you real again.*

Shayalin was raided again and again to make slaves of the Weavers of Dreams. What the Eolt had said about the killings hit her; before this, she'd been detached, not really listening to the sense, letting her Gift change the words for her and pass them on to Aslan. Now. . . .

The raiders came down on Shayalin, killing the Shallana males and the makers like her who were the fertile ones, the 'tween generation born single, not six. Carrying away the Weavers to dance dreams for men who had no understanding of what they really saw.

She burned with memory and sudden kinship and hatred for the Chave who were suddenly all the raiders who'd ravaged her world and destroyed her family. She knew what she should play.

She stilled the strings, then began to play. Just music at first, not calling her sisters' names to bring them back to memory.

As she played and prepared, she saw Maorgan bring forth his harp. It was a strange one, grown not made. Alive. Eyes closed, face taut with concentration, he stroked it and it changed shape. It was a slight change, but her eyes widened as she saw it.

When the shift was finished, he joined her, the harp new-tuned to match her own; the tone was more mellow and didn't have the volume of her own, but there was something about the sound.... *I'll have to have one*, she thought, *I HAVE to have a harp like that.* She closed her eyes and sought focus.

In her mind her sisters came. Naya, Zayalla, Annethi, Itsaya, Talitt, and Sullan. In her mind her sisters danced and she made the music for them.

She sang the ancient croon mated with that dance, a mourning dance for everything that dies. Her human throat could not produce the full sounds, but Maorgan's living harp seemed to read her need and he played the other tones.

And sometime later the Eolt began to sing.

The sound thrummed in her blood and bone and filled the court and spilled out of it; at the fringes of her being she felt the wonder in the Béluchar beyond the Meeting House.

The Eolt, the Denchok, the Meloach, the Fior—they gave her the fullness of her grief for the first time in the millennia she'd lived past the death of her world.

## 6

The blai was a low, rambling complex of rooms and arcades, a guesthouse for travelers, merchants and peddlers, Ard and Eolt, youths on their wanderyears. The area they were to occupy was at the back, little used, dust on every surface, a musty smell clinging to the walls.

Aslan came into the room where Shadith, Duncan Shears, and Marrin Ola, the laconic student Aide, were taking apart crates, turning them into work stations and stacking equipment on them. "Leave that for a moment. We need to talk."

Shadith straightened. "What the Eolt said?"

"Yes. And the implications. I want you in on this, too, Marrin. We have to decide what we're going to do."

Duncan's nose twitched. "Moment," he said and moved to a small crate at the top of a pile pushed into a corner of the room. He unsnapped the clips, lifted the lid, and took out a box. "Where?"

"My room," Shadith said. "It's the one with the least stuff in it."


Duncan opened the box, took out a privacy cone, and set it in the center of the braided grass floormat. He clicked it on. "Our business," he said and arranged himself on the floor beside it.

"Thanks." Aslan dropped to the mat, waited a moment as the others seated themselves, then said, "One of the Eolt made a speech at the meeting. It's a sentient being, connected somehow to the non-Cousin species here. Chave techs are hunting them for sport, touching them off to see the flare. Apparently they've already killed hundreds of the Eolt and are still doing it."

Marrin Ola blinked, leaned forward, then remembered he was only an Aide and subsided.

"Say it, Marrin."

"Do they know?"

"Good question. The Chave are not noted for their sensitive souls, but they aren't stupid. If this gets off-world with any kind of reasonable proof, they've got problems."

Duncan grunted. "Styernna."

"A lot like that. Yes."

"Um...." Marrin frowned. "Why? No courts, no laws. Shit happens all the time."

Aslan nodded. "Right. Prespace indigene comes close to meaning extinct. But there are a few twists in that. The Eolt are beautiful, especially wonderful when they sing; flakes passed around of what we heard yesterday and today would be very bad for Chandava business if news of the killing got out. And there's Helvetia. The Yaraka aren't important, Helvetia wouldn't listen to them. It doesn't get involved in trade wars. University is another thing altogether. Marrin, ever heard of a contract labor company called Bolodo Neyuregg?"

"Huh?"

"Right. They aren't around any more. They slipped over the edge into slave-dealing. I know because I was one of the slaves they dealt in. Helvetia doesn't approve of slaving. Blacklisted them. Cut off fund transfers, loans. Their client list evaporated. So did they. Helvetia doesn't approve of the gratuitous slaughter of sentients. If University got proof of what the Eolt said, Chandava Minerals would go the same road as Bolodo Neyuregg."

Shadith leaned forward. "You're going to tell the Goës."

"I thought about not, Shadow. Telling Goës Koraka hoeh Dexios would be the same thing as shouting it in the Chave Ykkuval's face. Both of them are bound to have spies busy as black biters on a summer day. But when you think about it, that doesn't really matter." She moved her shoulders, shifted her legs. "If the Ykkuval doesn't know by now about the Eolt's status, he will soon enough. And as soon as he does, he'll realize that he can't let news of this get offworld. It's make or break time, folks. Do we stay, or do we get out of here so fast we leave holes in the air?"

Shadith dropped her hands on her knees. "I'm staying," she said. "I'm separate, Lan. It's in the contract that way. What I do lays no burden on anyone."

Duncan Shears scratched at his chin. "Was wrong. Kinda wrong. Not Styernna. Got the gov on our side this time. Tell Goës we targets, want shields and stunners. I c'n do alarms, some other stuff. Good pay. No reports, keep the heat down." He twisted his mouth to one side, shook his head. "Not getting me on shuttle or anything else till Goës gets his house cleaned."

"Unh! Hadn't thought of that. Quick and dirty way of keeping news inhouse. So you say stay, ride it out."

He nodded.

"Marrin?"

The Aide grinned at her. "I come from a Baronial House on Picabral, Scholar. Fifth line-heir, male and healthy. I've made it past thirty still alive and I've scrambled a long way from home." He made an avert gesture. "May that way never get shorter. I've already earned one share of Voting Stock and this business gets me another. No caggin' bunch of heavy-world lizzers is going to chase me off from that."

"Right. Anything about the Eolt goes into deep code in the Ridaars. Keep it pristine for the Regents and Helvetia. Duncan, you'll be getting volunteers for the language transfer tomorrow. Copy out everything about the Eolt, set that down in a separate report. Privacy locked, hm? I don't want the Goës' fingerprints anywhere around it. He gets antsy about that, invoke Scholar's Necessity. Um." She chewed on her lip a moment. "I want a special flake of that session in the Meeting Room. Shadow, I want a translation of everything said, especially that last Lament. I'll go see the Goës tomorrow, arrange to transmit the flake to Tamarralda. Eyes only and classified to the max. Let her know what's coming so she can get ready. Any questions? No? Good. All of you, eyes open and shields up and don't let the bastards get behind you."

# 5. Grief

1

Ragnal tilted his squeeze pouch, swallowed a mouthful of yang, shuddered, and rubbed his mouth with the back of his hand.

He was lounging between two roots on a huge tree that was part of the woods between the fields and the Kushayt where the Ykkuval sat like a fat greedy spider. Sifaed called these trees kerrehs. She was one of the local femmes who worked the backroom of Drudge Farkli's lubbot, a big solid woman, not one of the wisps that broke in your hand if you touched them wrong. Reminded of her, he felt a stirring and thought about spending a few baks on chich and emm but took another drink instead and glowered out across his fields.

The scowl smoothed out as he rested his eyes on the sogan mounds with their circle-crowns of dark green leaves, giant spearpoints on broad stems. Now that he'd sterilized and remixed the dirt, it was good soil, rich and black and full of nutrients; the first harvest of sogan had brought tubers larger than a man's foot.

The Drudges were out on their floatboards, working the t'prags, snipping at weeds and stirring the earth around the tuber mounds. T'prags and boards alike were patched together castoffs, hiccuping along like yarks with a hangover because that ni Jilet kreash

Hunnar who was running this operation was too cheap to get the parts they needed. Ragnal was a Koroumak cognate like the ni-Jilets, which is why he worked for Company Koroumak-Jilet, but he kept Family tighter than that; far as he was concerned the ni Jilet sept were employers only.

Chains of local women were crawling along replanting the harvested mounds with eye segments of the seed reserve from the first dig, the bright orange chunks like dice in their busy hands. He smiled, pleased at what he saw. If there were any justice in the world, he'd get a commendation for his efforts.

Not chichin' likely.

Girs used to needle him about it. Dirtman, he called him. There's no honor in booting Drudges about and fooling with bugs and worms. And Girs didn't like Ragnal reminding him that he owed his education and his success to his older brother's job. *They sneer at me*, he said, *call me grubsuck and webfoot. It's holding me back. You're holding me back.* Same thing over and over—till Ragnal would lose his temper and pound him. Arrogant little ahmk. Last fight they had, Ragnal broke one of Girs' teeth and got his own neck twisted so bad he had to have heat packs on it.

*No more fights. No enough left of Girs to be worth burying. Taner! How'm I going to tell Mar her baby's dead?*

He squeezed out the rest of the yang, lumbered to his feet, nearly falling on his bum as the chichin' sad excuse for honest gravity tricked him again.

Grumbling under his breath he walked ti-tuppy along, heading for a refill in Farkli's lubbot, hating the strain he put on his muscles to keep himself on his feet, hating the bone leaching he knew had to be happening. Wasn't the first light-world he'd worked on. If he had a say, though, it'd be the last. *Say? That's a laugh.*

The lubbot was in the largest house still standing in

what had been a local village. Ragnal was using most
of the place to store his planting and harvesting equipment, but by old custom, he rented the extra rooms
to Farkli. He'd had most of the other houses dozed
and burned, leaving one of them for the Drudges to
sleep and live in, a second for a Drudge s'rag, and a
third for a sogan storehouse. They offended his eyes,
those structures. Garish colors. Flimsy. A hard wind
would blow them to kindling. Though it didn't seem
like this taffy world ever got anything like a real wind.
Those floating blobs would be smears spread half a
mile across those trees in a Chandava wind.

He pushed through the swinging door that old Farkli always managed to contrive wherever he was set
down and stood a moment letting his eyes adjust to
the dim, smoky light. The stink in the air was the
same, too, as if Farkli bottled it and brought it along,
a mix of sweat, lantern smoke, and the pungent stink
of the yang distilled from sogan and Taner only knew
what else he threw in the pot. Ragnal didn't ask. Old
man might just tell him. Better his stomachs didn't
know what he was running through them.

Lanterns. Rest of the place was lit properly but not
here. *The techs like it that way,* the old yisser said.
*What they call good ambience, whatever that means.
Drink more, too. Use the women in backroom 'cause
they don't like coming after some chicher Drudge.*

About a dozen techs from the Kushayt were spending some of their off-hours sucking yang and maybe
a few of them working up the nerve to waste some
baks on the backroom femmes. Always someone
ready to do the two-backed beast even with local
scum. Ragnal's mouth tightened and his scowl grew
darker. Scum. Each time he had Sifaed he got a
queasy feeling soon as he rolled off her, took a hard
shower to make him feel clean again.

The bar was three doors resting on piles of used
brick, the tables furniture from the houses Ragnal had

knocked down. He'd tipped Farkli a sign to get his scavenging done before the fire and took his fee in noggins of yang. Other Dirtmen he knew demanded and got a percentage of a lubbot's take, but that was dangerous. A bad batch of yang or a new Ykkuval cleaning house of side money and they could get broke to Unskill, just a notch above Drudge. Besides, Farkli's youngest girl had been Girs' wet nurse which made him Family of a sort.

*Girs, ah, brother....* He blinked hard and fast, his eyes burning. "Don't you ever trim your wicks, Fark?"

Drudge Farkli inspected him for a moment, then nodded and pushed a glass of yang across the bar, following it with a jug. " 'S a stinkin' oil t' yerets make. Don't even burn right."

Ragnal smiled. Yerets. Scum. Locals. He sometimes thought that was why Farkli kept signing on tour though he was old enough for a pension back home. Hitting places where there was something lower than a Drudge. He took a mouthful of the yang, raised his brows, and looked into the glass. "New batch?"

"Ayyunh. Ykk's Pet, he brung a pile of fruit over. Fed some to the women and watched them a couple days 'fore I shoved it in. And they's some weirds live in the Fen out there, they bring stuff. Like it?"

"Not bad."

"Pressin's from it burn better'n that oil." He hesitated, stared past Ragnal's shoulder. "Thought maybe some for lamps in Sef Girs' shrine?"

Eyes burning again, Ragnal squeezed hard on the glass and stared at the yang inside; agitated by the tremble in his hand, its broken surface was picking up yellow from the lanterns. He didn't speak until he was sure of his voice. "I'll tell the Birad to let you in." He didn't want to talk about it any more; he took the jug and his glass to a table in a back corner and sat sipping slowly at the yang, his head getting muzzier as the light that crept through the painted windows darkened.

For a long time he ignored the raised voices coming from a table on the other side of the room. He wasn't in a mood for company and he didn't care what techs got up to on their off-time. Only one tech he'd ever had time for, but Girs was cinders and they could all go to the Taner's lowest hell.

"... curse him, that ni Jilet kreash, incompetent thief, Genree the chich-up ... Chob tol' me ... he tol' me ... my bro' he tol' me ... Zanne had t' do 's own parts ... parts ... t' get flier in air. Zanne said ... Zanne...." The tech's voice lost coherence on the last words and died away. He sucked in a breath, shuddered, took a long pull at his glass, slammed it down, drew his hand across his mouth. "Cinsin' echt-born don' gi' moosh a kirg 'bout us. Genree ... pinch-nose idiot ..."

Swaying back and forth, inner lids at half-down, their translucent film gleaming in the lantern light, he muttered on and on, railing against Genree ni Jilet, saying it was him who killed Choban, pocketing the money for repairs and spare parts while the little he did buy was so worn and useless not even Zanne could get it to work right. "... and you know Zanne can fix anything with a chew of zam and a bit of wire and Hun the kreash lets that chich get away with it ... or maybe he's got his hand in, too ... licking the sweet off the top ... leave the dregs go through...."

The others at the table were nodding and muttering with him, the same glazed idiot look on their young faces.

There was a bowl on the table, white porcelain like a deathlight. Ragnal blinked to clear his bleary eyes. Probably was one, lifted from Stores. It wasn't burning oil but something else, looked like chunks of hairy bark—putting out a thick weighty smoke that hovered near the top of the table. As he watched, first one, then another and another of the techs leaned forward and sucked smoke into mouth and nose.

As Ragnal listened to the babble and smelled the sweetish acrid odor of the smoke, the drink chilled in his stomachs and his grief turned cold. *Tech Dihbat. Choban's baby brother. Like Girs was mine. Keeps on like that he's gonna get busted to Unskill. Maybe a spaz on chain at the Workfarm. Even listening to this kirg is dangerous.* He emptied his glass, set it down with the careful precision of the very drunk and groped his way out, exaggerating his state to look so far gone that he was seeing nothing, hearing nothing.

There were techs and Drudges in the lubbot who wouldn't have two thoughts about reporting Dihbat's rant. Or Ragnal's presence. He wanted to be able to claim he hadn't noticed what was going on because he was drunk and grieving. With that and his reputation for keeping his mouth shut, he should slide away from trouble. Ykkuval Hunnar wasn't vindictive, but he was a ruthless kreash and knew what letting such talk get loose could do to him. Dihbat was a fool.

As he pressed from the open fields into the wooded strip between the village and the Kushayt, his foot slammed into a root and he fell on his face. He lay without moving, gray dust settling on him, slow dust, so slow he could see it drift down. *Chichin taffy world. Fall and it's like a mattress. Ayee, Taner, not a mattress for Girs. Fire. Burning....* Body contorting with grief, he cried for the first time since he heard the news about his brother, pounded his fists on the road, beating and beating the insensate dirt. Girs was dead and this karolsha world didn't care, nobody cared, shovel the dead under and forget what made them dead.

A whistled tune. Footsteps.
Ragnal leaped to his feet, nearly fell over again,

scrubbed at his face, slapped dust from his coveralls.
As he straightened, he saw the local they called Ykk's
Pet coming round the curve in the road. Ugly chich.
A map of wrinkles wrapped around twiggy bones that
looked like they'd snap if you breathed hard on them.
Watery blue eyes with all the expression of polished
pebbles.

When the Pet saw Ragnal, his tune stopped, his
shoulders came up round his ears, and he shambled
to the far side of the road and stood there, eyes on
the dirt.

Ragnal snorted, then walked away. The less he had
to do with that one, the better he liked it. Even if they
weren't human, you could respect a local who gave you
a good fight. Something like this, though. . . .

When Ragnal emerged from the trees and into sight
of the gate guards, once again he exaggerated his un-
steadiness and the care with which he was moving,
pulling his perimeters in as if he were trying to walk
through a glass shop on a floor that was tilting
under him.

As he passed between the massive gate towers and
into the Kushayt, his body loosened and his breathing
got easier. Warped and distorted though it was, this
was a piece of home. The buildings in here had the
look of mass even if the weight wasn't really there;
they were built low to the ground with comfortably
thick walls and no stupid windows to weaken the load-
hold. The streets were straight and paved with grav
plates so they had an honest pull to them; the corners
square, the houses kept their hearts to themselves, no
vulgar display to tempt the weakminded toward theft.
It was everything the yerechs outside wouldn't understand.

In the tiny private suite that was one of the perqs
his status brought him, he stripped and stepped into
the shower cubicle, stood there with pulsing needles

of hot water beating at him, his forehead pressed against the wall, his eyes closed, the heat and massage of the water washing away more than the dust of the world.

When the hot water was gone, he stumbled out, dried himself, and fell into bed, his weight switching on the grav plate that made sleeping more comfortable. He started to think about what he'd heard, about Genree and Hunnar, about Girs' almost daily complaints about the equipment, but before he got beyond memory into planning, he plunged deep deep into sleep.

## 2

As Ilaörn watched the chav stump off, he smiled as he thought of the ravaged, tear-streaked face, the angry scowl. *One for us*, he thought. *I hope you burn like I am, I hope you're in pain that never stops.* He took a deep breath, adjusted the shoulderstrap of his carry sack, and moved on.

The mesuch killed Béluchar life down to the mites in the soil so they could grow their stinking tubers, but the Ykkuval wanted Béluchar plants in his Dushanne Garden. Wanted green and bloom under his eye. *Matha matha, gets me away from that place. Gives me a little time I'm not smelling them all round me, hearing those grunts they call speech, looking at those clumsy ugly buildings.*

His mouth tightened as he moved from under the trees and saw again the remnant of Dumel Dordan. The mesuchs killed and burned the Dumel with as little thought to what they were destroying as those bloody-handed barbarians who burned Imuë. A thousand and a thousand years of living and dying, birth and budding, gone. Dordan's song was finished. Trampled under the tracks of their monstrous machines.

He left the road and moved along the outside of

the light fence that enclosed the mesuch fields. He'd learned not to go near the mesuch Drudges. They had crude and painful ideas of what was funny. His knees would pay for the extra walking, but he'd been through one mobbing and shuddered at the thought of another.

The trees closed round him again, straining out the sounds of the mesuch machines and the shouts of the Drudges, the occasional yelps from the Fior women on the slave chains. They didn't bother slaving the Keteng, just killed them. The Denchok were at once too alien and too much like them, an abomination in Chav eyes. The Shape War songs told the same sad story, a thousand and a thousand years ago the Fior came here and killed with as little understanding and as much evil in their hearts as the Chave showed. And were killed until a harper made the first sioll bond with an Eolt. Ard Bracoïn and Eolt Lekall sang the grand Chorale of Peace, passed the song from Ard to Eolt to Ard again, spreading peace around the world.

The angies flitted through the upper levels of the trees, quadripart wings flickers of diamond, hard bodies ruby and emerald, topaz, sapphire and amethyst—flying jewels whose songs were clear pure notes as bright as their colors. There were more angies in the woods than he remembered, perhaps because they'd been pushed from the open fields.

The air dampened as he got closer to the sea and the Meklo Fen. Large patches of sky showed through the shorter, more scattered trees. Ahead he could see the light green of the rushes, the brown cones at the tips of their tall stems, the dance of light from a stretch of water, a cheled so shallow he could wade to the middle without getting his knees wet.

Eyes sweeping the ground, looking for budding plants he could take back with him, Ilaörn moved along the edge of the cheled, walking carefully to avoid stepping into one of the soft spots that could swallow before he had a chance to pull free. Hunnar wanted color and vigor, especially along his fake stream, which meant that the plants there had to be continually replaced.

He stopped by a clump of kolkrais, frowned down at it. The seven-lobed leaves were a healthy dark green, the buds had only a hint of gold at their tips. If he could get the greater part of the root system without breaking too many of the hair-fine feeders, that clump could be teased into blooming for the next two months.

He knelt on the damp, squishy soil, took a plastic container from the carry sack and set it beside the kolkrais, removed the hand spade from its loop on his belt, and began the delicate job of digging the plants loose. The slow, careful work brought a peace he hadn't felt in months.

And there were other satisfactions that drifted through his mind as he worked. The probe had missed his sneaking after Hunnar and watching him meet his spy. Ilaörn smiled as he dug, but his flush of triumph was quickly over. Once Ykkuval heard what the Eolt were, he wasn't interested in anything else and didn't let the probe dig around as he'd done before. Hard to read these Chav mesuchs, but he seemed angry about something. Angry, afraid, frustrated. *If I only knew what it was....*

As long as there was no suspicion and no direct questions to force his mind to focus, he could keep his secrets. No suspicion—that was the key. *I'll find out what you're afraid of,* he thought. *Somehow. And I'll sweep you all off this world.*

He lifted the kolkrais, eased it into the box, dipped his hand into the water and sprinkled it across the leaves, then cut some moss and tucked it into the corners to keep the plant from sliding about. He snapped the lid on, tucked the container in the carry sack and got to his feet.

*Money,* he thought. *If it costs too much, they'll go somewhere else. The mines. If we can get at the techs, stop the mining machines. . . .*

He saw a flash of color ahead and moved cautiously toward it, his feet squelching through the muck.

Before he'd taken two steps, a weight landed on his back, knocking him flat, face in the mud, carry sack flying he didn't know where.

Hands round his throat.

Heavy breathing in his ears.

Pull the chin down, shake and work the head, clamp teeth on one of the attacker's thumbs and try to bite it off.

Buck against the weight pinning him down.

Surge and work elbows and knees in the mud, getting them under him, pushing up, shaking side to side.

Grunting from his attacker, weight shifting.

He broke free. Rage put springs in his old knees and he was on his feet, kicking at the attacker who rolled away from the blows and got shakily to his feet.

For several moments they stared at each other, two old men panting and shaking as rage drained away, then Ilaörn said, "Danor?"

The other Ard spat at him. "Filth. Eater of me-such slach."

Ilaörn's shoulders dropped and he looked down; his hands plucked uselessly at the mud on his clothes. "I would die if I could. I am not allowed."

"Die! We aren't going to die until we wipe this world clean. I saw Hereom burn and I burned with xe and I burn with every breath I take. Dying is easy. We live and fight."

Ilaörn stared at the wiry little Fior standing hunched from a kick to his gut, face gaunt, arms and legs skeletal from bad food and worse sleep. "You? Phratha, Danor, look at you. You couldn't crack a nagal with a hammer. Chel Dé's Thousand Eyes, you couldn't even kill me and look at me!"

Danor's body sagged and the fire went out of his eyes; he looked so old and tired, for a moment Ilaörn half-seriously wondered if he were going to die on the spot.

He spoke hastily, slowing his words and putting stress on them as he got into what he was saying. "Matha matha, don't tell me anything important. When the mesuch put that crown on your head, you'd betray your mother or your firstborn or whatever they think to ask you."

He looked around and winced at the sight of the sodden carry sack half-drowned in the reeds. If he couldn't produce some living plants and account for all his tools, it meant a beating and a session with the probe. *Chel Dé! what I could jeopardize.* His mouth flooded with saliva, and he trembled as his body betrayed him as it had done so many times since Hunnar made a pet of him. He squeezed his eyes shut and turned away so Danor wouldn't see his arousal, crouched, and pulled the sack loose from the mud.

When he looked inside, the plastic containers seemed to be intact. Maybe the kolkrais would survive the mishandling. It was a hardy weed.

He set the sack back in the water, so he could rinse it off later. Without looking around, he said, "Find a place and sit down, then listen to me. Don't interrupt, don't say anything. Let me do the talking. Then just go." He stared out across murky water that turned a deceptively brilliant blue out in the middle of the cheled.

"The Chave ... the mesuch ... they came for metals and gemstones, that's what they deal in. They don't care who the land belongs to, they take what they want because they can. They kill the Eolt because it's a game they enjoy. They kill the Meloach and the Denchok because they are offended that such beasts should mimic their shape. It is not possible to reason with them. Would you listen if a bladal pleaded with

you not to slaughter it? Would you understand its
blats and honks or consider them speech? NO! I said
don't speak, just listen.

"This is important, Danor. If you kill even one of
them and it is known a Fior or Keteng did it, they
will take a terrible revenge. A thousand Keteng, a
thousand Fior burned alive to pay for one dead Chav.
Their honor demands it. I don't understand what they
mean by honor, but I've learned enough to know it's
a powerful thing to them. They can't live without it.
I'm not saying don't kill them, I'm saying it HAS to
seem an accident. Five days ago two died in such an
accident and one of their airwagons perished also. It
was smoke from the husk of a burning Sleeper that
killed them, it made them wild so they lost control of
their machine. What has happened before, you can
arrange to make happen again.

"There is another kind of mesuch across the sea on
Banitoëh. I have seen one of them. A traitor spying
on his own kind for money and spite. That kind are
enemies of the Chav. I could taste the bitterness of
that hate in Hunnar's voice and the voice of the other.
Consider an alliance with them. The enemy of our
enemy—you know how that goes.

"And one last thing. I say again, these mesuch are
driven by profit. Make this world cost too much and
they will be called away. Find our miners, ones who
know the lay of the mountains. Tell them to destroy
the surface crawlers, the ones like metal houses set on
tracks. These control the mining machines. It will stop
them and close down the mines. As much as you can,
make it seem an accident. But understand, no matter
how cleverly you contrive, the Chav are a bloody-
minded suspicious lot and will take payment in blood
for every loss."

"Ila, I've got a question."

"Be careful. Tell me nothing important or secret."

"Our Keteng are already moving south, away from

here. The Fior who've escaped the slave chains go
with them. Will the mesuch come after them, hunt
them out?"

"If it touches their honor or their profit, yes. Or to
make a lesson for the rest of us." He caught hold of
the carry sack's shoulder strap, began sloshing the sack
back and forth in the shallow water. "I wish you
hadn't told me that. It's something he'll be bound to
ask me when he needs to know."

"Your Chav know it already, word has come their
airwagons are following the walkers." Danor got to
his feet. Ilaörn could hear the sucking sounds from the
mud. "And if we do nothing, will there be less dying?"

"I don't know."

"You're the only Béluchar inside those walls. If you
have something to tell us, how can we know?"

"After the accidents begin, even if he lets me out,
don't come near me. I mean it. They have ways of
watching and listening beyond anything you can imagine." Ilaörn listened to the gentle splash of the water,
watched the black mud swirl off the c'hau cloth. "The
Riddle Mode," he said after a long silence. "I meant
to burn my harp when Imuë burned, I didn't, though.
I was taken too soon and afterward I hadn't the heart.
I haven't played since, but I've kept her oiled and fed.
I'll put my news in the Riddle Mode and you can have
ears listening to untwist the meaning. Do the same if
you have word for me." He sighed. "Matha matha, go
away and let me do my work."

### 3

Hunnar's shadow fell on Ilaörn suddenly, without
warning. The Béluchar's hand shook and he scattered
soil over the other plants; he bit down hard on his
tongue and continued digging out melidai so he could
replace it with the clump of kolkrais. Chel Dé's Thou-

sand Eyes, these bulky mesuchs could move like wisps of down if they took a notion.

"You're a mess. What happened, the Drudges get at you again?"

Ilaörn got to his feet, stood with head down, hands in the honor position. "No, O Ykkuval. I fell in the water, got tangled in roots. It was fighting out of them that did this."

"Mp. What's that you're planting?"

"It is called kolkrais, O Ykkuval. It will have a small, dark yellow flower, then a shiny red sporecase. As to use, I know none except as decoration."

"Ta'ma, go back to work, Cho, don't let it die on you." Hunnar strolled off, hands clasped behind him.

Ilaörn dropped to his knees, closed his hands into fists, and shook for a while. Then he pulled himself together and dipped up a dipper of water from the stream, moistened the soil with it, and began the delicate process of shifting the clump of kolkrais from the container to its new home.

"Doesn't look like much." Hunnar was back, standing on the far side of the stream watching him work.

"O Ykkuval, it will take a while for it to make itself at home here."

"Ta'ma, ground grubbing isn't my business."

"No, O Ykkuval. You have much more on your mind than a miserable little weed."

"Mp. You don't know how true that is." He began pacing back and forth along the path with its careful arrangement of flat stones, back and forth, his head tilted up so he was looking at the sky, not where he walked or at Ilaörn even though he made a pretense of talking to him.

Ilaörn eased the bits of moss beneath the lowest layer of the kolkrais, pressed it into the soil and poured more water on it. The moss would hold the moisture and keep the plant's roots happy until they'd tapped their own source of nutriment. This wasn't the first time Hunnar had used him as a sounding board. From what he'd seen of Chav life, the Ykkuval wouldn't dare talk like this to any of his own kind; it would be a weakness that they'd seize on and use to unseat him. *Able to trust no one. Didn't even have a wife to share his ambitions, at least, not here, not yet. I'm his wife for the hiatus, I suppose. He and I both know if I open my mouth about this, I'm dead.* He dipped up more water, splashed across the kolkrais clump to wash the grains of earth away.

"They don't know, they don't know, they spend thousands on com calls to chew me out for wasting time and money. Get rid of the Yaraka, they tell me, but don't you embarrass us, don't get caught with your hands sticky. When I ask what do they want me to do, they say that's your business not ours. When are you going to start shipments coming back to us, that's what we want to know. We've got commitments. We need product. We'll give you six more months, then expenses start coming out of your pockets. Hah! They foist that moron with the wide mouth on me, that Genree. Taner! What a lackwit. I'd like to do to him what they're doing to me, I'd like to say get your bolgyet together so you can face a real inspection or I'll fine your ass till you scream mercy. I'd like to, but I can't. His mother is Gatyr ni Jilet's sister and his sister is about to marry Tomar ni Koroumak. Cut my own throat if I tried it. I've got to do something, can't get product with half the plant down. Wall him off somehow, get him too busy to interfere. . . ."

Ilaörn let the spate of words flow over him, nodding and making small listening sounds as he moved along the stream bank, setting out the plants he'd brought back with him. Nothing useful in all that glagairh, nothing he hadn't known before. *Old men,* he thought. *Danor didn't tell me, but I know. A gaggle of old men plotting war.* He lifted the last plant from its container, purple delk, a young one with a small single bulb, washed the dirt from its roots and settled it in its hole, tamping the dirt around it with gentle taps from his thumbs.

Hunnar paced on, spewing his anger and frustration, his ambitions and annoyances, Ilaörn kept on murmuring encouraging noises and paying no attention to the words, shifting to make work when he finished the transplanting, pinching off dead leaves, stirring the ground to get air to the roots; he didn't dare leave the stream bed or just squat there doing nothing.

". . . and now there's this lot from University, cinsing prynoses interferring, if this thing with the jellies gets out. . . ." The voice stopped. Suddenly.

Ilaörn looked up.

Hunnar was across the stream from him, scowling at him. It wasn't anger, the Chav's inner lids weren't down, his eyes were shadowed and dull.

Ilaörn met those eyes briefly, then dropped his own. Chav reacted violently and without waiting for thought to a challenging stare even from one of their own. From a local like him, it was an invitation to a broken neck. Early days, before Hunnar had planted hooks in his head, when he was reaching out of grief for defiance, he'd earned himself broken ribs, a broken shoulder blade, and twice a concussion. Like a gath trained to bark and not-bark on command, he'd learned his lesson well.

"You won't talk about that," Hunnar said. "Not to Chav, not to anyone. Be sure I'll find out if you do."

"I have already forgotten, O Ykkuval."

"Hm." After a long glistery stare, his inner lids drew back. When he spoke again, his voice was quiet, thoughtful. "Those husks. Just what is the effect of that smoke?"

Ilaörn's mind skittered frantically as he fought to keep his face dull and incurious, to show no interest in what lay behind the question. *Chel Dé's Thousand*

*Eyes, what do I do. WHAT DO I DO!* If Hunnar really wanted the information, he could get it despite anything Ilaörn tried and he might pull out more....

"O Ykkuval, I'm not sure I know what you want."

"Your lot, not those vegheads, what does it do to them? You have anyone who gets a taste for that smoke?"

"I drank smoke when I was just become a man. There were reasons for it. You could call it a religious thing." He closed his eyes. *I'm not talking to him, but to you, sioll Imuë, to your spirit wherever it is.* "I have not done it since," he said aloud, "but I can remember the sweetness of that day, I can remember my senses expanding to embrace all of earth and sky and everything between. An angi's song was ... ah ... bright and piercing to my ears as its jewel colors were to my eyes. I could hear grass growing and the sap rising in the trees. I have had other pleasures since, but none that quite equals that." He opened his eyes. "And many of the aroch ... that is, those who tend the Sleepers ... they live year round at the Sleeping Grounds because they can't be without the smoke or they suffer. But how drinking smoke would affect a Chav, I have no idea. You'd have to test it."

Ilaörn stared at the water, wondering if the probe was going to be used on him to confirm what he said; a mix of terror and pleasure drenched his body and he couldn't have moved just then if Hunnar was whipping him.

After a long silence, he looked up.

Hunnar was gone.

# 6. Journey's Beginning

## 1

Yawning and still half-asleep after two nights of disturbing dreams, Shadith carried her harp and gear from the room assigned to her and stood in the arcade outside, shadows from the vine leaves flickering across her face. It was a hot day, damp and sticky; sweat stayed on the skin and breathing brought a load of insects, plant spores, and a whole stewpot of smells, ranging from the oversweet perfume of the fruits on the trees in the next field over to the acrid bite of pony urine.

*Peaceful.* She looked up. Through the vines she could see a flikit circling overhead. *Protection or spy?* She clicked her tongue. *Probably both. Koraka may be a slickery slider, but he's not stupid. I wonder if I am. Stupid. Staying here. At least I'm walking in with my eyes open this time, not falling through a hole.*

Followed by a line of 'bots like ducklings waddling after their mother and a hoard of curious children, Aslan, Duncan Shears, and Marrin Ola went down another shady walk toward the tech rooms at the back of the blai, going to log in before mapping and collecting began. *Better them than me.* She sighed. *Well, chatting to a lot of odd-shaped politicians isn't that much more interesting. At least there'll be music. I can live with that.*

She rubbed at the hawk etching, distressed because

the passion she'd felt only two days ago was draining from her, leaving her cold and dim again. Restless. Even thinking about the murdered Eolt only wakened an echo of feeling in her. She sighed. And this business of the cross-country trek on ponies wasn't helping. Stupid, the Eolt not letting the Goës send them in a flikit.

A Fior woman and two Ketengs with growths budding from their hips hurried past her, dragging a cleaning cart; they stopped a moment to stare at the troop of 'bots, then bustled into her room and set to work with much banging about, sloshing of water and unflattering comments about the mesuchs moving in on them.

Aslan leaned out the door of the workroom. "Shadow, if you'll come here a moment?"

"What's up?"

"Grab a seat." Aslan kicked a backless chair across to Shadith, settled herself in her own, leaning back, elbows braced on one of the work tables. "Bad news, folks. You may want to change your plans, Shadow."

"More bad news?" Shadith looked round for the privacy cone, raised her brows.

"No need. Anyone who's watching knows what I'm going to say." Aslan held up the flake, tossed it onto the table. "I took this over to the enclave this morning, saw Koraka. He got the point real fast and took me to the com room himself. And we got to watch the software melt to sludge. And the backup program follow it. Com's dead until the Goës' techs figure out what happened and make sure it won't happen again. A tech took the shuttle to the parking station. Same thing. He had to pull all personnel out of the station. Life support was going. No ship due for three months, so we're stuck here. We can do it two ways. We can move back to the enclave and stay there hunkered down till the ship comes, or we can go on with what we planned and take our chances with getting killed."

Shadith got to her feet. "Doesn't look to me like all that much has changed since the last time we talked." She pushed her arms through the straps of the gear sack and settled the harpcase beside it. "Count me irritated and on the job. I'll be flaking the trip, dictating observations. One way or another, word of what's happening here is going to get out."

Without waiting to see what the others decided, she left the room, strode along the walkway toward the staging area where Maorgan and the Metau Chachil were getting the pony train organized.

A Keteng with a lichen web so overgrown and complex that xe seemed to be peering out of a thicket stood by a string of twelve ponies, arguing with the Metau over the fee for their use, xe's voice getting louder and shriller with every word; xe'd been paid, but xe wanted an additional surety against return because xe said xe'd had reports that choreks were thick as black biters on a dry day. "... killing ponies or going off with them and everything else they can haul away. My eldest is in xe's third budding and the youngest is in slough, xe needs oluid to help with the Change. How you expect me to get xe through it if my stock ends up in some chorek stewpot?" Xe windmilled xe's arms. "What if the mesuch don't bring 'em back? Ard? What do Ard care about Denchok and their worries? Nothing. Living off the land's fat. HUNH!"

Ignoring xe, two Fior and three much younger Ketengs were cinching packsaddles on six of the ponies, roping supplies in place. Of the remaining six, three were saddled, three had lead ropes clipped to their halters.

Shadith raised her brows. *Choreks? Three ponies? I*

*wonder who the other one's for.* She yawned, moved her shoulders and left the shadows of the arcade.

"G' morning, Maorgan. When we leaving?"

Maorgan glanced at the sun, looking up through the golden shimmers of the drifting Eolt at the sun. "Won't be long now. Custom, Shadowsong, we start important journeys at the tick of noon, when Greiäsil shines on our heads."

"Why? Wouldn't it be better to get started early when the sun isn't so hot?"

"Ah, Shadowsong, that's the mesuch speaking." He drew the back of his forefinger along the neck of the nearest pony. "The caöpas browse on sunlight like the Eolt. They can go longer if we set out later. Besides, a journey's start ought to have a set point so you know where you are."

Shadith blinked. "You're right. My mind's in the wrong pattern. Which caöpa's mine?"

He pointed, what looked like mischief twinkling in his pale blue eyes. "Him."

The moss pony's eyes had long curling lashes and were a brown so dark it was almost black. Mixed in with his hair were a tracery of lichens that gave it a curious crinkly texture and a greenish sheen. Horses of any sort were generally associated with the multiform descendants of the Cousin Races, not with species native to the worlds where they settled, so the distant ancestor of this little beast would have come here with the first Fior as a fertilized ovum. *Hm.* Both it and the plant that grew on it must have mutated since—or were tampered with by the old Fior. She made a mental note to ask Maorgan when the first moss ponies showed up. Caöpas, he called them, but she found that hard to remember when she was looking them.

She scratched her caöpa's poll, cooing to him as he leaned into her, his eyes closing, his head resting heavy on her shoulder.

A boy's voice sounded behind her. "His name's Bréou."

She looked round. "Beä, Glois. Why Bréou? He doesn't stink."

"He makes stinks. You wait. You'll see."

Utelel giggled, stiffened xe's lips, and blew a loud BRRRUPPP!

"Ah. Now I understand why Ard Maorgan looked like that."

Glois scowled suddenly, moved closer to Utelel, took xe's hand. "We sh'd be going with you. We old enough." His scowl deepened. "Almost. What dif-f'rence a year gonna make?"

"You might grow a little sense in a year, dilt." Maorgan stopped beside Shadith. "You and your ac-complice in iniquity scoot over where you belong and stop bothering the Harper with your nonsense."

Glois wrinkled his face into a clown grimace, then he and Utelel went sauntering off.

"Shadowsong."

Shadith turned, leaned against the caöpa's side, her fingers idly scratching through the wiry hairs of its mane. He'd taken to calling her that when she ex-plained why Aslan called her Shadow instead of Shad-ith. Apparently he liked the image of a singer in shadow and the way the syllables slipped off his tongue when translated into Bélucharis. Chuulcheleet. She rather liked it herself. "Hm?" she said.

"We'll be three riders, not two. Ard Danor from Melitoëh comes with us. That's him over there a little behind Metau Chachil."

Danor was an ancient Fior standing apart from the noise and revel, his body pulled so tightly in on itself she could almost see the gap left in the air around him. Inside that wrinkled hide was a horrifying mix-ture of hate, fury, and grief. It rasped along her nerves as if she were being stroked by nettles. The thought of spending days in his neighborhood was not a happy one.

"Your friend is a skin around rage."

"He's a dead man walking." His eyes went somber. He shuddered as he looked up at Eolt Melech drifting delicately golden over his head. "You heard Eolt Lebesair's song. The mesuch on Melitoëh hunt Eolt to watch them burn. His sioll is ash on the wind." He looked past Melech at the Yaraka flikit circling overhead and moved his shoulders with distaste. "I almost think we were blessed that it was them who came to us."

She nodded. "If you have to entertain thieves, a subtle one is a better guest."

A Denchok with a mid-size lichen web sat on a stool, playing a large harp, a small herd of Meloach and Fior boys squatting beside him, joined with pipes and drums. Glois was there, playing a set of panpipes almost as long as his arm in his left hand. Utelel crouched beside him, stroking and tapping a doubled drum he held between his knees.

Off to one side Metau Chachil and Teseach Ruaim stood fingering the medals that marked their office. The rest of the Alsekumers were milling about, chattering in groups, laughing, asking questions, stopping to stare at the pony train, at Shadith and the others. Meloach and Fior children were running about, making noise, some in a chaotic tag game that involved tossing around a leather ball about the size of a boy's head.

When the sun was directly overhead, a chord of surpassing beauty came dropping down from the two Eolt. The folk of Alsekum hushed, the Dumel musicians let their hands go still.

Rising and falling as if they rode the waves of an invisible ocean, the Eolt made a symphony of image and sound and on the ground Ard Maorgan and Ard

Maorgan's harp sang with them, harmonies that
dipped in and out of the organ symphony completing
and complementing the Eolts in ways impossible to
describe or even understand.

Shadith heard the song and *knew* there were words
in it, celebrating the sun, the day, and the journey,
though there was no way the brain she had now could
fully translate it. Or appreciate the grief that screamed
from Danor as he stood, head down, listening to what
he could no longer share. She began to understand
just what the sioll-bond meant, what an Ard was, and
why they were so important to the joined peoples of
Béluchad.

## 2

Frowning a little, Aslan watched the pony train vanish round a clump of trees. She had wider latitude
than usual on this collecting run; University was tacitly
willing to see her do a lot more than record, but would
take a very dim view of her if she got carried away,
so involved with the locals that she embarrassed the
Regents. She sighed. Shadith knew that, but she wasn't
a Scholar and would never be one, her blood ran too
hot. *As mine does, they keep telling me. Phra, I don't
like being a Company snoop which is what I am if you
tear off the pretty wrapping. To work, Scholar, get to
work, no telling how long this window will last before
the Chave decide it's time to purge us.*

## 3

"My name is Budechil. It's a word from the old
tongue, out of the time before the Fior came. It means
Harmony. That thing will remember what I'm saying?
Show me."

Aslan shifted the Ridaar, clicked on the replay. An

image of Budechil crafted of colored light sat opposite the original, spoke the recorded words.

"Ihoi!" Budechil came heavily to xe's feet, stumped across to the image, passed xe's hand through it, then looked at the hand for a long moment before xe went back to xe's chair. "And who will see this?"

"One copy will be registered in University Archives for Scholars to study, a second will be left here with a reader so that your budlines a thousand and a thousand years on will see you and hear your stories."

"Meringeh! So what should I say?"

"Let's start with you, who you are, what you do. You've already given your name, we can go on from there."

Budechil tapped xe's tongue against xe's chewing ridge. "Glaaaa gla, talking is such a natural thing, why do I suddenly find words skittering away from me?" Xe closed xe's eyes, rubbed the fingers of xe's left hand along the arm of the backless chair.

For several moments xe sat there silent, then xe opened xe's eyes and started speaking again, slowly at first and then more easily. "I am Budechil the caöpa coper. Budline Chil-choädd. I am the Line Elder for the moment and direct the Chil-choädd lands of Ordumel Alsekum. I say for the moment because I feel the Heaviness of the Change coming on. Next spring when the melodach ripens, I will begin the eating and by summer's end will take my place on the Sleeping Ground. When I am Eolt, I will not have the sioll bond, I do not have enough music in my soul and I have not got close to a Fior. I think we will have a bond in Alsekum. Young Glois and Utelel of the Budline Lel-beriod seem to be building a music that has promise of being glorious. That is a good thing. It has been too long since Alsekum gave an Ard and a singing Eolt to Béluchad.

"I have budded five times. One died of the Withers before drop-off, one was chopped and eaten by the

chorek. The year those two dropped was Chel Dé-
cursed for sure. They were same-summer buds; it was
as if the dead one called the living. Two of the living
are Denchok, one is in bud, a single bud which is
more fortunate and easier to live with. The youngest
was a late comer, on the dying edge of my bud-time.
Xe has been sickly and has stayed close to home and
close to my reng. Ah, that too is an old-time word. It
means the organ that feels tenderness and love; it is
the same as crof which is what the Fior use as well.
The Fior are Béluchar now as much as the Keteng
and they do things we can't, our life is richer because
of them, but I still like to remember the time before,
when Bélucharis had no words for man and woman,
for birth and copulation and so many other things that
I have seen and known but do not understand.

"I've had to learn something about this business,
dealing with caöpas as I do, breeding them and raising
them, learning their seasons, when to separate them
and when to keep them together. It's hard, though, to
contemplate thinking people doing such things. I am
filled with delight when I think that Keteng need not
go through such contortions to continue the species."

Aslan leaned forward, lifted a hand to catch xe's
attention. "Would you care to talk about that? A Keteng would not need the explanation, but the Scholars
would like to hear your voice on this. If it is a private
thing and you'd rather not. . . ."

Breath catching in the odd hiccuping sound of Keteng laughter, xe rocked forward and back on the
cloth seat of xe's chair. Xe caught xe's breath, patted
at the mat of lichen on xe's chest. "Pardon me,
Scholar. I've always found Fior fussiness silly, and it
amuses me that you would think there is anything private about a dusting of spores." Xe dropped xe's
hands onto xe's thighs, the thin long fingers tapping
lightly at the heavy dark blue canvas of xe's trousers.

"It is like this. In the month Kirrayl when the sun

comes back overhead and the year begins, an Ordumel Circle gathers at one of the Dumels and holds a Kirrataneh. All day there is feasting and music and talk talk talk; there are people you haven't seen since the last Kirrataneh and won't see till the next. It has to be a night when the wind is soft and there is no rain or that year's spores are wasted. When the sun goes down, the Denchok gather on the dance floor, the Eolt are overhead to sing, the drummers are there to beat the heart faster and faster. You dance from the sun going down till the sun coming up. The fires that light the floor are perfumed with a thousand and a thousand essences. You dance till your spore sacs pop and dance some more while your kesamad open out and expose their sticky linings to catch the tiyid raining down on them and dance yet more in the joy of the getting time. There is always a first to pop, and you pray Chel Dé will not choose to make you that one, because you will be teased without mercy for the whole rest of the year. Once the first has sprayed xe's spores, all the spores are released. The pip-pop-pop grows louder than the drum beats. You dance in the rain of the tiyid and the pleasure of it is beyond words, something only an Ard and Eolt can express." Xe sighed and was silent for several minutes, then xe said, "I don't feel like talking anymore. Another day, perhaps."

## 4

The road was double in a way Shadith hadn't seen before. The part for wagons was paved with flat stone rectangles set in a tarry substance. The caöpas took the other part, a dirt lane planted with short tough grass that grew in fist-sized clumps, easier on the feet, no doubt. It ran parallel to the first with a shallow ditch between them.

On both sides of them, fields stretched to the horizon, a patchwork of plant rows and plowed ground

divided by narrow canals. Ordumel. The lands of
Dumel Alsekum. Keteng worked in some of them,
Fior in others, Fior children and Keteng Meloach ran
along the ditch banks, opening and closing valves to
feed the water where it was needed. Adults and children alike stopped what they were doing to wave to
the travelers, then went back to work.

Danor rode first, his body hunched in the saddle,
his misery like a hump on his shoulders. He never
looked round at them or at anything except the back
of his caöpa's head.

Shadith rode beside Maorgan, the spare caöpas and
the packers trailing along behind them. She was having more difficulty than she'd expected adjusting herself to this little beast—not so little, actually, when it
came to getting one's legs around him. Wide as a
house. Her hipjoints creaked and she was going to
know about it by day's end. Just as well it was going
to be a halfday this time. Another plus for the Béluchar habit of starting at noon.

*Bréou. No stinks yet. Probably when we stop to rest
and feed the string.*

*Katinka tinka walk. Find the rhythm? Wish someone
would tell me how. Like trying to fly a hiccuping flikit.
If this is what his walk's like, I don't want to think
about his trot. Chop-chop. Chop-chop. Clippety-
clippety-clippety. Head up in the air, short legs pump-
ing. Gods! My butt and my thighs are going to howl
tonight.*

The two Eolt drifted along overhead, now and then
improvising wordless music just to amuse themselves,
ripples of sound that dropped around the riders like
songs from enchanted flutes. Or perhaps they were
talking in a language so complex and abstract that the
translator in Shadith's head threw up its figurative
hands and went back to sleep.

"Are they talking up there?" she said. "Or just
making pretty sounds."

Maorgan looked up at the Eolt, smiled. "Both," he said. "Are your ears burning? They're talking about you. I can't tell you what exactly they're saying. When they go on like that, I can pick up about one idea in ten. You don't read them? I thought. . . ."

"No. I can pick up feelings and peripherals, but too many things are happening at once when they're talking to each other. My mind has too few . . . hm . . . channels, I suppose." She thought a moment. "My sisters might have, but they're long dead and I . . . that's an even longer story and unimportant besides. Tell me about the Meruu."

"It's a story I'd like to hear."

The road ahead was empty as far as Shadith could see which was about a half a mile on at which point it curved around a thickly planted orchard. "I'll trade," she said. "My story for the truth about things, or at least the truth you know." She frowned. "Though I'd prefer you didn't make song of it and spread it on the wind."

"If I do, I'll change the name and the face. You've made songs. You know how it goes. It's sound that rules what you say, far more than sense. And even a good story needs a bit of tweaking here and there."

"Tweak it hard, Ard Maorgan. I don't want to recognize myself. Ah well, this is how it goes: Once upon a time, a long long time ago. . . ."

"And how long is long?"

"Call it twenty thousand years, give or take a millennia or three. In that once-upon-a-time there was a world called Shayalin and on that world the Shallana lived and among the Shallana were certain families called the Weavers of Shayalin who could dance dreams into being."

"Dance dreams? Interesting. How?"

"We just did it. Like you and the Eolt. It's something Weavers were born with, that's all I know. I wear a different body now with different senses and different gifts, so I can't even show you what I mean."

"Now that's a trifle hard to believe. That bit about the body, I mean."

"Odd, eerie, maybe a little strange." She grinned at him. "Maybe very strange. The universe is full of weird things. Your Eolt, for one. Or could you explain how that flikit flies?" She waved her hand at the black dot intermittently visible through high, thin clouds.

"Hm. Think of a crystal that has the power to trap souls. Think of a soul that lived twenty times a thousand years inside that crystal. Think of a girl newly dead and a woman with healing hands who decanted the soul into the girl's abandoned body. Think that I'm a singer making a story just to pass the time. All or none or some of the above is true. Shall I go on?"

"Please."

"This is how the generations went among the Weavers. First there is the One. She is fertile and female, a singer who could not dance dreams nor bring them alive for others to see. She mates with an ordinary Shallana male and hatches the Six Daughters who were true Dancers, the Weavers. When they are grown and dancing, she mates a second time and produces a fertile daughter, a singer like herself. And so it goes, six and one and six again.

"I should say, so it went, generation upon generation until a free trader happened upon Shayalin and had Dreams danced for him by the Weavers of Shayalin. He stole a family of Weavers and ran with them. He was only the first of the raiders. In a hundred years there very few Weavers left." She went silent a moment. "When the Eolt sang of the burning, I remembered. . . ." She sighed and went on.

"And then there was another raid, more vicious than most, the raiders stupid and arrogant and above all ignorant. They killed Shallana a hundred at a time until a Weaver family was brought to them. Then they left. They shot the Mother/Singer and tossed her out an air lock because she was old and ugly. When they reached the Market world, they sold the Daughter/Singer for a pittance because she could not dance and was young and ugly and then they tried to sell the Weaver/Sisters and found no takers because the Weavers needed the Singer for the Dream. They tried to find the Daughter, but she was gone with her owner no one knew where, so they shot the sisters, too, and went back to Shayalin for another set.

"The Daughter wandered far, moving from master to master, acquiring a name that non-Shallana could pronounce. Shadith was the name she took. It meant Singer in the language she took it from.

"Her last Master/Teacher died and left her free to move on and she did. In the course of her travels she found work with an expedition of scholars digging in the ruins on a world older than most of the suns around it. She found a thing there, an exquisite thing, a shimmering lacy diadem with crystal jewels spaced round it. Because it was so beautiful, she set it on her head, and it sank into her and vanished.

"Time passed and the time came when her ship crashed. She died in that crash and as she went, one of the crystals in the diadem seized hold of her soul and it stayed there as the millennia passed.

"The diadem moved. And moved again. Shadith's soul moved with it and left it as I said before. That's my story. And that's why I said my sisters might have understood the Eolts' songs."

"Hm." The sound was skeptical, but that was Maorgan's only comment on what he'd heard. "And that bird etched into your face?"

"Think I'll save that one for another day. Tell me about the Meruu."

The trees in the orchard they were riding past had clusters of green spheres on long stems, the fruits about the size of her thumbnail. A scattering had a blush of pink mixed in the green. A few trees still had blossoms on them, odd looking things, a corona of round white petals circling a greenish yellow pod with cracks in it that showed off a crimson interior. Like the moss ponies, the trees looked an odd mix of Cousin and local that was more likely than not a result of the ur-Fior tampering with generative tissue. *Shape Wars. Hm. Must have killed off the techs and wiped out a lot of material or they'd be farther along than this. Sounds like the same old thing. Time to get Maorgan talking. Need to know what this place is really like. Chorek, that's something else. How they organize things. Weaknesses they've got to provide for. And what to do about the Chave. Gods, I wish Lee was here. Could use that ship of hers. No. Can't depend on her the rest of my life. It's MY life. Look at the man, off in a dream somewhere. Do I give him a jab to get him started, or let him surface on his own?*

As the road finished curving round the orchard and headed west again, a Fior driving a team of six heavy horned beasts came into view. They were red and white with heavy dewlaps, moving at a steady clip, a little faster than a man could walk. The wagon they pulled had composition tires and a padded seat. The sides were thin strips of wood that had been steamed supple and woven into high and relatively light walls. Canvas was pulled over the load and tied tight.

The Fior was a stub of a man as wide as he was tall, with a shaved head and bristly red mustache and beard. One ear was pierced, a wooden luck charm hung from a silver stud. He looked curiously at Danor, raised thorny red brows at Shadith, grinned at Maorgan, and waved the goad at him. "Ard Ma'gin."

Maorgan rode closer to the ditch, stopped his caöpa. "Barriall. Where you coming from?"

"Ord'm'l D'bak'mel. Watch y' back, Ard. Chorek round like lice."

"Hear you, Barriall. Chel Dé keep."

When the wagon had rumbled round the orchard, Maorgan clucked his caöpa into clip-clopping along beside Shadith and answered the question she thought he'd forgotten. "Matha matha, the Meruus. Meruu of the Air. A clutch of the eldest of the unsiolled Eolt. They hang together to chitter and chatter, sing a tune or two and report on the doings of their descendants, a litany of deploring and complaint. Meruu of the Earth. Much the same thing, Elders gumming out their last days pretending to run the place. Hold on a minute." He urged the caöpa into a trot that looked as uncomfortable as Shadith had expected, caught up with Danor, spoke with him, and pointed ahead.

When he was back beside Shadith, he said, "There's a lay-by with a well about an hour on. We'll stop and rest the caöpas a while, let them drink and nibble on some grain. Well, what I said was a bit of an exaggeration. We Ards are none of us all that fond of authority. The Meruus abide in Chuta Meredel in the Vale of Medon. Which is where we're going, by the way. The Circles of the Ordumels send representatives there to make laws for Banikoëh. There's a repository of memory and records, a place where teachers go to learn the history of the world. And a court where budlines go to lay quarrels and Fior to work out matters of property, where Ordumels go to settle boundary disputes, that sort of thing. But only if the problem's really serious. Bother them with something they think is frivolous and the fines they lay on you will take your last drop of sweat." He nodded at the smaller, paler Eolt drifting overhead. "Lebesair is what we call a Mer-Eolt," he said. "One of those that carries word from the Meruus to the Ordumels."

"Seems peaceful, all things considered. What was that wagon driver talking about. Chorek? What are chorek and why should we worry about them?"

"Chorek." Maorgan wrinkled his nose, shook his head. "Trouble, Shadowsong. Thieves, some of them killers. The milder sort attack travelers, strip them to the skin, carry off everything they own. Others. . . ." He shuddered. "They want to refight the Shape Wars. They steal to support themselves and kill to support their goals. Bad bunch. Ordinary chorek don't usually attack when there are Eolt on watch, but the ones at war with the world hate Ards and the sioll bond. Even if they couldn't steal, they'd kill us."

"Shee! Between them and the Chave, I'm going to be sleeping light for sure."

"They don't come this far from the mountains much. Sometimes we get bands raiding out of the Marishes. Like the Sea Marish down by the mesuch's enclosure. A lot of vermin in that place. Did us a favor when they sat down there, the mesuchs did. By the time we reach the edge of Dumel Alsekum's Land Right, we'll be close to the Kutelinga Marish. Then we will have to start sharing watch; it would be useful if you have offworld weapons." He fell silent a moment, brooding.

Shadith didn't answer the implied question; she wasn't ready quite yet to trust him all that much, didn't know how the Meruus would react to her coming to them armed. She sighed.

### 5

The two teachers moved about the room, putting away copybooks, picking up the scraps of paper that every classroom in every paper-using culture seemed to spawn by the end of each day. They were uneasy about talking to her, Aslan could feel that. At the same time, they wanted to talk. They were fascinated by the idea of University; they glanced at her repeatedly and every glance was a question.

The Keteng was the more aggressive of the two. Xe finished laying out the chalk in the tray that ran along the base of the slateboard, dusted off xe's hands, and turned to face Aslan. "So, what is it you want us to say?"

"If you could start with your names and what it is you do."

"Budechil said that thing," xe pointed at the Ridaar, "makes pictures and traps the voice."

"Would you care to see what it does?"

"Yes."

The Keteng contemplated xe's image, frowning at the sound of xe's voice. "That's me?"

"What you hear inside your head is never what other people hear. You'll get used to the difference after a while and won't find it strange."

Xe turned to whisper to the Fior woman, then fetched chairs and the two of them settled in the pool of sunlight coming through the roof.

"My name is Oskual, Budline Ual-beriod. I teach Meloach and young Fior song and history and all the things they should know about the ways of the world."

"My name is Teagasa Teor, I teach Meloach and young Fior writing, ciphering and drawing, dance and all the things that grace the world."

"We are bonded, Teagasa and I. It's not the sioll bond of the Ard and Eolt, but a sharing that crosses family and budlines. We dream the same dreams and when we share the fruit of the berrou in the High Summer month Orredyl, we can walk each other's thoughts. Teagasa was born and I budded and dropped free in the same month, the same day and from that time forth our bond was there, growing as we grew. From our experience when we went to the Vale of Medon to study history and other things, this bond is there in most who teach the young."

Teagasa smiled and touched Oskual's wrist near the hand. "On the Fior side, it doesn't matter whether the child is male or female, the bond is the same."

Oskual turned xe's wrist and took xe's companion's

hand in xe's. "You're interested in the Shape Wars, you said. To get the old songs about that time, you have to go to Chuta Meredel. Perhaps your Harper can arrange that for you. It won't be easy. The Elders hold their knowledge close."

"They're jealous of it," Teagasa said. "We tried for months to see just the old-Fior version of Bracoin's Song, without the music or any commentary, but we never got a smell of it. We had to make do with translations, and you can't ever be sure about them, can you."

Aslan glanced at the Ridaar, sighed. "It's a problem I've met before," she said. "I'd like you to think of people in the Dumel who have stories you think worth telling and wouldn't mind you giving their names. I'll send my Aide around later to collect the list." She smiled. "His name is Marrin Ola and he looks like bones held together with light brown skin. Right now I'd like children's songs and any explanations you have of how they came to be."

Teagasa's brown eyes went narrow with shyness and she looked away. "Wouldn't it be better," she murmured, the words barely audible, "if you had the children themselves singing?"

"The time for that will come. Clarity of words and tune is what's important now. And, of course, the explanations. This is more important than perhaps you know. It's often fairly late in the history of a people before the children's songs are written down. They're not considered serious material, though they will have information of considerable importance to a study of that culture imbedded within them."

"I see." The teachers whispered together for several moments, then Oskual clicked xe's tongue and smiled, xe's dark eyes shining with mischief. "We'll give you a sampling," xe said. "That's what you want anyway, catalysts to trigger more songs."

Oskual and Teagasa shifted their chairs, slanting them so they could face each other and still see Aslan.

"Charun, derun, comn and corr," Oskual sang, holding the long r at the end of the last word.

"In the cloudlands swoop and soar." Teagasa's higher voice wove about the drone of the r.

"Kere cherom busca madh." *Droned dh extending.*

"Creep and crawl, trot and plod." *Over and under the drone.*

"Elare, ehere, idus iäse." *Zed drone extending.*

"Dance and dart in deep green seaways."

"That's the start of one," Oskual said. "A namesong of birds, beasts, and fish. It goes on forever, a whole catalog of the creatures of Béluchad. There are a lot of catalogs children sing, lists of Ordumels in the Dumel Rings, lists of rivers, of mountains, of seas, of the continents." Xe grinned. "We like lists, we Béluchar."

Teagasa smiled shyly. "But we do songs just for fun, like the Caöpa song. Children do a clap-jump game to that one."

Oksual nodded, started clapping xe's hands in a strong steady rhythm. Teagasa joined xe, clapping on the off-beat. Together they sang:

> *"Caöpa Caöpa where do you graze?*
> *Upland and downland wherever grass stays.*
> *Caöpa caöpa how do you run?*
> *Clippaclop clippaclop under the sun."*

"That's another one that goes on and on," Oskual said. "And there's this one."

> *"Little Achcha Meloach*
> *Sitting in a tree*
> *Yelling down at Fior boy*
> *Can't catch me. . . ."*

The lay-by was neat and well-maintained, a grassy space inside a stake fence with fruiting vines woven through the stakes. Inside the fence there was a grassy area with two shade trees and several backless benches, a covered well with a hand pump for filling the water trough, a three-sided shed with a corral and hayrick for the caöpas or draft animals of those spending the night there, a resthouse with a roof made from pieces of shell scraped so thin they let the sun shine through. The only furnishings were a pair of wide benches built into the wall and a fireplace with an extension to one side for cooking meals.

After they finished tending the caöpas, Shadith strolled to the opening in the stake fence and stood looking along the road.

There was a dark blot on the horizon rather like a herd of something smaller than the ponies—something else coming down the road. She hadn't expected to see things so busy. Despite the Yaraka thrusting themselves into the lives of these people, once one got a very short way from the Enclave, the days of the locals seemed to be moving along much as usual.

She strolled away. Walking felt good, stretching muscles that the riding had tied into knots. She looked in the door of the resthouse, saw Danor stretched out on one of the benches with his face to the wall. *You want to be alone, I'll leave you alone.* She moved on. Maorgan was leaning on the corral fence, talking privately to Eolt Melech, the speech tentacle dropping to curl around his neck.

Shadith glanced at the Ard, shrugged and wandered back to the opening.

The blotch was closer, separating out into a crowd of children. She was beginning to hear fragments of laughter and words. She turned her head, called,

"Maorgan, something's on the road ahead, moving toward us. Come tell me what it is."

At first she didn't think he'd heard her, then he touched the tentacle round his throat. When the Eolt pulled free, he said, "According to Melech, it's the Mengerak. The twelfth year Circle." He walked over to her, looked out. "Right."

"That tells me a lot."

"Oh. Seven Ordumels make a Circle. In this Circle, we count Alsekum, Kebesengay, Bliochel, Melekau, Rongesan, Cherredech, Soibeseng. In the third week of Kerrekerl the Mengerak begins. The Children's Walk. Starts in a different Dumel each year, around and around the Circle. It's a time for learning, for bonding with the Circle, getting ready for the Kirrataneh and the Mating fairs. For trading. For holding the Circle in peace. What Glois was on about, next year he and Utelel will be making Mengerak. The kids think it's the greatest fun there is, going from celebration to celebration, but it's a lot more than that. It's a thousand and a thousand years old and it's important, it's one of the glues that binds us together. Ah, Shadowsong, if the Shape Wars come back...." He didn't try to finish, just shook his head and stood watching the horde of children coming down the road.

"What about the chorek? And animal predators?"

"If you'll look higher, you'll see half a dozen Eolt floating ward above them. Besides, if anyone harmed a single one of those kids, they'd have all of Banikoëh after them. We wouldn't stop till we cleaned the land of them." His face twisted with sudden anger, smoothed out almost as quickly. "It won't happen."

"It hasn't happened," she said quietly. "The Yaraka and the Chave, your mesuchs, they're changing things. Next year you'd better send guards with the children if you think they should go out. Not just the Eolt. Sounds like some of the political choreks would like nothing better than linking up with a set of powerful offworlders. And that means trouble of a kind you haven't seen before."

He looked past Danor at the band of children. They were close enough now that Shadith could begin to make out individuals. Two girls were dancing in a wild spiral along the grassy lane, hair flying, breathless laughter breaking to pieces on the wind. A Keteng Meloach was plucking strings and knocking his knuckles on an instrument that seemed rather like a lute crossed with a gourd. Behind xe other Meloach were clapping their hands and several Fior and Meloach were improvising mouth music. "We need this glue, Shadowsong. Without it Keteng and Fior could fall apart." He made an impatient sound. "Matha matha, we'd better get moving again. Holding on is what the Klobach is all about. The Meruus are expecting you to tell them how step by step, so we'd better get you there and let you do it."

# 7. Wheel of Fortune

## 1

Ceam handed the binocs to the Fior woman squatting beside him. "Look where they put the Crawler. They've learned. Take the canyon falling in on them to do serious damage there."

Leoca adjusted the focus. "Hm. I see what you mean. Good thing that isn't what we have in mind."

The Crawler was edged up against a stand of ancient kulkins and gumas, a swath of grassy ground between it and the creek that ambled down the canyon, the chuff of its air intakes audible above the muted sounds from the rest of the canyon. The day was warm and quiet, the rustle of the leaves, the murmur of the creek soporific as a lullaby; even the angies were staying close to their perches, their songs subdued, barely reaching the watchers on the rim. One of the mesuchs was stretched out on a blanket, sleeping in the shade of a young kerre just coming into bud.

"Doesn't look like they're expecting trouble. I suppose the storm meant you had clouds down to your ankles when Eolt Kitsek brought you word."

Ceam rested his chin in his hands. "Mm. You get caught in it?"

"Ihoi! did we." She took a long careful look at the canyon below, lowered the binocs, and rubbed at her eyes. "Makes you dizzy, this. Engebel, see if you can work out a way to get at that thing." She passed the glasses to her Keteng companion. "How many and what schedule are they keeping?"

He wriggled from the rim so the Keteng could take his place, stood when he was far enough that he wouldn't be seen from below, dusted himself off and sat with his back against one of the scrub gumas clinging to the slope behind the canyon lip. "Two mesuch. Four hours on, four off. The pair on duty when I got here were sloppier about it. Did a lot of leaving the machine to run itself. Next lot, though, they rung the changes by the bell. That's the way it's been since. Twelve days I been here, they've had three personnel switches, new mesuch coming in second day, sixth day, first lot came back yesterday. They were hot to hold sched, figure they got chewed out about it, but they're already starting to get lazy. I'd say tonight or tomorrow would be best time, they won't be cleaning up yet for next rotation." He glanced at the three Meloach squatting silent in the shade of the other gumas. "New kind of Mengerak?"

Leoca sighed. "In a way. Chetiel, Tengel, and Bliull were students of ours. Engebel and I, we're teachers. Cha oy, we were before the mesuch came. Story you probably heard a hundred times, they hauled Fior off to labor camps, killed any Keteng they could catch, and burned the Dumel."

Ceam grunted. "How you going to fix them?"

"Hokori puffballs. The spores get into the part that runs the machines and make it go crazy. Couple of the Meloach get under the crawlers between the tracks, pop a dozen spores into the air intake and, oh, twenty minutes later, the thing's junk."

"I was warned to stay telkib melkib from them. Alarms go off, I get roasted. How...."

"Something we found out by accident a couple tendays ago. Meloach don't register on their detectors. Our younglings there can slide right up to the crawlers before the mesuch know what's happening. About a dozen klids like us moving on Crawlers this tenday. Want to get as many of them as we can before they figure out what's happening and how to stop us."

Ceam glanced at the sun, eyes squinted against the glare. *Half an hour of light left, maybe a bit more.* He wriggled closer to the rim, trained the binocs on the trees behind the Crawler. The klid should be in place now. *Not a sign of them. Good thing, that.* His mouth pinched to a narrow line as he saw one of the mesuch move into the doorway of the Crawler living space and stand staring at the canyon rim. *Nervous, are you, scraëm? I hope you've got reason you don't know about.* "Ah!"

A small, agile shadow snaked from under the trees and vanished beneath the Crawler. As Leoca said, no alarm.

Ceam smiled. *If the teachers are right and hokori spores can poison that thing, Chel Dé be blessed, there'll be a dozen of the monsters dead soon. Not too soon for me.*

The Meloach slid out and crawled for the trees. Xe looked wobbly now, uncertain.

*Xe must have got a whiff of them xeself. Move, child. Go on, go on, keep going. Ah! good.*

One of the other Meloach slipped from the trees, caught the first by the arm, and half-lifted, half-dragged xe back into shelter.

Ceam moved the binocs to the door into the Crawler shell. As the sun slid completely behind the peaks, the light visible through the louvers that protected the windows were lines of yellow on a black ground, the open door a yellow rectangle interrupted by the blocky form of the Chav.

The mesuch turned his head, said something to the other one, his voice a grumble on the wind, the words unintelligible. He moved inside and pulled the door shut.

For half an hour nothing happened.

The door to the Crawler burst open, the two mesuchs stumbled out, choking, coughing, wisps of smoke following them, the yellow glow behind them flickering as if it were firelight rather than electric. As the mesuchs flung themselves onto the creek to wash the spore dust off them, the light pulsed a last time and went out.

Ceam smiled with pleasure. *It worked. The Crawler's dead.*

The smile vanished as the cliff groaned and shifted under him. He heard a horrible whining sound below him. When he looked down, he saw the nose end of one of the mole machines poke through the stone; a moment later the rest of it followed and it fell into the canyon, landing with a crash that echoed from wall to wall and a flare of light that started spots dancing before Ceam's eyes.

"Ihoi!" As the stone started shaking under him like a Keteng in the grip of berm fever, Ceam scrambled away from the edge and watched with horror as another of the machines screamed out where he'd been lying. It turned end for end and ate its way back into the stone.

He snatched his pack and bolted up the uneven mountainside rising from behind the canyon rim.

The mining machines screamed, the high whines lifting the hairs on his arms and neck; the groaning and cracking of the stone got louder. As the dirt slipped under his feet, trying to drag him with it, the mountain rocked and shuddered, the trees around him cracked and groaned, he caught at branches, brush, used them to pull himself along, fell to his knees again and again, the pack he held by one shoulder strap nearly wrenched from his grasp. He scrambled on, struggling to get over the shoulder of the mount, onto the far slope.

\*　　\*　　\*

Near dawn when the mountain had settled to its ordinary stolidity, Ceam crept back, keeping a careful watch on the sky to make sure no airwagons were around. At the edge of the still unstable scree, he stopped and looked down along what had once been a canyon wall.

The Crawler had escaped much of the slide, but a few huge chunks of stone had brushed against it and tumbled it onto its side. It looked like a dead nagal tipped on its back, the tracks like broken legs tucked close to the shell. Ceam set the binocs to his eyes and picked up glints of starlight from the twisted torn metal of the mining machines, mixed inextricably with the shards of stone. Near the Crawler he spotted an arm and a leg in the dull gray of mesuch worksuits poking from under a pile of debris. Either the second mesuch got away on foot or he was mashed to pulp under the fallen stone.

After a last scan with the binocs, he resettled the straps of the pack and began making his way down back around the mountain, a small contented smile on his round, lined face.

## 2

Ilaörn sat in the corner of the Ykkuval's consultation chamber, playing wallpaper music on the harp and listening to the reports coming in on the com. He kept his head down, his eyes on his fingers so he wouldn't betray the satisfaction he felt. Six Crawlers and their moles completely destroyed. Two intact but needing a complete replacement of the control system and new moles. Four Crawlers with only minor damage because the crews were alert enough and lucky enough to get the systems shut down before the spores had a chance to destroy them—all that working on information he'd passed out of the Kushayt. *Matha matha, it was a piece of luck, that, hearing the report about the spores.* He freed one hand, stroked it with loving care along the wood of the harp frame. *Your doing, my sweet mistress, all you.*

His heart had nearly failed him the morning a tenday ago when Hunnar's voice sounded behind him as he finished coding some information he'd picked up about movements of the Crawlers.

"Why haven't you played that before?"

Ilaörn eased himself away from the harp and got to his feet, moving stiffly, his knees aching because he'd sat so long on the cold damp earth. He folded his hands, bowed his head. "Oh Ykkuval, I was mourning. The time is finished now, so I play again. I was Ard, O Ykkuval. I was a master harper. It was my life."

"That was a strange piece you played. Jarring."

"Oh, Ykkuval, it was a study, not a finished piece. An exercise. Something to get my hands in shape again."

"Play something more ahh euphonious. Something more suited to Dushanne." Hunnar strolled off, glancing back now and again, a thoughtful frown on his heavy face.

Ilaörn leaned into the harp and considered what he should play. By way of their intimate connection through the probe sessions, he knew Hunnar better than most of his own people, knew the Chav's pretensions and limitations. Something simple but flashy. His mouth twitched into his first unbitter smile in months as he thought how like this mesuch was to more than one Ordumel Teseach he'd known. He started playing Ard Amorane's Trick—and tricked himself. He forgot about Hunnar and the mesuch, even about his sioll, losing himself in the sheer joy of the sound.

Hunnar's voice brought him back all too soon to the reality of his life.

". . . to judge with that primitive instrument you play, but the touch is lyrical, the tone most pleasing to the ear. An artist. Yes. Anyone can grub in a garden, but a true artist must follow his gift. We pride ourselves on our taste, we highborn. And our generosity. A gift like that puts a man outside of caste, makes him worthy of our patronage. . . .

Ilaörn stopped listening; he could guess what outside of caste meant. Pampered pet dancing to the whim of the patron. *I'd rather be your gardener than your "artist in residence," but I don't have a choice, do I. Hm. I can try telling you the garden refreshes my soul and I need to work here. Wonder if that'll work? If I can't get out . . . cha oy, it has to work.*

Endless sweet soft ripples flowing from his hands, Ilaörn watched the Ykkuval's anger rise as his eyes moved over screen after screen of reports on the destruction the spores had caused. Reports of villages burned in retaliation. Empty villages. Reports from the fliers scouring the mountains with motion and heat detectors. No locals sighted, either species. Empty land, but out of that land, destruction rising.

Hunnar tapped a sensor. "Memur Tryben, I want you."

Ilaörn touched the strings, the music he made barely audible, hoping Hunnar would forget he was there. He wanted very much to listen in on this conference, but he didn't know enough about the Chave to measure the weight of Hunnar's decision to make his native Harp Master an ornament and a testimony to his status. The lowering of the sound level backfired, though, winning him a glare from Hunnar. Without changing expression, he gradually returned to the way he'd been playing before.

Hunnar relaxed, closed his eyes, began tapping his claws on the chair's arm, not getting the beat quite right until Ilaörn altered it to match the clicking of those claws.

A soft buzz.

Hunnar sighed and sat up. He tapped the sensor and when the door opened, waved the Chav who came in to the honor chair at the end of the desk.

The Security Chief glanced at Ilaörn, his brow ridges drawn down. For a moment Ilaörn thought he was going to protest, but the Chav's eyes went dull as he slipped the Harper into the slot that Chave kept for such beings and forgot about him.

"We're hemorrhaging, Tryben." Hunnar waved a hand at the images frozen on the viewscreens. "I want it stopped."

Tryben's face went blank, his secondary lids glistening a moment before he caught hold of his temper and recouched them. "I hear, O Ykkuval."

Hunnar made an impatient movement with his eating hand. "Pull your claws in, Memur. I'm not blaming you." He flattened his hands on the desktop, his inner lids dropping till his eyes glistened as if they were greased. "Thanks to our illustrious Comptroller back home, none of us have the men or equipment we need." He drew in a long breath, snorted it out. "Have you discovered what it was caused all the damage?"

"Spores. From some kind of puffball thing. We had some trouble with it before. You remember? The Drudges' dirtboards went crazy and stopped working and when we opened them up, it was like they were coated with sooty hair. Same thing. All twelve. No way this was an accident."

"If they could do it out there, we're vulnerable here. What are you doing about that?"

"I've got the tech working on intake screens and baffles with burnclean sections. Should be fitted up in a day or two. We've set tingler fields around the rest of the Crawlers and stepped up the sensitivity of the alarm systems. The hayv won't get near enough to get their filth into the system."

"So they'll try something else. Hm. The locals in

the camps know something, I can smell it on them. Haul in the headmen and probe them to their back teeth. I want to know what their grandfathers had for breakfast." He paused, stared blankly past Tryben. "And pick up some of the vegheads. Try the probe on them, see what you come up with. I don't expect much, but you never know when your luck might pop hot."

"O Ykkuval, I'll set that going immediately." Tryben paused, straightened his shoulders.

In his corner Ilaörn's fingers fumbled and he almost lost the beat in his surprise at seeing that bloody-handed butcher nervous as a tadling at his apprentice trials.

"If the Comptroller would authorize the importation, I'd like to do an EYE sweep of the range." The words were slow and heavy, the Memur's gravelly voice devoid of inflection. "Ten fliers and two channels cleared for the pickup. It is the only way we can possibly find the saboteurs in all that forest and stone. Heat pickups, motion readers, and visuals just will not do the job. I suspect what we are looking for are small groups moving on foot, impossible to tell from grazing herds and other natural phenomena." He lowered his eyes to his hands and waited for the answer.

"If they'd listened to me, you'd have had EYEs weeks ago. No. I won't bother asking again. There's no point to it. I can give you five fliers. With all these Crawlers down, we've got that much excess capacity. Pick your men, tell them to do the best they can, ash whatever shows up on the monitors." A slash of his hand cut off the discussion. "Medtech Muhaseb. You've been watching to make sure he's not slipping word out about the husk?"

Memur Tryben lifted his head, settled into the chair, the dangerous moment had passed. This was business as usual and he was comfortable with it. "None of the techs working on the analysis have been given access to the com. Or to other techs. We've been monitoring them since you set up the project."

"Hm. There was an interesting com call last night. Jindar ni Koroumak. Making noises like he wanted to be invited out here. Hunting, he said. What could I do? He'll be here with his idiot followers in less than a month. Be prepared to have him nosing about the labs."

"Ah. I see. Your interest in this is kept close, I guarantee that, and Muhaseb's group is buffered. I'll make sure he doesn't get near them. News slipping out about the smoke is something else. The high that comes from burning the husks is common knowledge among techs and Drudges. You know how such things get about among the lower orders. Farkli the Drudge, the one who runs the lubbot, he's complained more than once about the stink and the drain on his income. Seems the smoke suckers don't drink as much as they did before." Tryben flexed his arms in the Chav equivalent of a shrug. "Techs coming off duty will raid one of the Sleeping Grounds and bring back as much of the husk as they can conceal in their gear. They have enough sense to keep their smoke sucking for off-duty hours. So far, anyway, but it seems to be quite addictive, so that may change soon. At least half the techs working on the analysis are showing signs of smoke dependence."

"Looks like we've got another Tirassci brewing. Kir and chich! As if I needed more trouble. How bad is it?"

"With our limited numbers here, it's not surprising that nearly all of the subclasses have tasted smoke. Without rigorous tests, any numbers would be hardly more than a guess, but I'll give them to you. Fifteen mining techs left. All have some degree of dependence. Six med techs. As I said before, four of the six are showing signs of dependency. Ten Drudges. Two of them got beaten for stealing Husk from techs. Most have no contact with the smoke. Twenty-four Guards. Six have drunk smoke on their off-hours, the others just get drunk. Six com and repair techs. All have tasted smoke. Two seem to be dependent, the others prefer Farkli's yang. Early results of the med techs' investigations seem to show smoke isn't as destructive as Tirassci chaw. At least not so swift a decay of nerve cells. Hard to say. We'd need to test long term users and we don't have any of those."

"Hm. Set a trap at one of the Sleeping Grounds. The Harper says those that tend the place are addicts. Find an old Cousin hanging around because he can't walk away from his habit, you'll get your long-term study with enough crossover to be useful."

"Ah. I'll do that."

They continued to talk for another hour and Ilaörn sat in his corner, playing his wallpaper music and stewing with impatience. He *had* to get into the garden. What he'd heard was important, he had to get it out. He closed his eyes and began setting the news into Riddle Mode. *Mesuch hunting mountain length, burning everything that moves.* Repeat. Repeat. *Trap at Sleeping Ground.* Repeat. Repeat. *Hunting and watchers.* Repeat. Repeat. *Leaders in the labor camps.* Repeat. Repeat. *Mesuch are coming to get them.* Repeat. Repeat. *Scrape their brains of everything they know.* Repeat. Repeat. *Anyone with secrets get away. Get away now.*

When Memur Tryben left, Hunnar got to his feet and paced the length of the room over and over, scowling at the tiled floor though it was obvious he saw nothing of the blocky design; he was walking off the anger he'd kept locked away as long as anyone who mattered was in the room. Back and forth, back and forth until Ilaörn was dizzy from watching him. Back and forth, back and forth—and then he stopped, stared at the wall of screen, went to his desk and reached toward the sensor board.

He drew his hand back, turned his scowl on Ilaörn. "Take your meal early. You'll be playing for my dinner tonight." He cupped his hand across his mouth, examined the worn gray tunic and trousers the Harper wore. "I'll have the terzin run up a formal robe for you. You'll wear that tonight. That thing you played in the Dushanne Garden. I want that. Something complementary to go with it. I'll leave that up to you. Impress them and you won't find me ungrateful."

"I hear and obey, O Ykkuval."

"Good. Be ready by ninth hour. I'll send a Drudge to fetch you."

Ilaörn sat in the dark outside the gardener's hutch, watching the stars shift overhead and soaking his left hand in an infusion of langtana leaves; he'd already soaked the right hand and was doing easy exercises with the wrist and fingers. Playing all day like this was tearing up his fingers even if it was music only by an extreme extension of the concept.

He smiled and did more finger push-ups, the thick springy grass cool and pleasant against his skin. More playing than he'd done since he and Imuë had grown old and creaky and stopped their wandering from Dumel to Dumel. He thought about Imuë and was surprised to find only a faint bittersweetness left of the pain that once tore through him when he remembered his sioll.

It was very late, past midnight. He was sleepy but not enough to hit the bed, not yet. He was happy. For two tendays he'd sent his Riddle tunes into the empty air without a hint that anyone heard them. Today, though ... today was payoff. Today made all of it worth the soreness in his fingers and the boredom in his soul. Twelve Crawlers out of use, six of them permanently. Ahhh.

The loud click of a door shutting snapped him out of his reverie. He got to his feet, stood wiping his damp hand on his old tunic as he watched two shadows walk along one of the Dushanne Garden's paths, both of them carrying bulky packs. Two?

Holding his breath, he ghosted after them.

On his belly among stinkweeds that had grown tall and thick as scrub trees, Ilaörn watched the cloaked figure climb from a sleek small flier. The spy from Banikoëh. As he had the last time, he started talking before he reached the shelter of the wall niche. "When I took the virus the last time, you said you wouldn't call me across any more; you said you'd work a way to get me called home. Chaos broke last night when they found out the com wouldn't work. How many times do you think I can shake loose before that lardhead tumbles to what's happening? What! What's that! Who's he?"

*Good,* Ilaörn thought. *I want to know, too.*

"You wanted to know why you're here. He's it. Look at this."

The spy took the flake Hunnar handed him, slipped it into a reader, then sucked in his breath. Hastily he covered his surprise and made to return the flake.

"Keep it. The money's in a special account, separate from the other. You'll need that flake for authorization to transfer the funds."

"And . . . mm . . . what's it buying?"

"Transportation." Hunnar set his hand on the squat dark figure of the other Chav. "You get him past Koraka's forward line and drop him at the edge of the swamp. That's all."

The spy opened his mouth to protest, shut it again. The fur on his face was ruffled, his mouth was pinched into a black pout. His fingers had closed around the small reader, his thumb was moving across them, as if he caressed both himself and the gelt enumerated on the flake.

The scent of mesuch fear and greed was bitter as the stench from the stinkweed. Ilaörn watched the spy weighing the dangers of doing and not doing. *You laid the stones for this the moment you let spite and greed goad you into taking your first bribe, fool. You might as well agree. You're dead if you don't.* His eyes widened as he saw the second Chav edging away from Hunnar; the spy didn't notice. He was too preoccupied with his struggle. *No, I'm wrong. You're just dead.* He caught his lip between his teeth, bit down hard as the Chav stepped swiftly behind the spy and drove his fist into the mesuch's back, jerked it away. No, not his fist. A knife with a blade hardly wider than a needle. The spy started to turn and the Chav struck again, this time driving the knife in under the chin.

The body dropped to the gravel. The Chav wiped his knife on the mesuch's cloak, then slipped it up his sleeve.

Hunnar touched the sprawled body with the toe of his boot. "Too bad. But I suppose we couldn't have milked much more out of him." He stooped, pried the flake and the reader from the spy's hand, straightened.

"Didn't think he'd wear it, taking me in."

Together they loaded the mesuch's body into the flier, then tossed the packs in on top of him.

Hunnar stepped back. "You're on your own, Kurz. As long as the Yaraka com system stays out, keep in touch. If you need supplies, I'll do my best to get them to you." He tapped the reader with the claw on his forefinger. "You don't make it back, this goes to your son. I promised it and I keep my word."

Kurz lifted his hand in the claws-in open-hand salute, reached for the sensor board.

The whine of the flier's lifters in his ears, Ilaörn crept backward through the stinkweed thicket, eased himself round the corner, and ran for the hidden door, moving as quietly as he could without diminishing his speed. His belly churned with the knowledge there was no chance of passing on what he'd heard before morning. Too bad too bad too bad ... the words echoed in his head to the padding of his bare feet.

# 8. The Ways of Béluchad

## 1

As the caöpa train rounded a hillock crowned with kerre trees, Shadith saw a Dumel ahead, nestled in a bend of the Menguid River, half a dozen sail barges tied up to the wharves lining the riverbank on both sides.

For some time now, they'd been out of the bottomlands into rolling countryside—brush and grass with browsing beasts, instead of wide fields of plowed and planted land. The road ran west with little deviation from the straight line, up and down, over hills, across small valleys, always gaining altitude no matter how many dips it made, though the gain was slow and subtle enough to be nearly imperceptible; the Menguid sometimes ran beside the road, sometimes curved away so that they wouldn't see it for several days, though more than once Shadith watched the tips of the stubby sails of the barges gliding past, just visible above the brush growing on a hillock, or the bright flutter of a burgee to remind her that there were other folk about.

There were no more lay-bys kept supplied by the Ordumel they were traveling through. No more Ordumels, only scattered farm houses and stock cabins.

This section of the road was poorly maintained, more ruts and potholes than paving, and few used it. Now and then they passed a farmwife on her way to market in a caöpa cart or a boy herding small animals that looked like cotton poufs on dainty black legs that her wordlist eventually told her were called cabhisha. Most of the traffic was on the river.

The Dumel ahead was flying bright pennons and oriflammes, burgees from the barges tied up at the river landing. Flowers blooming brightly on their heads and shoulders, Meloach were playing in circle games with Fior children dressed in red and orange trousers with brilliant white smocks embroidered in blue and green.

Overhead the two Eolt rose to a faster airstream and went gliding swiftly toward the Dumel.

Danor brushed his hand across his eyes.

Shadith winced as she saw how it was shaking. The happy scene below must be like ground glass on his nerves.

She kneed her caöpa closer to Maorgan. "What's this place called and why the celebration?"

"Dumel Olterau. I think. . . ." He clicked his tongue as he counted days on his fingers. "Time. How it slips and slides away. It's the first of Seibibyl . . . that means this is the first official day of Summer—and if I haven't lost track completely it's also Rest Day. Supposed to be good fortune next year when Summer begins with Rest."

As they rode into the town, a ring of dancers came from a side street, laughing and clapping, several of them singing, others beating out the rhythm with wooden clogs and tambourines. One of the singers was a pretty Fior girl with bright red curls and a spray of freckles across her nose; she glanced at Maorgan, looked up and saw the Eolt, then thrust two fingers in her mouth and produced a loud whistle. When she had everyone's attention she pointed at the Eolt, then at Maorgan. "Ard," she shouted.

"Ard. Ard. Ard." The shouts passed on and came back as more and more people crowded around them.

The singer caught hold of the caöpa's halter, looked up at Maorgan. "Will you come?" She sang the words, a ripple of pleased laughter in her voice. "Will you come stay with me, Ardcoltair?"

He laughed, lifted her onto the caöpa's withers, and kissed her thoroughly to the shouts and cheers of the crowd. "Take us to the blai, Sun-blessed. My friend there's in mourning and in no mood for pleasure. But once he's settled, we'll sing the Summer in for you."

Fingers sore, throat raw from the hours of singing and playing, soul still aglow from the joy of the music, Shadith moved wearily along the deserted walkways of the blai. There were no nightlights, but the blaze that was the Béluchad night sky made them unnecessary. Looking up was like gazing on a permanent fireworks display.

Where Maorgan was now she'd hadn't the faintest idea, and she was too tired to care. On the other hand, she had a very good guess what he was doing—the Béluchar weren't used to female harpers, but they didn't let that put them off. During the first break from playing, the Olteraun Fior had crowded round her, men and women both, offering themselves as bed partners, brushing against her, hands moving on her breasts and buttocks until she slapped them away and got the idea across that she wasn't interested in kaus and kikl.

She shifted the strap of the harpcase, dug in her pocket for the odd cylindrical key the Blai Olegan had given her, started to insert it into the lock hole—and stopped, sniffing. There was a peculiar pungent smell coming from the next room over. Danor's kip.

She frowned. *The way he was acting. . . .* She eased the strap off her shoulder, set the case down, and walked the short distance to Danor's door. She tried the latch. Locked. The smell was much stronger here, made her feel ... well ... odd. The closest she could come was that time on Avosing where the planet's air was permeated with hallucinogenic spores.

She leaned against the door and tried to get some sense of the man, but all she could read was a jumble of pain, rage, and a flood of grief so terrible she cried out against it. She closed her eyes, tried to concentrate, her head so tired from the music and the exuberance of the dance, from the excited attentions of Keteng and Fior, from the glory of the Eolt song, that her brain felt like mush. *Focus. Exclude. Strip away the flourishes of emotion, feel the beat of the body.*

By the time she managed to reassure herself about the strength of Danor's life flow, she'd breathed in enough of the smoke to send her floating.

She contemplated stretching out there on the walkway, melting with the smoke, absorbing just enough to keep her drifting, in a state where nothing mattered, all the twists and turns of need and rejection wiped away.... Her knees stopped holding her up. She didn't fall, it was a slow-motion folding down. It amused her. She kept folding until her face was pressed against the tiles. That was amusing. And pleasant. The tiles were cool and smooth.

She drew in a long breath—and sneezed violently, the spasm triggered by the pollen grains she'd sucked in with dust from the grouting between the tiles. She sneezed again and pushed onto her knees, appalled at what had happened to her.

Bones feeling like half-set gel, she used the latch to pull herself to her feet, then staggered back to her own door. She stood leaning into it, her forehead pressed to the wood, half forgetting what she was there for until her nose prickled again and broke her out of her trance. She unlocked the door, hauled the case inside, and stood slouched in the doorway, gathering herself.

As soon as she managed to get the bar down and into its hooks, she stumbled across to the bed and fell facedown on it, sinking into a sleep so deep that if she dreamed she never knew it.

## 2

Aslan clicked the Ridaar off. "That's enough for now. I'll show you more when you've talked a bit." She settled back in her chair and smiled at the four youngsters, two Meloach and two Fior boys, all of them around eight or nine years old.

I want children who are good friends, she'd told Teagasa and Oskual. They'll be shy at first, but having friends with them will help them relax and loosen their tongues.

Why children? Oskual asked. If you're gathering history. . . .

There's an official truth and a folk truth in every culture and often they don't coincide. Children pick up on folk truth, sometimes it seems from the air itself, and they aren't driven by politics and adult shame to conceal these things. I'm not a historian, Aslan finished. I record cultures. All facets of them.

She leaned forward, moved her eyes from face to face, a gesture meant to collect them and make them feel part of a whole that included her. "What do you do when you want to decide who goes first? Say in a game you're playing." She watched the scrubbed, sober faces, suppressing a sigh. So obviously on their best behavior, spines stiffened by parental admonitions. "No, don't tell me. Show me."

An eight-year Meloach named Likel had already proved to be the most talkative of the four, the leader insofar as this small group had a leader. Xe had bright red mossflowers blooming on xe's head and shoulders and already a beginning of the Denchok lichen web threading across xe's torso. Xe fidgeted in xe's chair, twisted xe's narrow pointed face into a comic grimace. "If it's just us," xe said, "and ev'one wants to go first, we do the Digger Count."

Xe turned to Colain, a short Fior boy with shiny black hair and eyes bluer than a summer sky. "Le's dig." Xe and Colain made fists, pumped them together through the air. "One. Two. Three. Diggit!"

Colain grinned. He'd kept his fist while Likel had flipped out his middle finger. "Stone b break knife."

Likel did the hand flutter that served Keteng for a shrug.

Sobechel, a younger Meloach with most of xe's mossflowers still in bud, though showing bright orange tips, played a knife to cut Colain's paper. Brecin, a gangly Fior boy with hair close to the orange of Sobechel's flowers, wrapped Sobechel's stone in paper. Then, with a nervously engaging grin, Brecin extended his fist to Aslan.

She raised her brows, grinned back at him. "Phra phra, why not."

"One two three," they chanted together. "Diggit!"

Aslan kept the fist, saw herself breaking Brecin's knife.

His grin threatened his ears. "You win, Scholar. You go first."

"Mm. I think I've been framed." She chuckled. "All right. What do you want to know?"

Likel scooted his chair closer. "You got any pictures in there of where you come from?"

Brecin pulled up his long bony legs and sat on his feet with his knees pointing out, his shoulders up, his arms hooked over the back of the chair. "And what's your family like?"

"And why d d do those mesuch want to c c come here and mess up everything?" Colain pushed at the lank black hair that kept falling into his eyes. There was an edge of anger in his voice that embarrassed him when his eyes met Aslan's; he went almost purple, looked quickly away.

"And what it's like riding between the stars." Sobechel had a dreamy look on xe's face, pale eyes the color of dust glistening with visions of distant places and strange things.

"Hm, that covers a lot of ground. Let's start with my family. My mother is a businesswoman, she runs her own company ... um which makes things sort of like locks only fancier with a lot of bells and whistles to discourage thieves. She lives on a world called Droom which is so far away you couldn't see its sun if you went out at night and looked at all the stars. Even from University I can't see Droom's sun, though it is a bit closer. My father is a poet. I don't see him much. He's always somewhere else."

"Like Glois' dad," Sobechel said. "He an Ard and he never comes back."

"Maorgan?"

"Uh-uh, another one. I think Glois' Da, he stays mostly on Melitoëh. Maybe he's dead. Those mesuchs over there are crazy they say."

"How c c come you live on ... um ... University and your Mum is way away somewhere else? D d do lots of people do like that?"

"University is a whole world that's a school where people go to study things, write books, teach classes. They come from a thousand and a thousand worlds. Some stay and some go home. I stayed."

"Ah." Colain nodded. "Like Chuta M m meredel. Our teachers went there to study. But they c come b back."

Sobechel clicked his tongue against xe's chewing ridge. "So it's different out there. And everyone don't come back. Your cousin Timag for one. He went for a bargeman and hasn't showed face here since Teagasa was beating the letters into you head. Scholar, you said you'd show us pictures. Can I see a starship?

Ol' Barriall, he use to deal with Free Traders and he said he'd bring me a picture of a ship, but he never did. Yours will be better anyway, his woulda been just flat and black and white."

She smiled. "Oh I might have a thing or two to interest you, Sobechel. If you'll all turn your chairs to face the wall, we'll have ourselves a show. Then it's my turn to ask questions."

Aslan switched the settings on the Ridaar and gathered her subjects into a circle around her. "Now. Give your name, then tell us a little about your family, whatever you're comfortable saying. Just to let your great great many greats grandchildren ..." she smiled at the giggles this started in them, "know a little bit about you."

"Cha oy, my name is Likel, Budline Kel-Poradd. My Parent has the Everything Shop, you know, you walk past it coming here from the blai. That's where Sobey got with ol' Barriall, he come here every month or so, down from the mountain lakes and the fac'tries there. 'Cept in winter, a course." Likel fidgeted in xe's chair, stared at the shell panels in the ceiling. "I've got three older sibs, I'm youngest. Um. There's Himtel, xe's Denchok now, got a bud growing, so I'm about to have a nexter. Then there's Iëtal and Iören, xes were same-summer buds. Xes finished school last year, looks like xes will be going into slough ... um ... that's turn Denchok ... soon's the olle bushes bud out. Himtel works at the store, xe going in partners with the Parent in a couple more years. The twins, xes work at looms in Sobey's Parent's weaving mill. Both of xes say xes going to go look for land when xes get enough money saved to put down a payment. Won't be in any Ordumels round here, though, land is family kept and don't change hands often. They thinking maybe Tatamoëh down south. Me, I don't know what

I'm going to do, maybe I'll find out come my Mengerak."

"My name is Sobechel, Budline Chel-arriod. Like Likel says, my Parent has the fiber mill. It weaves four kinds of cloth. The barges bring xe shearings from caörag and cabhisha runs up in the hills, the swampers haul in loads of c'hau bark out of the four Marishes, farmers sell xe the tatirou they grow and the finest of all are the threads from the cocoons of the deng-angi that only live on Tatamoëh Island way down south. That's really really expensive and my Parent only lets young Fior women weave with it, they have the nimblest fingers.

"I was the fourth my Parent budded. Two of my older sibs died of the Withers. My only living sib is the first dropped and xe's twelve years older than me. Xe's been Denchok most of the time I remember. I never saw xe much, xe was always busy in the mill. Xe's going to run it when our Parent goes Eolt. I'm glad xe likes it because if it wasn't for xe, it'd be me and I want to go for a scholar in Chuta Meredel."

Colain turned red again when Aslan glanced his way. "My name is C c olain Triü. My D da is the shoemaker. My M ma, she m makes things like saddles and harnesses. Mostly folk come to our shop for anything that gets made outta leather. My uncle Bort, he's the t tanner. I'm g g gonna to work with him when I finish school. He's already t teching me stuff. I g got one sister, Mevva. She's the oldest. M ma's teaching her to take over. I had a b b brother, but he got in trouble and run off; he was with the swampies for a while, but now we think he's either dead or g gone chorek." He bent his head so a wedge of straight black hair hid his face.

"My name is Brecin Gabba. Me, I'm with Colain. I like working with my hands. Besides, I'm my Da's only kid, Ma couldn't have more after me. He's the smith. The Forge, that's round the grove from the

Blai, handy there case travelers they want new shoes on a caöpa, harness rings or something like that. I been working in the Forge since I was old enough to know I sh'd stay 'way from the fire. I figure Da and me, we'll keep on working till we both drop. I mean, I LIKE making things. I like the feeling a good knife blade gives you, or an ax head or even mending a copper pot so folks can cook their supper."

"Hm." Aslan glanced at her notes. "Tell me about the swampies. Who are they, where do they come from, how do they live?"

Sobechel ran a finger across the moss growing like green velvet on the outside of his arm; it gave under the pressure, changed color slightly so a darker mark followed his fingertip. "I s'pose I seen them most. The biggest lot of them are Fior, but there's some Denchok, too. Some of 'em are stupid chieks who land up to their necks in trouble in Ordumels and get chuffed out. Some of 'em are people who just don't like having lots of other people around. And there's some I dunno why they went there. They live in the Marishes and collect stuff that grows wild there and bring it out and sell it. Like the c'hau bark I said, and melidai which is stuff we use on the bark and bibrek which makes a real bright yellow dye and bung which makes a dark red and lots of coloring stuff like that and medicines and stuff like that. The Fior swampies, they don't shave or nothing, weren't for the colors you couldn't tell them from Keteng, 'cause the Denchoks, they get all kinds of stuff growing in the lichen and they don't clean it out like our Parents make us do." He sighed, a trace of envy in the sound.

Aslan tapped a finger on the chair, asked, "But they're not chorek, not predators, I mean they don't attack people?"

"Not the ones I seen anyway. They just weird, that's all."

"Hm. I keep hearing about the Shape Wars, way

back, a thousand and a thousand years ago. Tell me what people say about that time."

Likel glanced at the others, saw they weren't going to say anything, so he started the story. "Well, there were these people who call themselves Angermans, they had to leave where they were 'cause a bad people were oppressing them."

Brecin nodded. "And the old Keteng, it wasn't like now, they din't have Ordumels and stuff, they live in grass beöcs and eat wild stuff."

"And the Angermans, their ship went blooey some way and they were 'bout dead when they got to Béluchad and their ship went bust all the way and it land kinda hard up round Rager Point, least that what the songs say. They get it part unloaded and Chel Dé hiccups." Xe put a hand over xe's mouth to mask xe's giggles.

Sobechel punched Likel's arm. "Snerp, how'd Scholar know what you mean?" He turned serious gray-brown eyes on Aslan. "That's what we say when there's a quake. Anyway, the ship it rolled into the Bakuhl Sea, right where there's a big deep hole. Some folks say the hole go all the way through the world, it that deep."

"And K k keteng they never seen anything b big like that, or people like that. And they were scared and run away. Then some of 'em get mad 'cause they figure these folk were messing up their fishing p places. And they g go to tell them go 'way ."

"And the Angermans they start acting just like the bad folk that chase them out of their old home and start doing things to Ketengs when they catch them."

"And it was a bad bad time."

"And it went on for a hundred and a hundred years."

"P people k killing p people."

"Till Ard Bracoïn and Eolt Lekall sang the first Chorale of Peace. And the Angermans took the name

Fior because they were freed of the angers of the past."

## 3

The nausea she woke with stayed with Shadith as they left Olterau, nothing serious, just an awareness of her stomach anytime she got near Danor and caught a whiff of the drug whatever it was. She thought about talking with Maorgan about him, but it really wasn't her business. Besides, she had a feeling he wouldn't like a mesuch interfering between two Ard. He was pleasant enough, she could feel that he liked her, but she was an outsider.

She glanced at him, suppressed a grin. Anyone talking to Maorgan right now would get a short answer and a sharp one.

Danor was following them this time, taking his turn at leading the packers and the spare mounts.

About an hour after they left the Dumel, the road turned suddenly, angling north and west, the grade increasing to the point that the caöpas started getting balky. And nervous.

Wind out of the northwest was picking up, damp gusts slapping dead leaves and other debris at their feet and flanks, blowing dry weeds past their bobbing noses, making them shy and toss their heads.

"Maorgan!"

The Ard's shoulders twitched as he came out of the half doze he'd been in all morning and he turned his head, a pained look on his face. "What is it?" He winced, screwed his eyes shut as he waited while she fought to control her caöpa and get him to walk the short distance between them. When she reached him, he glanced at the sweaty beast, then at her. "He giving you trouble? You want to change mounts?"

"No." She flicked a thumb at the black clouds gathering overhead. "You know this land. When's that going to hit?"

He tilted his head to inspect the clouds, eased it back down, a muscle twitching beside one eye, stared along the road ahead as it snaked over the hills and finally vanished into trees at the fringe of the great forest that clotted the higher slopes of the mountains. "About when we hit the trees."

"And the nearest shelter?"

"Inn. About a day's ride into the forest. We'll camp rough tonight."

"And the Eolt?"

"Waiting up ahead. They don't like to linger over Dumels up here. Some folk don't appreciate having Eolts around and can get nasty about it. And you do realize they'll have to get out of the storm's way? Mmm. Do you have offworld weapons with you?"

"A stunner. It'll put someone out, but won't kill them except by accident. Chorek?"

"Back in Olterau they fed me a lot of horrors about a band that's working the road. I discounted most of it, figured they wanted to hang onto us a while."

Shadith bit back a grin he wouldn't have appreciated. "So what do we do?"

"I'll call Melech to come back while xe can and take a look round, see if xe can spot anyone." When she looked skeptical, he shook his head. "Their looks are deceptive, Shadowsong. The stings on those tentacles can knock off a dammalt. You haven't seen those yet, shaggy things the size of a house."

Danor stopped his caöpa beside them. "Dammalt? Why you wasting time talking about them?"

"Never mind. We're talking about camping rough and watching out for chorek. What're you carrying?"

"Airgun. Darts. Minik on the points. Chorek come at us, serves them right what they get."

Maorgan grimaced. To Shadith he said, "Nerve poison. Fast and nasty. "Well, we better get moving again." He turned his caöpa, set him to moving at a quick walk.

Shadith rode beside him. "Nerve poison? That something the chorek will have?"

"Probably not. Amikta is a fungus that grows above the glacier line and distilling it is a nervous thing. Only a few can do it without killing themselves and everyone around."

"Mm. Remember what we talked about at the first lay-by? The mesuchs on Melitoëh could be arming them and sending them against us. No telling what we'll be facing."

He grimaced, winced, rubbed at his temple. "Complications. I wish all you mesuchs had never found us."

By mid-afternoon as the storm still held off, the caöpas had gotten used to the fluttering debris and had lost most of their skittishness though they were still nervous. At their rest break, they munched on the grain and browsed placidly enough on the new growth on the patches of brush at the edge of the small dry meadow. Shortly after Danor started a fire to brew up some cha, the Eolt appeared overhead, staying in place with some difficulty because of the turbulence in the air streams.

Eolt Melech dipped low, uncoiled xe's speaking tentacle and draped it around Maorgan's neck with a proprietary affection that made the Mer-Eolt Lebesair go pursy with disapproval. Xe was also pale and rippling with resentment at being brought back this close to the storm.

For the first time Shadith was aware of the personality differences between the two Eolt. She'd been seduced by their golden beauty, their music, and their untouchable quality into thinking of them as a peculiar combination of god and beast. To see one of them as irritable and petty startled her into realizing she was doing to them what others had done to the Weavers of Shayalin. God or Demon. It seemed every living creature could make one or the other of any species exotic enough in their eyes.

Melech withdrew xe's tentacle and worked xe's way upward through the turbulence to join the other Eolt in a quieter air layer.

Shadith walked over to Maorgan. "Well, what did xe say?"

"Melech saw a man riding parallel with us when xe got close enough to see us. Fior, not Keteng. Means we've got to watch nights as well. He'd stop on woody hills and use a glass on us, move on to catch up with us and do the same again. Right after the Eolt got back to us, he took off, riding north. Melech tried following for a while, but the currents were wrong and anyway the man disappeared into the forest and xe couldn't see him any longer."

The clouds thickened, the wind picked up, and the turbulence up where the Eolt swam grew so intense they struggled up to their maximum altitude and were blown out of sight.

A raindrop hit Shadith's nose, another landed in her eye. Her hair was short and close to her head, but she could still feel the wind tugging at it. A flurry of huge drops pounded her back, then no more fell for over an hour.

The caöpas turned fractious again as the road moved from open brushland into the edges of the forest. Sokli started sidling and cow kicking, trying to get his head down, trying to sink his teeth in any part of Shadith available. She hunched her shoulders, booted his nose away from her leg for the tenth time and let her mindtouch bleed into the twilight under the canopy, feeling about for the heatpoints that meant men watching.

The trees whipped about, leaves noisy and agitated, limbs groaning, creaking, occasionally snapping free to go juddering along the ground until they jammed up against a trunk.

Thunder crashed.

The darkness went white, and a tree not far from the road exploded.

Sokli squealed, planted his feet, put his head down, and wouldn't budge. Behind her she could hear the pack string snorting and squealing.

More thunder. And another tree gone, split apart, half of it crashing across the road. Maorgan muscled his caöpa around, came trotting past Shadith, heading for Danor and the pack string.

Shadith used her mindtouch to soothe the terrified caöpa as a surge of wind tore through the trees, followed a second later by hard, cold lines of rain that hammered into her. "Good, good, you're doing good, little Sokli. Turn round, I know, rain in the face is no fun, it's just a little while till we get back with the others."

The spare moss ponies and the packers were fighting the leadlines, kicking, rearing, bouncing about on stiff legs, snapping out with bared teeth, squealing, eyes rolling, all of them in a blind panic, struggling to escape, to run until they dropped while Danor and Maorgan struggled with equal urgency to keep the lines from breaking and the ponies in a compact huddle.

And the rain beat down.

And the wind blew.

Thunder rumbled.

Lightning danced around them.

Shadith opened herself to the ponies, breathed soothing things at them, calm, quiet, sense of full belly and sun warmth. One of the caöpas shook his shaggy head, snorted, and stopped his struggles.

That was the break. The others began to settle also.

Sudden pain seared along the top of her shoulder, the sound of the shot lost in the storm noise.

Sokli squealed, shuddered, dropped as a bullet hit him under the jaw and burst through his neck in a spray of blood and flesh.

Shadith flung herself down, hit the ground rolling, was up on her knees sheltering behind the caöpa's body, stunner out. She probed the windy darkness under the trees, felt the burn of a life-fire, zapped it with the stunner, and kept hunting for the others as more bullets slammed into Sokli's body or went past her, aimed at the others.

Ahead. Two of them. Each side of the road. *Gotcha! One down. Two. Other side. Gotcha! Last one ... kat'kri! Must be sheltering behind a trunk thick enough ... youch! Minging bastard. ...* Bleeding from a crease dug into hair and skin just above her ear, she flung herself over the caöpa's back legs, crawled round his hindquarters, and hunkered down as she scanned again for the shooter.

He started moving, darting for another tree so he could get a better angle on her.

She smiled, tracked him a beat, and zapped him.

Another scan confirmed he was the last. She got to her feet. Five of the moss ponies were down, one still alive but bleeding copiously from a shattered leg, screaming piteously. The others had run off. Danor was sitting up, cursing a steady stream, pressing his fist against a wound in his shoulder. Maorgan was sprawled on the road, facedown in a pothole that was filling with water.

Shadith swore and ran to him, the jar of her feet on the pavement sending pain shooting through her head. She knelt beside him, lifted his face from the water, sighed with relief as he coughed, then vomited water and bile over her knees. There was a hole in his arm, nothing serious, and a wound on his head, deep enough to show the white of bone, not a superficial crease like hers. It was hard to tell in the rain and dark, but what she read of his body signs told her he was in shock and in serious trouble. And there was nothing she could do except keep him from drowning.

Blinking rain out of her eyes, she left him lying face up and hurried to Danor who was close to passing out, hanging on with grim determination not to bleed to death. She sliced off one of his sleeves, folded it into a pad, then cut a strip of cloth from his shirt to bind the pad in place over the wound. "Danor, if you can shift yourself, get under the trees and out of the rain. I don't want you getting pneumonia."

"You kill them?"

"No. They're just stunned. Be out for around half an hour. I'll have to do something about that in a few minutes, but I want to get canvas up first, get the two of you into some kind of shelter."

"How many and where are they?"

"Four. Two on each side of the road, all of them ahead of us."

Her mouth set in a grim line, tears mixing with rain on her face, she cut the throat of the suffering packer, then checked to see what was left of their supplies.

The missing moss ponies were two of the packers and the three spare mounts. She felt almost a traitor when she felt a surge of joy that Bréou was one of them. Fortunately, what they'd lost to the runaways was mostly feed grain and some tools. The rest of their gear was on the dead packers.

The wet had made the ropes swell and the sheepshanks wouldn't pull free; by the time she got the tent pack loose and hauled it into the semishelter of one of the trees, Danor was gone. She swore softly, having a very good idea what notion he'd got in his head. She opened the pack and started trying to raise the tent without getting it soaked inside as well as out.

She dragged Maorgan inside, stripped and wiped him dry, wrapped him in a blanket, then went hunting for Danor.

\*    \*    \*

The first chorek was a burly man, short, a greasy beard covering most of his face, his clothes filthy enough to stand on their own if he'd ever taken them off. He was also very dead, a black dart in the center of one bulging eye.

She found Danor sprawled beside the last dead chorek, the darter clutched in his good hand. "Gods! What am I going to do with you?"

He didn't answer, being too busy dying.

Working carefully so she wouldn't dislodge the filthy, sodden bandage, she got him draped over one shoulder, powered herself onto her feet, and staggered back to the tent.

With the two unconscious men wrapped in blankets, their wounds coated with antiseptic and bandaged with sterile pads from her medkit, she stripped off her saturated clothing, hung it over branch stubs, hauled the rest of the packs inside the tent, set up a throway heat pac and hung a glow bulb from one of the tent poles. Aching with weariness, the crease on her shoulder sorer than a rotten tooth despite the plasskin she'd sprayed on it, the pain from the crease on her head beyond description, she swallowed a painpill from her personal pharmacopoeia, pulled the last blanket about her, and sat a moment gathering strength before she even tried to think of what else she should do.

The rain pounded down on the canvas, a soothing steady beat, the heat eddied from the throway, seeping into her muscles and bones. Sitting up was too much trouble, she shifted position, shifted again, curled up beside Maorgan, closed burning eyes for just a moment. . . .

## 4

Marrin Ola jumped, caught the leather ball as it flew out of bounds, sent it looping back to Glois and the others playing on the bare patch of ground out beyond the blai.

He squatted outside the line drawn in the dirt and watched the game progress with flurries of activity as the ball was kicked and butted from end to end of the field, flying a few times through vertical loops barely wide enough to let it pass through, watched shouting arguments between the two sides, two Fior boys bracing nose to nose, chest to chest until Utelel teased them out of their fury, watched a couple of players go stalking off when they were called on fouls.

He muttered a few field notes into the Ridaar remote, but didn't bother with a detailed description. It was a game so typical of prepubescent youngsters in dozens of the cultures he'd studied that he could have recited the rules without even asking the boys. Besides, that wasn't what he was here for.

As the game broke up, he beckoned to Glois and Utelel.

They came over and squatted in front of him, smeared with dust and sweat, scruffy and grinning.

"Back home on Picabral when I was your age, my cousins and me, we knew everything that was happening round home. I figure you two're about the same."

Utelel pursed his wide mouth, opened his eyes wide and managed to look as innocent as the yellow flower dropping over one ear.

Glois turned wary. "Maybe so," he said. "Why?"

"Because there's a problem. Our problem, not yours, but we could use some help. The other mesuchs, you know, the ones on Melitoëh, they're probably going to send spies to kill us." He sighed as he saw the two pairs of eyes start to sparkle with excitement. Aslan wasn't going to like this, but he wasn't going to tell her unless he had to. "This isn't a game, Glois, Utelel. I'm talking to you because I think you're smart enough to understand that."

Glois' tongue flicked across his upper lip, he turned

to Utelel. The boy and the Meloach looked at each other for a moment, then Glois turned to Marrin. "You want to know if there's strangers hanging about, asking questions, right?"

"Maybe not just strangers. Anyone acting different than they usually act. You know what I mean?"

"Uh-huh. You think maybe somebody been bought?"

"That's the trouble with this kind of thing. You never know." Marrin scooped up a small smooth stone from among those at the edge of field and sent it slamming against the goal post. It hit with a thunk, bounded off. "Don't you go doing anything you wouldn't ordinarily, huh?" He found another pebble and sent it after the first. "Otherwise you could warn 'em we're watching. You know what I mean?"

"Uh-huh. But nobody much looks at kids. Unless they should be in school and aren't."

Marrin snorted as he saw hopeful faces turned to him. "You start skipping school and I'll haul you back myself should I see you round." He got to his feet. "Seriously, you two. You watch it, huh?"

He walked off wondering if he'd just cut the throat of his own career. If those kids got hurt and it came out he'd recruited them. . . .

As he went back to mapping the Dumel and counting the population, he eased his conscience with memories of his own turbulent youth, the things he'd managed to survive until he finally got offworld.

# 9. Incursions

## 1

Kurz landed the flikit on an island in the middle of one of the Marishes and started unloading his gear beside the spring of clear, clean water that welled up between the high-kneed roots of a tree, smiling as he thought about the meltdown in the software of the Yaraka satellites that made his security possible. *Clotheads too dumb to suck tit.*

He worked quickly and silently; the faster he got the flikit out of here, the safer he'd be. Too bad it was only the longcoms gone down. Yark security not connected with sat tech was still running and the furheads were a sneaky lot.

Chav satellites had located this fleck of dry sand in the middle of one of the seacoast Marishes. Though the islet wasn't all that far from a knot of shacks used by a band of choreks that made a habit of attacking travelers on the road that passed close to the edge of the Marish, the satwatch reported they never visited it. The others in the Marish also avoided the place, the swampies who lived in the heart of the wetlands in widely scattered hutches, none of them less than a day's walk apart. They tended to make constellations, not settlements. If one could have a collection of hermits, this might be the way they organized themselves.

He knew there had to be a reason for this careful avoidance, but the satwatch hadn't discovered anything in the three weeks before this—no large predators, no wash-over with flood water, not even any insect swarms. Whatever it was, he trusted himself to deal with it. He'd met and defeated hairier things before this. No chichin-haunted islet was going to get him.

The weather was so perfect for his purpose it might have been engineered for him, clouds gone black with rain, boiling overhead, darkening the day to twilight. He braced the Yaraka kreash in the pilot's seat using burnaway straps, clicked his foreclaw on the sensor square and stepped hastily back as the flikit's motors began to hum.

He watched it spiral upward then dart away to the north, forgot it as soon as it vanished and started pacing the edges of the islet, inspecting the sand and the water for problems before he set up his camp, humming his pleasure at being on his own in a monotone not unlike the buzzing of the black beetles that clustered on the trunks of the odd bare trees that clustered at one end of the island.

He'd been born to a Drudge and would have stayed one if Hunnar hadn't chosen to lift him into Unskill and train him as spy and saboteur/assassin. To this day he didn't know why it was him that was picked, but he was grateful to the highborn for that and for the good things that had come from it.

A wife and children for one. They had a comfortable life on the edges of the tech sectors; his children would be tech class, not Unskill like him and, Taner be blessed, not Drudges. He saw them for a few months every few years, but didn't miss them much. In a mild, mostly abstract way, he was pleased with his family, but more with the idea of them than their actual physical existence. They gave him a sense of being rooted in something while he wandered the universe in Hunnar's service.

He was no longer young, pressing the far edge of

middle age, and everything he did took more effort these days. He didn't like to think of retiring, but he was a meticulous methodical chav and one not given to avoiding hard truths. For the past several years he'd been looking around for a position he could retire into, preferably one offworld. He'd been running study flakes every spare moment, economics, xenopsychology, the languages native to the worlds Chandava Minerals controlled and anything else he thought might be useful.

He wanted work offworld because he was shorter and slighter than the ordinary chav and had always been the butt of jokes and booted about by those stronger than him—which had included almost everyone his age and older whether they were male or female. He'd learned very early that his wits were all that would protect him—but he couldn't be seen to be clever because that just made things worse. Invisible wits. The ability to maneuver others into protecting him while keeping them ignorant of what he was doing. Perhaps that was what Hunnar had recognized in him.

He noted a line of large depressions in the sand at the upstream end of the island, the print closest to the water's edge clear enough that he could count the toes and see what looked like claw marks. He set his hand on the damp sand beside it, pressed down, extruded his claws, walked the hand out of the depression. Claws longer than his, with a broader splay to them.

He examined the other prints, noting that their spacing increased suddenly about halfway across the island, as if the creature had gone from stroll to all out run between one breath and the next. What would scare into flight a creature with such formidable defenses? And without coming close enough to leave traces?

*No other tracks on the sand. A flier of some kind? A firejelly? Not likely.* If there were any hanging around here, the satwatch would have noted it. They were too big to miss. *Hmm. Smaller version? Predator with poison on those dangling tentacles?* He looked up, noted that the trees that grew here were mostly bare trunk, with small hard leaves the length of his shortest finger, nothing to impede the path of a flying predator. *Good. Make a note. Watch overhead.* He took a step, stopped, thinking about the clinging, yielding sand, thinking about the lethal burrowing worms in the Kumar Waste back home. *Note, too, watch underfoot.*

Happy with his choice of first camp, he went back to his pile of gear and began hauling it into the area under the trees. A dangerous place would provide its own watchbeasts and the privacy he needed. He strung a hammock between two trunks, settled the steelskin shelter in the webbing while he used the spare rope to weave other nets to hold his gear and his food supply off the ground. He left the miniskip and its drag trailer to the last, fired them up, and roped them into the highest crotch that would support the weight.

When he had everything else settled to his satisfaction, he dropped onto an upthrust root knee and sat contemplating the largest of the packs, a locked box that held the weapons he meant to pass along to these choreks—which was a delicate process since he didn't fancy being sliced apart by one of his own cutters, but it was one he'd done before and he'd worked out a procedure that got his business done and kept his hide intact.

By the time he had the cache hoisted up beside the miniskip and tied securely in place, it was nearly sundown. He expanded the shelter, sealed it in place about the hammock, then collected a cup of water from the spring and a hot pack of stew and went to watch the sun go down while he ate his dinner.

## 2

Ilaörn closed his eyes so he wouldn't see the faces of the lab techs, but he couldn't close his ears because he had to keep playing that chertkum noise that Hunnar considered music. He couldn't stop hearing them talk about the plundering of his world, his people, because the Keteng were as much his people as the Fior.

". . . the organics involved are extremely complex. We don't have the facilities for a full investigation. Nor, I'm sorry to say, the expertise. It's much more Yarak's sort of thing. Would you know if. . . ."

Hunnar grunted. "Classified."

"Ah. Ta'ma. We've put the Drudges you sent us through a number of tests. If you will follow on the screen. Yes. This pair we put through a saturation test. We kept them for a week in a sealed chamber. There. You see the haze? They were hm in smoke you might say for a full week at a level just below suffocation. Then they were strangled and autopsied. We have examined cell structure insofar as we were able, we are somewhat limited since there has been little need for more sophisticated instrumentation hm none beyond that necessary to maintain the health of hm our techs. If the Ykkuval could hm . . . No? I will go on.

"The female Drudge was pregnant. It is one of the reasons she was chosen. We examined the fetus and are reasonably certain the smoke is not teratogenic. As to the adults, there seems to be little effect on the structure of the brain and none of the other organs show any stress. However, I must remind you that this is a very short-term study and effects could be too subtle for us to notice. We are arranging a long-term study with smaller doses, with your permission five years would be a suitable length for this project."

"Leave your proposal on my desk, I will consider it later." His claws click-clacked on the wood. "In the meantime, I'll have Memur send his men out to collect a sampling of the local Cousins addicted to the stuff. You can put them through your grinder. Surely at least some of what you learn will have application to Chave. We are, after all, a branch of the Cousins, however much some of us like to forget it."

"A branch that has diverged rather significantly from the others, by your leave, Ykkuval. Nonetheless we will appreciate the addition to our knowledge. If you will look at the central bank of four screens, you will see the results of our second study. We selected a second pair of Drudges, one male, one female to study the pleasure factor, to determine what happens to the mind when one breathes that smoke. We made this a separate experiment because the probe alters conformation when employed as extensively as we intended to use it this time. We wanted to be sure the physical stats were not corrupt."

Ilaörn's eyes came open when he heard the word *probe*. Despite his misgivings he stared at the screens, his fingers plucking absently at the strings, falling into an old exercise, one he'd played so often when he was a boy he knew the trick of it without needing his mind at all. There was an ache in his loins that distressed him; it made him feel soiled, his soul compromised beyond redemption. He'd been dreaming recently about the probe sessions with Hunnar and more than once come half-awake to plot how he could force another probing without betraying half the Béluchar left on Melitoëh. He wanted those orgasms again, that total plundering of self, wanted them with a passion greater even than any he'd shared with his sioll. And despised himself for all of that.

He fixed his eyes on the screens. If he couldn't participate, at least he could watch.

"You will find, O Ykkuval, that the visuals are both interesting and disturbing. We have censored nothing, but naturally the flakes will be put in your hands for disposal as soon as this presentation is complete. No copies have been made. We begin with the female subject."

Two of the screens expanded to fill the wallspace. The Drudge was stretched on an examining table, wide straps about her arms and legs, another crossing over where her waist would have been if she'd had much of one. She had broad shoulders and hips, a thick layer of fat between muscles and skin hiding her bone structure and making her look like an ugly rag doll. A lab tech in white with a breathing mask that obscured most of his face came into view carrying the probe crown. He set it on the bed, gave the woman's shaved head a hard polish with a cream he took from a small jar. When he was satisfied, he placed the crown on her head, taped it down and began a series of tests.

Sensing Hunnar's impatience, Tech First Muhaseb said hastily, "We left all that in place on the flake so that you would see that it was done properly. Indeed we have done no editing at all of what follows. What the probe finds will appear in the second screen."

Thick yellowish smoke boils up from a bowl set on a tripod beside the head of the female Drudge. The heavy features of her face begin to twitch. She fights against the straps, turns her head restlessly from side to to side for several minutes, as if she were a riding beast trying to shake off a pesty persistent fly. After a few minutes of this

nothing
nothing
nothing
nothing
Murky colors swirl in slow turgid whorls, coil along the edges of the screen, eddies of color about a pool of ink. The blackness is still, then lights begin flashing erratically, brilliant, near blinding light, like a strobe at a light show. A shape slowly takes form in the broken blackness, a

her movements grow more violent. A masked attendant appears in the image, draws up a broad strap, passes it over the lower part of the woman's face, draws it tight and locks it down, then retreats from view. The woman struggles a moment more, then shudders and lies still. Her eyes open but her inner lids stay deployed and her eyes glisten in the rage sign of both sexes of the Chandavasi. Her body jerks and twitches for several minutes, then the smoke seems to get to her at last and she lies quiet for a few moments, her hands open and close several times, then curl into fists. Her outer lids droop lower until her eyes are glistening slits. After a moment she begins to pant, her legs move under the strap, her knees try to come up, to spread. . . .

misshapen woman, tiny then swelling until the image fills the frame and is thrusting against the edges as if by sheer power of rage and will it would burst free. This image shrivels suddenly into a small ancient baby with a huge distorted head and limbs atrophied until they are little more than boneless tentacles. This happens at the exact moment when the strap tightens across her mouth and chin. The ancient infant begins to melt as if it were cast from wax and left beside a fire. The runny wax begins to coil into a whirlpool, bits of the wizened form still recognizable, an eye slides past, a horribly distorted mouth, an ear, a breast like an empty sack with a huge brown nipple. The shapes melt into the mud-colored whorl and for a brief while the frame holds only ugly ochers and dirty reds. Then another form begins to. . . .

The images in the dream screen grew murky, muddled, a birthing scene with the cord wrapped about the bloody infant's neck, strangling it, shifting to increasingly violent sexual imagery, violence the woman directed at herself and at the males in her fantasies, all of them techs and admins, one of them a distorted but clearly recognizable version of Hunnar. The sounds of breathing in the Ykkuval's conference room quickened, went raspy. Ilaörn kept his eyes on the screen, he didn't want to look away, he didn't want to see their faces, knowing they would be echoes of his own.

Both screens went suddenly dark.

Tech First Muhaseb cleared his throat. "At that point the subject began having um aaa physical difficulties. It was deemed appropriate to bring this portion of the study to a close for the moment. She was taken from the straps, her um convulsions dealt with, then she was placed in an observation cell. We have been following her recovery, testing her mental state such as it is. So far there seems to be no physical damage from the smoke session, though the effect on her psyche is less easy to quantify since we won't put the probe on her again until she returns to her baseline stats."

He coughed, fiddled with the sensor board a moment, shrunk the blank screens, and brought up the other two. "The male Drudge had an equally um aaah disturbing but quite different reaction. There is a um point to be stressed here. It is quite likely that the history and personality of the subject interact to determine the content of the fantasies."

The left screen held the image of the same observation theater as before. The male Drudge was an anatomical study, each muscle group clearly delineated, the heavy bones in his face prominent in the typical Drudge mask. His hands and feet were thick with rough dead skin as if he'd glued cork pads to them. The tech went through the process as before, oiling and polishing the knobby head, settling the crown in place, taping it down. He pulled his breather mask into place, emptied a specimen pac of shredded husk into the brazier by the Drudge's head and set the fibrous pile on fire. Then he stepped back, moving out of view.

The Drudge lies still, only the twitching of his eyelids and the slow rise and fall of his chest to show he was alive. He doesn't try testing the strength of the straps, though his eyes keep sliding round to the no longer visible tech. The smoke from the brazier thickens over him, he is holding his breath, but used air explodes out of him and he gulps in a lungful of the smoke. His mouth stretches wide, he is screaming, though there is no sound recorded on this flake, unlike that of the woman. His face is suffused with blood, his chest is vibrating as he pants faster and faster as panic seizes hold of him. Like the woman he turns his head from side to side, the movements increasingly violent, then he jerks his head loose from the strap, lifts it as high as he can and slams it down on the headrest. As he lifts it again, the tech

nothing
nothing
nothing
nothing
nothing
nothing
nothing
a stirring in the greenish black ground as if something is trying to take shape
nothing
nothing
the screen goes white, branching black patterns race from edge to edge, smaller and smaller patterns until the whole screen is black. White patterns start in the upper left corner and race outward, downward until the white has overlaid the black. The screen pulses black to white, again, again, eye-straining flashes timed to the pants of the subject. Then there is an explosion of harsh primary colors, jags of red stabbing into splotches of green, pinwheels of yellow with razor-edged arms

rushes into the viewfield, jerks the strap taut. The subject tries to scream but cannot. His body surges against the straps, then collapses in on itself. The smoke is very thick now, swirling about the subject whose breathing has steadied; he is limp, pacified, deep in the spell of the drug. . . .

slashing across both . . . then the colors and forms vanish or rather mutate into a pastoral scene with an extremely idealized but recognizable male, the subject, striding across the grass, sword in hand shining copper and silver in the sunlight. He is walking toward a woman who is also idealized, but recognizable. . . .

"That. . . ." Hunnar watched a moment longer. "He dares. . . . I'm right, isn't that the Bashkan's youngest daughter?"

"Ah um yes, I'm afraid it is. And it gets much worse as the fantasy progresses. There are references to you also, O Ykkuval. Um aaa, you will definitely not appreciate the subject's thoughts about you. They are um aaa highly subversive. Of course there isn't the sliver of a chance he would ever act on such dreams. Remember, this is a Drudge."

"A dead Drudge." He glanced at the screen, scowled as he watched the image bowing before the woman, laying his sword at her feet, moving to unsheath a sword of another sort while she was unfolding like a flower before him. "Stop that now. I don't care to see more."

"Certainly, O Ykkuval." The screens went black. "We will be dissecting both subjects in the near future after we've put them through some psychological tests so we can test the mind state after continued use of the drug against the baseline tests we took at the beginning of this investigation. Do you wish the personal reports to continue or would a flaked notation be acceptable?"

"Flakes have a way of sliding through cracks in security. The personal reports will continue. This is to remain on Samlak status, forbid to all eyes but mine."

"It will be done."

### 3

Kurz woke with the sun, crawled out of the shelter, and took a quick run round the islet. His were the only prints visible. There'd been a windy thunderstorm late last night that left the damp sand as neat as if it had been raked. He came back to the trees, pulled on his clothes, and inspected the shelter.

There were hundreds of small discolorations speckled over the upper curve. They'd bleached some color from the polymer sizing applied over the fabric but hadn't done damage to the fibers themselves as far as he could see. Not yet, anyway. It was the first time he'd seen anything that could get that polymer to admit it existed. He didn't touch the spots until he'd rinsed the shelter repeatedly with water from the spring.

He listened to the noise made by the tip of his claw passing over one of the tiny splotches. Rough. Catching on the edges of broken bubbles. The cloth underneath seemed intact, but it was woven from Menaviddan spider silk and there wasn't much that could injure that. He checked over the gear he'd hoisted into the trees, but that was untouched. It was after him, whatever it was. He shrugged. No matter, he wasn't going to be here long. He clipped a yagamouche and its holster to his belt, pulled his tunic down over it, slipped a stunner into the pocket built for it inside the tunic, checked to make sure his other weapons were in place, then he peeled a trail bar and started toward the chorek settlement, jaws working on the hard sticky confection as he splashed through water and muck, pounded across sand spits.

The satwatch reports were enough to give him a good notion of the habits of the chorek who lived there. Six men, four women. Two of the women seemed bonded, the other two available to all the men. Even the women never rose much before noon, though they were about earlier than the men, getting meals fixed and doing other chores. There were no sentries, just one man each night taking his turn to keep the fire going in the round stone firepit at the center of the village.

When he viewed the reports, he wondered why a fire in a place that warm and humid. He understood it now, understood the stack of poles beside the firepit, poles with bundles of rags bound round the ends, rags saturated with a dark, sticky liquid. Whatever it was that had come after him last night—that's what they'd got ready for. It was a comfort to him that crude torches would drive the thing off; his yagamouche could melt a hole through the hide of a Sancheren tantserbok.

He slowed his pace as he got near the settlement, began choosing his path carefully, keeping himself sheltered from view as much as he could. It only needed one restless kreash stumbling out to relieve himself to see him and rouse the camp.

When he reached the shack he'd pinned as the leader's hole, he ignored the doors and windows, caught hold of a projecting rafter, and hauled himself onto the roof. Using his claws as pries, he extracted shakes until he had a hole large enough to ease through and balance on one of the crooked beams that supported the roof.

A man and a woman lay snoring, tangled in a nest of filthy blankets, a clumsy jug beside then. Kurz wrinkled his nose at the stench that rose to meet him, a mix of sweat and sex with a sour overbite from that jug. Must be something on the order of old Farkli's yang. He reached inside his tunic, eased the stunner free, and put both of them out.

A few beats later he had trees and sawgrass between him and the settlement and was trotting easily through shallow water, the naked and filthy chorek wound into an equally filthy blanket and draped over his shoulder. Though he hated touching the creature, Kurz held him in place, arm across the backs of his knees. The chorek's arms hung loose behind him and slapped against him with every step he took. He closed his mind to this and to the stench, concentrated on getting back to his camp as quickly as he could. Trying to hide his trail would just waste time; he couldn't beat the trailcraft these swampbyks were likely to have.

When he reached the islet, he bound the chorek to the trunk of one of the trees, clipping off a loop of the filament cord and passing it under his arms and over a thick stub of a branch so he couldn't work the loop down and step out of it, knotting a much shorter length about his wrists. He left the man sagging over the chestrope and lowered miniskip and the weapons cache. He collapsed the shelter, loaded the rest of the gear into the drag trailer, and clicked the lid down. He didn't lock it. This was only the first of several sites he planned to visit. Having the weapons cache out and open, giving the chorek a taste of bounty that could be his, that was part of his plan. And there was even a chance he'd have to kill his captive and haul all the weapons to another site. If the male was locked into challenge mode and unwilling to listen, there'd be no point in continuing his speech.

He pressed his hand against the palm lock, then threw the lid back so his captive could see the neat rows of cutters in their velvet niches. He set the stim spray in the turned back lid and, careful to pick a spot upwind from the chorek, hunkered down to inspect his captive.

The skin under the oily patina of the forever unwashed was sickly pale and the chorek's long thin arms and legs, the torso with its ribs showing, his incipient pot belly made him look half-starved and diseased. Kurz discounted both impressions. Though Hunnar's Pet was clean and a lot older, his skin was like this one's, fragile as a kaliba's soaring skins, but he was spry enough. And his body shape wasn't that different. This chorek was reasonably set up for his age and circumstances.

A scar wandered down the side of his face, a thin line with dots along side from the sutures. Knife cut. Probably a fight. Which he won, otherwise no one would have bothered to sew him up. Puncture wound just above his left hip. That one could have killed him if it had been a hair to one side. Small red dots on his belly and thighs. *Good thing the bugs on this world don't like the way Chave taste.* Odd puckered scars on his arms, one on his shoulder near the neck, several of them with what looked like burn marks across them. He'd lived hard and used up more than his share of luck in staying alive.

Kurz frowned. He'd taken this one because analysis of the satwatch data showed he was the leader. Easier to convince one kreash than trying to herd half a dozen hostile mud-humpers. And he'd chosen to begin with this band because they were among the most active—and successful—of the choreks working out of this Marish. A bloody, greedy collection of sublife.

Kurz glanced to the west. The sun was a red blur behind a thickening layer of clouds. They were blowing inland faster than he'd expected, starting to fade the shadow cast by the trees. Not to his taste, flying in that muck, but hanging about here was even less attractive an option.

He took up the stim shot, pressed the end against the side of the chorek's neck, stepped back as it took hold, and stood watching him come back to awareness.

The slack mouth with its sickly pink lips opened and closed, the matted beard and mustache moving greasily with it. The eyes that blinked open were that peculiar blue that many of these mudhumpers had. Surrounded by those straw-colored cilia, they were disgusting. The chorek jerked at the braided strands holding him against the tree, stopped when he decided he hadn't a hope of breaking them. He realized that quickly enough to warn Kurz that he was clever and therefore not to be trusted.

The chorek hawked up a glob of mucus and spat it at Kurz.

It fell short, of course. Such a trite reaction. Kurz was disappointed, but was careful not to let it influence his estimate of the man. "You will listen," he said and was pleased at the effect of the words on the chorek. He didn't like language transfers, they made his head hurt, and all these subhuman langues put ideas in his head he didn't like to see there, but it was indeed useful to be able to talk to them. "You don't like me," he said. He picked up one of the pods the tree had dropped during the night, used his thumb claw to dig a bit of fluff from inside it, then blew it away. He sat watching it a moment, then turned back to the chorek. "What you like and don't like is worth that to me. I come to offer a trade which will get us both what we want."

The chorek glared at him. "Mesuch. I wouldn't give you a handful of wet chert."

"Unless you're very stupid, you will. Listen to me. It hurts nothing to listen, and you're certainly going nowhere. We want this world cleared of Yaraka. You know them. The furfaces. You want that, too. You want to be rid of us. We will confine our activities to Melitoëh, leaving Banikoëh to you. We want metals and minerals. When those are gone, we are gone. This is a light world. We don't like light worlds. We live most comfortably on worlds that would crack your bones and suck your guts out through your crotch. The Yaraka are different. They are after drugs and botanicals. Plants is what that means. Plants never run out, they make themselves over and over again. The Yaraka are here forever unless you get rid of them now."

The chorek's eyelids flickered and his face softened. "I can see that," he said and his mouth moved in what he must have thought was a guileless smile. "So cut me loose and we can make our deal."

Kurz sighed. *They always think it's so easy.* "In a while I will, but not yet." He reached into the cache and lifted out a cutter. "This is a weapon that regenerates its force if you push this slide back ..." He used the claw on his forefinger to snap the thin metal cap along its grooves, exposing the collector beneath. "Thus. Set the weapon in full sunlight for a minimum of four hours, and by the end of that time it will be strong again. It is a fire at your fingertips, one that will only burn your enemies. Thus." He shoved the slide home, lifted the cutter, and sliced the outer end of a limb not far above the chorek's head. It brushed his shoulder as it fell. "You can see what it does to wood. Consider what it would do to flesh and bone."

He got to his feet, walked out of the shadow under the trees, exposed the collector and set the cutter on the sand to replace the small bit of energy he'd expended.

When he was back hunkered beside the cache, he said, "It is as easy as that. The weapon will be at full strength again in less time than it will take me to say these words. There is no danger of overcharging. It was developed with folk like you in mind, men who have little acquaintance with such weapons." *Made to withstand the stupidity of fools like you.*

There was a shine to the chorek's eyes and a tension in his shoulders that told Kurz he'd got his first customer well and truly hooked. "So I see what you're offering," he said. "What you asking?"

*That you don't massacre each other, but go after the Yaraka. I wonder if this is worth the cost. Hm, if nothing else, you'll keep the Yarks chasing their tails a while.*

Kurz went to fetch the cutter. He showed the chorek the green light that meant the weapon was fully charged, then replaced it in its niche.

"We want the group from University dead. Whoever supplies proof of this will receive two bods of gold for each person removed. The proof must be convincing, but we will leave that to you to figure out. For the death of any of the Yaraka we will offer a bounty of five kolts weight in pure gold. For the death of the Goës Koraka hoeh Dexios, I mean the Yarak who is the chief of all the Yaraka here on Béluchad, for him we will offer seven bods of gold. Again, upon proof that he is truly dead."

"So we fight your war for you."

"It's one way of saying it."

"Get ourselves killed for a crann of mesuch?"

"No. For yourselves. We don't want this world, just its metals. We'll leave you alone when we've got what we came for."

"You say it. Do your folks back home say it?"

"Either your accept what I say or you don't. I'm not going to play stupid games with you." He lifted a section of the top tray from the weapons cache, six cutters in their velvet niches, set the section on the sand, closed the lid and palmed the lock shut. He took hold of the handles, grunted to his feet and hauled the cache to the drag trailer, popped the lid, and slid the cache into the place he'd left for it.

"Ihoi! You're not going to leave me tied here. Hoy! Let me loose."

Kurz turned and gazed at him. There was panic in the hoarse voice. He was really terrified of whatever haunted this islet. "I slept here last night. I was not disturbed."

"Maybe they don't like the way you taste. Come on, let me loose. My word on it, all I want to do is get away from here."

"They? What are they?"

"The melmot. They hang round here. It's the water and the fruit from those caor trees that pulls them. And the salt lick there next to the spring. They don't need salt, they get all they need from your blood, but it draws critters here."

"Describe the melmot."

The chorek was calmer now, his brain engaged. He was using his voice and information to hold Kurz there, to persuade where pleading hadn't worked. Kurz was pleased. That quickness to grasp a situation would make him a dangerous enemy to the Yaraka.

"They are like the Eolt, but no bigger than the palm of an open hand. They move mostly at night and in herds, twenty, thirty at a time." The tip of the chorek's tongue flickered across his bottom lip. He looked nervously upward, a tic pulsing by one eye. "They sting you till you can't move, then dissolve your flesh and suck it up through their eating tubes."

"At night? It is my understanding that Keteng go dormant at night."

His shoulders hunched, the chorek tried another of his impossibly guileless smiles. "They store sunlight. And there's energy from the food." He spoke slowly, trying to hold Kurz's eyes as the muscles tensed and shifted under his filthy hide. He was rubbing the wrist knots against the tree's rough bark. He didn't know about polymer fibers and how futile his actions were and Kurz wasn't about to enlighten him. "Most Keteng can, though they don't do it much. They don't like the way they feel after. One of 'em told me once it was like a hangover without the fun of getting drunk."

"You know a lot about this."

The chorek managed a shrug. "I spent a few years studying at Chuta Meredel." A rustle in the leaves brought his head up, but it was only an angi carrying off a stem of caor berries. "I don't like Eolt much. Got on my nerves. So I left."

Kurz stared at him, watched his eyes shift, his face pucker into a scowl. *Kicked out, most likely. I'm going to leave him another sixpack. He's a better choice than I knew. Nothing like the spite of a failed academic.*

After he'd set a second section of cutters on the first and locked down the drag trailer, Kurz moved behind the chorek and cut his hands loose. The strain the chorek had put on the filament had tightened it so his hands were red and swollen, falling uselessly at his side when they were released.

Kurz walked back around the tree and thrust the knife into the ground a short distance away. If he stretched the chorek could reach it with one of his feet.

"Ihoi! I can't do you anything. Cut this stuff. Hoy!"

Kurz straddled the miniskip, bent, and tapped on the lift field, settling himself in the saddle as it rose. Ignoring the shouts from the chorek, he rode the skip into the open, took it and the drag trailer to canopy level and started for the second of his chosen drop sites.

### 4

Ilaörn sat in his corner, hands moving gently, calmingly over the living wood of his harp as he watched the mountains burn.

The wall was a single screen now. In it, he could see bits of six fliers in addition to the one that was making the pictures; they flew parallel paths along both sides of the mountains, burning the forest and any structures that came into view, sparing only the Sleeping Grounds when they came across them.

Ilaörn was beyond tears, beyond rage. It was too much to take in, too much destruction, too much greed, too much grief. And nothing he could do would change anything he saw. *All our little schemes,* he thought, *they're worth nothing against this. Caida bites that raise a momentary rash until they're squashed and washed away.*

Hunnar worked at his desk, glancing up now and again to watch the progress of the burning and make sure the Sleeping Grounds and their cocooned Eolt were left untouched. Then he went back to his reports and his plotting.

# 10. Scrambling to Stay in Place

### 1

It was still raining when Shadith woke.

The beat of the rain was lighter, but just as steady. The heat from the throwaway pac was way down and the warning light was flashing. She'd slept for over five hours. The crease on her head had scabbed over, the scab dry and pulling a little, but the pain was gone, even when she touched the wound. When she lifted her arm, there was still some soreness in her shoulder, though not enough to restrict movement.

Afraid of what she'd find, she bent over Maorgan, touched his forehead, jerked her fingers away. *Hot. Well, at least he's still alive.* She checked Danor and relaxed enough to start thinking again.

"Com. Where's the com? I've got to call in help. I can't handle this." Eyes closed, she tried to remember where she'd put the handcom, swore softly when the image came to mind of a hand tucking the black rectangle into the bag attached to her saddle.

She listened to the rain for a moment longer, shivering at the thought of going out in that, then she gathered herself, dug out a raincape, pulled it round her, hung the glowbulb to the collar and crawled from the tent.

The bulb was a feeble gesture against a night as black as the inside of a coal sac. She'd grown so accustomed to the bright glare from the cluster stars, she'd almost forgotten what such darkness was like, how difficult something as simple as walking could be when she couldn't see her feet. The wind was down to a teasing breeze that flipped about the flaps of the cape as she trudged through the mud and water puddles to the road and the dead ponies.

Sokli was a lump in the middle of a pool of water dimpling under the beat of the rain—and he'd come down on the bag she wanted. She sloshed over to him, knelt in the muck, and began the nauseating business of working the saddle bag from under all that stiff meat.

The icy water complicated the job, made the leather swell, and turned her fingers stiff as she tried to work buckles she couldn't see, but it also helped once the bag was free of its tethers. She rocked it back and forth, the washing of the water carrying off some of the dirt under it, eventually giving her enough room to jerk it loose.

Back in the tent, the raincape hung on a branch stub outside, she stuck the glowbulb back on the tent pole, dried her hands and feet on a blanket, found another throway heater and started it going. Then she worked loose the leather straps and dumped the contents of the bag on the canvas floor of the tent. Everything was soaked. She wiped off the foil containers of the trail bars, set them aside, tossed sodden underwear out through the door slit, and found the handcom under a pile of disintegrating paper.

She wiped the com off, wiped her hands, slid the cover off the sensor plate, and touched it. The working light didn't come on; that worried her, but she tapped the sensor again and waited for the squeal the recorder back at Alsekum used to acknowledge a call.

Nothing.

"Well, if anyone hears this, we've got trouble and need help. Attacked by chorek. Maorgan and Danor seriously wounded, need doctor bad. Caöpas dead or run off. Come get us soonest."

No response.

"Gods. The wet shouldn't have damaged you, you're supposed to be sealed against damp, good to half a mile down in your average ocean. Even the moss pony falling on you shouldn't have knocked you out. Must have been defective to start with. Curséd cheap trash!" She was about to pitch it through the crack in the doorflap, shook her head and dropped it beside the sodden saddlebag. "Get some cha in me first, some food, then I'll give you a look again, see if there's some way I can jar you alive."

She dug a pot from the gear pushed up against the side of the tent, pushed it outside to collect rainwater, then crawled over to check her patients.

A touch told her that the fevers were still going strong, maybe getting worse. She didn't have a baseline temp for Fior, so she couldn't be sure how bad it was. Stupid, stupid that Koraka hadn't bothered to get a medkit calibrated to Fior metabolism. "Not only the Goës. Why didn't I think about that?"

Her own body was from a distant offshoot of the Cousins, far from the standard model. Add to that the time the Fior had been here, separate, in what was apparently a mutagenic environment—the moss ponies and other things she'd noted were evidence of that—and she didn't dare try her own spraycopeia on them. Or wouldn't until one or the other of them seemed about to die.

Such a simple thing. Ride along a peaceful roadway, traveling by invitation and under escort. Into the back country where neither Yaraka nor Chandavasi had penetrated. What could go wrong? She only had her medkit along because Aslan had insisted. She certainly hadn't expected to need it. *I can take care of myself.* She remembered saying that. *Look, Aslan, you don't know what I've survived without all this fuss.* "What was I thinking of? Gods!" *Why didn't I say something about the Fior? Gods! Talk about stupid. . . .*

As the night wore on, Danor's fever fluctuated and he slid in and out of delirium. Maorgan was very quiet, settling deeper and deeper into coma. She grew afraid that both would die on her before she could collect the caöpas and haul them to help. The years in the diadem and the talents of the brain she'd inherited when Aleytys slid her into this body had given her the translator (which was convenient), the ability to mindride beasts (useful and occasionally a pleasure), and a touch of telekineses; she could nudge forcelines if they weren't too strong and play about with small objects, but Aleytys' healing gift hadn't transferred. This wasn't the first time Shadith had mourned that fact.

She bathed Danor and laid damp compresses on his brow; she worried over Maorgan and added water to the cha pot, and when she had a moment, held the handcom and tried to feel her way into it, to find the break or the short or whatever was keeping it from working. These were throwaway units, sealed and meant to be replaced when they malfunctioned. Nobody said what you were supposed to do when you were sitting in a storm out in the back of beyond with two potential corpses on your hands and no 'tronics store within a dozen light-years.

The crash of the rain shifted suddenly to a faint patter and the wind dropped until the flutter of the leaves above the tent was audible over its whine.

She crawled to the door flap and pushed it back enough to let her see out.

The sun was up and the clouds overhead were ripping apart. The puddles in the glade glittered silver where they puckered from the last of the raindrops. The cold was retreating, too. The air smelled of green and wetness, invigorating as cold cha.

She pulled the flap to, gave Danor another bath, replaced the cold compress on Maorgan's brow, then pulled on a shirt and pair of shorts and went out to see what else she could find to help them survive this impossible situation.

She was stripping the rest of the riding gear off dead Sokli when she saw Eolt Melech coming against the wind, pulling xeself along with xe's tentacles, tree by tree fighting xe's way toward her. Xe's dread slapped at her, so powerful it was almost strangling.

Xe saw her and called out, a bass organ note that hammered against her heart. Then xe was singing to her, demand and plea at once, chords of meaning.

Where is he?    My Sioll.    He suffers.
   I throb to it    I am wrung with it
Where is he?    My Sioll.    Bring me to him.

"Follow," she sang in approximation of the Eolt song/speech. She left the dead caöpa and moved into the trees to the glade.

Working to the sung instructions that battered at her with their urgency, she lifted Maorgan from his blanket cocoon, carried him from the tent, and laid him on the mud and grass close to one of the trees.

Eolt Melech grasped the branches with xe's holding tentacles and brought xeself down until xe could touch Maorgan. Shadith could feel xe's terror at being so close to earth. If xe's lift failed or a windshear developed, xe could be dashed to the ground and xe would die there, slowly, agonizingly, xe's membranes rotting while xe still lived.

She watched, worried. Maorgan had said the Eolt weren't as fragile as they looked, but it was like watching a glass vase she valued rocking back and forth on the edge of a shelf.

Xe unrolled a tentacle different from the others,

one xe had kept tucked up and hidden in the rootstock of the many other trailing tentacles. The end touched Maorgan's face, splayed out across it, the translucent flesh conforming to the bumps and hollows of the Fior's face.

For a moment nothing happened, then she saw that the skin on the tentacle was pulsing, in out in out and it glowed then went dull in the same rhythm, light and not-light, in and out. The tentacle flushed to pale pink, the pink to blood red.

The pulse quickened.

In her half-sync with the Eolt she felt Maorgan reacting, something was happening in him, she didn't know what. She had to trust Melech, she knew the strength of the bond between xe and Maorgan, she knew he wouldn't harm his sioll, but it was a strange thing to watch.

The edge of the sun passed into the widening rift in the clouds, the glade went suddenly much brighter. Melech's battered, wrinkled membranes plumped out and began to glow again. Xe was golden and strong, xe sang as xe went on with what xe was doing.

The tentacle mask came free with a faint sucking sound and Melech let xeself float upward. Xe sang xe's triumph, wordless organ notes that filled the space beneath the sky. Shadith turned her face upward, her whole body throbbing to the glory of that sound.

When she looked down, she saw that Maorgan's face was dotted with tiny red spots as if a hundred black biters had settled on him to suck a meal. His eyes were closed, he was breathing slowly in the shallow breath of sleep. As she watched, he sighed, moved uneasily on the muck he lay in, but didn't wake. She knelt beside him and checked his pulse. It was strong, steady. When she set the back of her hand against his face, the tight hotness of fever was gone.

Tired, irritated, and at the same time happy that one of her problems was lifted off her shoulders, she hoisted him again, carried him over to the tent. She eased him onto a bit of canvas from the packs, washed the muck off his body, then dragged him inside and wrapped him in his blankets again. He sighed a few times as she did this, muttered and twitched, but didn't wake.

The second throwaway was beginning to flag. She sighed, took the hatchet and went out to cut some wood; her patients were going to need the warmth and whatever food she could get down them.

She found a downed tree a short distance from the glade; it was old and crumbling on the outside, but the inside was firm and mostly dry. She laid down the square of carry canvas and began cutting and prying lengths of wood loose. She was sweating and developing blisters when she heard a rustle. She dropped the hatchet, flung herself onto the far side of the tree, then sat up, laughing, as a moss pony edged from behind a tree.

It whuffled plaintively and a familiar smell came on the wind.

"Bréou." She stood. "All right, bébé, come here, luv."

The caöpa came sidling toward her, head turning and eyes still a little wild, tail swishing.

"Ahhh, that's a splendid pony, that is." He leaned into her, head pressing against her breasts, making small contented groans as she rubbed his poll and dug her fingers into his roached mane. He was wet and stinky, but she was almost crying at his pleasure in their reunion.

One of the packers came easing into the small clearing around the downed tree, the pack listing, the straps of the packsaddle distorting the round of his barrel. As she worked to ease the strain and get the pack resettled, the rest of the pony string gathered around her, nuzzling at her, pushing at her as if they wanted to crawl under her skin.

She gathered what wood she had, slipped the hatchet through her belt, and led the small herd back to the clearing where she stripped off their gear and salvaged some corncakes from the packs she removed and piled beneath the thickest of the trees, resting them on high-kneed roots to keep them out of the muck. The corncakes she broke and put in their nosebags, left them munching away while she took her meager gleanings of wood over to the tent and got a fire started.

The light dimmed a bit as the sun passed behind a clot of dark clouds, but Melech was still bright gold and shining as xe hovered above the tent, tentacles anchoring xe to the tree. She sang a few notes to xe as she moved about, getting the grate settled above the fire and soup fixings into the cookpot.

## 2

Marrin heard the hissing whispers and smiled as he recognized them. He didn't turn as the scuff of bare feet told him Glois and Utelel were edging into the workroom, just kept at his work refining the map of Dumel Alsekum, drawing on the lightpad, his crude lines cleaned up and made elegant on the screen.

They edged up until they were leaning against him, watching the marks he was making on the pad, seeing how they were changed on the screen. "What's that?" Glois said.

"It's a map of the Dumel. I'm putting in where people live and the kind of gardens and trees they have. See, this square with roundish corners is the Everything Shop and I put a smaller square on top for the place where your friend Likel lives with xe's family. Those marks there are the names of xe's Parent and sibs."

"I know what maps are. How come it looks different up there?"

"There's a bit that thinks in there and it knows what I want so it does it. There's a bit that thinks in all our machines."

"Oh."

Marrin set the pen down, swung his chair around and scowled at the pair. "It's the middle of the day, why aren't you in school? You know what I told you."

"Ah, Aide Mar, it's Rest Day. And it's first Seibibyl and that means it's Summer now and us Sekummers we getting ready for a biiiig party. And we got chased, so we come here and anyway we found out some stuff you maybe want to know."

"Ihoi, we did," Utelel said, his lighter voice as filled with triumph as Glois'. "There's this Fior swampie, his name's Sabhal, he carves stuff, you know, like cro-galls, he makes hinges so their mouths come open and even sets in bitty teeth from something, I dunno what's got teeth that little, my Parent buys stuff from him for my sibs and me, so he knows us pretty well and. . . ."

"And you go round the Dumel when you try to explain anything, Utta. He want to go see Ut's Parent, 'cause xe can talk to Met 'n Tas for him, he don't like officials and won't go round them. We got him to talking to us 'cause Ut's Parent is busy with Summer Day business. He forgot what day it was and he almost run off when Ut tells him. Anyway, what he said was, there's a funny looking mesuch fossicking around in the Marishes. Like a big crogall with xe's snout pushed in. Anyway, the mesuch, he's got this weird stick thing that flies and he's messing around with choreks and giving them these things like our mesuch got, you know, fire comes out one end and burns through just 'bout anything. Sabhal, he says the choreks are getting real stirred up, like you kick into a mutmut nest and they go running round like crazy. Sabhal, he says one bunch of 'em nearly set Marish on fire, burn down all their bothys, and if it didn't rain woulda took a lot a grass and trees with 'em. Anyway is that the kinda thing you want to know?"

"It certainly is. Chorek with cutters, that's not a happy thought. Have you talked to Ut's Parent yet?"

Utelel shook xe's head, the orange and yellow flowers dancing with the movement. "We just heard and we come here first."

"Well then, you'd best scoot along and take the message like Sabhal wanted you to. Tell them that you told me and that I'm passing the word on."

Glois wrinkled his nose and looked at Utelel, but before he could say anything, Duncan Shears walked in.

He raised his brows when he saw them, but didn't comment. "Here, catch." He tossed Marrin a flake in a portable reader. "List of parts the Goës swore he'd send us. His signa included. Haven't had a smell of 'em. I want you to get hold of the Molyb Oschos, see what's holding things up. Use the authorization on that to build a fire under him if he's dragging his feet."

"Right. By the way, I've just learned that the Chave have an agent over here passing out cutters to the chorek. Think I should get hold of Security there and let them know?"

Shears scowled. "How sure are you?"

"Pretty damn."

"I'll give a call to the Scholar, let her know. If she decides better not, she can get through to you on the jit's com. Button up before you leave, but don't worry about the alarms. I'll set web once you're out." He glanced at the two young Béluchar, sighed, and went out.

"Gonna take the jit? Take us with you, Marrin, hunh? Give us a ride, huh huh?"

"No way, my young friends." He powered down the port, tapped on the datalock and got to his feet. "Besides, you have something you've got to do, remember?"

"Ahhh, we can do that anytime. Ut's Parent don't

want to see us now, xe said xe don't want to see us, said it loud."

"Well, you've just got to change xe's mind. Look, Glois, I'm a target, like all the rest of us from University. Any shooting, it's going to come at me. You want me to have to live with knowing I've got one of the people I'm supposed to be studying killed?" He lifted the jit's keypack from the hook by the door, shooed the still protesting pair outside, pulled the door shut behind him. "And I'm really serious, Ut, Glo. It's important that your officials know what the swampie told you. It could save lives. That's on your shoulders. Now you go and do right by your folks."

He watched the youngsters drag off along the shadow-dappled walkway, then went to the main workroom and stuck his head inside. "Dunc, how about letting me trade for a heavy-duty stun? Don't want to sound too nervous, but cutters floating around makes me sit up a bit."

"Done. Let me get to the cache. . . ." He palmed the lock box open, turned back the lid. "Hm. Another thing . . . come over here, I'm going to load you down with a few telltales. Won't do much, but maybe could give you some warning."

"Did you get to Aslan?"

"She's in the middle of an interview, but I set the flasher going so she'll be coming through any minute now."

Marrin swung into the jit, set the telltales on the shelf in front of the stick, then took a good look round to make sure Glois and Utelel weren't anywhere near. He sighed. He liked that pair, they reminded him of himself and a cousin of his. *Wonder how close we came to getting ourselves killed?* he thought with a pleasing sense of nostalgia only possible because he had no intention of going near his homeworld again. *And how many times.* He started the jit, backed it from under the tree, and started around the outside of the Dumel. Now that he was out of the workroom, he could hear the voices, the snatches of music, could see the pennants being raised and now and then catch the wisps of aroma from the food and the mulled cider being heated in a vast pot outside the Meeting House.

As he turned into the road, he started the telltale and immediately punched the volume lower when the beeper went into hysterics as a laughing dancing chattering band of Keteng came round a grove of oilnut trees. They heard the beeping and milled about the jit for a while, clapping their hands and shouting Summer blessings at him. As they broke off and headed for the Dumel again, two meloach with bright blue flowers on their heads and shoulders grinned at him and tossed a handful each of sugared nuts into the jit.

Smiling and crunching on a nut he picked off the seat beside him, Marrin sent the jit humming along the road, his worries forgotten for the moment. He liked this world. No doubt it had its dark side, but he'd come up in a world that was mostly dark side with only small flashes of light and he felt very protective of places like this. Aslan wanted to preserve the brightness so later generations could retrieve it; he was more like Shadith, he wanted to stop the plundering now. He thought about Shadith and the things he'd heard about her, rumors and jealous bitching both. Thought about the restrictions of the Scholar's life which were starting to bear down on him.

He wanted enough Voting Stock to have University as homebase even if he didn't go for Scholar at the end of his training—which meant he had to restrain his actions and keep inside the rules for another decade or so while he played politics with his sponsors so he could get onto the projects that brought him the stock. Which also meant he'd better not revert to early training and go play commando raid with the Chave Enclave as target.

The handcom's bell jolted him back to the present. He tapped it on. "Ola here."

"Marrin, Duncan just told me about your young friends. We'll decide what to do about that tonight, till then silence is best."

"Right, Scholar. Will do. Out."

His thoughts kicked along to the intermittent beeps from the telltale as the jit hummed past fields with large beasts in them and the occasional Keteng or Fior herder drowsing in the sunlight. The road itself was empty now, the Béluchar coming to the celebration in Alsekum were mostly already there.

Half an hour from the village, the open fields grew smaller and smaller; there were groves of nut and fruit trees, also occasional woodlots filled with shadow and cut-glades where thickets of young trees were bright green patches between the darker trunks of the mature stock. Excellent ambush spots, his mind informed him and he started tensing again, though the telltale had gone quiet once there were no more herds to trigger it.

The woods grew denser as he neared the bridge over the Debuliah River, an arm of the Sea Marish reaching along its north bank. The road turned into a causeway above stagnant, weed-filled water, and the trees closed in around the road. Over the hum of the jit's lifters he could hear angi-song and the occasional splash from a crogall or some other water monster too cold to register on the telltale. By the time he reached the approach to the bridge, he was so tense a sudden burp on the telltale sent him reaching for the stunner. A glance at the telltale gave him distance and direction. He stopped the jit, swept the beam at full stun through a 180 arc, dropped the stunner on the seat beside him, and jammed the accelerod as far to the right as it would go.

When he saw the glimmer of the Enclave forcefield, he slowed, tugged a k-rag from the doorpocket, and wiped at the sweat on his face. He loathed cutters and he'd had enough of assassins a long time ago. Muttering anathemas under his breath, he headed the jit toward the Enclave gate, wondering if he'd just put a stray caöpa to sleep or pinned a swampie or did anything more than dunk a few fliers in some murky water. At least it wouldn't be anyone heading to the 'Clave to trade. The paved ground was empty and there were no barges tied up at the landing today. Rest Day. Summer Day. Just as well.

### 3

Eolt Melech made a song of her name and woke her from the sudden heavy sleep that had descended on her after she tried feeding soup to her patients, spilling more on the canvas than she got down them. Danor's breathing was harsh and labored, but Maorgan was lying on his side, curled like a child, sleeping sweetly. She made a face at him, then crawled out of the tent.

The day had turned lovely, the sky was clear of all but a few wisps of cloud, the wind had died down to a whisper, and the caöpas were busily browsing on the tender new growth on the brush growing between the trees. She got her to feet, wiped her hands on her shirt, and moved to the middle of the glade.

Melech was drifting above the glade, holding xeself in place with a single anchor tentacle. Xe looked plumper and more contained after a morning of sungrazing, delicately lovely again, the ragged edges smoothed flat. Xe unrolled xe's speaking tentacle but didn't try to touch her with it, waiting for her permission first.

She understood why. It was easier to convey xe's thoughts through that link and besides, xe didn't want to wake Maorgan. *Tetchy as a mother with a sick child,* she thought. *Just as well, listening to that chord speech hurts my head.* She reached out, let her hand brush against the tentacle as a way of granting the permission.

And gasped.

What poured through the Eolt's flesh and into her was indescribable—more intense than the deepest physical joy she'd ever known, even when she was a Weaver on Shayalin.

She snatched her hand away at the same time xe recoiled from her, then stood looking up at xe, her fingers moving over and over the hawk etched into her cheek. "Shall we try that again?" she said finally and put out her hand again.

The shock wasn't so great this time, though it was still there; it was like grabbing hold of a live wire and feeling electricity flowing into her.

They both carefully ignored this.

Eolt Melech mused for a moment, then spoke quickly, xe's words coming at her like yesterday's rain-drops, hard and fast.*I have quartered the Forest ahead and I have seen no more chorek sign, although with the thickness of canopy so various it is hard to be sure. The Mer-Eolt Lebesair has gone ahead to watch the road for us. . . .*

Even through the quick pelt of the words she felt a sense of things-not-said in that last bit, underlined by a powerful irritation that xe could not quite hide.

*Xe will sing to me of any dangers xe finds and I will pass these to my sioll. Maorgan is well?*

*He's still asleep, though it's been rather a long sleep, there is no fever, his pulse is strong.*

*I thought it must be so, but it is good to hear your confirmation. The other?*

*Is not well at all. Could you do for him . . . ?*

*No. It is not possible. The touch would kill, not heal. If you can manage to preserve him alive and get him another half a day's ride along the road, about ten sikkoms that is, you will come to Dumel Minach. It is a miner's settlement and there will be healers there who can deal with puncture wounds and broken bones. And the Inn at Minach is forted against forest choreks, so you will be safe there. Will you look at Maorgan again and bring me sight of how he is?*

*I'll do that.*

She watched xe drift upward to hover near the high clouds, then the fatigue that her broken sleep had not cleaned from her system flooded over her again. She returned to the tent, fell on the blankets, and was deep asleep almost before she'd stretched out her legs.

She woke again, an hour later, to see Maorgan bending over the older Ard. And there was more wood stacked inside the doorflap of the tent. He'd been out and busy while she slept. She rubbed at her eyes, once again amazed at how quickly he'd recovered, definitely more in that sioll bond than was apparent on the surface. No wonder Danor had been so filled with rage since his sioll was burned for the pleasure of a pair of Chave techs. He must have felt the burning as intensely as his sioll did till the Eolt was dead.

Maorgan turned when he heard her moving. "He's really bad. Have you talked to your people?"

"Com's dead. Sokli fell on it when he was killed. You look better."

"I feel better. I see the caöpas came back."

"Last night. I suppose because they're tame creatures and don't like the wild. Besides they wanted corncake and that doesn't grow on trees." She pushed herself up, grimaced at the throb in her head. "I hate interrupted sleep, I always feel like I'm three thoughts behind and a hundred pounds heavier. Would you bring Danor outside? And a blanket to put between him and the ground. I'm going to try something."

She opened her medkit, set a scalpel in the sterilizer, scowled at the antiseptic spray, then at the red and yellow matter pressing against the scab on Danor's shoulder. It was the bullet that was causing the trouble and probably a fragment of shirt it took in with it. She rested her fingers as lightly as she could on the hot dry skin and let her mindtouch drop through the flesh. *Yes. There. Dark heavy mass. Have to get that out. Can I shift it .. unh ... slippery ... yes, I can, yes.*

She looked up, met Maorgan's worried gaze. "I have to do something," she said. "I think I can get the bullet out and the wound cleaned, but I can't be sure. See if you can fix up a litter we can put him on and carry him to someone who knows what they're doing."

He nodded, got to his feet. "And I'll see about getting the packs ready."

She checked Danor. His fever was up another notch and he was moving his head and muttering things she couldn't catch, his hands were scrabbling weakly at the blanket. She wanted to put him out for the cleaning of the wound, but she didn't dare, she was worried enough about reaction to the spray. She set the antisep bulb on the folded-out worktray of the kit, then took the scalpel and opened the wound, jerking back as blood and pus spurted out.

She set the scalpel back in the sterilizer, sprayed a pad with antisep, and began wiping and pressing, wiping and pressing, getting as much of the yellow matter out as she could, trying to ignore the groans and screams from the man she was working on. When there was just blood and clear liquid coming out, she knelt with her hands resting lightly on his chest, the red raw hole between them.

She could move small objects, she'd done it before. She'd even drawn a bullet before, it just took concentration and time.

*Bullet. Yes. Shred of something foreign in there, too.*

*Grasp both. Yes. Gotcha! Ease them up. Easy . . . easy . . . damn!*

Danor was coming further awake, starting to writhe around on the blanket. One arm came around, slammed into her, nearly knocked her out of her trance and off her knees. Then he was quiet again, she didn't know why, she could feel life beating in him still, didn't matter, the only thing that mattered now was getting that bullet and that shred of cloth out of the wound. She'd lost hold for a moment, but retrieved it now. *Easy . . . easy . . . come along . . . up . . . where's the path . . . ah! around there, when he moved, he shifted things . . . just to make this harder . . . up another inch. . . .* "Ah!"

The battered cone of lead popped out of Danor with a comical little spt!, rolling down his ribs into the grass. The thread of cloth swam beside the wound in a pool of blood.

She wiped the back of a bloody hand across her eyes and saw Maorgan when she opened them. He'd used his body to pin the old man down, keep him from moving.

"Finished?" When she nodded, he rose. "Oddest thing I've ever seen," he said. "You're a talented lady, Shadowsong."

With a little bark of laughter, she shook her head. "No more than you, Harpmaster. Now if you'll go back to your packing, I'll finish this up. By the way, thanks."

He grinned and walked away.

She wiped the shred of cloth away, cleaned the wound again, sprayed antisep on a new pad, and taped it in place. "Now if you'll just stay alive till we get you to Minach."

### 4

Marrin Ola stopped in the doorway to the work-room when he saw Aslan sipping tea and listening to

Duncan Shears. "Get the cone up, I've got something to show you."

A moment later he was back. He stepped through the haze of the privacy cone, took a cutter from inside his shirt and put it on the table. "Not a rumor. Not any more."

Aslan looked at the mucky weapon. "Looks like it took a bath in mud." She sniffed. "Very stale mud where something died a while ago."

"It did." He wiped his hand on his shirt, pulled up a chair, and gave them a sketch of what happened at the bridge. ". . . and I managed to pry about half what you want out of Oschos, the stuff is locked in the jit, I'll bring it in later. It took a while, though, so I was irritated and in a hurry and I'd almost forgotten about the wobble at the bridge, so I hadn't turned on the telltale. So when Glois and his pal rode out at me, I nearly had a heart attack. The young idiots. I'd told them to keep away, but they saddled up and rode after, I think they thought they were going to protect me, I don't know WHAT they were thinking. Anyway, Glois was excited about something but he wouldn't say what. He got me on his caöpa and climbed up behind Ut and they took me to this mucky islet with a huge oilnut tree growing at one end. The cutter was there, one end of it sunk in the mud, the other end caught on a root. And the chorek who had it, he was facedown in the water, about as dead as you get. Drowned. I'd hit him with the stunner and down he went. There were pieces out of him, a crogall or something like that had started eating him. Kids thought all that was terribly interesting. Reminds me of me when I was a kid, but my stomach's gotten weaker since those days." He glanced at the cutter lying dark and lethal on the table, leaned back, and crossed his legs.

Aslan swore.

Duncan Shears rubbed at his chin. "You can interview from the Enclave."

"We've been over that and over it, Duncan. It won't work." Fingers tapping at the worktable, she stared at the wall, her eyes narrowed, the corners of her wide mouth tucked in. "Shadith should be getting to Chuta Meredel soon. End of the week she said. When she calls in tonight, I want her to try getting permission for the three of us to fly in. From what I've heard, I doubt any Chav spy will be getting close to that place. Center of learning, repository of history, center of government such as it is. I've been salivating at the thought of getting there, but I didn't see how . . . even Shadith had to ride there . . . no flikits allowed . . . and the Metau and Teseach went rabid when I barely mentioned the place . . . without an invitation I'd given up hope . . . funny, this business might even be what makes it possible." She blinked. "Well, enough of that. Marrin, what about the com and the satellites, are they anywhere near getting them back on line?"

He uncrossed his legs and straightened his back. "Very sneaky and thorough virus. Hm. It's hard to believe a Chav invented that virus. They're not usually so . . . um . . . indirect. That is to say, they have few graces not directly related to the extraction of minerals. I suspect the presence of a Freetech and I think I know the man. Family had me locate him and send him out to Picabral not so long ago; I talked to him first. Most amoral entity I've ever come across and one of the cleverest at what he does. If I'm right, Koraka has about as much chance of resolving that virus with the personnel and equipment he has here as we have of walking home. It ate through the defenses as if they didn't exist. All they needed was someone to get it into the system and they bought that. Software's unusable, the techs are trying to pull something together to get the com going, but everything they try, the virus eats. We are cut off completely for the moment. And there won't be a ship from Yarakan for another six weeks. They know who it was that the Chave bought, by the way. You remember that phora, Galeyn I think was his name? The one who looked like he had a burr up his nose? Well, he disappeared along with his private flikit. From what I could get out of Oschos, the Goës is raving, he suspects all the rest of them and is talking of putting anyone who sneezes funny under probe." He shrugged.

"And he can't afford sitting there much longer looking like a fool. And if we hand him this business of the cutters and the Chav spy ... Gods, that'll start a shooting war. It's all the proof he needs, isn't it. A weapon, a body, a spy he can capture. Active aggression against University residents, stockholders, and a full Scholar as well as damaging Yaraka equipment. He could go under a truthreader and come out sweet." Aslan got to her feet. "I want both of you thinking about options. See if you can dig up a third choice for us. We'll meet tonight, my room, see what Shadith can tell us."

# 11. The Ways of Secret Wars

## 1

Ceam stood in the gloom under the trees and watched smoke rising as the mountains burned. The fire the airwagons set was eating toward them, but it was still miles off and not yet dangerous.

"So you made it."

He turned.

Leoca stood with her arm around the shoulder of her Keteng companion, her face weary. Engebel looked bleached, xe's lichen brittle and gray. Behind them, in among a patch of half-grown guma trees, the three meloach in their klid were squatting on the mossfern groundcover, huddled together like new-hatched kerrut.

"So I did. You look like you had a hard run."

"Yes." After a minute, she added, "But we didn't lose anyone."

He took a last look at the peaks, moved into the shadow toward the two once-teachers. "How many made it here?"

"Twenty-three, and you're one of the last we're expecting. Eolt Kitsek said that was all he dared take time to find."

"Had a long way to come. With all that fire, seeing xe was shall we say a surprise."

They walked together through the trees with the meloach following silently behind. Ceam took a drink from his flask, offered it to Leoca and Engebel, they declined, so he slapped the stopple back in and hung it from his belt. The flon burned hot in his belly, gave him the illusion of energy, and helped him hide from himself how bad the situation was.

The saboteur klids and the solitary spies met beside a spring that welled up between two roots of the largest oiltree for miles around. A double dozen weary and angry Béluchar, about half Fior and half Keteng with a scattering of children among them, sitting silent and grim among their elders.

For some time most of what happened was irritated wrangling, none of them willing to give up the right to speak or give way to any of the others; most of them came from different Ordumels in different sections of Melitoëh, some of these traditional rivals. And the times had made them suspicious of strangers. All the rules were washed away. If there'd been an Ard left on Melitoëh, the harper would have had their deference, but most of the Ards had died from heart attacks brought on by unbearable pain or by their own hands when their siolls burned. The few that were left were like Ilaörn and Danor, crazy or caged.

After a while, though, Leoca and Engebel moved to the center of the surge, touching an arm here, whispering there, spreading a calm, bringing order out of chaos with the skills they'd learned in fifteen years of teaching.

Engebel stood on a root beside the spring, the height raising xe's head above the rest. "It would be a shame," xe said, a dark sad note thrumming in xe's voice. "If we destroy ourselves before the Chave can do the job. You, Ceam, you Heruit, you Deänin. . . ." Xe named them all and with the names, caught them in xe's web. "You all . . . we all have hurt the mesuch or they wouldn't have done that horror. Cha oy, we just have to hurt them more. Heruit, sounded to me like you've been thinking about something. Tell us."

Heruit was a Fior with a freckled bald head and the remnants of a comfortable plumpness. "We started this to run them out of profit and patience. Ihoi! we've done the second all right, but the first doesn't seem to have happened. I don't really care why, I make this point only to remind you all why we've left the center of poison alone. The mesuch fort. I say that is our target now. There's not much worse they can do to us, so there's no further point to forbearance. Ard Ilaörn has done well for us, let us ask him to do more."

With a slash of his hand to say he was finished, he dropped to a squat on the mossfern.

Engebel pointed a blunt finger. "Rebek."

Xe was a small, wiry Denchok, thinner and shorter than most. "I think we're agreed there. It's just a matter of how we do it. What with this and that, I was run into the Meklo Fen a few tendays ago. Some of my budline are living in there with a clutch of swampies. Saw a patch of hokori ripening nicely in the Meklo Fen, so that's useful. And there are other things in the Marishes that we can use to fight with. The swampies were telling me about the trading they're doing with the mesuchs. . . ."

The mention of trade brought some of the listeners to their feet roaring with outrage.

Leoca jumped up beside Engebel, thrust her fingers in her mouth, and cut through the noise with a piercing whistle.

When Leoca brought her hands down and dropped to sit on the root, Engebel said very softly, "Quiet. You're acting like fools. Xe has a point, let xe make it."

Rebek nodded. "Xe is right. The swampies trade fruit and dried shroon and fresh fish for whatever they can pry out of the techs and Drudges around the mesuch fort. And they make quite sure that some of these things have dormant chiro spores in them. A portion of the spores will pass right through whoever eats them, maybe contaminate the water system, maybe not, but some will set their hooks. I would not like to be a Chav with chiro worms growing in my gut."

Heruit chuckled, then he whooped, slapped his thighs, jumped to his feet and hugged Rebek, startling the little Keteng. Still chuckling he stepped back. "What a ploy! What a demondream of a ploy! Who thought that one up?"

Rebek coughed, patted xe's mouth. "From the little I know, I'd say it just sort of happened. And that is not the only thing they are passing on. But that, while pleasant to contemplate, is not why I brought the matter up. Even with Ard Ilaörn inside the walls, we don't know enough about that fort to attack it with any hope of real damage. We need information first. And we need to get it without having the mesuchs suspect what we're up to. It is Summer Day today. Did you remember that, all of you? Summer Day. You know what that means. Hot and humid and the Scacca wind blowing day after day off the Bakuhl Sea. They'll start going crazy when mold grows on their hides and every surface around. They're desert folk, Ard Ilaörn has told us that. They won't stay trapped behind those walls. They'll want distraction, amusement, anything to cut through the whine of that wind and the stink of the mold. I say, think about that."

Engebel swung xe's fingers, deliberately choosing a Fior woman this time. "Deänin."

Deänin was a stocky woman in late middle age, her hair cut short and mostly gray, her face lined, her eyes almost lost in nets of crows's-feet. "Before I came to the mountains, they set me to running their whorehouse in Dumel Dordan-that-was, the house that Drudges used. You don't want to know what a rutting Drudge is like. Male or female. Rebek is right. When the Scacca blows, that's when we have a chance, but we have to be ready to take it. Before I came away, I saw Drudges and techs both drinking smoke. That's the trade we can work on, get them so drugged with smoke they get careless. The big Muck, he's trying to get hold of the trade all for himself, he's trying to cut off the techs' supplies, it's like he's working for us. Let them think they ashed most of us with the trees. Let them think what's left of us have gone tame with terror. Let them get real comfortable. Then we hit and we wipe them off Béluchad."

## 2

Brion blinked at the ceiling, wondering what it was that woke him so early.

A moment later Temuen came in with a tray, two mugs of timel tea steaming on it, sticks of husk burning in a holder, a bright bunch of silny flowers in the little vase he'd carved for her. "Greet the Summer," she sang. Her voice quavered, but it was still as true and sweet as it had been the first time he heard her sing.

He pushed up, made room for her beside him on the bed. "Summer Day already?"

She patted his hand. "You lose count, you know."

When they woke from the smoke trance, they left the shelter and stood at the edge of the Sleeping Ground watching the smoke from the fires coiling above the peaks. Brion caught hold of a vine twisting about the pergola, weak tears filled his eyes "Why?"

"Because they look at us like we're bugs. Been stinging them, I 'spect. Smoking us out, burning us down like we would a nest of chups." There was a scratchy irritation in her voice as if she'd said the same thing too many times before. After a moment he felt the echoes in his mind and knew he'd stood here, said this, she'd said that, all of it before.

"Sorry. I forget."

"I know. Takes some like that."

There was an odd burring in the air. Not loud. Like a cloud of kekads swarming above a lake. The image pleased him, brought up a memory of a time when he was just a boy and dreaming of being an Ard and bonding with an Eolt. He felt again the jolt when he realized it wasn't going to happen. Fifty years ago, yet the hurt was still fresh. He leaned against the pergola and wept for that and all the things he'd forgotten in the years since.

A hand tugged at him. Temuen's voice was shrill in his ear. "Come on, old fool. The mesuchs, they coming here. We gotta get away."

"Wha ... where?" He brushed at his eyes, saw the dark blot of the airwagon dropping down beside the Sleeping Ground. He started to move then, but it was already too late. A force of mesuchs came bounding out of the wagon and moved in an arc toward the ground. He turned only to see another airwagon and another arc closing in from the other side.

A grating sound from the first airwagon, then words. "Stop where you are. If you try to run, we'll take your legs off. Come to the Bonding Court...."

Agitation made Brion's limbs twitch. *The words ... they shouldn't know the words ... they stole the words....* Muttering his distress, he let Temuen tug him along to the court.

All the other Guardians were there, the young ones and the old failing ones like him. The mesuchs had trapped them all.

The airwagon was still talking at them. He'd missed part of it, so it was a while before he took in what was being said and then only because the wagon repeated it twice. "... will choose four from among the oldest of you, the rest won't be harmed. You can go on about your business as soon as we leave. Any disturbance or disobedience will be punished immediately."

A mesuch walked past them, staring at them. Brion shivered as the hard metallic gaze seemed to peel his skin back.

A moment later the mesuch was back. He had a short brass wand in his hand. He moved his claw, a ray of light went out, touched Camach. "You."

The light touched Sulantha, the oldest of the women here. "You."

The light touched Brion. It was cold light, but it burned him. He shuddered when the mesuch said, "You."

The light touched Temuen. "You."

The mesuch stepped back. "The ones I marked, step forward. You'll be coming with us."

*At least I'll have Temuen.* Brion took a step toward the airwagon. *At least I won't be alone.* He reached to take her hand, but she wasn't beside him. He turned.

Her face had gone red, her eyes were little and squinty. She got like that when she was angry. And she was stubborn when she was angry. "No!" she shouted at the mesuch. "I'm not going anywhere."

Brion rushed to her, took her arm and tried to pull her along. "Temmy, don't, I need you. Don't. Don't. Temmy...."

The mesuch didn't bother trying to persuade her. The light that touched Temuen this time burned a hole clear through her and she crumpled at Brion's feet.

The marker light flashed out, touched Teärall. "You. Now. All of you. Move. I will not accept hesitation."

Teärall took Brion's arm. "Cha oy, Brio, what's done is done. Come along."

At times during the flight to the mesuch's place, Brion would forget about Temuen and stare out at the clouds or at the ground moving with such stately deceptive speed below them. Then he'd look around to find her and show her the wonders and she wasn't there and he'd remember and the pain was new again, new each time as if the horror happened over and over. He'd gotten used to Guardians dying, they did it all the time. Old men died. Old women died. They went into the ground and their souls came back as Keteng and flowered into golden Eolt. But those dyings were shared things, with songs and stories and the Passage Feast to celebrate the freeing from the body. Even when young Rudiam had a heart attack when he was only fifty-seven and dropped dead in the middle of a Song Smoke, it wasn't like ... Brion looked out and saw a herd of blackface caörags spooked by the shadow of the airwagons rippling across the grass, smiled at how silly they looked from up here, turned to nudge Temuen ... and screamed, remembering....

The mesuchs drove the four Guardians ahead of them into a small gate in the backside of their fort-place. After passing through a maze of corridors, all rigidly square with glow bands that produced a glaring white light that seared Brion's eyes, kept him blinking and rubbing at them, a hand in the middle of his back shoved him into a small square room, with walls and ceiling a smooth white ceramic.

The others came stumbling in after him, dazed and eyes streaming from the glare.

The mesuch's voice came blaring into the room, as hard on the ears as their lights were on the eyes. "Strip off your clothing and drop it in the opening provided."

Brion blinked, stood staring at the wall, not sure he'd heard what he thought he'd heard. Teärall patted his arm. "Brio, take off your clothes. We all have to do that." She turned, began helping Sulantha with the ties on her robe.

Liquid came at him from everywhere, hard lines that hurt where they hit. Not water. It stung his eyes and had the greasily sour taste of soap when it got into his mouth. Then the water was gone and something like fog gushed into the room. It caught him in the throat and started him coughing. He could hear the others hacking and wheezing.

Then the fog was sucked away and they stood shivering on the smooth cold floor. A part of a wall slid back. A door. Not the one they'd come through.

"Leave the room." The mesuch's voice had a weary impatience as if he spoke to really stupid animals. "Leave the room. Leave the room now. Walk down the corridor till you reach the first open door, go through it. Leave the room. Leave the room now."

Wet and shivering, they turned into the new room to find towels there, gray soft rags with an acrid herbal odor and voluminous white garments hanging from hooks shoulder high on the wall. Brion rubbed his hair dry enough so it stopped dripping into his eyes and sending driblets of water down his neck. He dropped the towel on the table where he'd found it, took down one of the garments. It was a loose sleeveless smock that reached his knees and left his legs and feet bare.

He'd barely gotten it on, was still tying on the cloth belt when the mesuch's voice sounded, startling him as it seemed to come from the air. After a minute he remembered that was the way it was before.

*Sorry. I forget.* He said that to Temuen a while ago. When was that? A while ago.

*I know. Takes some like that.* Temuen said that to him a while ago. Temuen. . . .

"Leave the room. Now. Leave the room. Turn to

your left. Do not go back the way you came. Turn to your left. Keep walking until you are told to stop."

Obediently, Brion shuffled down the corridor until the voice stopped him beside a door.

"Put your hand on the yellow oval."

It was a pale spot, seemed more brown than yellow to Brion, but he wasn't going to argue the point. When he set his hand on the spot, the door slid open.

"Step inside."

He shied as the door slid shut behind him, cutting him off from the others.

"What is your name?"

"Brion." His mouth quivered. He wanted to ask what was going to happen, but he couldn't get his tongue around the words. His body was beginning to lose the smoke; his fingers twitched, and a tic pulsed beside one eye.

"Brion. This is your room. Do what I tell you and you will know how to use its functions."

There were more yellow ovals scattered about. One brought a bunk bed sliding from the wall. One a toilet. One opened a hole in the wall he was told would have food for him at the proper time. The one that pleased him most opened a narrow door that led into a small square patio. There were four concrete benches set against the windowless walls that enclosed the place, a tree and a fountain in the middle, a hideous squat thing, but at least there was moving water in it. As if the builder that made this ugly heap had designed the bare minimum for folk who need green and sky to stay alive.

He shuffled to one of the benches and sat down. A moment later more doors opened and the others came out to join him, sitting silent, staring at the fountain and the single finger of water rising to dance with a grace that damned its surroundings.

Teärall was the youngest of them, the most impatient. She pushed gray-streaked brown hair back from her square bony face. "Why? I thought we were dead. This is almost as bad as dead, but not quite. Why are we alive?"

Brion stared at her a moment, then his face crumpled and he started crying. She was there instead of Temuen. Temuen was dead.

Though there was no answer that first day to Teärall's question, the following days gave them ample reason. They were questioned, poked, prodded. Samples were taken of all their body fluids. They were laid out on tables, lights shone at them, they were drawn through long machines. Do this, do that, they were told. And they did whatever they were told, moving like cabhisha before the nipping and barking of a herd dog.

For the first tenday they were given no smoke to drink.

Sulantha died on the third day, falling against Brion as they walked about the bleak garden.

He wept for a moment, then forgot why as soon as her body was removed. He was flashing in and out of awareness. His body ate and slept and moved about, but most of the time he only knew that when one of the mesuch guards slapped his face to wake him from his trance of nonthinking. By the end of the tenday, even this barely reached him. He spent most of the time sleeping in the sun in the patio, curled up knees to chest, Camach and Teärall nestled beside him.

On the eleventh day he woke in his cell and found a bowl with fragments of husk on the floor beside the cot, smoke rising in blue white twists. He dropped off the edge of the cot, sprawled on the floor, his face close to the bowl as he sucked in the smoke.

When he woke from the trance, he went outside and sat on his bench, watching the water dance. There were drawbacks to awareness. Grief and pain and anger churned in him. He thought about opening a vein. He also knew the mesuch would not permit him to die on his own time. He thought about Sulantha. Thought she was luckier than she knew. Her soul was free and would be rebodied in a quieter time. He didn't think about Temuen, turned his mind away whenever the image of her flickered behind his eyes.

Teärall came out. Her eyes were red and wild, her plain face made plainer by a scowl. "Do you know what they're doing?" She didn't wait for an answer. "We're test animals. They're using us to figure what the husk does. They're using us to find a way of growing husk. Like Keteng breed cabhisha for their hair and their meat. Do you hear me, Brion? Do understand what they're doing?"

Brion blinked at her, then he nodded. "Yes."

"We've got to do something." She waved away his warning. "Cha oy, I know they're listening. What does that matter?" She turned as Camach came slouching out, his eyes seeing things in the otherwhere. "Cama, do you know what they're doing? Listen to me, do you know?"

His body shuddered and his gaze shortened till he was looking at her. He said, "They told me to tell you, they'll be coming for the three of us this afternoon. More tests."

"Oh."

### 3

MedTech First Muhaseb shifted in his pulochair and looked nervous as he waited for the Ykkuval's attention.

Hunnar was leaning back, eyes closed, hand waving to the lively stomp that Ilaörn coaxed from his harp.

Ilaörn watched that hand and brought the stomp to an end when he saw the movement go ragged and lose even an approximation of the beat. He segued into pale background paste that Hunnar could ignore. He would have pushed it longer if he'd dared; he didn't want to see Muhaseb's pictures, his stomach still burned from the last time. He leaned his head against the wall and closed his eyes though he knew he would open them later when the picture show began.

Hunnar's chair hummed as he swung to face the med-tech. "You said you had a report."

"Yes, O Ykkuval. You asked us to keep you informed on progress as we made it."

"And?"

"Ah mmm, this phase was rather more mmm incomplete than we liked, however, we do have sufficient date to make the next phase more successful."

"Incomplete?"

"Ah mmm, unfortunately the subjects had to be dispatched before the series was complete. We have mmmm taken them apart and examined the pieces. . . ." His mouth twitched into a sour smile. "Mmmm, boiling jam from spoiled fruit as it were. Would you prefer to examine the conclusions first or do you wish to see the process develop?"

"Skip the beginning. I want to know why you wasted the subjects I had my guards collect for you."

"Mmmm. Yes. I must repeat, O Ykkuval, our experience in this sort of exploration is minimal at best. We are trained to deal with illnesses and injuries among the work force and must proceed from the most general of principles in this study. If you will watch the screen. Scenes from the day in question. We had deprived them of the smoke for a tenday and observed a growing disconnect from reality until sometimes they failed to respond even to the most intense of pain stimuli. Examination of body fluids and cells taken from various organs indicate what seems to be mmmm a nearly complete integration of the drug with the cell structure so that deprivation leads to a shutting down of most functions. The oldest of the subjects, a female, suffered a massive disruption of the brain on the third day and died. As I said, the others were shutting down more completely with each day that passed and would probably have followed the woman into death if we had continued the deprivation for a second tenday. While testing to destruction would be of some value, it was determined to begin a new phase. If you will observe the screen, O Ykkuval."

The wall screen came alive. It was divided into four cells. In three of them skeletal figures are lying on wall cots like corpses laid out for burying. The cell door slides open, a pole pushes a bowl of smoldering husk into the room. Before the door closes, all three have rolled off the cots and are hunched over the bowls, faces stupid with a combination of ecstacy and need as they suck the smoke into mouths and nostrils. The fourth cell is the patio, empty now, the only movement the flutter of leaves and the dancing of the column of water.

"You will observe how quickly function is restored once sufficient smoke is ingested. The need is different for each of the three as evidenced by the duration of their intake. It is interesting also that the first thing each of them does is move into the open, into the semblance of a garden we provided them with."

Hunnar listened to Teärall's speech, held up his hand.

The tech stopped the movement. "Yes, O Ykkuval?"

"Was there any discussion in the hearing of the subjects as to why this is being done to them?"

"None, O Ykkuval. We were careful only to give the necessary orders. Not a word beyond that was spoken at any time. Not even in Chava."

"And they're peasants. Drudges. How does she know?"

"Ah mmm. O Ykkuval, we know almost nothing about local culture or how developed it might be. There are reports that there was a primitive kind of electrical system in the village we took over. It is quite possible that certain types among them have developed a certain philosophical sophistication somewhat beyond their technical capacity."

"Ump."

"Our mmm miscalculation of their potential arose from their passivity. Only the one showed any resistance at all, that was, of course, the woman shot by your guard when he gathered these for us. She should have been factored into our expectations, but that was not done."

The image on the wall flickered and shifted to a single screen showing a corridor and three people shuffling along it, meager, almost skeletal figures, shoulders rounded, heads down.

"As you can see, passive, low energy, wasted bodies. However, watch what happens next."

Another jump, from the corridor to the testing facility. Lab techs herded the three subjects into cubicles, ordered them to undress and lie down.

There was no signal given, no word spoken, but in the same second all three jumped their techs. They did no damage, but the sudden attack provoked the Chav defensive reaction and they ended as ragged fragments splattered against the wall.

"The techs have been disciplined. Level one only because of the provocation and the previous passivity which made the attack such a surprise that they acted automatically and killed rather than restrained the subjects." He touched the sensor and the screen went blank. "If you wish, O Ykkuval, I can take you through the autopsies and the examination of brain cell development, or I can give you a summary of what we think as of now."

"Leave the flake with the details, I'll examine it later. Summarize now." He glanced at a wall chron. "You have three minutes."

"Ah mmm every cell we examined departed widely from the Cousin norm, insofar as there is a norm and considering the limited resources of our filing system. Some were wasted until they were hardly recognizable as cells, some hyperdeveloped, all of them, even the atrophied, had a patch of odd-shaped receptors which we believe is the site where one component or other of the smoke attaches. That is not necessarily true. Ah mmm we would appreciate your including a nonaddicted young form of the species in the next collection. We need a base form to validate our conclusions. At the moment these are that prolonged exposure to the husk smoke induces physical changes in the brain and body structure. The functioning of the body and thus life itself becomes completely dependent on the continued use of the smoke, but what those changes do to thought patterns, indeed, the ability to think and reason, we don't at present know." He rose to his feet, placed hand over hand and bowed. "Within my three minutes, I believe. If you have further questions, I will be happy to return."

When the bell sounded, Hunnar clicked on the speaker, snapped, "Quiet."

Ilaörn took his hands from the strings, and sat silent and disregarded in his corner.

A small voice said, "Kurz."

Ilaörn recognized both name and voice and set himself to listen carefully and remember what he heard. He'd gotten word out about the spy, but in the past tenday the harpist who usually answered him had been silent, so he had no way of knowing if he'd played to empty air or listening ears.

Hunnar hunched forward, the inner lids drooping down so his eyes glistened to show the intensity of his attention. "Listening. Speak."

"Have visited the four Marishes and some fifteen bands of choreks. The cutters have been distributed. The information about the bounties on the heads of the University team is passing quickly from mouth to mouth and I have already seen several bands making their way toward the village where the team is now. Unless they are warned by a bungled attempt and take precautions, they should soon cease to exist. Also there will soon be severe disturbances in the lives of the villagers and the local farmers as the chorek use their new firepower to enrich themselves, which will further dampen the efforts of the Yaraka to ingratiate themselves with the locals."

"You want more cutters?"

"Yes. At the drop as arranged. Plus a new unit for the miniskip. The damp and local fauna have damaged the old one to the point that my freedom of movement has been severely curtailed. This is the more frustrating since I've heard of forest chorek and meant to cross to the mountains and begin enlisting them. I have achieved a tentative connection with one of the political choreks with ties in that direction."

"You are well?"

"Yes. Though rather bored. This business has proceeded with an almost ludicrous ease."

"May your boredom continue. Good work, Kurz. But take care. I've just been reminded that the locals have teeth and can use them."

"Pitiful teeth, O Ykkuval, along with an ignorance so vast it is astonishing. How soon can the drop be made? I am lying concealed near the area."

Hunnar glanced at the wall chron. "Three hours till dark here. I'll have Asgel load the flik and start across an hour from now. He should reach the drop a little after sundown. Congratulations again, Kurz. You have exceeded expectation, as usual."

Ilaörn sat in the Dushanne Garden listening to a distant harp with a relief that he carefully concealed although he was alone for the moment. In the rhythms was an acknowledgement of his message and a warning to be listening for news later in the tenday. He sighed and brushed at his eyes as he saw the airwagon rise above the Kushayt and go darting westward. Somewhere out there an Eolt would be riding the wind currents in the same direction, making xe's relatively slow and labored way to Chuta Meredel. Time. The mesuchs ate time the way crogalls ate meat, swallowing in chunks what other beings nibbled at.

They were going to eat this world like that. Hunnar and his lot. *We're to be fodder for their appetites, especially the Keteng. Kept in herds like caörags, raised for the husk from the Sleepers, the hatchling Eolt for the pleasure of the hunt. I will die before I see that. I hope I will die.* The thought twisted his stomach in knots. He groaned aloud. *How can I with this ... this burr in my head that won't even let me think the thought without....*

The distant harp had settled to an old song, one of those from the flight time, from so long ago and so far away that even dreams couldn't reach there.

> *"My lover has gone away, gone away, oh*
> *My lover has gone across the wide sea*
> *My heart is sore, my heart hurts, oh*
> *Bring back my wandering lover to me...."*

He listened until the sad pure notes faded; his eyes burned with the need to weep, but he had no tears left.

209

# 12. The Price is Right

### 1

Dumel Minach was the first walled town Shadith had seen on Béluchad. The blai was outside the walls and reflected that isolation with tiny slits for windows and shutters that looked as if they could repel cannon balls. A branch of the Menguid ran past the place, a narrow rushing stream full of rapids and waterfalls. Paired wooden rails with a skim of iron nailed to the top of each ran along the leveled riverbank, laid across the squared-off trunks of large trees set a long pace apart. A walkway was laid down between the rails, with slats of wood to give purchase to the clawed feet of the draft dammalt used to pull the lines of tramcars loaded with roughly refined ores from the mines and flatbeds loaded with lumber.

One of those trains was moving along the rails as Maorgan rode past Shadith and yanked the bell chain dangling beside a kind of gatehouse set like a wart on the wall beside massive doors. It was late, the sun was already down, just a few streaks of red and purple touching the clouds and the near dozen Eolts drifting above the Dumel.

They were singing the night in, the great organ notes echoing back from the peaks with a beauty that made her heart hurt.

Danor stirred. His hands and arms were confined by the ropes that tied him onto the stretcher, but his head turned back and forth and he muttered. His fever had begun to rise again half an hour ago and she was getting increasingly worried about him. She set her hand on his brow, tried to sooth him with a brush from the mindtouch. It seemed to help. She suspected that grazing of the mind brought back sense memories of the sioll bond and made him forget his loss for a moment or two.

Maorgan was standing now, his caöpa groundhitched beside him, browsing wearily at the new green tips of a bush at the edge of a small green garden. The wind was rising, and between that, the Eolts' song and the noise of the passing train, she couldn't hear what he was saying, but the set of his shoulders told her he was angry.

One of the Eolt left the others, rose to a higher air stratum, and began gliding toward them. Melech, probably. Though she hadn't yet seen enough Eolt to be able to distinguish between them. Xe rode the winds down, slapped a tentacle against the shutter, slid the end of the tentacle across Maorgan's face with an affection a blind man could read, then let the winds carry xe aloft again.

The argument was over.

Maorgan came striding to her, raised his voice so she could hear above the noise. "Bring the caöpas round to the side. We'll go in through the stable. It'll be easier on Danor that way."

She slid down, took the reins of the litter ponies while he led his own mount, Bréou, and the single packer they had left. "What was the problem?"

"We're late. They'd already shut the doors and didn't want to open up again, especially not for strangers. Wouldn't believe I was Ard until Melech threw xe's snit. We're lucky in one thing. There's a doctor in the blai. Accident at one of the mines. He got back after the Dumel gates were shut."

*   *   *

A stocky Denchok with a rifle under xe's arm was standing inside the stable waiting for them. Xe had lifted the bar on the massive portal, but left it to them to haul it open and drive the caöpas inside. Xe glanced at the litter. "What happened to him?"

"Chorek. They're dead."

"Good." Xe relaxed when xe saw the harpcase Maorgan lifted from the packer. "Said you was Ard. Playing for us tonight?"

"We'll both be playing once we get Ard Danor settled. My companion is also a harpist."

The hostler looked past Maorgan, looked away without comment. After a minute he said, "You want help moving him? Said I was to ask."

"No, we can handle it. You just take good care of the caöpas, they've given good service and need a little coddling. Leave the packs by the door inside, someone will come pick it up later. Shadowsong, shall we get started?"

The doctor was an old Denchok near xe's transformation, the lichen-web so thick it was almost continuous. Xe bent over Danor, peeling the bandage away, interested in the tape because it was something that both lines of Béluchar had simply not thought of; for one thing, neither Meloach flowermoss nor Denchok lichen was compatible with adhesive tape. Xe pointed to the redness and swelling where the tape had been. "While I can see that this was an emergency and you used what you had, Shadowsong, this adhesive substance has provoked an allergic reaction which makes complications." His voice was a pleasant rumble. "You say the bullet is out?"

"Yes."

"Cha oy, it was done very cleanly with little damage to the flesh. I commend you. Is the water boiling yet?"

Shadith stepped to the narrow window, where the

doctor had set up his brazier, looked into the pot. "Just starting."

"Good. Would you bring it here, please."

Xe dropped a gauze packet of minced herbs into the water and set it aside. "So you're finding our world an interesting place?" Xe fished in xe's bag and brought out a small ceramic jar, began unscrewing the lid.

She chuckled. "In every sense of the word."

Xe began spreading cream from the jar across xe's hands, working it into xe's greenish-gray skin. "Political?"

"Don't think so. Maorgan says the politicals always yell at you when they shoot. These didn't."

"Take the sieve and strain that decoction in the mug. Then you can see how much you can get down him. That's a mix of roec and cliso, a feverbane, plus it'll mute the pain and put him to sleep. About half for now. Save the rest for later. I've heard about the mesuch down by shore. Didn't seem too bad, sort of like the traders who drop by now and then. Caused some stir, though, they did. Say they have fur all over them. Must get hot now that Summer's here. You now, you're more like the traders I've met. Got drunk once with one of them, man called Arel. Said it was anniversary of something. That's good. His throat's working, so he's swallowing. Talked a lot about a girl ... or a woman ... he was real confused about that ... with a flier etched on her face. Like that thing you've got. Said more than he meant to, the old gray empties had him by the scrot if you get what I'm at. I think that's enough for now. If you'll get one of those wipe rags and keep the field clear, I'll deal with that wound."

Shadith set the cup aside, wiped Danor's mouth with one of the rags, and gave him a brush from the mindtouch again to help him settle. He looked so frail and ancient a loud sneeze would break him apart. "He gets around. Arel, I mean."

The doctor opened the wound, then stood back while she wiped away the matter that oozed forth. "You be harping with the Ard tonight?"

"We sing for our supper, or so I understand." She looked up, smiled at the sudden widening of xe's eyes. "No no, that's only a saying, Tokta Burek. Yes, we'll be playing once we've had something to eat and wash up. If you have a favorite tune, let Maorgan know."

"That I will. That's enough of that." He took a sterile cloth and began applying cream from another small jar.

Maorgan began a lively tune with laughter chuckling through the notes. After a moment Shadith caught the rhythm and began weaving her own themes round it, smiling as she did so at the glee on Burek's face.

"Little Achcha Meloach," Maorgan sang, his rich baritone filling the room, Shadith chanting unwords in harmony with him.

*"Little Accha Meloach*
*sitting in a tree*
*yelling down at Fior boy*
*can't catch me.*
   *cha oo cha me oh bam ba oh*
*Little Arja Fioree*
*running through the wood*
*chasing yellow angies*
*catch them if she could.*
   *ja ooo fee ree fee ree ra oh*
*Little Cheon Fior boy*
*paddling in the flood*
*throws a fish at Achcha*
*be-bumping in the mud.*
   *chee oh fee oh ba bum bum ba oh."*

Round and round through the antics of the three they went, Achcha, Cheon, and Arja Fioree. The audience—merchants and their clerks, the miners down too late to make the town, along with more anonymous travelers heading across the Medon Pass to Chuta Meredel and the workers in the blai—they smiled at first, then snapped their fingers to the beat and began singing along.

"What was that song?" she asked as they climbed wearily to their rooms, released finally by the lateness of the hour.

"Children's rhyme. Silly thing, but it's got a good tune and everyone knows it. I used to play it a lot at dances." He looked wistful for a moment, then sighed. "Even without the mesuch, the world's turning sour. I wouldn't have thought it before, but this could be a good thing in its way. Lance the poisons and let them out like you did with Danor's wound."

## 2

Marrin Ola woke with the irritated feeling that the day was starting wrong and was going to get worse as it went along. Three times last night the alarm went off, but by the time he and the others got to the set-off point, there was nothing to be seen. If they'd needed more warning about what was going to happen, they'd gotten it. He was angry with both the Yaraka and the Chave but not much surprised. Assassinations of every sort were the prime means of politics on Picabral, with blackmail, abduction, bribery, and threat following close behind. He lay with his fingers laced beneath his head, staring at the ceiling, smiling a little. His growing-up time had given him a fine training for the subtler games on University. These he actually enjoyed. Most of the time. He was good at playing them, too. But he counted on these

Jo Clayton

projects that took him offworld and into quieter, often kinder societies to renew his enthusiasm for staying alive. The Chav spy and what he'd introduced were corrupting and destroying that, forcing him back into a situation where he had to play those games again. Marrin took those actions very personally.

He rolled off the bed and went through his exercises until sweat was dripping off him, then he showered with the pulsing spray head he'd brought with him, a bit of lore he'd picked up from more experienced Aides on earlier field projects. By the time he was dressed, he was still angry, but a lot readier to face what had to be done.

Aslan looked down at Duncan Shears. "Just get things buttoned up. If the Goës can figure a way to catch the spy, we might be able to come back."

Duncan chuckled. "That's the ... what ... fifth time, Scholar. You worry too much."

"I know, I know, worse than a nervous horse." She settled into the jit's passenger seat. "Right. Let's go, Marrin. And if you see that pair of young trouble-on-the-hoof, pull up and let me take my turn at them." She sighed. "All we need is a dead child."

Marrin drove slowly on the dusty circle road that curled round the outside of the dumel. "Maybe they listened this time. Or maybe their parents dusted salt on their little tails and made sure they were in school. Look, Scholar, I'm sorry. I shouldn't have involved them."

"You couldn't know the Chave would be so brazen about targeting us."

"I should have. It's an obvious ploy once they managed to take out the com."

Aslan snorted. "You and my mother. You'd get along well, I think."

"Um. That's as it may be. Listen, Scholar, I've been thinking. Shadith has been off air for three, four nights

216

now. She wouldn't know about the spy because we didn't the last time she called. From the description the youngsters picked up, he's got a miniskip, wouldn't take him long to cross the plain and start working mountain choreks. Because we haven't heard of any doesn't mean they aren't there. Could be she's either dead or hostage by now."

"We went over that last night. And over it. There's no way of knowing. Those handcoms aren't supposed to go down, but when you don't have a store handy to replace parts, anything can happen. I know I should have tried to pry another one out of the Goës, but he turned frugal on me. 'I have to account to headquarters,' he said. 'We agreed to finance you,' he said, 'but not put you up in luxury.' Luxury!" She sighed. "They do it all the time, Marrin, you might as well get used to it. There's some little niggle they get caught up on. So?"

"Turned frugal? Or thought he'd got all he needed from you. I'd wager my University Stock that's what it is. Once you got the Béluchar calmed down and the language transfer, he thinks he doesn't need us any more. We're just a nuisance and an expense." He took a deep breath, clamped down on his anger. "Well, I expect you know that."

Aslan chuckled. "Well, I expect I do."

He glanced at the workers in the fields. In one, a man was plowing a team of two red and white spotted blada; the next field over two Meloach were guiding water from a flume into furrows between rows of diokan. Beyond them was pasture where a herd of caöpas grazed. "I hate this, you know. I know what it's worth, this kind of peace. Picabral. . . ." He shook his head.

"Marrin, do I need to remind you?"

"No. Lost causes only give me heartburn." He managed a weak grin. "Listen, I've been thinking." He took the jit up onto the causeway, cut speed to a crawl. "Scholar, the Chav Ykkuval has till the next

Yarak supply ship arrives to gut the Enclave. Chances are he's finished being subtle about it. If you can call bribery and sabotage subtle. I don't think our Goës is up to his weight and I certainly don't think we want to be inside that fence when the Ykkuval decides it's time to move. As long as there's no one to contradict him, he can claim it's locals' work, armed by smugglers with him sitting across sea innocent as a haloed saint. I think we should use Shadith as an excuse and head for the mountains. If you can squeeze a flikit out of the Goës, that'd be best, but passage on one of the sailbarges might do. As long as it's understood we go armed and we'll shoot back if attacked." He glanced in the mirror, swore and stopped the jit.

Standing on the seat, he faced back along the road. Cupping his hands round his mouth, he yelled. "You two get back in school. You know what I told you."

Aslan twisted around. The road was empty back to the place where it curved around a small wood lot and up onto the causeway. After a minute, though, a pair of caöpa heads poked round the trees and slowly, reluctantly, two riders edged into view.

Marrin dropped into his seat, brought the jit whipping around, and sent it roaring at them.

They shied, glanced back as if they were thinking of taking off, then sat their saddles, faces pinched with chagrin, thin shoulders slumped, waiting for the jit to reach them.

He stopped under the noses of the nervous ponies, got to his feet, and stood leaning on the top of the windshield while they quieted the little beasts. "Cha oy, just what did you think you were at, kekerie?"

Glois and Utelel exchanged glances, then Glois took the lead. "Ute's Parent had these caöpas he wanted exercised, so we did."

"Uh-huh. And you're not going to tell me this is another holiday?"

"Um. Ute and me, we got all our lessons done, we

din't see reason to scrunch round in some hot room list'ning to teacher bababaing on about stuff we already know."

"Uh-huh. Let me tell you something, young keklins. This isn't a game. It never was. And I never should have opened my mouth to babies too young to know what it means to keep a promise."

"We didn't promise you nothing!" The last word ended in an indignant squeak.

"Equivocation and silence, young keklins. You know what I mean." He spoke slowly, watching them wince as if the words were switches hitting them. "How do you think I'd feel, if my doing got you killed? You want to load that on my head? How do you think your parents would feel if you got killed doing something like this? Glois, you told me you don't have any brothers or sisters and your father's gone? Who's going to take care of your mother? Utelel, you're going to be Eolt someday, do you want to miss that for a silly game that isn't a game at all?" He stared somberly at them, shook his head. "You did a good thing, warning us about the spy. You saved my life, maybe all our lives. Now go home and stay away from the Marish."

He watched them ride slowly away, then collapsed into his seat, pulling a handkerchief from his sleeve and wiping the sudden sweat off his face. "They're good kids. Bright and full of the devil in all the right ways. Gods, I hate this!" He cracked his palm down on his thigh. "I HATE THIS."

Aslan put her hand on his arm. "I know. It's why we do what we do. Save a little so when the bad times are past people can reclaim what they had."

He pulled his arm away, started the jit turning. "That doesn't help right now, Scholar."

He tensed as he took the ramp back onto the causeway, slapped in the accelerod until the jit was roaring along at its top speed. "Don't hesitate, Scholar. If the telltale whispers, sweep that stunner through a one eighty, then drop."

They were almost to the bridge when the first buzz sounded.

He slowed the jit to a crawl when they reached the far side of the river and mopped at his head again. "I'm going after him," he said. "That spy. I'm going to kill that bastard." He glanced at the single barge tied up at the landing and took the roundabout instead of the direct route to the Gate since the trade ground was busy today.

"Marrin. . . ."

"Don't tell me to leave it to the Goës. He may be slick as a greased sikker when it comes to trade, but he hasn't got a clue how to fight this kind of war."

"I'm not trying to tell you anything, Marrin. Only think about what you're risking."

"I get kicked off University?"

"No. That's not the problem. You could get killed."

"That's not a problem."

"You so sure of yourself?"

"No, but the dead don't give a hot jak about anything."

"It'll be harder for you to find projects."

"You saying you won't recommend me?"

"Tsah! Marrin, you want to get killed?"

"I'm not suicidal, if that's what you're thinking. You didn't answer me."

"Yes. I'll recommend you. But you know how rumors bloom round those halls. You'll be giving away a big edge if you get a reputation for jumping in the sun."

"If that's all that's bothering you. . . ." He stopped the jit outside the gate to the Enclave, hit the horn.

"Ahhh! Sometimes. . . . You remind me far too

much of a man called Quale. Nice guy, but he drives me crazy sometimes."

Carefully not smiling, Marrin watched Aslan smiling and subtly flattering the Goës before she got to the hard bargaining. The Yarak was enjoying it, too, quite aware of what was happening. It confirmed that part of his opinion about the Goës, a really good trader and exec. But he had the weakness that went with the gift, a conviction that people were always persuadable and that, ultimately, reason won over passion. An illusion, that. Sometimes a fatal one.

". . . nearly finished what we can do in the Dumel. I'd like to shut down the station in Alsekum and head out along the Menguid on one of the sailbarges. More than just for study, I must confess. For the past several nights the harper Shadith has not been in communication with us. University will be most unhappy if something serious has happened to her. While she is quite competent at taking care of herself, I am determined to discover what happened." She drew in a long breath. "All the more since something very troubling has happened."

Marrin looked down at his hands, concentrated on keeping them relaxed as Aslan sketched out the events of the past several days.

". . . from the gossip of the swampies. Not just gossip now. In my eyes, the reports are amply confirmed by the cutter my Aide discovered beside the chorek's body. And by the crease you'll find cut into the body of the jit, if you go down and examine it. A souvenir of today's attack."

"If you'll wait here a moment . . ." The Goës rose with the elastic grace of the Yaraka, leaving the room with as much haste as he thought comported with his dignity.

Aslan leaned back in her pulochair, closed her eyes. Marrin looked round the luxurious office. Only the

Goës' second best office at that. *Running the show on gall and charm, a double-hinged tongue his best weapon. Seven techs, a handful of aides, a few guards and god only knows how many laborers. Less than a dozen probably. Contract labor. Won't arm them, so they're no use. Spies? Who knows. Yaraka and Chandavasi don't usually go head on head like this. They stay in their own realms. Bad time to be low on the learning curve.*

Aslan and Marrin stood as the Goës came striding in. "As always in an entry situation," he said with a graceful wave of his hand that meant they should sit down and be comfortable—which they carefully refrained from doing until he was seated. "We are short of hands to do the work. However, I have managed to detach a few guards from other duties. They will take a few locals with them and check the fringes of the Marish to dislodge any ambushes and carry in any of the um choreks you might have caught with the stunners. As to your intention of traveling in-country, I don't see how I can permit that. Not until we know more about how deeply the spy has penetrated into local society. You did say that the young musician you brought along is not associated officially with University?"

"Shadith is rather more than a simple musician, Goës Koraka hoeh Dexios. She has a number of interesting friends whom you might not care to annoy. You will have heard of the Hunters of Wolff, more specifically a Hunter by name Aleytys; they are closer than sisters. You will also have heard of the Dyslaera of Voallts Korlach on Spotchals. She was adopted into the Voallts clan as daughter of Miralys. There are others I could name. Life could be very unpleasant if these folks somehow got the notion you interfered with our efforts to locate her."

"Threats, Scholar?"

"Certainly not, Goës. Merely an objective and measured assessment of the situation."

"I see. And if a flake of this conversation were sent to the head of your School?"

"That is your privilege, Goës. Feel free to do whatever you choose."

"I see. If I allow you to leave, you'll sign a release?"

"For myself and if I'm allowed to write it, yes. And if you have a Register File intact. University has a standard form which should be acceptable to your legal department." She smiled. "This isn't the first time the problem has arisen. As to Aide Ola and Manager Shears, they will have to speak for themselves."

"If you'll provide a flake for the legalware to look over, I'm sure we can work something out. When were you thinking of leaving?"

"That will depend upon how soon we can get passage on a barge. I wanted to clear matters with you, Goës Koraka, before I started making arrangements." She stood. "If you want my testimony under Verifier, it is yours without condition. I do not like what is being done to these people."


Marrin drove past the track parked at the beginning of the causeway. "And we hope they're finally doing their job since their being here makes Shears' telltales useless."

"I know. You rank me right up with the Goës for cluelessness, don't you."

"From what I can see, Scholar, you've led a singularly sheltered life." He kept his eyes moving, scanning the silent green front of the Marish as if the flicker of the leaves and the flutter of hanging lichen webs could give him the answers the telltale wouldn't.

"Tactful. And very like my mother." She was silent a while. The darkness under the trees, the stagnant water with its reeds and clouds of insects, the gauzy lichen like ancient webs of gigantic spiders, the stillness of the place, all of that seemed to settle over her and give her voice an oddly muffled quality when she finally spoke. "It has always amazed me how most physically competent, practical people have such a low opinion of a Scholar's imaginative competence even when they are very bright themselves."

"In my case, if you want a serious answer, Scholar. . . ."

"I would prefer one, yes."

He frowned at the stretch of causeway left, glanced over his shoulder, reached up and tapped on the tell-tale. "On Picabral, men whose skills lay only in the mind generally died before puberty. It gives one a viewpoint perhaps a little skewed."

"I see."

"A dull and bloody place, Scholar. You wouldn't find much interesting there. Such a world tends to a deadly uniformity, the more so since anyone with a touch of your imaginative competence . . . by the way, I rather like that phrase . . . removes himself at the first possible moment." He sighed with relief as he started down the ramp. "Though I wouldn't put you among those who only dream. But you have been sheltered from a great deal that might help you plan right now."

"Hm." It was a small and exceedingly skeptical sound almost lost in the hum of lifters. It trailed off into a sigh as she leaned back and let the stunner rest in her lap. "We'll have to crate the gear and get the Metau and Teseach to give it storage room in the Meeting House. That should be safe enough. You and Dunc start running the analysis of the interviews, get everything encrypted and duplicated into flakes. Just in case. I've three more interviews set up for tomorrow. Might as well finish those before we leave. Besides, one of them is a bargeman's wife. Won't be direct help, no doubt, but maybe I can pick up some useful information."

"No more argument?"

"About going after the Chav? I don't waste my breath." She wrinkled her longish nose, laughed at him. "Besides, Shadow may already have dealt with him. She can be a very sudden woman when she chooses."

"I've heard rumors. That the truth you told the Goës?"

"Now, Marrin, I'm surprised at you. You think I'd lie?" She grinned. "When every word I spoke is going through analysis by traders used to listen for nuance?" She sobered. "And I'll probably have to submit to the Verifier when this business is over. You, too. Remember that."

"Me?" He blinked, looked startled. "Why? I'm only a student."

"Because this is a Trade Matter. Which means Helvetia. I've been through one of their condemnation trials. They pick nits like no one else. Which means everyone, including you, Dunc, and a sample of the Béluchar who can speak as direct witnesses to the burnings. Goës Koraka hoeh Dexios knows all of this, Marrin. It's why he's being so very very careful in everything he does. This is life and death for Yaraka and Chandavasi."

He looked out over the placid fields with the herds and their drowsy keepers, the farmers working in their fields, weeding, irrigating, planting things whose names he didn't know, whose uses he had even less idea about. The sky was empty of Eolt, but a few clouds stretched in long arcing wisps across a deep blue dome. Such peace was deceptive, he knew, this was no godhome perfection, but filled with stresses and strains and the thousand thousand ways that life can go wrong for people, especially when two such disparate species tried to live together. But they did try, and there had been peace. This wasn't a stagnant world; things changed, but they had changed at Béluchad's own pace and in ways peculiar to this dual species called Béluchar. And the Eolt were a wonder. The first time he'd seen them, they'd been like jewels carved from amber, and when he heard them singing in that grand chorus ... the memory stung a sterner anger out of him and a determination to pull together for himself the Chandavasi files. They were there in the Rekordek, he'd just been too busy to look into them.

Duncan Shears was waiting in the stable the Blai Olegan had cleaned out to house the jit. "Metau and Teseach have been by," he said. "They want to see you soonest, Scholar."

"About what?" Aslan swung down from the jit, pushing her hair back from her face. "They give you any idea?"

"Probably Glois and Utelel," Marrin said. "Finally got around to doing what they should have done yesterday."

"Hm. Dunc, were they angry or what?"

"Serious but not hostile."

"Then that's all right. I'd better get cleaned up first. Marrin will fill you in. Things are going to start changing very quickly."

"Enclave?"

"You don't sound happy about it."

"I'm not."

"Well, we're not. We're going to go inland and hunt for Shadith."

"I was thinking about that. Away from here to anywhere is a good idea."

## 3

"Ihoi! I'm weak as a rotted rootbulb." Danor grunted, tried to push himself up.

Shadith rose from the cot where she was drowsing,

opened the slide on the nightlight and carried it across
to the bed. "So you're with us again." She set the
nightlight down, bent down, touched his face. "Good.
For a while there I thought you were going to burn
this place down around you, that fever had you so
hot."

"Place. Where are we?"

"Blai at Dumel Minach."

"How long . . . ?"

"Six days. You nearly died from the fever and the
allergies, but Tokta Burek got you through."

"Allergies?"

"There was a point when I had to use things from
my medkit on you. They worked enough so we didn't
kill you by moving you but caused some problems
later." She managed a smile. "Might have fried a few
nerves, but with some rest you'll do all right."

"Rest. We've already lost six days." His voice went
shrill on the end, and he tried to push himself up.

Shadith clucked her tongue, bent over him, her
hands on his shoulders, not applying pressure yet, just
letting him know she could. "And we'll lose even
more if you tear open that wound. Relax. Mer-Eolt
Lebesair went on ahead to let the Meruu know what
happened. Xe got back yesterday. They'll wait for us."

"The dying won't wait. Leave me and go on."

"Yes, we could do that, but you've seen what we
could only report second hand, Ard Da. . . ."

"Don't call me Ard. My sioll's dead." That outburst
used the last of his energy; he went limp, turning his
head so she wouldn't see the tears coursing from his
eyes.

She touched his hair lightly, straightened, filled a
glass from the ewer on the bedtable. "I've poured you
some water. It's on the table here, just stretch out
your hand when you want it. I'm on the cot by the
window, call me if you need anything."

She stretched out, yawned, but couldn't recover the

drifty doze she'd been in when he called out. She'd done everything she could think of to get the handcom working again, but repairing solid state electronics with a screwdriver and a talent for mindlifting small objects wasn't a very hopeful project to start with and she got the results she'd expected. She thought about throwing the thing away as useless weight, but she couldn't quite bring herself to do that. Not yet.

Aslan would be bothered over no reports coming back, but she wouldn't worry too much. Shadith smiled into the darkness, remembering the Scholar's acerbic comments on administrative stupidity. *Not one to suffer fools lightly, Aslan. Talking about fools. Smugglers bringing in guns. Those were offworld pellet shooters the choreks had. I should have taken them apart instead of just leaving them beside the corpses. Well, no time for it, I'll just have to live with that. Won't be Arel. How odd to come across word of him again. Or maybe not so odd. The Callidara was part of his round before Bogmak. And won't he be pissed if the Chave win the prize and shut the world on him.* She sighed.

She was deeply tired, but sleep kept eluding her no matter how she tried to clear her mind. In a few days, less than a week, she'd be answering questions for the Meruus. *What happens after that? I've done what Aslan brought me along to do. Now what happens. What do I do? What do I do? Burning Eolt.* She shuddered. *That has to stop. I have to help. Somehow. Aslan can testify, say we make it offworld. Which may be a very iffy thing. The Ykkuval has to know he doesn't dare let us get away. What do I do? Go after them. Use what I can do ... animal armies ... I haven't tried it with budders ... I wonder if I can mindride local vermin? Hm. No, don't try it now, you get started, you'll never get to sleep.*

She heard the clink of the glass, thought about going over to help the Fior; after a moment, though, she decided he'd feel better doing as much for himself as he could. *In the morning, soon as Maorgan gets back from whatever bed he's found, I'll ask him to give Danor a bath and a shave. Gods, I hope we get out of here soon, this place is growing on me like mold.*

### 4

Amalia Udaras was a middle-aged woman with gray-streaked brown hair. Her face was round, comfortable, still pretty, her eyes big and a dark strong blue. She'd chosen to be interviewed in the garden of her house where she had a good view of the river.

"I like to sit out here when I have a little time and the day's a clear one. My Tamhan, he's Kabit on the *Ploësca*, my eldest boy, Dolbary, he was good at making things even when he was barely crawling, he's carpenter's mate on the *Morrail*, and my second boy, Beill, he's prenticed to the pilot on the *Grassul*. Never a one of them ever had a doubt in his head that he'd be working the river when his time came. I've always wished I'd had a daughter or two, but Beill came hard and after him, I couldn't have more. Cha oy, Chel Dé has his reasons."

"Kabit. An interesting word when you look at the roots. A well/source. The rule. Will you explain it, Amalia Udaras?"

"Ah. The Kabit of a sailbarge is two things at once, Scholar. He holds coin, lends and collects interest on coin lent. Because he is moving continually along the river, this is convenient for traders and storekeepers. My Tamhan is a clever man, numbers dance for him, though he hasn't as much time for them as he likes. He has two apprentices who do much of the actual accounting. He is also the chief officer of the barge, concerned with cargo, crew, and safe sailing. Is that sufficient?"

"Not only sufficient but interesting. I'd like to interview him if he can find a moment to talk with me. But that's for later. Go on with what you were telling me."

"As I said, I like to sit out here and watch the river. It's like it ties me to my Tamhan and Dolbary and Beill. There, you see that bit of slickery there on the water, means there was a storm up near the mountains a few days ago, there's something in the soil up there that makes that glitter when the river's carrying new mountain mud. I used to worry when I saw that and understood what it meant. I still do, a little. You know every ten years we have the Blianta Simur which is rather like the Mengerak. The Children's Walk. Did they tell you about that? Cha Oy. The Blianta Simur is a pilgrimage like that. People travel to shrines or just go visiting, or go to Chuta Meredel to study something. Not everyone, of course. Most folks only make one Blianta in their lives, though some do three or four. And if you're always traveling like my Tamhan, cha oy, you just don't bother. But one year he got permission for me to come on the barge with him so I could make my Blianta. What? Oh, yes. They do take passengers sometimes. Some barges. It depends upon the Kabit. Some don't like having dirteaters on their boats. That's what they call us, you know, even me, though I'm married and mother to the river, you might say. Anyway, we went through a terrible storm, but the barge it was tight and rode easy enough, so I haven't worried near so much since. Mostly, if you're on a barge and not part of the crew, you're expected to keep out of the way at all times, otherwise you might find yourself on shore and walking."

"Barge season. It's high season now. You will see a lot of traffic on the river these days. The season generally runs from Kirrayl through Termallyl, that's thaw through to the first big snowfall, though if it's a mild winter in the mountains sometimes the first barges will leave in Diokayl, unless it's a Fifth year when Diokayl loses a day and is called Getrentyl, that's an old word for Sorrow, you know. When Dio-kayl is Getrentyl, no one starts anything. It is very bad luck. The children who are born in Getrentyl have a curse on them, they either die young or go bad some way. The Denchoks never bud in the winter months so they are spared that."

"How long is Tamhan usually away? That varies according to how far upriver he goes and what loads he finds. If he fills up early, he comes back sooner. In general, though, in season he is away between forty and fifty days each trip and each season he will make around five trips. In the winter, when the barge is in drydock, he consults with the owners, works on the books, looks over the loans to see which are current and which look like they might go bad on him, makes plans for the next season, and oversees repairs and cleaning of the barge. Time he has left over, he plays dissa or droic with the other bargemen, works on our house—he's neat fingered and clever, Dolbary gets his talent from his Da—goes to Council meetings and does the thousand small things he's had to let go since Spring."

"Me? Oh, what I do isn't very interesting. Just a lot of little things. I make the boys' clothes and keep them mended. Tamhan gets his shore clothes made by the tailor, of course. He has to look just right when he's talking with merchants and mill owners and miners. I do make his workshirts, though. And I make the covers for the furnishings in his cabin on the barge. I do needlepoint, it's something I take pleasure in. I make up my own designs and Tamhan tells me they are much admired, so perhaps Dolbary gets a little of his gift from his mother, too. I take care of the house. I take my turn fixing lunch at the school. I help the Denchok and the other Dumel wives arrange things for the fetes and rites and celebrations. Why just this last Summerday, I baked the suncakes and the berry bread and kept an eye on the children as they strung pennants and looped poppers around to make the fine noise of the Summer Greeting."

"I am also a perfumer. I distill and blend, do concentrates which I sell to the soapmaker. It is easier to do this when Tamhan is away; some of the smells are a bit overpowering. He is always bringing me new essences, flowers and other things for my distillery and glass bottles and tubing from the Glasshouse at Dumel Olterau. And he sells my perfumes in all the Dumels he stops at. I enjoy very much the creation of new blends and it helps the family prosper."

"I do keep busy when Tamhan's gone, though when he comes home I like to keep a lighter schedule. I like to fuss over him a bit, listen to his tales. He's always got interesting things to tell me. I've been on two other Bliantas with him since that first time and it's always good to hear again of places I've seen."

"It is sad that Dolbary and Beill are almost never home when Tamhan is. Nor do they see each other all that often, except to wave to if their barges happen to pass. A time or two they've tied up together, but not often. Their rounds are just too different. Cha oy, if you live from the river, you live by river's time."

## 5

Shadith glanced over her shoulder at the litter ponies. Danor seemed to be handling the jolting all right.

Night before last, after xe had inspected Danor, ignoring the Fior's agitated complaints, Tokta Burek let Shadith tug xe from the room.

"He won't listen," she said.

Tokta Burek had just shrugged, xe's lichen-web creaking with the movement. "He'll fret himself dead," xe said, "you might as well start on again and see if you can get him to rest come nightfall. He'll not let the jarring stop him getting better, you needn't worry over that. The chert's too dammalheaded to die.

You said he's been drinking smoke. That's where those blisters come from, his body fighting the need, trying to revert to the way it was before. Can't be too far gone, or he would be dead. I'll give you some doses of the roec and a lotion to spread on his skin for the pustules. It will take a few weeks to work the irritants from the smoke out of his system."

"Hunh! He's an irritant to my system."

Burek chuckled. "A talking boil," xe said. Xe touched her cheek, the one with the hawk etched on it. "I have deeply enjoyed your art, Shadowsong. By next year I will have spun my husk and be dreaming the change time away and you will be part of those dreams."

Remembering, her eyes stung. Impatiently she drew her hand across them and once again set her mind-touch to probing the dark silent forest that closed in around and over them, only a few flickers of sunlight reaching the road through the heavy canopy. She was riding a few pony lengths in front of Maorgan who was leading the single packer and the two litter ponies and looking a bit strained.

That was because Melech had gone on ahead with Lebesair. With their gas sacs and thin membranes they were vulnerable to pellet guns. One hit wouldn't bother them much, the hole would seal itself before too much of their lift leaked away. Enough hits, though, and the weight of lead as well as the loss of gas would bring them down. An Eolt on the ground was a dead Eolt.

Wild lives brushed against her touch, feral beasts descended from the fertilized ova brought by the Fior, budding beasts that had developed here, and the curious mixes that she didn't know how to explain. No, mix wasn't quite the right word. Blend? Alloy rather than compound? Like the moss ponies, two strands of life style woven into a quirky whole.

In any case, no danger to them.

They stopped at intervals to feed and water the po-

nies. That was doubly important now that they had
no spares. They stopped at noon to eat and let Shadith
check Danor's bandages and see how he was holding
up.

Tokta Burek was right, the journey seemed to be
speeding up the healing rather than setting him back.
His temper wasn't improved and his weakness meant
it came out in spates of complaint and jabs at Shadith
and Maorgan. Shadith caught him watching Maorgan
with an evil satisfaction at seeing the Ard suffering
the absence of his Eolt.

Mid-afternoon Shadith rode round a bend and saw
a group of Fior and Denchok leaning on shovels and
contemplating the bridge over the creek that crossed
the road. The water foamed around rocks and hit the
bridge piers with a force that made them shudder visi-
bly. She waved Maorgan to a stop, then rode forward
till she reached the group.

"Oso, Meathlan. Is the bridge safe for the crossing?
We carry an injured Fior to Chuta Meredel and can't
stretch too much circling."

They turned and stared silently at her with a blank-
faced stolidity that was as intimidating as it was irritat-
ing. She'd met this response many times before in her
long life, so she simply sat with her hands resting on
the pommel, waiting for one of them to make up his
or xe's mind to speak.

A Denchok set hands on xe's hips, looked from
Shadith to Maorgan just visible behind her. "Injured?"

Maorgan raised his brows. When Shadith nodded,
he rode a few steps forward, enough so the Denchok
could see the litter.

"Chorek," Shadith said. "Tokta Burek fetched his
fever down, but we've got to get him to Meredel."

"Best keep a hard watch out, the choreks're bad
round here. Politicals, lot of them, chased out of Ordumels down Plain and landed on us. And there's no

dumels for shelter 'tween here and Medon Pass. Take
it slow, maybe better get the litter over first. Storm
winds last night kicked a couple planks off and the
water loosened the piers some when it rose. We were
just figuring how to shore them up till we can get a
builder from Minach."

When Maorgan tried to lead the litter ponies onto
the bridge, they set their feet, hunched their heads
down, and wouldn't budge. Shadith clicked her
tongue, slid from the saddle. "Best let me do that,
Ard."

Danor swore weakly as she edged past the ponies.
She ignored him, rubbed the poll of the off bearer
and considered how much control she should exert.
These tough stubborn little beasts liked ground solid
beneath their feet, not shifting about with little
screeching whines. She rather did, herself. She could
feel uneasiness on the verge of solidifying into fear.
That wasn't good. She eased into the mindfield, not
trying to see through the pony's eyes, only to give him
a sense of warmth and security.

After a minute of her massaging his poll and his
brain at the same time, he relaxed a little. She repeated the process on the other litter pony, then
stepped away from them and pulled off her boots. She
tossed them onto the road and walked the bridge, feet
clinging to the worn planks, feeling them shudder
against her soles. Through the openings left by the
windripped planks, she could see the water hammering
at the supports. They were right, though, it would hold
if she could keep the ponies calm.

She came back. "Ard, your harp, play us across,
hm? The Mad Mara's Lament I taught you a while
back so I can serenade our little friends here."

"Wild things fluttered in my head," she sang and
remembered another time she'd sung that song, sitting

in a cage, waiting to be sold to a bunch of bloody-handed priests.

> *"Wild wings fluttered in my head*
> *And wild thoughts muttered there*
> *In waking dreams I saw you dead*
> *Your body rent, your throat gone red*
> *Your splendid thighs ripped bare.*
> *I cannot sleep, cruel love*
> *Memory's my Mourning Dove*
> *Cuckoos call out, hornéd maid*
> *See your faithless lover fade*
> *All oaths broke, all hope betrayed...."*

With the last notes, the caöpa stepped from the bridge, snorting as he let her lead him clear. She hitched the leadrope to a convenient sapling and ran back across the swaying timbers, collected her boots, pushed them into a saddlebag, then went back to work coaxing the other caöpas across.

The swaying was worse, the footing more uncertain, so this time it was harder to get them going, even with her mindtouch soothing them, but the harp music helped. They were used to the sound and it covered all but the worst of the noises from the bridge.

As Shadith swung into the saddle, the Denchok on the far side of the swollen creek cupped his hands about his mouth and called, "Watch out for choreks. Thick as fleas."

She waved to him, then rode Bréou around the litter ponies and took her place in front. "Let's go."

It is the peculiar quality of water sounds that they can be quite loud and yet inaudible a few minutes off. Before they'd gone more than a few score paces along the road, all Shadith could hear was the wind creaks of the trees and the pattery sound of the leaves. Now and then a flurry of sound broke across this background and once she saw a small flier turn into jewels when it darted through a sunbeam, ruby and emerald on the carapace, with diamond wings. The Forest hummed around her, the peace as thick as the shadow that lay across the road, the trees giants now, rising ten or twelve times her height. Their trunks were rough textured, the bark deeply incised and so loose that they looked like they had the mange, patches of old bark in place, dark gray and spongy, patches of new pale green and rough as if someone had used a rasp on them. The distance between the trees increased with their height, but the forest didn't open out like others she'd seen. Even though the light under the canopy was minimal, spikes of fungus rose everywhere, pastel and pulpy, pale pink, ocher, grayish-green, ivory. Lichen vines spread from trunk to ground in fan-shaped webs and giant slimemolds spread like golden syrup across the ground. The air had an odd mixture of conifer bite and fungal musk.

She kept the mindtouch sweeping from side to side, reaching as far as she could. Back and forth, back and forth, almost soothing in its regularity. Back and forth, back and forth, the road a green and pastel tunnel ahead, gently curving, following the swell of the mountains, rising and falling only a little, sometimes a small cut into the mountain to keep the level easy, sometimes a hardpacked fall of scree glued in place with concrete.

They stopped to feed and water the caöpas. Danor feigned sleep so she'd leave him alone. He needn't have bothered. She was too tired to fool with him. She sat a while wondering if she should put her boots back on, at the same time rather enjoying the freedom for her feet. Probably not a good idea in this place, no telling what bacteria or parasites she was picking up. She didn't move. It was hot and the air was heavy and her feet felt good as they were.

Maorgan made her some tea and scolded her into

eating some dried fruit he'd cut into small pieces so they'd be easier to swallow. She needed the energy and got the fruit down, though her gorge rose at the thought of eating and her throat tried to close on her.

On the road again. Back and forth. Back and forth. Drowned in deepening green twilight and the heavy odor from the lichen, molds, and other fungi. Back and forth. Back and forth.

Late in the day, when it was almost time to stop for the night, she felt a burn at the farthest point of her reach.

"Hold it. There's something. . . ."

*Rage/satisfaction/anticipation. . . .*

*Male aura. Fior. About a kilometer on.* She slid from the saddle, walked a few steps from Bréou, set herself and swept her mindtouch in a slow arc, focusing all her attention into the touch, dragging in as much information as she could.

*One man. One caöpa. No backup, just him.*

With an exploding sigh, she came back to her body, started as she saw Maorgan standing beside her.

"What is it?" he said.

"Ambush. One man. Angry. Must be a political." She untied the thongs on the saddlebag and took her boots out. She sat in the middle of the road, wiped her feet with her kerchief, and began the painful process of getting the boots back on.

"What are you doing?"

"Going after him, of course. You lead the caöpas at a slow walk, I circle round behind him and nail him with the stunner." She grunted as her heel finally dropped home, then started working the other foot into its boot.

"Shadowsong. . . ."

She looked up. "Don't be tedious, Maorgan. It was the truth I told you back there on the first day out, not just a story to pass the time. This is what I do, what I have done a hundred times before." She wig-

gled her foot, yanked on the boot tops and seated the
second heel, got to her feet and brushed herself off.
"As far as I can tell—and this isn't all that accurate,
mind you—the chorek's in a tree about half a sikkom
ahead. If I'm not on the road waiting, do what you
have to do."

She waited until she heard the clip-clop of pony
hooves and Maorgan's whistled tune winding lazily
past the spears of fungus. Wrinkling her nose with
distaste, she began circling around to get behind the
chorek, pushing her way through those spears, the
pulpy stalks breaking apart and squishing under her
boot heels, the smell intensifying with every step. The
slimy pulp from the fungus made her bootsoles dan-
gerously slick. She fell twice, the first time when her
foot came down on one of the slimemolds while she
was concentrating too hard to keeping the touch on
the chorek, the second as she was trying to hurry
across an open section and get to shelter.

The smell worried her and she stopped to check
the wind. It was slow, sluggish—and blowing from the
direction of the chorek so that was all right. *Have to
be careful*, she thought, *funny to think cracking a stink
would be as big a danger as cracking a twig underfoot.*

She saw him finally, a dark blot in a rope cradle
about three meters up one of the trunks. He'd sunk
spikes into the wood to hold the rope ends and pulled
the thick loose bark out from the wood, using the curl
to mask him from the road. She saw him stiffen as he
heard Maorgan's whistle. He moved slightly, brought
something gray and short up from where it had been
resting, sighted it on the road, and waited. *Not a pellet
gun. What is that?*

Shadith wiped her hands on her shirt, eased the
stunner from the leather sack dangling from her belt.
She wiped her hands again, made a last sweep of the
surround to verify he was alone, shot him.

The weapon fell with a clank onto the tall roots of the tree, rolled off toward the road. The chorek was draped over the ropes, his mouth open, eyes rolled back, the whites glistening in the murky light under the canopy.

Watching him intently to make sure no twist in his genes made him a tricky candidate for stunning, she made her way to the foot of his tree and collected the thing he'd dropped. She stood staring at it for several moments, deeply shocked. Pellet guns were one thing, in a pinch most smugglers would carry a few for trading, but energy weapons? That was big time trouble. The only time she'd seen it happen was on Avosing, and that was only because there was major value being exchanged. But one ragtag bandit on a nondescript world?

She tested the cutter on the limb of a tree close by, then used it to burn loose one end of the rope cradle, not caring a whole lot whether or not the man survived the fall.

He was limp from the stunning and not that high up. He hit the downslanting roots, rolled onto the ground, and finished the roll not far from where she'd found the cutter. She checked his pulse, nodded, straightened his legs, then moved to the center of the road, waiting for Maorgan to show.

Maorgan looked down at the man. "Don't know him. Where was he?"

She flicked a hand at the tree, then frowned as Danor came tottering around the ponies. The Melitoëhn's eyes were focused on the chorek, his face was flushed, his body tense despite his weakness, there was a bulge inside his shirt that didn't come from bandages. Where he'd got the knife or whatever it was, she didn't know. "Danor, no." She spoke deliberately, then put herself between the stunned man and the Ard. "We need to question him first."

"Him?" The old man's voice was stronger than it'd been in days. "He wouldn't tell you the sun's shining though you could see it for yourself."

Shadith smiled grimly. "He won't have a choice. I've got some babble juice that will no doubt kill him eventually so you can rest easy about that, but before then he'll cough everything he knows."

He looked at her a long moment, then nodded. "Get on with it, then."

Maorgan crouched beside the chorek, searching through his pockets, laying out their contents on the ground beside the man. He looked up as Shadith came back, her medkit in her hand. "Nothing here to say who he is." He flicked a finger through the meager pile, sent a luck charm rolling away, uncovered a bit of paper, passed it to her. "Someone in Dumel Minach, laying out our route and what speed we're likely to make."

"Confirms he's a political, if we needed such confirmation. Here." She handed him a tape braided from fine colorless filaments. "Wrap that round his ankles and make sure the metal bits on the end touch. You don't need to tie it."

He raised his brows. "Looks like it'd melt in my hand, let alone hold a grown man."

"Try to cut it if you don't mind dulling your blade. Don't worry, you won't even scratch it. Give me room to work, hm?" She took his place, strapped the chorek's wrists with a second come-along tape. When she glanced at Maorgan, he was looking at a nick in the knifeblade.

He shrugged, wrapped the tape around the chorek's ankles, touched the locktights. Nothing obvious happened, so he tried to take them apart and redo the seal.

Shadith chuckled. "Useful gadget, right?"

"How do you get the things off?"

"I've got, mm, call it a key. Otherwise, to get him out of those loops we'd have to amputate his hands and feet. Well, well, so you're coming awake on us now." She got to her feet and stepped back to wait for him to exhaust himself and recognize futility.

The chorek's eyes cleared. He saw them, and his face suffused with rage; he tried to break loose, throwing his body about, but all he succeeded in doing was cut himself on the filament tapes. After a useless struggle he lay panting and glaring hate at them, especially Maorgan. "Jelly sucker, you a dead man. And all your kind a perverts."

Shadith opened the medkit, took out the spraycopeia, clicked on the mostly illegal canister of babblers Digby had sent her on the day she'd adopted as her birthday, the day Aleytys had decanted her into this body. She set the blood sampler in the sterilizer and deposited the medkit on the road. "We're going to ask you some questions, chorek. Now I know you think you wouldn't tell us the time of day, but you will." The sterilizer chimed. She took the sampler out, caught one of his hands, set the nozzle against a finger tip and triggered it. In almost the same move, she was back on her feet and he was staring at the red drop welling on his finger.

"You needn't look like the world fell on you, chorek. All I did was take a little blood from you." She clicked the sampler into its slot on the spraycopeia. "I don't want to kill you too soon." She glanced at the readout, sighed. "In a laboratory with a much wider range of ... mm ... ingredients, I could probably guarantee not to kill you at all. As things are ..." she touched the sensor, made a few fine adjustments, "the least this brew will give you is a course of boils from hell. Now. Such ethics as I have tell me I must ask if you will answer our questions freely and without stint. Well?"

He spat, the glob of spittle landing on the toe of her boot.

"Sit on him a moment, will you, Maorgan?" She detached the canister from the spraycopeia. "Hold his head so I can get at his neck."

In spite of his struggles, she got the injector against his carotid and triggered the jolt of babble. She straightened. "That's good. You can get off him now, Maorgan. Don't talk to him yet, wait till I tell you."

Glancing now and then at the chorek, she repacked the medkit, set the sampler in the sterilizer, and closed the lid. By the time she was finished, the chorek had gone limp, his face greenish white under the tan, his eyes closed, his breathing deep and slow.

"Good. Maorgan, let me talk first, then you can ask your questions. It might be a good idea to make a note of his answers." She moved along the road, knelt when she was just beyond his head. "What is your name?" She almost sang the words, her voice soft and unthreatening. "Tell me your name."

"Ferg. Fergal Diocas." His voice was dragged and dreamy, the syllables mushy.

"Ferg. You have a friend in Dumel Minach. Tell me your friend's name. What is your friend's name?"

"Paga. Her name is Paga Focai."

"That's a pretty name. Is she pretty, Ferg?"

He laughed. It was an ugly sound, mocking and angry. "That silly bitch? Big as a dammalt with a laugh like a band saw. Always at you. Chel Dé, I have to be drunk as a dog to get it up when I do her."

"I see. It was her gave you news about the Ard and the rest of them?"

"Oh, yeah, and wetting herself because she knows I'll come do her when I finish the scum. She gets off on blood, nothing gets her hotter."

"And how does she get word to you? How does she do that, Ferg?" She kept her voice soft and insinuating, slipping the words in between the rustle of the leaves and the dirt grains rattling along the road as the wind picked up strength with the waning of the day.

He snickered. "Leaves me notes, doesn't she. Silly kueh. Games! Love post she calls it like she was some just blooded girl. Hollow in a tree down by river. Ties a bit a yellow rag on branch when she put something in hole."

His eyelids flickered, his eyes darted side to side, a buried awareness worked the muscles of his face. Shadith stopped the questions and sang to him, a low, wordless croon like a mother singing a child to sleep. After a moment he relaxed and the smug grin twisted his mouth again. "Kueh," he said.

"No doubt. You had a weapon. A strange looking thing."

"Cutter," he said after a while. "Ol' frogface he say, point it at a stinking jelly and you got yourself one krutchin' Summerfire tree high and mountain wide. Hooooeeeshhh!"

Shadith heard a scuffling behind her, curses. She ignored them, crooned a bit more to settle the chorek again. "Old Frogface, hmm, I think I know him, tell me what he's like."

"Ugly anglik. Shorter'n me but twice as wide. Skin's like lehaum bark. Made me want to see 'f I could peel him like them there." He waved his bound hands at the nearest tree. He blinked at the hands, waggled them, started snickering. "Peel 'um. 'Ould d't too, he come back at me. Peel 'um. Peel. . . ." He let his hands drop, scowled at the branches arching high above the road. "Mesuch, filthy. . . ."

Shadith leaned closer to him, began one of the Shalla croons, drawing him back into dream with the help of the drug. "Tell me about his hands. What were they like?"

"Curséd claws, black as his stinking soul."

"Tell me about his eyes. Was there anything odd about his eyes."

"Stuff crawled over 'um sometimes, made 'um shine."

"What did he say to you? Tell me exactly what he said to you."

His eyelids flickered again, then closed completely, the energy drained from his voice as he droned what he'd been told about how to recharge the cutter, about the price on the heads of the University team. Toward the end of the speech he started getting agitated again and this time the crooning only seemed to exacerbate the disturbance. Words drooled from his mouth as he jerked his head back and forth and tried to pull his wrists apart, jerking so hard the tape cut into his wrists. He ignored the blood and kept jerking, as if he meant to saw off his hands and set himself free.

His face got redder and redder, his eyes glassy, his mouth hung open, working, working . . . until, abruptly his body spasmed, arced up from the ground, then went limp.

"He dead?"

She looked round. Danor was hunched over, his legs drawn up, his head buried in his arms. Maorgan stood beside him. It was he who'd spoken. "I think so, but I'd better be sure. Bring me the kit, would you?"

Shadith keyed the locktights loose, rolled the come-alongs up, and shoved them into a saddlebag. "You heard what he said. There'll be dozens of others out there hungry for that gold. We'd better start pushing the caöpas as hard as we dare. We're targets till we get over Medon Pass."

# 13. Ploy and Counterploy

## 1

Ceam, Heruit, and his cousin Bothim squatted in the shadows under the trees at the edge of the Meklo Fen watching the Chav get off their floatcart and walk toward the swampie Porach who was sitting cross-legged on a thick mat woven from reeds, reed baskets placed around him, filled with fresh fish, herbs, nuts and the round red fruit of the bilim tree that grew deep inside the Marish.

The damp heavy breeze coming off the grass brought the snake-smell of the mesuch to Ceam. His stomach knotted and he felt himself getting hot; it didn't seem to him he could take his eyes off that massive form with its oddly bobbly walk.

As if the mesuch could feel his gaze, the creature turned his head and stared at the group of men.

Ceam fought his eyes down and stared at the black muck he could see through the grass. After watching the techs up in the mountains, he hadn't expected them to be so formidable and so quick to notice up close. And he hadn't expected the smell and what it would do to him. The rage it would rouse in him. It was all he could manage to squat there with his eyes on the ground.

No more game. No more detachment. This was the Enemy. The things that had slaughtered his friends and burned the Eolt, who'd stolen his peace and his joy from him.

The smell got stronger as the mesuch inspected the fish, bit into one of the bilim fruits.

Eolt Kitsek had slid through the clouds last night to tell them the mesuch and their crawlers were back eating the hearts of the mountains. Fewer of them, though, and cautious. A roving tiogri paddling through the ash for roasted carrion set off an alarm, a squalling oogah and a firewand from the crawler singed the spots off the tiogri's tail, though he got away alive, his only hurt a bare behind. That was briefly satisfying, making them waste supplies and their own peace on a danger that wasn't there. No one was interested in the miners, the new target was their home fort.

Heruit moved slightly, dropped his hand on Ceam's shoulder, squeezed. It was both a comfort and a warning. And it helped and did not help, it warmed Ceam with fellow feeling and it irritated him that the older man could read him so easily. *I'm not meant to be a spy. At least, not this kind. This feels so useless, hanging about listening to that beast haggling over how many needles for needlefish.*

The haggling went on and on. Ceam rocked restlessly on his heels, pulled a spear of grass, peeled it into fine strips, pulled another, then another and wondered if he could last much longer without leaping to his feet and running at the monster who was so absurdly acting like all the other merchants he'd seen from the time he was whelped. Obscene that the two of them out there should look so much alike, Porach and the mesuch. Both old. He didn't know how he knew that, mesuch didn't have hair to go gray and they all seemed wrinkled to him, with skin like tree bark. He was, though. Old. Temperish. Yellow cast to eyes that were still far too sharp for Ceam's comfort.

Finally, though, the chaffering was done. Porach was tucking his goods in a c'hau cloth bag, needles and thread, a coil of cord, fine and colorless, some packets of dye. The mesuch snapped his fingers and the two younger ones came and loaded the reed baskets onto the floatwagon.

Porach got to his feet, swung the strap of the bag over his shoulder, caught up the mat, and stood rolling it into a tight cylinder as he watched the floatwagon go gliding off. When it disappeared into the trees, he pulled loose the long stick he'd thrust into the muck and came over to them, swinging the stick and moving with the peculiar long glide of a swampy, his bare feet barely bending the grass or so it seemed to Ceam.

Heruit cleared his throat.

Porach shook his head. "Not here."

They followed him deeper into the Marish. He went back on a new path; Ceam had noticed that the two tendays he'd spent living in the Marish. Swampies almost never used the same path twice in the same day. It might have been to keep down any signs of wear, or perhaps some predator they didn't discuss might be alerted and avoided by this. His curiosity was itching at him, but he knew better than to ask. Swampie wanted you to know something, he told you. Got snarked if you kept pushing at him and one day you'd turn around and he wasn't there any more and you were out in the middle of the morass and didn't know where you were and didn't dare go anywhere because there were softs and crogall burrows where if you stepped in them you were dead.

Porach moved swiftly along the edge of the water, jumped onto the kneed roots of the mekek trees that grew along here, ran across the knees with a curious, irregular, tied-in gait. Ceam followed more slowly. He wasn't used to going about in his bare feet and his soles had picked up some parasites that itched like fury and hurt when his feet slapped down on the slippery, hard wood. Behind him he could hear the sound of Heruit's feet, the muttered curses that got louder the longer they ran. And Bothim's panting snicker as the smaller, more limber man trotted along behind them.

Porach jumped from the roots onto the dimpled sand of a long thin island like the scar from a knife wound. He flung up a hand to stop them, then dug the end of the stick into one of the dimples, inspected the result, and jumped back onto the root. He took a whistle from inside his tunic and began blowing into it. Though it produced no sound that Ceam could hear, it made a tightness behind his eyes.

He smothered an exclamation as he saw the sand shift and shiver as something ran along beneath the surface and vanished beneath the water without giving him the least glimpse of what it looked like.

Porach slipped the stick under his arm, jumped onto the sand and ran along it. The others followed.

He led them on a winding difficult route deep into the Marish, till they reached the twinned isles where they'd been living for the past tenday. The one with their hutches on it was round and barren, thick bug-ridden grass and lichen webs crawling everywhere, a single raintree at one end. Porach's isle was a long pointed oval with a small spring of clean water welling up between two trees into a stone basin. Porach and Meisci his wife had brought stones from outside and cement powder and had built a neat cup with knee-high walls. The stream from the spring ran through it and kept it filled and a shell lid on the top kept it clean.

Porach blew into his whistle again, this time drawing a strange echo from inside the thicket at the end of the island. A moment later Meisci came out and brought for them a long narrow board with folding legs, the portable bridge between the islands.

He'd shown them what swam in that water and Ceam got the shivers each time he got his feet wet, no matter that Porach was along and knew what he was doing.

When the bridge was settled in place, Porach turned. "You are welcome to share a sip of tea and a word or two."

Meisci was a thin, worn-looking woman with strands of gray in her long brown hair. She was shy and half-wild, uneasy with strangers about, though when they came to visit, she knelt behind Porach for the courtesy of it and listened to the talk with curiosity enough to forget herself from time to time. She brought out her china cups, no two of them alike, and filled them with hot strong tea, added slices of ullica fruit and small rounds of unleavened bread.

Heruit emptied his cup and let Meisci take it for a refill. "I can't see as that gets us any forwarder. Unless you got more than I heard out of that ulpioc."

Porach's mouth thinned and curled into a secret smile. "More'n you'd guess."

Heruit made an exasperated sound that pretty well expressed what Ceam was feeling.

Porach's smile widened. He played with the moment, then capitulated according to some schedule of his own. "To start with, that's not one of the big 'uns inside the walls, that's what they call a Drudge. It's him runs the mesuch drink house in Dumel Dordan that was, I picked up other trades isn't first time he done that, easy enough to get him running on about old days. He's an old 'un as mesuch go. Likes to natter on about nought. He pretty pissed at techs for bringing husk to his place and stinking it up and ignoring his brew. He got a pride in his brew and it's like they slighting him when they do that. Besides, it takes 'um funny, he says, sometimes they just get sleepy and hit floor snoring, othertimes they like to go crazy, bust the place up. He says he can tell old hands at it, their haws come half down all time, that's those inside eyelids they drop when they getting fire-bellied."

He pressed his lips together again, no smile this time. His shaggy brows drew inward, a deep trench dug between them. "Couple things to worry on. Less'n a hundred of them right now, but they expecting lots more in a couple months, maybe a bit more. We could maybe wipe the hundred. When it's thousands, I dunno. Worse, was something else ol' Farkly said, one time he and me, we was trading brew, had to sample it like, and he gets feeling loose and one thing he says is mesuch has same problem a while back. 'Nother world. Something on it messed up their techs. Couldn't stop them getting at it, so they stop the world. Cracked it open like you'd stick a nut 'tween you teeth and chomp down. Mucks get too fussed with husk smoking, could be they do the same here."

Heruit scowled. "World's a big nut."

"Cha oy, but when you figure how they get here, maybe they can do it." He supped up some tea, handed his cup to Meisci for a refill. "What I know is bits and pieces. Techs getting itchy one way 'nother. High Mucks not paying 'ttention to what they supposed to be doing. Like when you kick into mutmut nest and watch the itchies run round like crazy. One of ol Farkli, that's his name, one of his humpers, he sidle over to me couple ten days ago, wants to buy husk, I say I don't have any, but I'll ask round. What I think is, you can use that Drudge to get to techs over to Dordan-that-was and worm outta them what you gotta know."

## 2

"You've come to make trouble, haven't you." Parlach was a broad strong woman a little younger than Deänin, with a round face, pouty lips and pale blue eyes. Bland blue eyes, mouth falling into a meaningless smile when she finished speaking.

Deänin looked at her a long moment. "Yes," she said finally and waited for a response.

"Good. Think you can keep it away from the House?"

"Likely."

"Good. What you want?"

"For the moment, information. Discreetly gathered. The inside workings of the mesuch fort."

"Hm. Time limit?"

"No."

"Good. I'm shamed to say I don't have many I trust who have the brains to do that work and not get caught at it."

"Not getting caught is more important than the information."

"I can see that. Someone else you ought to bring in. Sifaed. She works the back room at Farkli's lubbot. Gets more techs than we do, ours is mostly Drudges, and one of her steadies is the Chav who runs the Drudges."

"She tied to the lubbot or does she get out?"

"After she and the other women clean the place, she's mostly loose till noon. I could set up a meet if you want. Best not here. She goes walking round the edges of the Fen when she needs to get away from the mesuch, that's as good a place as any. You know what she looks like?"

"No."

"Big woman, not fat, just heavy. Taller than most. Wide shoulders, wide hips, light brown hair with a lot of red in it, fine flyaway stuff that kinks into tight curls with the least damp in the air. She was a teacher back before the mesuch came, bonded like they do with a Keteng teacher, a Denchok called Bolabel. Mesuch killed xe when they broke up the Dumel. Like they did all the Keteng they saw about."

"I see. Yes, set up a meet two days on, tell her I'll watch her backtrail, make sure she's clear before I show. I'll call her bond's name to show her it's me."

"You sure you want to do that?"

"Yes. How she handles it will tell me things I need to know."

Sifaed was grim-faced, eyes hooded, anger in the set of her shoulders as she stepped into the shadow under the trees and stood waiting for Deänin to show herself.

"Bolabel," Deänin said quietly, then stepped from behind a tree. "How long do you have?"

"That isn't the question. Convince me I should stay."

"We've quit trying to drive them off. We're going for the head now. Get that and the body dies."

"How?" There was an edge to her voice. "You didn't see what happened here when they came. You weren't here. I'd remember you. All the faces are graved in my head, everyone, dead and alive. I've searched for a way, Chel Dé have I searched. You can't get in there and I don't care how big an army you can get together, you won't even get close. They'll kill you faster than my father mowed a hayfield."

"So we just have to be cleverer than they are. What do you know about inside that fort?" Deänin pulled a pad from a pocket in her shirt, took a pencil from its loop and waited.

Sifaed's eyes went distant. She moved over to the tree, lowered herself onto one of the knobby root knees and scowled at the reedy grass growing round her feet. After a short silence, she said, "One of my regulars is the Muck of the Dirtmen. That's what they call them that grow food for the rest. Hunh! Not that they actually touch dirt, that's for Drudges. Ragnal, his name is. Touchy. Full of resentments. You know the kind. Every time someone looks at him, he turns it into a slight. His baby brother was in an airwagon that went down. Crashed. He blames the Muck in charge of equipment, says he's so corrupt, he'd get rid of all his workers if he could and eat their pay. He says Hunnar, that's the High Muck of Mucks, he got this job because his wife is important, that he's messed up a couple of other times and this is his last chance before he's hauled home and put out to pasture. And that most of the other techish Mucks are the same sort, rejects put together because no one else will have them."

"Hm. You said he's a resentful man."

"Cha oy, but he's not the only one grumbling at the way things are run, so I suspect it's close to true. Let's see. The Drudges live in Dordan-that-was. Seven male, six female. Was more, but guards took four off and that was the last anyone saw of them. Inside the fort, maybe fifty guards. They go on staggered duty, fifteen at a time, two on the High Muck's workcenter, another two on duty in his quarters. They like that duty, it's just watching the clean Drudge do her work, then sampling the Muck's drink stock and poking through his picture stuff. What they hate is walking the walls and punching in at the call stations. It's boring and they can't slack there. There'll be one or two in the watch towers and four walking the walls. The rest off duty, or wherever the High Muck says, lately they've been hitting the Sleeping Grounds, bringing in Guardians. Right now, he's got around ten of them out looking for Denchok, don't know why, guards don't either, they're grumbling because it messes up the schedule. Um. Don't know how many techs exactly, but you folks have whittled them down by at least a dozen. Four kinds, mining, med, communications, and repair. I've counted round thirty at Farkli's, probably more than that. Four Mucks under Hunnar. Never see those. Um. Some support staff for day to day business the Mucks won't mess their hands with. Borrow that pencil and pad?"

Sifaed turned to a clean page and drew a square. She frowned at it a moment, then started filling in the square with smaller squares and numbering these. When she finished, she wrote the numbers on the facing page with a note beside each number, then handed the pad back. "Far as I know, that's how things are arranged. Those Chave go on and on like drunks on a talking jag when they're with me. Cha oy, I admit I encourage them, you know why." She looked at the pad in Deänin's hand. "I can't see what use any of that is. You're not going to get in there. Nobody gets in there except Chave."

Deänin slipped the pencil into its loop and tucked the pad away again. "We'll let you know when we figure it out. Take care, Sifaed. And don't push things, hm?"

Sifaed nodded. "I hear. Chel Dé grant the time be soon."

3

Feoltir ran her fingers nervously through hair she'd bleached until it was white enough to pass for age. She glanced at the Guardian who'd volunteered to stay behind, wondering at the withered serenity in his face. He was wandering about, sliding his hand along the rough brown fibers of the Sleepers as if he were caressing cats. He was saying his farewells, that was clear. Farewells to things that looked like wooden eggs with the bark still on. She knew well enough that Eolt were developing inside, she'd been to a Hatching, she'd watched the embryonic Eolt emerge, small and slippery like egg yolks, watched them hunt blindly for the sky, pulling themselves up the posts of the pergolas and crawling shapeless and really rather revolting onto the lattice. She'd watched them suck blood from the Guardians and begin making the gas that would plump them out and carry them aloft. She watched them put on beauty and go floating upward, watched the making of the bonds.

That was why they were there. Her brother wanted the sioll bond. He sat with the other boys and in his turn played the song he'd made to call the new-hatched Eolt to him. He had the gift, an Eolt dropped the speaking tentacle, draped it lightly about his neck. She'd never forgotten the wonder and joy on his face, nor the pain in the faces of the two boys who weren't chosen.

*And I didn't even have the chance to be rejected.* She closed her eyes. *I had as much music in me as he did, but no one listened.*

A touch on her shoulder. She shivered, looked round.

"They're coming." Eagim pointed. "You're ready?"

"I'm ready."


The guard shoved her into the cell. He was rougher than he meant to be but not deliberately; he'd just forgotten his own strength. She caught her foot on the sill and fell heavily onto one hip, her right hand twisted under her.

By the time she got to her feet, the door had slid shut and she was alone. Fear churning in her, she moved to the sink in a corner of the cell and ran cold water over her wrist. It was already starting to swell. In a little while she wouldn't be able to use it and she was ridiculously right-handed.

She moved to the cot, lay down on it, and pulled a blanket up over her. Ignoring the pain and the weakness in her fingers, she curled up and began removing the nutshells she'd inserted into herself. One. Two. A sharp pain in one finger. The third shell was broken. She lay still a moment, then worked her fingers deeper and brought out the fourth and last shell. *When I hit the floor*, she thought. *That must have been when it happened.*

She fetched out as much of the shell debris as she could locate, then uncurled and lay with her injured wrist across her eyes. The shells were filled with spores, borer worms and chigger nits. Making their way into her now. Into her flesh and blood and bones. No matter. There was time enough to break the other shells on the faces of the techs when they took her for their tests.

She slept a little, woke with her wrist throbbing. She wet a towel, wrapped it tightly about her arm and lay down again, dropping after a while into a restless sleep with dreams of worms eating into her, worms emerging from her skin, waving their slimy heads about.

A bong from the wall woke her from her nightmares. A monotonous chant told her to strip and follow the blinking red lights.

Her mind sodden with sleep and pain, she unwound the towel from her arm, pulled off the guardian robe and looked blearily around for the lights.

Red dots eye level on the wall blinked in swift series over and over as if the red light raced from the cot to a narrow door that stood open now, a door she hadn't seen before. She stepped across the raised lip into a room like a closet with smooth white walls. The door slid shut and jets of hot water came at her from several directions, stinging at first then wonderful, washing away pain and fatigue.

The water stopped long before she wanted it to.

"Put on the robe you'll find in the meal slot," the voice boomed at her. "Tie on the slippers."

Her wrist was so swollen now she could barely use the hand. She managed to tie on the slippers, then leaned against the wall, her head roaring, her face and body slick with pain-sweat, nausea threatening to empty her stomach.

"Go to the door. Go to the door. Go to the door."

She ignored the voice. When she could move, she

went to the bed, collected the three nutshells, took them to the sink and washed them off, then slipped them into her mouth.

"Go to the door. Go to the door. Put your hand on the yellow oval. Put your hand on the yellow oval."

The guard was waiting outside. He was angry, she could tell because his inner eyelids had dropped and his eyes glistened. But he said nothing, nor did he touch her, just gestured with a long black stick, relaxing when she obeyed without fuss.

In the long examining room she saw the other woman she knew and a few male Guardians. Except for a few quick glances to map the place and set the script for what she planned, she kept her eyes down, shuffled docilely along until one of the techs noted her swollen wrist, swore with exasperation and pulled her away from the others. "Taner's Claws, Guard Tibraz, I told you to watch your hands. This is the third one damaged."

She kept her eyes on the floor, so he wouldn't know she'd learned their ugly speech.

Hand on her shoulder, he took her to the workbench with its organized clutter of tools and instruments, placed her hand and wrist in a hollow much too big for it since it was shaped to Chav dimensions, closed the top over it and started the scan working. "Hm." He switched to Belucharis. "Two small bones cracked, woman. I'll put you in a pressure bandage and give you some pills for the pain. Should be all right."

He freed her wrist, turned away, reaching to a sensor on a cabinet door. She looked up. The other women were watching her. She nodded, spat a shell into the palm of her left hand.

The guard started toward her. Smiling fiercely, she spun away from his arm, slapped up and over it, smashing the shell against his face. Still spinning, she spat out the second shell, slapped it against the face of the tech, then threw the third shell onto the floor and grabbed a small smooth-handled blade from the clutter on the bench, set it against her throat, and cut deep.

## 4

MedTech First Muhaseb's face bloomed on the screen. He showed worry in the Chav way, the inner eyelids dropping but not all the way down, a trickle of drool unnoticed at the corner of his mouth, his color faded to a pale gray green. Hunnar waved Ilaörn to silence, scowled at the screen. "Well?"

"We've got a problem, O Ykkuval."

"Explain."

"The batch that the guards gathered from the Sleeping Grounds this time, most of them were women. They ah mmm used their mmm body cavity to bring in an extraordinary mix of spores and microscopic borer worms. Four techs and six guards got smeared with these and they're close to panic now. They can feel themselves being eaten and rotted out. It's mostly imagination, but, I'm afraid, not wholly. They're demanding we drop them in stasis now and send them home with the next ship for more specialized treatment. They say it's in the contract with their subclans and mmmm I'm afraid it is."

"You didn't search the women?"

"Hindsight is easy, O Ykkuval, but Taner's Claws, they were women. Acting docile as pet keddin. And to use such mmm means! No, we didn't think to body search them. We washed them down, did a visual search, put them in robes we provided. It should have been adequate if they were normal women. Ah mmm most of them managed to kill themselves, but we salvaged three and put them under probe. It wasn't any accident that we got mostly women. And not Guardians either, they were planted at the Grounds waiting for us, called themselves freedom fighters and they'd volunteered though they expected to die one way or another, from the infection they spread or at our hands." He hesitated. "And we had to close and steril- ize the lab. Ah mmm, several instruments were dam- aged and despite the cleansing, the few med techs I have left are hesitant about going into that room. We will, of course, find some means of continuing the ex- periments if you order it, but my recommendation is to let them drop for the moment anyway. We really aren't set up for this kind of work."

"Very well. Write up your preliminary results. You know what I want. Complete honesty of course, but perhaps a stronger emphasis on the positive aspects?"

The image of the Tech First bowed, his eyes dulled as the inner lids slid home with his relief. "I hear and obey, O Ykkuval."

When the screen had faded to a glassy gray-green, Hunnar brought his fist down hard on the desk and spent the next several moments cursing the techs, the load of losers and blockheads he'd been saddled with, the hunting party due in less than a month now, Béluchad, the women and all the varieties of Béluchar life. Finally he straightened, flicked a hand at Ilaörn, claws still extended though his anger had cooled. "Play something soothing. I've got to think."

Ilaörn lifted his head, fighting to keep the smile in- side, the glee that was bubbling in his blood. For the first time since the Ykkuval's guards had captured him, he felt a real touch of hope. *We're going to do it. We're going to win.* His hands were shaking, but the touch of the harp wood calmed him; he set his fingers on the strings and began improvising a muted paean to his happiness.

It was quickly interrupted by a pattern of chimes.

Hunnar swore again, touched a sensor and rose to his feet. When the image bloomed across the screen, he bowed until his head nearly touched the desk, straightened with his hands folded in the submission display. "Ykkuval Hunnar ni Jilet soyad Koroumak is humbled by the honor of your presence, O Bashogre Aila O Rozen ni Jilet soyad Jilet, O Jiletah Jilet."

The figure was swaddled in robes heavily embroidered in square designs with jewels and gold and silver wire, couched on a ground of silken crewel work. His hide was bleached with age until it was a pale greenish white, and thinned so that the heavy bones of his skull made a caricature of his face. "Honor, hah! Hunnar, that kadja Hayzin comes to me bleating you're sucking coin like a black hole. What's going on out there? This wasn't supposed to be a messy one, just get the ores out and back to us. And deal with the Yaraka, of course. They been making trouble? You want me lodging a complaint with Helvetia, trade interference?"

"O Bashogre, it would be perhaps wiser to let that rest a while. Ah mmm. The locals have been hostile and managed to do us some damage and mmm if I may say it, our Finance Tech Genree has been less than efficient at anything but lining his own pockets. It would improve matters considerably if he were called Home."

"No doubt, no doubt. Unfortunately, that is ... not possible in present circumstances. What is that music I hear? It is charmingly delicate."

"Ah. The locals have a cult of the harp. I have taken one of them as bond-kerl. He's thoroughly tame and quite gifted. And not allowed to get out of the Kushayt, so there's no breach of security. If you find him pleasing, then it will be my joy to give him to you."

"When this matter is complete, I will accept your offer, young Hunnar. At the moment better not. Helvetia is difficult about the institution of the bond-kerl; they refuse to understand the reciprocal nature of the relationship. A collection of kadja nicmerms with spines so limp they can fellate themselves—but they control the flow of coin, so we have to humor them. I've read your flakes on the Yaraka matter and the use of the Freetech's aaah contribution. Well done. But don't wait too long to end it. Things can go wrong when you hold back your finishing stroke."

"Your wisdom is beyond bounds, O Bashogre. My agent is at this very moment stirring the locals into rebellion. As soon as he reports the proper degree of heat has been achieved, we will strike under the cover of a local attack and the Yaraka will be erased from this world. We will be properly contrite and point out that we have voluntarily confined our activities to a single continent and have had our own difficulties with a rebellious populace."

"Most commendable. Now as to the other matter. We are most interested in your plans. We will be sending a separate cadre to continue the studies of the effects of the smoke and deal with the logistics of collecting the ... what did you call them ... ah! the Keteng and confining them on reservations for breeding purposes. A fascinating life cycle that. The pictures of the flying creatures and the blaze when they expire make me regret my advanced age will not permit me to see this with my own eyes."

"Mmm, O Bashogre, there is a complication. It would be well to send parasitologists and equipment for identifying and countering a wide variety of borer worms and dangerous spores. There is ordinarily no problem with such things, but we have had an incident in the lab. Several of our techs and guards were exposed to such matter through actions of local terrorists."

"I see. How many involved?"

"Four techs and six guards, O Bashogre. They have requested stasis and return. My Tech First reminds it is in their contracts so it has to be done. It would be helpful if they were sequestered while they were being treated."

"Definitely we do not want word getting out too soon. There will be complications enough to setting up the hunting preserve. You will keep me informed." The screen blanked.

Hunnar sucked in a long breath, let it explode out. He glanced at Ilaörn squatting on his pad in the corner. "Come. I need thinking time in the Dushanne Garden."

# 14. Getting Together

## 1

"What!" Aslan grimaced at the Barge Kabit as she listened to the voice from the Ridaar remote repeat what she'd just heard.

Kabit Laöful was a short broad man with one of the few beards she'd seen on Béluchad and a moustache that was a flourish in itself, the ends waxed and curled up so high they nearly tangled with a pair of bushy eyebrows.

Duncan Shears' voice came tiny but clear into the conference room at the Meeting House, his tones dry, noncommittal. "I have an envoy from the Goës standing beside me, Scholar. He has brought a flikit for our use and a message. The Goës has come to a stronger sense of the urgency of the situation and the necessity for more speed and flexibility than river traffic would allow."

"Pleased as I am to hear this, Manager Shears, I could wish he'd made up his mind a trifle sooner, before I wasted the time and patience of Kabit Laöful. When will the flikit be available?"

"It's here now. I've set Aide Ola to stowing your gear and supplies."

"Ah. Thank you. Is there anything more?"

"No, Scholar. Out."

Aslan slipped the remote into its slot in the Ridaar strapped to her belt. "As you heard, Kabit, other transport has been provided. I apologize for having wasted your time. If there's anything I can do...."

He smiled and his mustache ends wiggled absurdly. "You can join me for a glass of brandy at Seim's Tavern and you can explain to me what is this flikit thing."

She smiled. "If you'll allow me to buy the brandy. The explanation comes free."

## 2

The sun was low in the west, what was left of the day hot and still. The road was little more than a pair of faint ruts winding through the forest, rising at an increasingly steep angle. Shadith was in the lead, weary to the point of nausea. The litter discarded, Danor was tied to the saddle, clinging to the pommel with both hands, his face set, his eyes fixed on the twin peaks crawling so slowly higher as they neared the pass; Maorgan followed with the pack pony and the spare. They'd gone watch on watch since they left the dead chorek, snatching a few hour's sleep each night. The moss ponies were tough little beasts, but even they were close to quitting.

Shadith's mindtouch brushed repeatedly against men moving through the trees parallel to them, but each time she dismounted and left the road to go after them, the touches faded away. They were being watched, but so far no ambushes had been set. She began to hope they'd make the pass without more trouble.

## 3

"You'll probably know one of us, our harpist, was invited to speak to the Meruu Klobach." Aslan took a sip of the siktir brandy and smiled at Laöful, amused by the skill with which he maneuvered his own drink past his beard. The brandy was rather too sweet for her tastes but produced a nice glow as it went down. She made a note to ask the Denchok taverner about his brews and where he got the distillates. "She took a communicator like the one you heard in the conference room and reported her observations of the day's journey to us each night. Not quite a tenday ago the reports stopped. Cha oy, one day was no worry. Things happen. Two days of silence and we started wondering. Three days and we knew we had to do something. It was a matter of finding transport and security. Hm. A flikit is a small flying machine. You've no doubt seen them buzzing about around the Yaraka Enclosure."

He brushed lightly at the short bristly hairs in the middle section of his mustache, then smiled again. "It will make searching for your friend much easier, so I'll not complain though I'll miss the conversations we might have had. The little harpist, I hope nothing has happened to her. I heard her play with Ard Maorgan and the Eolt on the day you first came here. She is a wonder, that one, she would be Ard if she weren't a woman and a mesuch."

## 4

Shadith dragged herself from the blankets, huddled shivering and half awake as she tried to get herself together enough to wash her face and give her teeth at least a cursory brush to get the taste of too many nightmares out of her mouth. She looked up as Maorgan came out of the shadow under the trees, Danor leaning heavily on his arm. He helped the older man sit, then went to check the pot of water he had heating on the fire, scowled down at it, touched it with the tip of his forefinger. "Barely warm and it's boiling."

"It's the altitude," she said. "We won't have a really hot cup of cha till we're on the other side of the mountains." She yawned. "Anyway, I'll take it however I can get it."

"Mm. The peep still hanging around?"

She closed her eyes, pressed her palms against her temples and got her mind touch moving, slowly and creakily at first, barely beyond the trees, then more surely as the effort completed her waking. "Yes. Fidgeting. Mm. Two of them, actually. Up ahead. They seem to be watching the road. Road, hunh. Beats me how they get supplies in to Chuta Meredel."

"Free Eolt carry things when they're needed." He finished filling the pot and set it aside to steep. "The Meruus don't want to make it easy to reach the valley."

"I see. Thus anyone who comes to them with a complaint has work for his hearing."

He got to his feet, shrugged. "I suppose. I've never thought a lot about it."

While he fed the moss ponies and gave each of them a mouthful of corn, she lay back on her rumpled blankets and made a wider sweep of the area. There was a blurred response out at the very edge of her reach. She thought it was a band of men, but they never got close enough for her to tease out the various life strands. It bothered her that they seemed to know so much about her abilities. Then her hand closed in a fist and she cursed her stupidity in every language she knew.

That chorek set his ambush in a tree because people just don't look up. *I saw him there. I knew why he did it. I congratulated myself because I wasn't such a fool. Fool! Gods, I keep forgetting what he said. The Chav spy has a miniskip. And of course he'll have spotting equipment. He's been up there in the clouds watching us. Watching me. He knows. . . .*

She got to her feet and began twisting through warm-up exercises she'd neglected because she'd been too tired to bother with them. By the end of the day they should be in the pass. Whether that meant more danger or less she wasn't prepared to say. Still, there should be some sort of guard posts if choreks were as thick in these mountains as everyone said. *And I can get some rest.*

The day unreeled like the past several, plodding uphill through hot still trees, sweat rolling down the back, matting hair to the head, walk a stretch, ride a stretch, Shadith stumbling along, eyes drooping half closed as she kept the sweep fanning back and forth back and forth, worry rising as the amorphous shape paralleled the track, peaking as the pair ahead of them stopped for whatever reason. Stopped, but always moved on before she decided to go after them.

The three were silent when they stopped to feed and water the ponies, Danor hoarding his strength, Maorgan growing morose as the separation between him and his sioll stretched out, Shadith too tired to bother talking.

Clouds occasionally blew thicker above them but didn't stay long enough to lessen the sun's heat, just tore apart and flowed on westward. New clouds came to be shredded in their turn. There was no wind, though, beneath the canopy. The air was still, it felt stale, stagnant, the breaths she took brought no refreshment, as if the air were so old and used up it wasn't any good any more.

The forest began to thin, the trees grew shorter and more frail, twisted by thin soil and storm winds; their leaves hung limp and the needles of the conifers were still and gray with old dust. A saddle began developing between two peaks, one lower than the other. Thin straggly grass dried yellow by the summer sun began to fill the space between the trees. The fungi were suddenly much smaller, ankle high at best, or climbing the sheltered side of trunks. The lichen webs that hung from tree limbs were paler and more thready.

Danor shriveled as the sunlight strengthened until

all that was left of him were bones and a pair of burning eyes focused without deviation on the saddle ahead where Medon Pass was bound to be.

Maorgan brooded. The opening out of the canopy gave him more sky to watch, a sky without Melech hovering overhead.

Shadith relaxed a little and dropped the frequency of her scans. She could see far enough around to pick out possible ambush sites and probe them at need.

They reached Medon Pass shortly after noon, left the stony, barren slopes to ride along a track between crumbling stone walls, moving carefully past falls of scree. Stone and more stone, lichen, moss and assorted mycoflora she couldn't put a name to, clumps of yellow wind-dried grass, patches of low-growing twisty brush. The clippety-clip of the moss ponies' hoofs echoed loudly along, overhead a flier shrieked and plunged out of sight, rose again with wriggling in its talons. On and on they went, the Pass replaying the same themes in their varied permutations.

Shadith stopped Bréou, waited for Maorgan to ride up beside her.

"How long is this Pass?"

"Over a day's ride. We'll reach watchtower in about an hour. There's water and shelter. We'll camp there and start on again tomorrow morning."

"Watchtower? That mean guards from the Vale?"

He rubbed at his eyes, gave her a weary smile. "Yes."

By the time the sun was low in the west, the wind sweeping down from the peaks was cold and piercing, crawling in every crevice in Shadith's clothing, biting to the bone. Her body was born to a warmer climate, hot and humid with few cold days. Despite the thermal underwear, she was shivering and unhappy by the time the track leveled and they moved into the mouth of the Pass.

Some distance ahead she saw a massive tower built into the side of the mountain. The narrow window slits were a pale yellow against the dark granite of the walls; she brushed at the tower with the mind touch. Two lives in there. The guards Maorgan mentioned. She sighed with relief, closed her eyes and slumped in the saddle. *Just a little longer and we can rest.*

After a moment, though, she straightened. *Can't let down too soon. Right, let's see who's with us. . . .* She swept the mountainsides, reached as high in the air as she could.

No sign of the spy. The blob was behind them now, still too far to count the individuals in it. She swept the mindtouch across the tower again, more energy in it this time, got a clearer picture of those inside. . . .

Without stopping or looking around, she said, "Maorgan, is there any way out of this defile?"

He slipped off the caöpa's back, tossed the reins to Danor and strode forward to walk at her knee. He looked up at her, one brow raised. "Not that I know of. Why?"

"We've got a problem. Ambush. Them in the tower, they're choreks, not Vale guards. Keep looking at me, hm? I don't want them getting itchy. They're that pair who've been riding ahead of us."

"You sure?"

She bit back the snarl, said, "Yes. I'm sure. Waiting for us in the tower because they knew I'd expect someone to be there and not get bothered by it." She wiped her hand across her face. "We need time. . . ." Still carefully facing forward, she called, "Danor!"

There was silence a moment, then he said wearily, "What?"

"Ambush ahead, they're watching us, we need an excuse to stop. Throw a fit, scream, whatever you think will do it."

Silence. The scrape/clop of the caöpas' hooves on the gritty track, the whuff of their breathing.

A hoarse cry filled with pain and fear.

Shadith gulped though she'd been expecting something, then she swung from the saddle and ran with Maorgan to Danor's side.

The old man was swaying in the saddle, his mouth stretched wide, his trained voice producing a tortured sound that filled the hollow between the mountains and bounced off the peaks.

Maorgan cut the ropes that bound Danor to the saddle. He and Shadith got the old man down and stretched out on the road.

Shadith squatted beside him, touched his face. "You all right?"

Danor grinned up at her, the first time she'd seen his face lighting with laughter. "You wanted a fuss."

She grinned back. "Well, I must say it was a noble fuss." She took the cup Maorgan handed her, held it out. "You can sit up on your own. The caöpas block their view."

He pushed up, wincing, his face paling at the pain and the pull of his weakness. "You're sure, Shadowsong?"

"Like a pup knows his mama's scent. They've been with us too many days for me to mistake them. A moment. I want to check something."

She reached back along the road, brushed across the blur. It wasn't a blur any more. A band of men. Mounted. Getting closer. She teased out the different life fires. *Ten . . . fifteen . . . twenty. Twenty! Gods! And moving up fast. We've got an hour. Maybe.*

"Those men I told you about? They've stopped hovering and are coming at a trot. They'll have pellet guns and cutters. Both of which outreach my stunner." She glanced from Maorgan to Danor and saw they were waiting for her to tell them what to do. They were musicians, used to being welcome wherever they went. It was something she'd noted before; ordinarily there'd be a lot to admire about this Eolt and Ard managed peace. Right now, however....

She looked around. The pass had high steep walls. There was a lot of scree right here and some scrubby brush that grew in lines and patches wherever it could get a foothold. That gave her an idea.

"Maorgan, unpack one of the tents, start putting it up. Danor, start yelling again, throw in a few loud groans, go quiet and repeat."

"And you?"

"While you're holding their attention, I'm going to try wiggling through those bits of brush till I'm in stunner range of the tower. I'll try to take out those choreks so we can get in there alive. The walls will give us some protection from the cutters, especially if they have to stay back, and they'll make the pellet guns close to useless. I figure we can hole up there until Medon Vale wakes up and sends help. All right. Let's get started." She bent and began pulling off her boots.

Maorgan grimaced. "Your puppets hear and obey." He began working on the ropes.

Danor gulped at the water in the cup, cleared his throat and yelled again, pain and anger and endless sorrow embedded in the ululating cry.

The sound sent shudders along Shadith's spine as she shifted the stunner around to the middle of her back and crept away from the road, keeping larger boulders between her and the tower when she could, slipping along in the shadow of the brush.

A fold in the cliff occluded the tower. She got to her feet and moved as quickly and lightly as she could, stepping from boulder to boulder in the long slanting landfall. Pebbles and coarse sand slipped into new slides or bounced down the steep slope. She tried to ignore them since there was nothing she could do about them. When she reached the edge of the out-thrust, she dropped to her stomach and eased her head around it. There was a patch of brush in a damp spot snuggled up against a vertical section of mother stone. She snaked round the fold, crouched in the shadow, and scowled at the tower.

The window slits told the tale all too clearly. Thick walls. A good four feet through. She closed her eyes. *Two heat sources. No change there. Sense of impatience mixed with gloating. No puzzlement or alarm. Good. That meant they didn't notice me leaving.*

She chewed on her lip a moment, decided she wasn't close enough. Dropping onto hands and knees, she began edging forward again, moving more carefully now because she had neither distance nor a fold of stone to protect her. Behind her, she could hear Danor creating his noise. He was enjoying himself, but dropping into too much of a pattern. She ground her teeth and tried to hurry. The choreks were bound to see through that any time now.

She set her foot carelessly, shoved against a stone sitting in precarious balance on a smaller stone and sent it rumbling and bouncing down the slope, knocking other stones loose. She swore under her breath and crawled on, hurrying hurrying knocking more stones loose hurrying to get close enough. . . .

A spear of light flashed from a window slit, hit the heartrock just behind her, sending drops of melted granite flying. A drop landed on her leg, she shook it off and scrambled on. The brush behind her started smoking, she could hear flames crackle and pop.

The next try was closer, and the chorek had figured out that he didn't need to take his finger off the sensor, just wave the rod back and forth. She stayed ahead of the sweep, but just barely, dived behind the largest boulder she could find and brought the stunner around.

She aimed it at the window slit where the cutter's lance came from, touched the sensor, and smiled when the beam cut off. She swept the tower top to bottom, then reached out with the mindtouch.

One heat source on low, but the other was hopping about like a drop of water on a griddle. She swore and began crawling closer, keeping her attention divided from the ground under hand and knee and the tower. Stones rattled under her, knocked against the scrub sending the tops shivering though she was nowhere near them. The brush was taller and thicker here. The tower had obviously been built near a water source.

She felt the chorek's flare of anger, rose swiftly to her knees to pin the location, then dropped flat as the beam lanced over her. She thumbed the sensor, played it across the tower, smiled again as the chorek dropped and the beam went out.

"Information," she said aloud. "It all comes down to who has the data right."

## 5

Aslan leaned from the flikit and looked down as Marrin Ola brought it round a half circle over Dumel Alsekum. The tractor and the trailer with their gear was crawling away along the road, Duncan Shears just visible inside the cab. She sighed and straightened. "As any kind of scholarly study, this is a disaster." She wriggled in the chair until she was settled more comfortably. "Yes, yes, I know. It was set up to be. And we've done with admirable efficiency what we were brought in to do."

In the distance two Eolt floated like golden glass bells, heading on one of their enigmatic errands. She watched them as Marrin flew above the road, following its twists and turns. "I wonder about them, you know. We look at them and enjoy their beauty and listen to their song speech, but what are their stories? What are their lives like?"

"Likely we'll learn more in Chuta Meredel. You want me to keep on along this road? We know she was all right until they left Dumel Olterau. There's this big bend coming up, if I cut across it we'll save about an hour."

"Go ahead. I've got a bad feeling about this so the sooner we catch up with her the better."

Aslan watched the wide flat riverplain change to small rocky hills with lots of brush, the neat lush farms become ranches with grazing, browsing herds of cabhisha which from above looked like powder puffs with black heads, herds of bladlan, lean leathery beasts with short stubby antlers that were bony imitations of lichen webs.

As the river curved back toward them, she saw a riverbarge gliding with the current, only enough sail to provide steerage way. Bright crimson jib, emerald main reefed to a small triangle. She unclipped the Ridaar, flaked the image, dictated a description along with her own reactions to the colored sails, the broken glitter off the river, the more muted colors on land, then tucked the Ridaar away. "It's a beautiful world, this."

"Mmm."

"I've never been to Picabral or had occasion to study it. Anything like this?"

He shrugged. "Could have been. Picabral is harsher world, colder, a little heavier, and almost as isolated. It was settled in the Fifth Wave by a band of game-players with illusions of bringing back royalty, nobility and a rigid caste structure to support them. And rich enough to set up the physical analog to their fantasy world. You could tell me the story, Scholar, it's that common."

"Isolated, hm. You broke away."

"It was easy enough." The air being steady enough for him to let the autopik handle the flight, he leaned back in the seat, hands laced behind his head, his eyes on the clouds hovering above the mountain peaks. "Enforced ignorance is a splendid way of controlling the peasants, but the rulers can't afford an equal ne-science." A flicker of a smile on his lean face. "Those among the male heirs who show a certain aptitude are sent to University for their schooling. I simply stayed." He was silent a moment. "They lose a certain number of us every generation, but I think that's as calculated as the rest. They weed out the rebels that way, the ones who might cause trouble."

"That's not an especially good idea if you want to have a viable society."

"My adult cousins don't tend to think that far ahead. Besides, holding onto power is more important and immediate than some illusory thing called society."

"Yet I think you miss it sometimes."

"Ah, it's home. Nothing's ever home like the place where you were a child."

"Hm. for you, perhaps. For me, University is home and it has been from the moment I touched ground there."

The land unreeled beneath them as the flikit covered ground it had taken Shadith days to cross on ponyback. Marrin slowed as Olterau slid toward them, a busy place with ore trains from the mountains creaking along twin tracks, pulled by huge lumbering beasts that looked like animated haystacks. Wains from the cabhisha runs shook and swayed along a road paved with granite setts, loaded with canvas wrapped bales of sheared fleece. Now and then Meloach or Fior children drove small herds of bladlan—two, three, five beasts at most—or flocks of ground walking birds toward the Dumel. The streets in the town itself were filled with sailors off the six barges tied up at wharves on both sides of the river, with men, women and Denchok moving in and out of shops, stopping in taverns, milling in clusters—all of them stopping to stare as the flikit passed by overhead. At the western edge of the Dumel a shift was changing at the fiber mill, workers pouring out into the yard with slips of paper in their hands, the next shift waiting for them to clear off so they could get work—these, too, paused to stare.

As the road turned north, the trees began growing more thickly, turning from scattered groves to forest, with the dark spikes of conifers showing up for the first time. The sky ahead was thickening with cloud and the winds were picking up. Now and then a splatter of rain hit the top and side of the flikit. As the light dimmed before the coming storm, Marrin took the flikit off autopik and flew it as low as he could, holding it just above the treetops so Aslan could scan the road with the all-wave binoculars and pick up any signs of trouble.

Aslan used her eyes as well as the more narrowly focused instrument and kept a tight watch on the road. About half an hour into the forest she spotted the remnants of a caöpa, mostly scattered bones and patches of hair. "Marrin, I've got something. One. Two. Mark. Right. Circle back and land at Mark."

They found the mostly consumed bodies of five caöpas by the side of the road or a little way into the shadow under the trees. They also found three bodies stripped mostly to bone. A touch from Aslan's medkit told her they were male and Fior at that. Not Shadith. Maybe not the two Ard who rode with her.

Another brief search found signs of a camp, rope ends, charred wood, scattered piles of caöpa dung. And a bloody pad that had blown up and caught in a crotch of one of the smaller trees, protected from the rain by the nest of some bird or other. She tested the blood and relaxed. Fior.

Marrin came back into the small clearing. "Found

more caöpa sign back that way. Looks to me like they were attacked, most of the caöpas were killed, one or both of the men were wounded. Either Shadith or one of the men killed the attackers. And that's probably when the handcom got bust."

Aslan dropped the bit of cloth. "No doubt." She shivered. "I don't like this. Let's get going."

When they reached Dumel Minach, the storm had blown the Eolt away. As soon as he saw the place, Marrin turned to Aslan. "Scholar, you want to stop here? If one of them was injured, they probably lay up here for a while. The people down there would know what happened."

She shook her head. "No. Let's keep going. If we don't see sign of them and they haven't reached Chuta Meredel yet, we can always come back."

"Not all that much daylight left."

"If you're tired, we can trade places."

"You've got the better eye, Scholar. But I don't feel good about setting down in the dark, not after what we saw."

"Hm. You're probably right. Depends on what we find. Let's move."

The moon rose shortly after sundown, a gibbous blur behind the clouds, the road narrowed, then disappeared beneath the canopy, and only the bridges over the innumerable creeks kept them on track; it was like the game children played, connecting the dots.

Marrin was flying half-speed now and had the telltales turned on. Animals kept away from the road, so the soft bongs were rare enough for him to send the flikit swooping through the canopy to check them out. They never saw anything, not even one of the mountain ruminants. Aslan kept the binoculars scanning the trees, but it was frustrating. Should Shadith and the two Fior be dead, they could have flown over bodies anywhere and they wouldn't even know it.

As she searched, Aslan worried. It was the right decision, going ahead. They'd find Shadith if she was still alive and if she was dead, a little delay wouldn't matter a whole lot. Knowing that didn't help a whole lot.

"Cutter." Swearing in Picabralth, Marrin hit the speed slide and sent the flikit curving away from the road in a long sweep.

Aslan pulled the binoculars off her head, smoothed her hair as she scowled at the dark ahead, winced as a line of light cut through the night, the sideflare illuminating what looked to be a tower of some kind; it cut off suddenly and the telltale flared. "Ah! Stunner. Guess who, hm. Take us into the clouds, Marrin. I want to see how many there are out there. With cutters I'd rather not have surprises."

He nodded and took the flikit higher.

## 6

*I'm getting good at blind firing. Gods curse them for giving me the practice.* Shadith eased up to a window slit, jerked quickly back as a cutter beam struck through it. *Good eyes, damn him.* Behind her the beam melted gouges in the ceiling, brought down spatters of melted stone which were too far back to touch her. She shut her eyes, felt about for him, lifted the stunner and touched the sensor. The beam dancing up and down the slit blinked out and the lifefire dimmed, so she knew she'd got another. *Trouble is, there's too many of them. . . .* She held the charge plate near her eyes, swore softly. The stunner was one issued by University to field studies and had a large reservoir, but getting in here had drawn that reservoir down, which meant sooner than she wanted, she'd have to start using the cutters.

She heard the pellet gun from the room on the other side of the tower, the sound coming oddly doubled through the window and the room's open door. So they were trying to slip by on the cliffs and Maorgan spotted them. For a moment she wished she could split in three. Getting inside here had saved them for the moment, but they were two defenders facing an attacking force of at least twenty. She thought about the price the Chav spy had put on her head and fought down a surge of anger that blanked out the mindtouch for a moment.

She knelt with eyes closed, brow pressed against the cold stone, calming herself, transmuting the anger into resolve. It wasn't just the spy, he was only a tool, it was the Chave sitting in their enclave across the sea decreeing her death, stealing the last few years left to her. For an instant the thought amused her, after twenty thousand, getting so het up about a hundred or so. Then she sobered. Well, it was the reason she'd begged Aleytys to find her a body. Now that her ending was always before her, the days, even the hours, were jewels beyond price. Brighter and more glowing. Or they were supposed to be. She considered this moment, sighed. "I'm only alive when I'm about to be dead. Gods, what a ... Digby, it looks like you've got yourself an agent. If I live through this."

She set the stunner on the floor and lifted one of the cutters she'd taken from the choreks she'd stunned. Danor had begged for one of them, but there were some things she still wouldn't do; arming a crazy man with an energy weapon was one of them. Not from exactly altruistic motives, but she was going to have to testify under verifier and she didn't want that sort of thing popping up.

Slave trading and arms dealing. She closed her eyes, felt four life fires creeping toward the tower. With a soft curse, she dropped the cutter, snatched up the stunner and swept the beam across the line of creepers. She dropped back and felt around with the mindtouch. And swore again. Three were out, she must have only grazed the fourth because he was crawling away; the tic in the body heat told her that she hadn't completely missed, got him in a hand or foot, not enough to put him out, but enough to keep him worried for a while. *Foot.* She giggled, stopped when she heard the strain in the sound. Not so long ago she'd stunned her own foot trying to get away from someone. *I hope you feel as weird as I did.*

She sighed and gathered strength for another sweep. She was so tired it was hard to keep the concentration she needed. The touch would soften, spread out so she couldn't pinpoint anything, and twice it'd gone dead on her.

At least a dozen still on their feet. If they got close enough that the thickness of the tower walls would protect them as much as it did her and the others, the iron door would keep them out about two minutes, then she and Maorgan would have to try and hold the stairs and the floors weren't thick enough to stop the cutter beams, not that close. . . .

A loud whine broke through her concentration. She popped her head up for a quick look through the window.

A flikit plunged from the clouds, swept in an arc across the pass and out of sight.

She dropped back onto her knees, leaned her head against the cool stone and pulled together the mind touch for what she hoped would be the last time in a long while. Every life source she touched had the dimmed down dark red glow characteristic of stunning. She shifted, sought out the flikit—and nearly melted with relief. Aslan and Marrin.

She collected the cutters, slipped the stunner into its holdall, and got to her feet. Her whole body aching as if someone had been beating her with wet towels, she crossed the floor, stepping carefully over the still hot spatters of stone melted from the ceiling, stood in the doorway leaning against the jamb. "Maorgan, Danor. It's over. We're in the process of being rescued."

Maorgan came to the door, the pellet gun tucked under his arm. "That flier?"

"Cha oy, the Scholar and her Aide. She must've gotten worried when the handcom broke and I couldn't report."

"Took her long enough."

"Probably because she had to talk the Goës into going against the strictures of the Eolt and giving her the flikit." She yawned. "Ihoi! I'm tired. Open the door for them, will you?"

"You're sure?"

"Have I been wrong yet?" There was weary exasperation in her voice and he looked affronted. Too bad.

She yawned again. The light from the oil lantern sitting in the middle of the floor shivered like stirred water. Behind her she could hear the scuff of his boots as he fidgeted, then the series of clumps as he went down the wooden stairs. She lowered herself to the floor, sat leaning against the wall, trying to stay awake until Aslan arrived.

# 15. Choices

## 1

Ilaörn lay in the dark, listening to the rain beat against the roof and walls of the garden shed. *First stormy night, the harp said. Kitsek will float over the mesuch fort and drop the weighted sack.* He didn't want to think about that. He didn't want to deal with what it meant. Instead, he played over the dinner scene, savoring the simmering resentments among the Chave leaders. The Ykkuval Hunnar, the MedTech First Muhaseb, the Memur Tryben, the Bursar Genree, the ComTech First Chozmek. All of them scratching at each other like jealous cats.

Most of the day clouds hung thick and low over the Kushayt; the air was still and stickily humid. Sundown brought rain, a few flurries with huge drops splatting down, then a steady fall that pounded on the Kushayt's roof, a ceaseless hammering that brought a deep melancholy to the Chave dining at the Ykkuval's table. In his corner Ilaörn played sprightly dance tunes (Hunnar's orders), but put a subtle drag on the beat that he hoped would amplify that wet weather gloom and the pall that the failures and deaths in the experiments had cast over them.

One way or another, scratching at each other's nerves. Hunnar digging at Genree, lifting his lip in a smile that had nothing to do with humor and everything to do with exposing his threat-teeth. Genree digging at Hunnar for wasting money on fool's games, wasting lives and equipment. Digging at Tryben for laziness, letting a bunch of grubbers who hadn't even gotten to electricity run rings around him and his guards. Digging at Muhaseb, questioning his competence.

It was an uncomfortable meal and Ilaörn enjoyed it very much.

Hunnar dismissed him early for once, confirming what Ilaörn had long suspected. The Ykkuval liked music about as much as he liked meditation. He had a Dushanne Garden and a tame musician as outward signs of his status, no more. It amused him to keep Ilaörn about as long as the music didn't interfere with what he was doing.

The rain was coming down hard when he ran from the main building to the garden shed, beating on his head and shoulders, soaking him. The harp was in her carry sack of c'hau cloth and dry when he took her out, but he wiped her down carefully with an oil rag, loosened the strings and wrapped her in a blanket, then stripped, rubbed himself dry and stretched out in the bed, his second blanket wrapped about him.

*We're hurting them. We're really hurting them. We haven't gotten them out yet, but I begin to think we will.* He cut off that thought before it went further, began running children's songs through his head, the simple repetitive rhythm thumping along with his heart. He matched his breathing to the beat, closed his eyes and concentrated on the song . . . *caöpa caöpa where do you graze? Upland and downland wherever grass stays. Caöpa caöpa how do you run? Clippaclop clippaclop under the sun. Caöpa caöpa when do you play? Dawnlight and noon bright and all the long day. . . .*

A deep organ note broke through his disciplined reverie. He squeezed his eyes shut and huddled the blanket closer about him, then sighed and sat up.

When he stepped into the rain, the downpour had slackened a little, the beat of the drops against his head and shoulders not so painful. He shielded his eyes and looked up.

To his relief there were no light lines lacing the clouds. These dead-eared Chave must have thought it was only thunder.

A small dark blob fell from the clouds, slanting in its plunge as the wind caught it. He could see that it was weighted, otherwise the wind would have carried it away; even so, it was only the top branches of the kerre tree that stopped it from going over the wall. He swore and ran toward the tree, caught the packet as the swaying branches let it drop.

Back in the shed, he dried off again, lit a candle and sat crosslegged on the bed to open his prize.

Nested in a springy mass of thread lichen he found half a dozen smaller packets, neatly labeled and sealed with wax. At the bottom of the packet there was a brief letter. He held it close to the candle flame, scowled as he struggled to make out the writing.

*Ard Ilaörn, we greet you and bless you for the great service you have done the people of Béluchad. We call upon you now for even more sacrifice and devotion. Place the packets of reka spores inside the air intake in the Ykkuval's office; we believe this will carry them into the basement where the head machine lies. We hope the reka will take root in there and kill the machine. Since the attacks on the crawlers, the water taken into the fort passes through a series of filters in order to keep spores from entering the system. It is refiltered and reused several times, but the inner filters are less efficient and will let some things pass. Find a way of delivering the packet of powder marked ederedda into the drinking water. It won't kill them, but they would prefer death over the way they feel for a few hours. There are two ederedda packets. If possible, slip them into the system around five hours apart. In the packet marked dok you will find two airgun darts. The tips are coated with fresh minik so be very careful of them. If you have a chance, set those darts in the Ykkuval's hide. We have tested minik on Chave. They die even faster than Béluchar. This will be difficult because the Chav skin is too thick for the darts except in a few places. If the Ykkuval will let you get behind him, the area where his ears attach to the skull is vulnerable. Also the palms of his hands and the inside of his elbow. His eyes if you can get them before the inner lids come down; these look fragile, but they aren't. The inside of his mouth. The inside of his ear. Unless you think you can get at one of these areas, it would be best not to try. The minik will stay potent for seven days. Do not try to use the darts after that much time has passed. In the packet marked tugh, you will find two wax covered pills. There is liquid amikta inside. One is for you, the other can be dropped into any drink at less than boiling temperature. If it is a cold drink, crush the pill between your fingers. You should know that it's quite likely the amikta will kill you also if you touch it with your bare fingers. There is apparently no smell or taste, at least none the Chave can detect. This too we have tested on captives. Chel Dé bless you, Ard Ilaörn, and give you peace.*

> *The Council of Béluchad in Peril*

He rubbed the tip of his forefinger across the signature, sighed and shook his head; whatever happened the world he knew was gone forever. He twisted the note into a spill, put the end in the candle flame until it caught fire, then sat holding the paper and watching it burn.

The thought of actually doing the things they wanted him to do started his belly churning and his hand shaking so much the fire went out and he had to rekindle it from the candle. It wasn't that they were difficult. He knew Hunnar's office as well as he knew the strings of his harp.

What they were asking was suicide.

Even if he didn't try to kill Hunnar, once the damage was discovered, it couldn't be anybody but him that did it.

"I can't." He shivered. He started crying. "I can't. I can't. I. Can't. . . ."

# 16. Plots and Deeds

## 1

*Banikoëh, Medon Pass, sun not fully up yet*

The morning was cool with dew glittering in the long shadows that filled the pass. Shadith stood with Aslan outside the tower's iron door, watching Maorgan lead the moss ponies down the switchback from the tower to the road. She rubbed at her eyes, yawned, her body still aching with sleep-need. "If you'll take Danor, it'll be easier on him riding in the flikit than trying to sit a pony."

"You're sure you won't come along?"

"Can't leave the ponies, Scholar. Besides, this is how we were told to come. I think it's better we stick to the script."

"Right. We'll give you an hour's start and stay low when we follow."

Shadith grinned at her. "You're enjoying this, aren't you?"

Aslan raised a brow, then grinned back. "Right." She sighed. "This is a fascinating society. Isolated all these years, working out a way for disparate species to live together and like it. There's the sioll bond. I want to know more about that. Other bonds. Something about the way the two species interact. Maybe part physical. Interesting to see if over time the Yaraka that stay here long enough will go the same way.

Ah! Shadow, this is a lifework, the one I've been hunting for."

"Unless the Chave take over."

Aslan grimaced. "If they do, we'll all be dead, so I'm not going to worry about that." She turned the grimace into a grin, made a fist and thumped Shadith's shoulder lightly. "I'm going to let you do the worrying, Shadow. And the figuring out how to keep that from happening."

"Oh, thanks."

Aslan chuckled. "Yes. And there's something else we'd better get settled." She unclipped a remote from the Ridaar. "I'm going to register the completion of your contract, if you don't mind. That way you don't have to worry about University constraints."

"Hm. Let me think about this."

"Shadow, you know you might be doing things that University would have to take notice of if you were still under contract. Listen, this protects your base. If you're not acting as their agent, the Governors can ignore a lot more interference in local matters."

Shadith sighed. "All right, let's do it."

## 2

*Melitoëh, Dushanne Garden, Kushayt, night*

Hunched over, mind eating at itself because of his inadequacy, Ilaörn crouched beside the stream listening to the harped messages hammering at him from outside the walls. *When?* the sound asked him. *When will you act?* He shuddered. *We have to know, Ard. When?* He'd left his own harp inside. He didn't have an answer. He couldn't say *Not yet*. The answer might be *Never*. All day he'd watched the air intakes, watched every move Hunnar made. He'd walked behind the Chav, provoked nothing but an irritated sweep of a hand.

*I can't*, he thought. *I can't do it. I can't make my hands do it.*

## 3

*Banikoëh, Medon Vale, approaching noon*

The Vale of Medon was a squat oval with the lake at one focus and a continual shimmer of mist from the hundreds of hot springs that bubbled up through layers of moss and lichens, geysers that sprayed upward higher than trees, as if the Vale breathed in and out, water not air.

Hundreds of Eolt floated over the city, drifting in and out of clouds like fleece. Half a dozen were hovering at tentacle length above a herd of small warty beasts, rather like frogs on deer legs. These beasts stood head down, legs set, the Eolt tentacles sealed to large humps above their shoulders, dark fluid rising up the tentacles to spread swiftly through their translucent bodies, fading as it spread. As she watched, one by one the Eolt broke free of the beasts and rose to join the others.

Maorgan was busily scanning the Eolt. *Hunting for Melech*, she thought. *I wonder if he can recognize his own?* She glanced back at the feeding fliers. How and what the Eolt ate wasn't something she'd thought about before, and definitely something Maorgan hadn't wanted to talk about. It was a prettier thought, that that shimmering beauty fed on sunlight but more of a dream than reality.

Part of the valley floor was broken into a patchwork of fields, lush green punctuated by small figures. Odd how easy it was to tell Denchok from Fior even from this distance, a difference not in shape but in the way they moved. She watched them, trying to find words for that difference but could not. There were groves of fruit and nut trees around the edge of the valley, and in the rolling foothills grazing herds of bladlan and cabhisha and the food beasts of the Eolt.

Beyond the field there were clusters of houses set haphazardly here and there. It was the rocky land with thin soil, land not suited for farming, that the Vale folk had built on. The places where the hot springs bubbled up.

Near the far end of the lake there were a series of massive buildings unlike any others in the Vale. They were faced with marble and gleamed eerily white in the light of the nooning sun. The steep-pitched roofs shimmered like fish scales, the same translucent shingles that she'd seen on all houses where Denchok lived and worked. The area around these buildings was crowded with Fior and Denchok, male and female alike, some moving in pairs, some alone, some in large fluctuating groups. She noticed for the first time that she saw no children, no Meloach and no young Fior.

Beyond this complex was a kind of arena. A round flat open area surrounded by tiers of benches and a broken circle of tall marble columns tied together with stone lintels and capped with odd bronze arrangements that puzzled her until one of the Eolt brushed low across the arena, caught hold of a bronze rod and used it to hold xe in place. Xe rested there a moment, swaying gently.

Maorgan thrust two fingers in his mouth, let loose a whistle that made her ears ring.

The Eolt at the arena loosed xe's hold, rose till xe found an air layer traveling the way xe wanted and came rushing toward them.

Xe dropped and coiled xe's speaking tentacle about Maorgan's neck. Maorgan's eyes glazed and his face relaxed into a shapeless joy that made Shadith uncomfortable—as if she had inadvertently broken into someone's bedroom. She looked hastily away, went back to examining the Vale.

A number of other Eolt had started drifting toward

them and there was a stirring in the crowd outside the large buildings, a swirl that gained definition and direction as half a dozen Fior and Denchok started marching along the road that ran from the lake toward the pass.

They were at least ten miles off so it would take a while to get here, but she didn't want to wait. She glanced at Maorgan, sighed and looked away again. They'd been apart for days. She could remember the burning excitement when Melech had touched her that once. She moved her shoulders, shifted the strap of the harpcase and started Bréou down the trail. He could follow with the other ponies when he felt like it.

It felt good to be riding finally without the need to extend the mindtouch and sweep the land in front of her. She was still very tired and relaxing the stress made it hard to keep her eyes open, even with so much interesting strangeness about.

An Eolt tentacle brushed against her, sending a jolt through her body. She looked up. Eolt were circling thick above her. As she watched, another tentacle dropped. Hastily she extended her arm and let it touch the back of her hand. It was easier on both of them that way. Touch and touch and touch till she was near drunk with them. Power surges ran through her body, Bréou squealing as they passed through her and stung him.

Behind her Maorgan shouted and the Eolt cleared reluctantly away.

She looked round. His caöpa coming at a jolting trot, the packers following free, he was riding toward her, Marrin in the flikit close behind, holding the flier only a few feet off the ground. That was dangerous, but tactful under the circumstances.

"Shadowsong!"

She wrinkled her nose at the irritation in the word. "Calm yourself, Ard. No harm."

He stopped the caöpa beside her, grabbed her hand,

inspected the palm, turned it over, inspected the back. He let it drop. "I told you, Shadow, they're dangerous. Especially free Eolt like these. Sometimes they get . . . cha oy . . . funny when they're very old. And there are a lot of Old Ones here."

"We've got an escort coming to meet us, Maorgan. I doubt the Eolt would get that funny when we're expected."

"You don't know that, Shadow."

"Well, I do, Ard. There was only curiosity, no malice."

"I forget you can do that. Cha oy, there's still clumsiness to figure in. So be careful."

She smiled and shook her head, then urged Bréou onward, thinking fond thoughts of the sturdy if stinky beast. He'd done well by her on this long trip. She glanced back at the flikit and giggled. It looked so silly trailing there behind them, sitting on top of billows of white dust that the lift effect etched from the unpaved track. Like an odd-shaped black balloon. More balloons overhead, golden and bell-shaped. She looked up. Not so dreamlike when you saw the underside with its nests of coiling and uncoiling tentacles, the multiple mouths the Eolt used for their singing—and, no doubt, excretory functions. That thought made her giggle again.

They met the escort an hour later. Shadith dropped back, let Maorgan do the talking.

"Buli Terthal. Buli Dengol."

The Denchok Buli banged xe's official staff on the dirt of the roadway as a prelude to speech, then glared at Maorgan with a down-browed annoyance. "Ard Maorgan. We summoned one mesuch and one only. Who are they?" Xe swivelled the staff up, pointed it at the flikit.

"They are the reason we're alive and here," Maorgan said. He extended his voice into song mode so it reached beyond the speaker to the Denchok and Fior who'd gathered to watch the show. "We were attacked at the Pass Tower by a score of choreks. The watchmen there are dead; we laid out their bodies on the lower floor. Unless you insist on keeping us out here when we're tired and hungry, this can be explained to the Meruu."

## 4

*Melitoëh, the Kushayt, morning in the office*

Ilaörn knew he must look bad when even Hunnar noticed. "I am not a young man," he said in a response to the Ykkuval's abrupt inquiry. "And I did get wet last night."

"Remind me to have a med tech look at you. Don't want you getting sick on me. Keep the music light and easy, hm?"

"Of course, O Ykkuval." Ilaörn flexed stiff fingers, slid them across the strings without plucking sound from them. His body wanted to be as inert as his mind, but the time he'd spent in here had taught his a lesson all his years as Ard had not—that he could produce sounds he loathed and do it to a schedule, not when he felt like playing.

He closed his eyes, forced them open again. The heat in the room and a night without sleep were almost too much for him. Eyes on the blank screen that took up the whole of the wall opposite, he plucked a single note, added another, worked his way into a children's song. The music brought its usual relief, easing away the bitter remnants of a night filled with unresolved questions. Distantly he heard Hunnar's voice as the Chav talked with his guards and techs, the hum of the machines as he worked on things incomprehensible to Ilaörn.

A soft bong woke him from his haze. He knew that

sound. It was Kurz calling from Banikoëh, a warning to Hunnar that shielded matter was coming.

A cell near the middle of the screen flashed to life, the face of the Spy assembling from broken bits of light and color.

The image steadied.

Hunnar leaned forward. "Well?"

"O Ykkuval, I could wish I had better news. The University group are either more competent at defense than we suspected or are gifted with large helpings of luck. Luck is impossible to fight, one must simply wait till it turns. Fortunately it always does."

"What's all that about?"

"O Ykkuval, my information is that there have been five separate attacks on the group, all of which have failed. Also, a number of cutters have fallen into the Scholar's hands."

Hunnar swore. "That is what comes of leaving things to incompetent dirt grubbers."

Ilaörn watched him master his anger and make a superior/inferior apology gesture at the screen. He found this interesting. Hunnar must be more desperate than he thought, more dependent on this spy.

"No, I'm not blaming you, my friend." The Chav's voice was as syrupy sweet as it'd been with the mesuch traitor. "It was my idea to make the grubbers my surrogate. Where are they now?"

"The manager is in the Yaraka Enclave. The other three are in a place called Chuta Meredel. My informants are not especially reliable, but I have no reason to doubt this. They are very bitter about the inhabitants of that place, rabid about the jellies, they want to burn them all. When I showed them what a cutter would do to a jelly, they went into rut like a bodj driven mad with must. They're too stupid and too impatient to plan anything which is why they are where they are. Which is why I have to be careful how I approach them. Given half a chance they'd try knocking me on the head and getting off with everything I have, no matter that I am a source of more weapons and other useful commodities."

Hunnar grunted. "You've dealt with worse material before this. You have a plan?"

"Yes, O Ykkuval. I spoke of the inadequacies of the locals not to complain but to make clear why it will take a while to implement my plan. I am organizing an attack on Chuta Meredel, trying to get the idea across that hitting the Vale of Medon at several points simultaneously with smaller forces will enhance their ability to kill and destroy. While attention is distracted by these attacks, I can slip into the Vale, hunt down the University group, and shut their mouths permanently."

5

*Banikoëh, Chuta Meredel, the Meeting Place, early afternoon*

The seats in the first ring of the tiers were elaborately and individually carved from white marble, these were for the Denchok and Fior who belonged to the Meruu of the Earth. Between each of the seats was a tall slender marble column with grasping bronze bars on the capital. These were the holds of the Eolt who served the Meruu of the Air. Behind these were the tiers of plain seats, painted white, enough wear on them to let the dark dull brown of the wood show through here and there. Behind these were sets of columns ranged in arcs to form a broken circle about the arena. These were for the Eolt who were not part of the Meruu of the Air.

Shadith squatted beside her harp on a raised platform in the center of the arena, wiping sweat from the wood and from her brow, watching drifts of vapor from the hotsprings bubbling up all around the arena, wondering peripherally about quakes and other instabilities while she chewed over the things she'd planned to say. Full of a high-minded zeal, she'd meant to give a series of lectures on how they could live with outsiders and protect themselves from the worst aspects of exploitation. That zeal had dribbled away on the ride here.

Aslan had seen their truth before she had; Keteng and Fior had managed to merge two very disparate species into a generally peaceful and productive society; they didn't need to be lectured or treated like children just because they'd been isolated for a very long time. And they wouldn't listen to her if she tried it.

She glanced at the clouds. If they didn't hurry up and get this thing started, they'd have to postpone it or shift it indoors. She checked the strings again, plucking individual notes to make sure the tuning held. This moisture wasn't what her harp liked, but the composite strings would hold tune better than Maorgan's, though she'd seen that strange wood swell under the stroking of his hands, change shape slightly to keep the tuning or shift to a new one.

Maorgan stood beside her, Aslan and Marrin a step behind. Too agitated and angry to rest, Danor was stumping along the rim of the oval dais, leaning on a cane, glowering at the Denchok and Fior who were swarming into the arena, arguing over seats, spreading out, getting pushed together as more people moved onto that tier. Overhead, Eolt were singing irritation at each other, pushing and shoving to get a tentacle hold on the outer columns. The noise from groundling and fliers seemed to pile up inside those columns and hammer at them. The swirl of emotions was almost as loud. Shadith's head started to ache.

After a while, though, the chaos sorted itself out. The tiers were filled, all the Eolt that could crowd onto the bronze holdbars were in place. Danor stopped his nervous walking, stood leaning on his cane, waiting.

The Eolt SANG.

Shadith closed her eyes, breathed sound, soared on sound, was permeated by sound, was SOUND itself as if her body had changed into vibrations and no longer existed as flesh.

The SONG ended.

Eolt Melech sang a long drone. Maorgan's harp melded with the sound, wove variations on it.

Shadith touched the strings of her harp, felt her way into the harmonies, and joined them. As the Eolt had tasted her on the way here, she tasted them now, the mind touch unfocused and encompassing.

The semi-meld with the fliers and their residues in her blood brought her sisters to dance for her. Warm mist drifted into the arena from the hotsprings, silver streamers of heat and damp that shaped themselves into graceful swaying images, black and silver similitudes of Naya, Zayalla, Annethi, Itsaya, Talitt, and Sullan. Six sisters, weaving dreams just for her now, dead in the body for twenty times a thousand years, living in her memory and her mind's eye whenever a new matrix in a new world brought them forth for her. Once again she thought she saw Itsaya wink at her, saw Naya smile, saw Zaya shake her hips and grin over her shoulder, saw her sisters greet her each in her own way.

Distantly she heard a singing sigh pass from Eolt to Eolt, from Keteng to Keteng to Fior and in a corner of her mind where it didn't interfere with her own joy, she knew that her voice and the harps, Maorgan and Melech had combined somehow to bring the Weave of Shayalin to life for more than her.

It was a joy and a wonder, but fleeting.

Her sisters turned through a last step and were gone.

She laid her hand on the strings and stilled her harp.

Maorgan and Melech felt silent also.

Danor threw his head back and howled, a sound so full of grief and rage it seemed to darken the air inside the columns.

"I cry out to you," he sang, his voice full and vibrant despite his weariness, age and wounds, fueled by the rage that swelled in him.

I cry out to you                Hear me, Meruu
       Fear in the skies, fire in my eyes
         Who will assuage my rage?
I cry out to you                Hear me, Meruu
       Golden blaze in sapphire skies
     Windborne and alone my sioll dies
          A sudden brief sun
           My soul cries
          For nothing, xe's gone
       For diversion, distraction
      A mesuch's measure of fun
I cry a warning              Hear me, Meruu
       Fear threatens your skies
       Fire burns at your border
       The torch and its terror
      Waits the torchbearer's will
I cry a warning              Hear me, Meruu
I cry my grief                 Hear me, Meruu
I cry for vengeance         Hear me, Meruu
     Kill the destroyers, O mighty Meruu
         Fill them with dread
           Let the dead rest.

Danor dropped to his knees, his arms hanging limp, his head down. He was trembling so violently he could barely keep his place.

An Eolt among the Meruu of the Air spoke, slowly, formally. "I, Bladechel, am Voice for the Air. You have seen these things with the eyes of your body?"

Danor cleared his throat, forced his head up and

his voice out. "I have seen mesuch in an airwagon direct their weapons on my sioll. I have seen xe turn to a tower of fire when the beam from that weapon touched xe. I have seen the airwagons chasing Eolt, free and siolled, burning them for the joy of it. I have seen Denchok and Meloach chased and corralled like beasts and slaughtered like beasts. I have seen Fior driven from their Dumels and Ordumels, the women taken for whores, the men as slave workers. I have seen these things with my own eyes." He let his head fall again to hide the tears he couldn't stop.

As soon as he was finished the Speaker repeated his words to make sure all heard them. Then xe said, "The Scholar from University, step forth. Speak your name that all may hear it."

Aslan moved to stand beside Danor. "I am Aslan aici Adlaar of University and of the School on University that follows the study of the cultures and histories of many peoples."

"Do you know the history of the mesuch that kill Eolt for pleasure? Can you attest that this has happened before?"

"They are the Chandavasi. They call themselves the Souled Men. Let it be understood that what I say now is a caricature of their truth because all generalizations can only be caricatures."

"We do hear and understand, Scholar."

"Then I will proceed. It is their belief that all other creatures are little better than beasts and thus may be treated as beasts, even those that share their shape. They will restrain themselves only in the face of a perceived danger or a force greater than they can overcome at that moment. They have strong clan bonds, a long history of bloodfeuds and a weak central government that does little more than provide certain services to the clans and attempt to mediate quarrels between them. This is important because the homeworld Chave will not send help to the mesuch on Melitoëh beyond what the mesuchs' own clan provides. Defeat them and they will cut the names of the Chave who have failed from the lists of their people and the name of Béluchad will never be spoken again. This being so, I can't have any way of knowing that such actions have happened before on other worlds."

The Speaker repeated her words as she had spoken them, then xe asked, "Hearing this, it seems to me they will fight like trapped behabs and destroy utterly what they cannot have if they see defeat before them."

"That is so. There is evidence of such already. Among the starfaring it is considered a very bad thing to give energy weapons to those that don't have them. This is almost as bad as the slaughter of intelligent beings. Yet they are doing this." She held up the cutter. "Should news of these weapons get back to University, the Clan and perhaps Chandava itself would be named Pariah and cut off from many services that they need. It would be as if the Kabits on the sailbarges refused to lend or buy from a person in a Dumel. How long would that person manage to prosper?

"The Chave have destroyed all means we have of reaching out with this information and they are now trying to destroy us. They are passing out these weapons and they have set a weight of gold on our heads. We have been attacked repeatedly by chorek. And will be again once we leave here. By the way, I'll have a suggestion about that when the time comes for such things. Indeed, I doubt we are safe even here. Or you. These weapons the chorek have are hand-held versions of those mounted on Chav fliers, the weapon Danor spoke of. Should a beam from the cutter touch any Eolt, xe would burn like Danor's sioll."

"This is true? How many of those weapons are out there?"

"I don't know. Perhaps dozens, perhaps hundreds. There is a Chav spy come across from Melitoëh; he's passing them out like pieces of candy. Twice chorek attacked me and my aide at Dumel Alsekum. Each time they used a cutter. Of the twenty chorek who attacked the tower in the pass, fourteen had cutters. We have collected these. From some of the things the chorek said when they woke and found themselves bound, these are what you call political chorek and are filled with hate for all things Keteng and all those who deal with Keteng."

There was wailing from the Eolt even as the Speaker was repeating Aslan's words. Xe finished and was silent for a moment, xe's tentacles coiling and uncoiling, xe's filmy membranes pulsing. When xe could control xe's voice again, xe said, "Is there any way you can demonstrate that weapon here without endangering the Meruus and those who watch?"

"I can't demonstrate without destroying something. Would you mind replacing part of the arena floor?"

Once again the Speaker had to fight down xe's agitation. Xe said, "Show us."

Aslan walked to the edge of the dais, stood holding the cutter pointed down while she spoke. "This is a modification of a mining tool. Chandava Minerals is a mining business and can justify their presence by claiming these weapons were stolen from their crawlers. It is enough to keep them from the Verifier, which is a machine starfarers have that can judge the truth or falsity of a statement. That is why it will be necessary to capture and keep alive some who received the weapons and the spy himself until we can take them offworld and turn them to weapons against the Chave. If you will watch." She touched the sensor, played the cutter beam along the white marble floor, gouging long deep lines in the stone, parallel, a hand's width apart.

She touched the sensor again and stepped back. "As you see," she said. "Thick stone will defend against the beam, flesh will fry on the bone, glass will melt and metal will cook what's inside it or touching it."

There were no groans or moans this time, only a shocked silence. The Speaker shuddered wildly, then fought xeself to control. "You had a suggestion, Scholar?"

"Two suggestions, actually. One, that you allow my Aide and I to remain. We can discuss matters in considerable more detail so you will have the data you need for planning your defense. The flikit will also be useful, since the Eolt should stay carefully away from Medon Pass. There are devices in it that allow the pilot to locate large life forms. Chorek in other words. And there is a stunner set into the base."

"A stunner is a nonlethal defense weapon. It acts rather like a block of wood brought down on your head, puts you out for a while, gives you a sore head when you wake, but does little additional harm. We are forbidden to give these to you. Even if we could, we have very few of them. Our goal is learning, not conquest."

"The second suggestion is that the harpist Shadith and my Aide Marrin Ola be sent to capture the spy. They are both fight trained and very good at the arts of survival."

"That child? That glorious gifted child?"

"That child has done things you can't imagine, O Speaker. Cha oy, I will let her speak for herself. You asked what I would suggest, but this is your world. You will do as you must and we will hold ourselves bound by your decisions." She lifted a hand, moved it in a flat slicing motion, a Keteng gesture that meant *I have done.*

There was considerable muttering among the Meruu of the ground and touchings of tentacle to tentacle among the Meruu of the air.

Stretching muscle against muscle to relieve the strain from the tension and standing with her neck bent so long, Aslan eased back to stand beside Shadith. "You're up next, glorious gifted child."

"You're not going to let me forget that, are you."

"How often is one presented with a line like that." She grinned at Shadith, then sobered. "I saw your sisters dancing out there. Mass hallucination or whatever, that is amazing, Shadow. Do you know how you do it?"

"No. You still haven't said how you'll explain sending Marrin off with me. Doesn't he have more to lose than I if University disciplines him?"

"I haven't decided. He made up his mind a while back and nothing I said changed it, so I'm left to find a way to cover him. Maybe use you as a reason, him going along to protect you. Mind?"

"No. I ..." She made a face and stepped forward as the Speaker called her forth.

The afternoon wound slowly on, questions to Shadith, questions to Marrin Ola, questions to Aslan, questions to Maorgan, interminable arguments within and between the two Meruus, proposals raised, rebutted, brought forth again. The captive chorek were brought down from the tower, questioned to no great result since most of them refused to say anything, just spent their time staring at Denchok and Eolt with hungry eyes that was a more powerful warning of their intent than any words might be.

The Klobach came to an end when the sun touched the tips of the western mountains.

**6**

*Melitoëh, Meklo Fen, mid-morning*

Denchok and Fior trickled into the fen a few at a time but the trickle never stopped or even slowed. Though so many people around made them profoundly uneasy, the swampies came out of the twilight under the trees to guide them and help the newcomers get settled. They faded into the heart of the fen as soon as they could, but came back again and again when they were needed, bringing food and other necessities for living in the swampland.

Leoca looked up as Engebel ducked under the overhang of the stem and leaf roof that Porach had taught them how to make. Xe'd been off all morning getting leaves to repair that roof and had been fiddling with it for an hour after Leoca got back from the swampie meet with fish for supper. "Fixed?"

"Hope so. We'll know in a minute. Starting to rain again." Xe shivered, dropped to xe's knees beside the tiny fire. "If I get much wetter, I'm coming down with root rot." Xe glanced at the fish. "Any news from Ilaörn?"

"Nothing yet. I saw Ceam. He's just back from a run to outside. Ilaörn's gone silent. Won't answer the harp calls. Ceam says he thinks it was putting too much on him. He reminded us that Danor said Ilaörn had gone soft in the middle. He said we shouldn't rely on him, that he'd go squish on us."

"Cha oy, Danor wasn't all that sane himself. Think he got all the way to the Meruu? The Eolt don't say anything about seeing him."

"Who knows." Leoca reached behind her for the pot they'd got from the mesuch traders, lifted her head. "Listen to it come down. This is going to be a drencher." She stretched out her arm, held her hand under the spot where the leak had been. "Looks like you fixed it."

7

*Banikoëh, Guest House*
Shadith set her cha mug down when a Denchok came into the room where the University group mem-

bers were breaking their fast, a short wiry Keteng with a lichen web so thick that his eyes looked like beetles burrowed into bark. She suppressed a weary sigh, expecting to be summoned to another day of questions and endless arguments.

"I greet you, Scholar, Singer, Aide. I am called Daizil. I am Metau of the House of Knowledge and Speaker for the Meruu of the Earth."

Aslan stood, Marrin left his chair to stand behind her. Shadith brushed toast crumbs from her mouth and joined them.

Aslan dipped her head in a sketch of a bow. "We greet you, Metau Daizil. May we ask why the honor of this visit?"

He inclined his upper body in answer, a stiffer move, his neck too thickly imprisoned in lichen to make a nod feasible. "The Meruus have conferred throughout the night and have reached a decision, Scholar. You yourself will remain as advisor, explaining to us the soul of the Chandavasi and giving us what knowledge you have of means of defense. We accept your characterization of Shadowsong and Marrin Ola and honor their gift of their skills to the preservation of our people. Whatever they will need in the way of supplies, they have but to ask and we lay Chel Dé's blessing on their search. We are winnowing our own for those with landskills that we may send forth two or three small bands of searchers. If nothing else, these might serve to drive the spy into the arms of your people. The Scholars of the Meruu will welcome you, Aslan aici Adlar. A student will wait in the hall outside to guide you when you're ready." He inclined his torso again, marched out.

Aslan stood watching, silent, frowning.

Shadith stretched, rubbed the back of her neck. "So it begins," she said.

*Melitoëh, the Kushayt, after moonrise*

Ilaörn dug the packet from under the delseh mint, closed his hand on it, closed his eyes. After a minute, he thrust it into his sleeve and moved on to the next cache. He hadn't resolved anything. He didn't know what he was going to do. But he wanted to be ready if the resolve ever came. He knew it would be a matter of seconds. The indrawing of a breath. If he couldn't act before that breath was gone, he never would.

When he had them all, he stood a moment looking speculatively at the wall, wondering about the hidden door. He shook his head. It was bound to have some kind of mesuch latch that only Hunnar could open. He moved his eyes along to the kerre tree where Eolt Kitsek had dropped the packet. There was cord in the garden shed ... if he could get up that tree ... onto the top of the wall ... the cord would be strong enough to get him down without breaking his legs ... if he chose the right time ... when the wall watch was past. ...

# 17. Killing Games

**1**

Shadith settled in the flikit's co-chair, closed her eyes and let her mindtouch sweep over the forest unreeling below them. The mountains were spiky with a few peaks high enough to have small glaciers in their cracks and crannies. The clouds were thick, the winds erratic with treacherous sheers that shook the flikit and sent it slipping and sliding until Marrin got control back. Shadith and the telltales both had limited ranges so he couldn't take the flier above the clouds and out of the rough air.

Medon Vale was surrounded by tall cliffs and steeply tilted hill waves humping up toward the stony peaks. The trees on the slopes were thick as fur with scattered open spots like a touch of the mange. Room to hide an army or two if they could get over the peaks without being seen.

Marrin started the round at the end of the Vale opposite the tower, where the cliffs were high with thin streams of water falling over them in several places while the highest peak of the local section of the mountain range was here, Rois Orus, looming above the Vale. He took the flikit slowly along, eyes on the instruments.

Now and then the telltale bonged softly. When Shadith probed the slopes to locate the lifeform, she usually found only a large predator or a herd of ruminants—the difference in feel was unmistakable when she touched a beast, not a man.

As Marrin eased the flikit around the end of the Vale, the telltale bong started chattering like a gossip who hadn't talked all week. Shadith concentrated. A band of men was moving through the trees—single file, so they were easy to count. Fifteen. "That's them," she said, "take them out, then let's find us a talker."

## 2

Kurz hitched himself higher in the tree, settled in a crotch that would hold his weight, then used the cutter to remove foliage so he could see the Vale. He estimated the distance to the main cluster of buildings, slipped the binocs over his head and dialed in the magnification that would give him a fair view of what was happening down there.

As he watched the two female scholars come out with the male aide trailing behind and a small crowd of locals circling and shoving around them, he thought regretfully about the rangegun the Ykkuval wouldn't let him bring out of the Kushayt. With a bit of luck and explosive loads he could turn that plaza into a crater and no more worry about the University group; they wouldn't have mouths to open. Trouble was, it left detectable residues and with the Yaraka involved here, that wasn't on.

The Harper and the Aide climbed into the flier, but the Scholar stayed on the ground; she and the Aide talked a while, then she stepped back and watched while the flier lifted and circled to gain altitude. Kurz took a moment to watch her as she turned her head, said something to one of the locals, then started striding back toward the buildings, the locals scurrying to keep up with her. Then he shifted the viewfield, located the flier just before it vanished into the clouds.

He switched to infra and followed the pulsing blur north toward the end of the Vale. *What are they up to? North?*

He followed the blur as it curved round the end of the Vale and started south along the eastern line of peaks, winced as the binocs picked up a sudden flare of energy. He switched back to visual and swore again as he saw the flier slant steeply downward and vanish into the trees. He pulled the viewer off, rubbed at his eyes. "Hunting," he said aloud. And was grimly sure he knew what game they hunted.

It was over an hour before the flier rose again. It hesitated a moment then darted into the clouds. He followed the blur south until there was another energy flare. He took off the binocs, slid the instrument into its padded case, checked to be sure the cutter was clamped solidly to his belt, then he swung down the tree, dropped to the ground and trotted to the mini-skip. Speculation was all very well, but seeing with his own eyes would give him a better measure of what was happening.

He walked along the line of red-faced, angry men, shouting at him to untie them. They were bound with thin tough cord. Not filament. Must be some local fiber. When he reached a face he remembered, he stopped. "What happened?"

The man glared at him, then looked away, shamed to be found so helpless. "Mesuch," he said after a moment. His voice was hoarse and full of a violence he couldn't let out any other way. "That thing you call a stunner. They took the cutters." He wriggled closer to Kurz. "Turn us loose. They said they coming back for us. Turn us loose."

"Before I do, explain him." He pointed at a man who lay in a huddle next to some bushes, his face contorted, drying foam on his mouth and chin.

The chorek's throat twitched. He still wouldn't look

at Kurz. He didn't say anything until Kurz turned and made as if he were going to walk away. "They wanted to know about you." The words came out in a hurried mumble. "The woman wanted to know why we were here, where we got the cutters, where you'd got to."

"I see."

"Garv din't tell her nothing. She put some kind of poison in him, but he din't tell. He's dead, in't he."

"Oh, yes," he said. *And you're a liar. Babble of some kind, he talked his fool head off before it got him.* He unclipped the cutter and sliced through the chorek's neck. Ignoring their struggles, screams, and pleading, he killed the rest of the bound men, then trudged off for the miniskip. Put any one of these grubs under a verifier and what they'd say would be very bad for Chandava. Which meant he had to follow the flier and do the same with the rest of the choreks the woman stunned. It wasn't pleasant work, but it had to be done.

His plan for the multiple invasion of the Vale was as dead now as those choreks were going to be. Underneath his calm mask he was angry, he wanted that Harp player dead. He was impatient with the need to finish the choreks, he wanted to start the stalk now, but he didn't dare. If he failed, Hunnar and Jilet would fall, his family with them. He couldn't afford anger at Hunnar or any High Jilet, so he channeled it all onto the Harper's head.

### 3

"When we found out there were six different bands getting set to raid the Vale, we couldn't ignore that." Shadith nodded to Daizil. "Marrin can give you the general locations where we found them. We stunned them, tied them into neat parcels for you and left them to be collected later. You'll find a few of them rather dead. The babble drug has unfortunate side effects in some Fior."

She waited until Marrin had left with the Speaker, sighed, and turned to Aslan. "We collected over seventy cutters, Scholar." She laid three of the weapons on the table. "In case you need them. We have the others locked in a cache in the flikit, didn't think it was a very good idea to have them floating loose. Too much temptation."

"I agree. Did you get enough information to go after the spy?"

"Enough to know he's probably about somewhere. We'll spiral out looking for whatever we can find." She wrinkled her nose. "And try not to get shot down. You be careful, Lan. I mean it. You didn't hear what they told me. I don't want you thinking you're safe, just because you're here surrounded by people."

## 4

Kurz whirled the bolas over his head, the weights at the end whistling loud enough to bring up the heads of the grazers. They were domesticated beasts so they didn't panic, but they did move away from it, scattering as was their habit, to give a stalking predator a number of targets. He let the bolas go and grunted with satisfaction as it tangled round the legs of a female with a calf. He ran forward a few steps, slipped a second bolas off his arm and brought it up to speed, downing a second beast not far from the first.

He slipped his improvised halter onto the first, drove the tether's holding peg into the ground with a powerful blow of his fist. As soon as he'd dealt with the second, he cut them free and let them get to their feet. Then he backed off and squatted next to a bush where his silhouette would be camouflaged.

They pulled at the tethers for a moment, blatting their distress, but when nothing more alarming happened, they forgot about the intruder and went back to grazing.

He waited patiently. Grazers were grazers on every world he'd visited, the same narrow acuteness and the same stupidity. When he thought the time was right, he moved slowly, a step at a time, away from the bush. They retreated as far as they could, but he didn't chase them, just dumped two small heaps of grain on the ground beside the pegs, then went back to his bush.

They nosed at the grain, then began eating it.

He took some more.

They shied a little, but only retreated a few steps.

After about a hour, they were used to him and after a little practice on lead, ambled contentedly along behind him, the calf trotting at its mother's flank. They were his shield against the devices in the flier, large warm bodies that would camouflage his warmth. It wouldn't work against a military filter, but a clutch of Scholars wouldn't have that kind of equipment. For one thing, they wouldn't need it.

He set up camp near the last of the killing places, climbed a tree and watch the flier hunt. It was in the air on the far side of the Vale, casting about, shifting from side to side to cover the forested area between the floor and the peaks. Looking for him and being very thorough about it. He watched with calm approval, he would have done much the same, sweeping the ground to make sure he missed nothing on that first circle, widening the circle to the far side of the mountains on the second round. It would have caught him on foot or riding. Using the miniskip would be like shouting *here I am, come get me.*

Another thing he approved of. The flier barely missed the tops of the trees. It was in easy range of his cutter.

He left the tree and took a shovel into the small meadow where his animals grazed. He dug out rectangles of sod and set them aside, then settled to deepening the hole until there was room for him to lie down in it. He trimmed thin branches, used them as supports and replaced the sod so that all but a small opening at the end was covered. The flier was equipped with a stunner, but he knew those clunkers, they were energy gluttons and the Harper wouldn't use it until she spotted him.

That was what he had to prevent. He needed them close enough to let him disable the lifters.

He dropped the last sod pieces into the hole and went back to his tree to watch the progress of the flier.

## 5

The telltale bonged softly. Shadith closed her eyes, extended the mind touch.

"You can relax, Shadow. It's only a couple of grazers."

She sighed and sat up. "This has been one of life's more tedious days. Wonder if we're wasting our time."

"Fivescore dead choreks say he's out here somewhere. And there's been no energy output from the skip."

She shivered. "If I ever had qualms about going after him. . . ."

"He's a thorough cattif, give him. . . ."

The flikit screamed as the cutterbeam gouged through the lifters, broke through into the cabin, grazing Shadith's thigh. The flier turned into a rock and went plunging down, not much forward movement because they were going so slow. Marrin slapped in the lever for the emergency rockets. This triggered the crash belts. They came slapping around both of them, locking them into the seats.

For a moment Shadith thought the rockets weren't going to blow, then they roared awake, slowed the fall, the flikit trembling and shaking and threatening to veer onto its side and go slicing down again. She clung to the seat with both hands and stared at the trees rushing toward them.

They slammed into a tree top, bounced, hit another, tilted crazily, bounced from tree to tree, metal screeching, the stench of hot sap as the trees started to smolder, the snap, groan, creak of the mangled trunks.

The motion stopped.

Silence.

Tilted at an acute angle, the flikit was wedged into a thicket of thornbush that grew up against a large squat tree that was still shuddering under the impact of the crash.

Shadith unclipped the crash belt. Marrin was bent over, his belt loose, his head against the readouts, a trickle of blood wandering down the side of his face. "Tsa! It would happen. . . ." She stuffed two of the cached cutters down her shirtfront, climbed onto the seat, reached for the stub of a branch and used it to swing clear of the thorns. After a quick scan of the area, she raced for a pile of boulders where the cliff looming over this strip of forest had crumbled in some long past earthshift.

She'd barely got settled in a niche between two boulders with a bit of scrub as a screen when the spy burst from the trees, heading toward the wrecked flikit with a velocity that startled her so much he'd vanished into the trees before she could turn the stunner on him.

She left her plans in the dust behind the boulders and went across the scree as fast as she could, slipped into the trees away uphill from where the Chav had entered them and ran to reach the spy before he found Marrin, cursing her own stupidity because she'd forgotten he was heavyworld, a hunter.

She tried a sweep as she ran, hunting for the hunter, but her foot slipped on a patch of fungus, her ankle turned under her and she fell hard. When she stood, pain shot up her leg. She took a step, the pain was bearable if she went down heel first and didn't bend the ankle, so she went ahead, walking more carefully. Stopping at intervals to do a sweep because she didn't want that Chav coming at her out of nowhere.

She heard the humbbbzzapp of a cutter. She stopped, probed.

Frustrated fury. That was the Spy.

Pain, cold anger. That was Marrin.

She tracked the Spy for a moment. He was shifting continually, moving too fast for Marrin as he'd moved too fast for her. She followed him for a moment, hunting for a pattern. When she thought she'd found it, she began limping forward, pain sweat streaming down her face, her stomach knotting as she kept hearing the cutters go off. Marrin would be pinned in the crashed flikit with cutter beams coming at him from a dozen different places. Must feel like he was under siege from half the world. Still, he had the cutter cache at hand and was keeping the Chav away. For the moment.

She pushed through the lichen and molds and fungus, footing treacherous, trying to move as silently as possible. From the intensity of the Spy's focus on the crashed flikit, she suspected he didn't know she was out, that he perhaps thought she'd been injured in the crash.

She heard him crashing across the mycoflorid forest floor, mashing and tearing mushrooms, mildews, slimes, lichens, and all the rest of the fungal forms. With a sigh of disgust, she lowered herself to the mucky ground and crawled forward. It was easier to move on knees and elbows, the weight off her injured ankle, but the smell was indescribable. She slid along, flicking out the mind touch every other breath to keep track of the Chav.

She flattened herself behind a pulpy growth as he came charging past, still maintaining that terrible speed and power, an ogre in seven-league boots. A moment later she caught a glimpse as he stopped, fired, flung himself aside as Marrin answered the blip with a sweep from his own cutter, moving it side to side around knee level. It missed the Chav only because there was a hollow there that gave him a kind of shelter. Obvious that he'd planned it that way. Not just powerful meat, but a hunter's brain.

She eased the stunner from the holster in the middle of her back, sighted on him. She had to hit him full on the first time; it would take a large and protracted jolt to put him down. Before she was ready, he was up and gone.

She edged forward until she was close to a tree, hidden by the lichen webs that dropped thickly from the lower branches, settled herself to wait, praying as she did so that Marrin's present luck would hold.

Once again she heard the crash of the Chav's feet, got herself set.

He circled behind her this time, flashing through the trees, choosing an alternate route to keep Marrin confused. She froze, but he ran on without even a stutter in the pound of his feet. He was already out of sight before she recovered enough to start breathing again. She couldn't believe he hadn't seen her, though she was fairly well concealed by the lacy drape of the gray-green lichen, yet it had to be true because a tap on the firing sensor and she'd be in two pieces right now. He wouldn't even have had to break stride.

*Stick to your pattern, Chav. Stop trying to be clever. Come on. Come on, stomp right past. Give me a shot. O gods, Marrin must be half crazy wondering what happened to me. No, Shadow. Keep your mind on what you're doing. This is no time to measure the whichness of the why.*

She eased a little forward and tore a hole in the lichen veil.

The flikit had settled more since she'd left it, it was almost invisible down in the thornbush. The bush was too damp to catch fire, but it was smoldering as were a number of the trees around. There were no flames, just smears of stinking smoke that for the moment tended to give additional protection to Marrin since the thornbush thicket and the huge tree it grew around were for some reason at the center of a large glade. There was little shelter for the Chav. As she watched, Marrin followed the Spy's beam pulse with one of his own.

For several moments the play was on the far side of the clearing, then she could hear the Chav heading her way. She drew in a long breath, held it, then let it trickle out slowly, counting as she did so, steadying the stunner on her forearm, waiting. . . .

He came bounding through the trees, his head turned away; he was watching the thorn patch.

Shadith centered the stunner on him, swore in frustration as he flung himself back and to one side as a pulse from the thorns came at him. He retreated farther into the trees—Shadith stiffened, wondering if her luck would hold again—and turned back on his path, moving more silently this time, more slowly. Marrin had ears like a bat—she'd noticed more than once how acute his hearing was—that was probably the reason he'd kept the Chav off.

A moment later the Spy's cutter pulsed, this time cutting at the thorns rather than the flikit.

A pause. Another cut.

Marrin answered, took a chance this time and held the beam longer than a pulse.

No response.

Shadith chewed her lip. *What are you up to now?*

Nothing and nothing. Not a sound from the Chav.

She heard the foof as a puff ball exploded, then a faint brushing sound. A moment later a dark solidity undulated swiftly along the ground. The Chav. Crawling.

*Marrin, don't you dare fire, I don't care what you*

*hear. That's right, sweet spy, just a little closer, little little little. . . .*

She touched the trigger sensor, held her finger on it.

The Chav roared, fought to his feet and leaped toward her. She didn't move. She kept the stunner full on him and prayed the power would last long enough. By the third step he was falling, he moved his foot clumsily for another step, tumbled onto his face.

She got to her feet, backed away several steps to put more distance between them. "Marrin," she called. "He's stunned. I don't know how long it'll last. Bring the come-alongs. If you can. I don't want to take the stunner off him."

"Shadow." The relief his voice was almost a sob. "Don't think I can do that. Something wrong with my legs."

"Oh, kortch!" She edged around the Chav, keeping as far from him as she dared. She gave him a last shot from the stunner, ran limping toward the thorn patch trying to ignore the pain that shot up her leg. The ankle was badly swollen, she was going to have to cut the boot off her foot. *What a clutch of cripples.* When she reached the edge of the thorn thicket, she said, "Weight them with something and toss me the ties. I want to turn our Spy into a package soon as I can. Oy! he's fast. And I can see him pulling trees up by the roots and using them as quarterstaffs."

When Marrin's face showed above the thorns, it had a greenish undertone and his eyes a feverish glitter. His hand was shaking as he swung the bundle until he had some momentum then released it rather than threw it.

The comealongs were straps woven from Menaviddan monofilament inside a sheath of graal cloth to keep the filament from cutting to bone. With metal closures that could be shifted at need, then locked in place. And even a Chav's full strength wouldn't break the closures once they were in contact and activated.

She bound his wrists in front, used a second strap to link his elbows so he couldn't move them from his sides. The third strap she used on his ankles, giving him enough play so he could shuffle along, but not enough for a full stride.

He showed no sign of coming round, but she didn't trust that and got away from him as soon as she was finished with the tethering.

She limped back to the thorns and stood looking at the tree and remembering how easily she'd jumped, caught the limb and swung down. "Marrin, you still with us?"

"Just about."

"Think you can get a line over that limb?" She pointed. "I can't make it by myself."

"What happened to your leg?" She could hear him shifting about, moving with a painful slowness.

"Stupidity. Stepped wrong on a slime patch and twisted my ankle."

"Wondering what that smell was."

"You should meet it up close and personal like I did."

The rope came over the limb and snaking down to meet her hands. She got her hands set, began pulling herself up.

### 6

Kurz came to awareness slowly, head throbbing, inner eyelids half lowered, his body twitching. When his vision cleared enough, he found himself on his back, staring up at a sky full of dark clouds threatening rain. *No*, he thought as several drops splatted onto his face and arms. *Not threatening. Doing it.* His mouth twitched. *What an odd thing to be thinking about. Rain. What. . . .*

He tried to move, but there was something holding his arms close to his sides, pinning his hands together.

He closed his eyes.

His body twitched again, he stopped seeing for an instant, thinking, existing ... as if for that flicker of time neither he nor the world existed.

*Stunner*, he thought suddenly. It had happened to him a few times before, the same in-and-out spasms, the same agony in the head, the blurred vision.

He lifted his hands until he could see them, saw the comealong strap around his wrists. He couldn't remember being stunned, but it had to be the Harper. *She wasn't in the flier, after all. I assumed she was. That was stupid of me.*

His ears finally extruded and he could hear again.

Voice. The Harper. She had a clarity of speech that made even a whisper travel and she wasn't whispering.

He listened.

". . . no, Lan, we're in fair shape, but not for walking out of the mountains."

Sound of squeaky woman's voice. Com voice. He couldn't make out the words.

"That much, hum? Might be a problem keeping the prisoner in our hands if that's the case."

More squeaks.

"I think you're right. Better we don't even go back to the Vale. The Goës has agreed about sending a flikit to collect us? Good. We're provisioned for at least a week and should be able to manage the wait with no problem. Marrin was the worst hurt, but the daggnose in his kit doesn't seem to be worried about him and now that I've got the pressure bandage on my ankle and a little palya in my blood, I'm doing fine."

Squeaks.

"Oh I will. I saw our Spy in action. Oy! he's impressive. I'm taking no chances with that one."

He lay without moving, without threat as the Harper stopped a long stride away.

"The stunner is recharging," she said. There was a

calm determination in her voice, no anger, no judgment, just determination cool and powerful. "I mean to keep you alive, you know. I don't need to explain why, you're not stupid. If you do something threatening before the stunner's ready, you can't make me kill you. I'll just take your leg off at the knee."

He didn't look at her or answer her. There was no need. When she tossed him a blanket and a food pac, he got himself to his knees and sat sucking on a paste tube. He was waiting. They always got careless sooner or later. His chance would come. It had to come.

# 18. Nibbling Down to Bone

## 1

Long after moonset on a heavily overcast night, Ceam and Heruit slipped into Dordan-that-was, groped through shadow to the blai that was now Drudge barracks. They took waterweed bladders from the string slings and squeezed them flat, expelling fish oil across the doors and walls of the rambling structure. Ceam dug a small hole, filled it with the last of the oil, coiled a fuse made from an oil impregnated length of vine into the hole and lit the end. He lit the end, tapped Heruit on shoulder, then the two of them slipped along a back street to the lubbot/storehouse where the Chav Muck kept his machines and repeated the process. Ceam set a shorter fuse and the two men ghosted from the Dumel to the fringes of the Fen.

A few minutes after they reached shelter, they heard a shout and the wind brought them the smell of burning oil, the crackle of flames. Ceam sucked in a draft of air, slapped his hand against his thigh. "Gotcha," he whispered.

A breathy chuckle from Heruit—then, "Let's get outta here before they get us."

## 2

Leoca and Engebel watched from the fringe of trees as four small forms flitted across the open ground and vanished into the shadow of the wall without being spotted.

Leoca let go of the breath she'd been holding. She reached out, took Engebel's hand. "One," she said.

It was very late, about an hour before dawn, the time chosen after days of watching the wall patrols. When were the mesuch most alert? When did intervals between the wall patrols lengthen, when did the Chave walking them drag their feet and give only perfunctory attention to what was happening around them?

"Two," Engebel said as a small dark lump appeared atop the wall to vanish almost immediately inside, then another and another until all four were in. "It's holding. No patrol yet."

Fighting the pull that was like weights on xe's bones, Orebli led the other Meloach down the metal road between the heavy square blocks these mesuch used for houses. Heart beating too fast, eyes blurring with the strain, xe counted off the blocks until xe and the rest of the klid reached the airwagon storehouse. It was an open grid with four fliers stowed on each of three floors.

Orebli stepped from the road and nearly fell over when the extra pull vanished. He grinned and ran to the fire ladder, began pulling himself up. There were no guards in here, what old Ilaörn had said, the mesuch depended on the walls and the wall guard to keep intruders out. They didn't have enough Chave left to set guards anyway, Chel Dé bless the Béluchar who died to make it so.

The four Meloach each took a flier. They brought hokori puffballs from their carry sacks and set them into the lift motors, then emptied small fishgut sacks of bloodworm larva over the seats. The only sounds in the structure were the gusty breathing of the Meloach.

When they finished they plodded back along the

road, too weary to force more speed from their laboring bodies.

The climbing line was where they'd left it. Orebli crouched, reeling up the inside line, while the others slid down the other. Xe followed them down, shook the line to free the grapple hook. It wouldn't come loose. Xe shook it again, heard the tramp of mesuch boots and hesitated, crouching in the mass of bushes and weeds growing near the base of the wall.

He heard an exclamation from the guard, saw the knotted rope go swooping upward. Then a shot. The other three had almost made the outer fringe of the trees. Two of them vanished into the shadow, but Sorhan flung out xe's arms and fell. Orebli pressed xe's fist to his mouth to hold back xe's griefcry.

Xe crouched where he was, waiting for the shot that would end xe.

It didn't come.

Xe heard a confusion up top, then running footsteps and a moment later, a blatting horn of some kind. Xe flattened xeself against the ground, began creeping along the wall, staying in the muck of weeds and such until xe rounded the first of the eight corners.

Xe lay still a moment listening, then turned onto xe's back so xe could look up the wall and see what was happening.

Shadows flickered, there was the pound of boots. Then silence.

Xe jumped up and walked rapidly toward the next corner. The night was hushed, waiting for the storm to break, and sounds carried a long distance. Inside the walls there was a mess of confusion, orders being shouted, clangs xe couldn't place, thuds of feet on the metal roads. Nonetheless, xe was very careful how xe set xe's feet. Xe couldn't know what ears might be listening for sounds out of place.

When xe reached the fifth corner, xe stopped, looked anxiously at the line of trees. Xe chewed on xe's lip and fought the urgent need to run, to get out of there. The open space was waste land, patches of grass, a bit of scrub and humps of fungus. It didn't look like much cover, maybe it was enough, though, especially when the mesuch would be focused somewhere else.

Xe went on xe's belly again and started crawling, moving from bush to clump of mycota to shallow dip in the ground. The back of xe's head itched and every bone in xe's spine and it took all the will xe had left not to look around, just keep crawling, but xe did it.

Leoca waited anxiously in the shadow under the trees watching the small form creep slowly toward her, sometimes visible, sometimes swallowed by shadow. *Hurry, baby. Fast as you can. They're starting to beat the woods now. We have to get out of here. Come on, Orbi. Faster if you can. Ihoi, you're a bright one, baby. I don't want to lose you. Don't want to lose me. Come on. . . .*

Xe reached the woods not far from where she waited. She could hear the sob of xe's breathing, the soft rustle of xe's movements. "Orebli, over here," she whispered, just loud enough to reach xe. "It's Leoca."

Xe came rushing through the trees, flung xeself at her, pressed xeself against her, trembling so fiercely xe could barely stand.

"I know, ti choi. Keep it in just a little longer, we've got to get out of here."

### 3

"Why didn't somebody know those vegheads don't trigger alarms? Why was it such a big surprise that three veg kits—Kits!—could waltz right past the guards and not even get a wiggle out of the sensors?" Hunnar slammed his fist on a corner of the desk, went back to pacing.

*Meloach killed because I sit here useless. Meloach hurting them like this. Babies.* Wallowing in self-disgust, Ilaörn sat huddled in his corner, his fingers moving automatically through the soft nothing-music that sat like wallpaper around the talkers while he watched the Ykkuval rampage back and forth while the Memur Tryben sat stolid and unresponsive in his pulochair waiting for the storm to pass over.

"Well?"

"I've had Chozmek put his techs on an analysis of sensor data from last night. Used your name for it otherwise he wouldn't have cooperated. No reports yet on what went wrong."

"They didn't notice at the Farm that the vegheads don't register?"

"O Ykkuval, you only authorized two men to handle business at the Veg Farm. And one of those is a Drudge. They haven't had time for anything more than getting the veggies moved in."

Hunnar swore and flung himself into his chair. "I've got a promise of more personnel, but that waits the next ship from home."

Tryben lifted a hand, let it fall. "Which is still two weeks off and, I don't need to remind you, brings trouble in the form of Jindar ni Koroumak." He cleared his throat. "There's something else."

"You've found the target these weeds were after."

"Yes. The flier stack. None of them are flyable at the moment. Not one. The weeds contaminated them with those miserable spores; they're dust fine and once they're established it's like every surface they touch grows a crop of hair. The mech techs will have to take the drive systems apart and clean them. And three guards are in sickbay. Some kind of borer worm. They were spread on the seat, the guards we sent to go after the intruders got in and sat down without checking. Their ... hm ... organs are very seriously compromised."

Hunnar shuddered. "What a foul . . ."

A sudden terror put a lump of ice in Ilaörn's gut. What if Hunnar decided to question *him*? If he were put under the probe, they'd know. . . . He glanced at his sleeve. The packets didn't show. It was heavy Chav cloth and the Drudge who'd made it for him was clumsy with the shears; there was room for two inside that tent. *Dé's Silver Cups, if he didn't do it now . . . Kitsek's daring wasted . . . that child dead. . . .*

"Grubbers have no honor." Tryben's voice was weary, flat. He was going to go on when a bong from the screen interrupted him. "That may be the techs working on the kephalos. I told them to call me here if they came up with something, no matter what."

Hunnar tapped a sensor and a section of the screen woke to show a weary, worried face, inner eyelids drooping out of their folds, ears drawn small.

Tryben leaned forward. "Well?"

"O Memur, we have something. An anomaly, or rather a series of them."

"Show me."

"I can't. I told you, we're all right on the hardware, but for this sort of thing you need someone who knows the running ware inside and around. Kephalos smooths out the blips as soon as they appear and we can't get it to leave them alone. It seems to be interpreting them as errors and suppressing them whenever they surface. You have to be here to see them and, O Memur, the Ykkuval is the only one who can authorize entry for major changes in the security ware."

"And what do you think they represent?"

"I can't say. All I know is it's the only indication we've found. You need to see for yourself, maybe you can come up with something."

Memur Tryben turned to Hunnar.

The Ykkuval got to his feet. "We'll both go. Tech, be ready to show us what you've got." He tapped the sensor and the screen went dark, tapped another and the lift door opened.

Holding his breath, keeping his eyes down, his mind blank, Ilaörn got to his feet, slipped the harp's carry strap over his shoulder and moved after them, expecting at any moment that Hunnar would notice him and order him back.

The two Chave paid no attention to him at all, even when he brushed past Tryben to stand at the back of the lift. It was an odd feeling, to be invisible like that. After a moment he was angry, an anger with a base of chill desperation.

*Don't think about it*, he told himself. *Just do it. Don't try waiting for the RIGHT moment. You know what you are. Just pick a moment and do it.*

The lift door opened and he followed them into a vaulted chamber set deep in the earth. The air was so hot and dry he could feel the inside of his nose drying and cracks starting across his lips. The center of the chamber was filled with a mass of metal. He stopped to stare at the thing. It was like nothing he'd seen before, like an enormous junkheap with faint light halos here and there, small screens like glowing eyes— and he could swear he heard the thing breathing.

He edged closer.

Hunnar and Tryben stood with the two techs watching one of the larger screen with enigmatic shapes flickering across it. Ilaörn didn't understand any of that and the continual repetition of the pattern irritated him. He examined the monstrosity carefully, looking for breathing holes. He didn't want to waste his spores. He shifted about, feeling for currents of air, moving very slowly, careful not to attract attention.

"Hakh. I think I've got it. Let me have the board, tech." Tryben settled himself before a sensor paten, blanked the screen, and ran his fingers over the finger squares, calling up another pattern. He touched a square, another, ran the pattern through a few permutations until he had one he was satisfied with, wiped it, repeated the process twice more, pulled up the first two patterns and merged them with the third, enlarging the result until it filled the whole screen.

"You know it better than I do, tech. Take a look."

"I can't say for sure, but seems to me it's a lot like the anomaly."

Ilaörn stopped his fidgeting a moment and smiled at the sullen resentment in the tech's voice.

"O Ykkuval, if you will permit, an eyeprint will authorize adding this pattern to the Library. Then we'll see if the anomalies remain."

"Do it."

Ilaörn watched with interest as a curious helmet was brought from a locked cupboard, clamped on Hunnar's head, a lead plugged into the kephalos. *Now*, he thought. *Do it now.*

He slipped the strap of the harp off his shoulder, set the instrument on the floor. *Chel Dé bless, old friend.* After a last caress on the smooth live wood, he took the spore packets from his sleeve and tore them open. Holding the packets between little finger and fourth finger, he slipped the sheaths off the airgun darts.

Expelling the breath he'd been holding, he cast the spores in the face of the kephalos, leaped forward, drove one dart into Hunnar's neck and the second into his own.

# 19. Fire in the Sky

## 1

Shadith took another length of rope from the storage bin, tied it to a strut on the front seat. She tossed the free end over the limb, looked down at Marrin in his blanket sling. "You ready?"

His hands were hooked around the crudely tied net that helped support the sling, his face was gray-green with pain, shiny with sweat. "No." His mouth squeezed into a thin, wry smile. "Get this going, hm. The sooner it's over, the sooner I can faint."

She made a face at him and swung out over the thorn patch, careful to land on her good foot. She tottered a moment, then picked up the staff she'd cut from one of the trees and shaped into a crutch of sorts. She used it to bring the sling rope to her, tossed the staff up to Marrin and carried the rope end to the tethered cow grazer, one of the pair the spy had used as camouflage. She fastened it to the harness she'd improvised from rope and strips of padding, pulled the knot loose on the tether and spent a moment scratching the curly black poll while she tightened her hold on the cow's impulses. It wasn't a full mindride, she wasn't looking out through grazer eyes, but she could prod her into moving where she wanted, at the precise speed and direction. She straightened, called, "Ready to go, Marrin. Yell if you get snagged."

The grazer leaned into the harness and step by step

hauled Marrin from the crashed flier. When he was swinging free and had the staff ready to shove himself clear of the thorn patch, she called again, "Ready?"

He grunted, set the end of the staff against the trunk. "Ready."

Shadith clucked to the grazer, got her to take an awkward step backward, then another and another. The cow mooawwed her displeasure and shook her head angrily. She didn't like backing up, she didn't like the rubbing and pressure from the harness, but it only needed half a dozen steps to lower Marrin gently to the ground and the job was done before she balked and wouldn't move again even with Shadith's mind-tickling.

After a last scratch of the curly poll, Shadith used her belt knife to cut the rope off the harness, then the harness off the beast. "My thanks, lady." She patted the cow on the flank and watched her run off, heading back for the ambush-clearing and her calf.

As Shadith hobbled wearily back to Marrin, she saw the Chav watching her. Before she moved out of sight round the bulge of the thorn patch, she gave him a broad smile that she hoped irritated him intensely.

She squatted beside Marrin. "How you doing?"

"I have been better."

"Well, let's get you in the tent. Then I'll see if I can get hold of our rescue service."

"What about the spy?"

"He's contemplating cloud drift right now. No doubt plotting like mad and waiting for an opening to set those plots going."

"Don't leave him alone long, Shadow." He tried to lift himself and help her move him but his arms had no strength left and there wasn't even a twitch in his legs. "I'm no use."

"Feeling sorry for yourself, are you? Hmp. You'll be fine once we get you in the ottodoc at the 'Clave."

He smiled up at her. "And we can be sure the Goës will come for us. We've got his proof."

"Sorry and cynical." She chuckled. "And very right. Brace yourself. I'm going to have to slide you along on the blanket and it won't be comfortable."

## 2

"I am a Scholar with a Scholar's constraints. And while I sympathize deeply, your people are not my people, this is not a fight I have any business joining." Aslan spoke slowly, with a weightiness that made her cringe a little; but she wanted no mistakes about what she was saying. "I can suggest this, treat with the Goës Koraka hoeh Dexios. He will probably provide transport and medical services—but the price he'll ask for these is something that you might not want to pay. He will not sell you weapons."

They were in a sun-filled tree-shaded patio with Eolt graspers on the eaves and a fountain playing gently in the center, water from a hotspring below the blai shooting at intervals into high jets but mostly bubbling up, then dripping musically from bowl to bowl and into a small stream that vanished under a wall. Aslan found the humid heat uncomfortable, but the Eolt and the Denchok who'd come to talk with her seemed cozy enough.

Daizil Voice for the Earth leaned into the speaking tentacle of Bladechel Voice for the Air. After a moment, xe sighed and straightened. "Why? We fight the same enemy."

"The Goës is not a warrior, he's a trader. He takes the long view. Which is that what you use to defeat the enemy will be turned on him once the enemy is gone."

Again the two Voices consulted, then Daizil said, "Ard Danor implied that if the Chandavasi triumph, they will be harvesting Eolt on Banikoëh also. Do you think this is likely?"

"Once this is a sealed world, yes. There will be no place for Eolt or any other Béluchar to hide from them."

"And there will be no help from outside. They take what they want."

"There will be protests from University, but yes. Without witnesses to raise their voices in protest and start a campaign against the Chandavasi, essentially no help."

"And you?"

"The Chave are not likely to leave witnesses from outside, especially those who know how to make their stories heard. This is a world visited by smugglers and free traders. There would always be a chance one of us might escape."

"I see. So your fate depends on our deeds."

"To some extent, yes."

"And still you're unwilling to do more than advise."

"To be a credible witness—which will be of greater use to you than my own inadequate fighting skills, I can do no more."

"There is no chance of talking with the Chandavasi?"

"I would never say don't talk. I would also say that their history as I know it doesn't indicate a willingness to listen."

"I see. Would you use your communicators to speak to the Goës for us, should we decide that is what we will do?"

"Yes. You must do your own bargaining, however."

"That is understood." Daizil smiled at her. "We know traders, Scholar. We have many of our own."

### 3

The sound shook the building, a great deep note that resonated in Aslan's bones. She'd been stretched out on the bed, eyes closed to facilitate memory, subvocalizing a report to herself, getting down impressions, questions she needed to ask and anything else that occurred to her. She sat up, startled, removed the throatmike and went outside to see what was happening.

The sky was thick with Eolt, swirling in a wide golden vortex, singing as they circled higher and higher to join the streams heading east. The flow seemed endless, more Eolt arriving every moment, coming from all directions.

"Scholar." Daizil joined her and stood looking up, xe's mouth set, a sad droop to his eyes.

"Voice. What's this about?"

"The Eolt have decided. There will be no bargaining. Whatever the cost to them, the Chave must be destroyed."

## 4

"You'd best keep a close watch on him. He's tried to kill himself twice."

The Goës smiled grimly, his mouth open to show the tearing canines. "I thank you for the warning, Harper. We have some potions that will take his mind off his troubles." He contemplated her a moment, eyes like chocolate ice, then he smiled again, this time the closed-mouth pleasure smile. "Bringing the Scholar and her team was one of my better ideas," he murmured. "Will you join me for a glass of cha or something stronger, Shadowsong?"

"Of course, Goës Koraka. I would like to be kept posted on Aide Ola's progress, though. He is a man to be valued." She glanced at the procession leading the spy away, met his eyes and felt a chill lance through her. Even the creepy Ginny Seyirshi had never treated her to so intensely personal a hatred.

The Goës noted that. "Yes. We'll make very sure he's kept chemically restrained, Shadowsong."

He poured the cha from an elegant white pot into a small drinking bowl. "Will you have citra or glemm? And I believe there is some toz in that pot."

"Nothing, please. What cha is it?"

"Smoky sill from the highlands of Molot."

"Ah. A favorite of mine." She smiled. "I see we share the same smuggler."

He chuckled. "An odd little man with interesting connections, by name Arel."

"Mm." She sipped at the cha, relishing the clean tang of the liquid and the silky texture of the bowl. The she sighed and set the bowl on its saucer with a small decisive click. "Reluctant as I am to disturb the peace of the moment, how far have you got on the repairs to the splitcom?"

"We captured one of the Chave sats, Dulman be blessed that the shuttle was not linked into the system when it went down, and we're attempting to cobble up something with those parts that we can use to hook into another of the sats and go from there. Chave thought patterns are not all that complex and we've managed to work out the codes. With a bit of luck and some hard work we'll get word out within the next tenday. Which should take some of the. . . ." He looked up, frowning as a phora came in without knocking. "What?"

"Something you have to see, Goës Koraka. We don't know what it means."

The sky was filled with golden bells blowing east on the high airstreams—first a scattering, one, two, half a dozen, the sun shining through their translucent veils, then rank upon rank of Eolt, turning the western sky bright amber with their numbers.

"You don't think about there being so many of them," Shadith said. "A world's a big place and they get lost among the clouds."

They stood in the middle of the Enclave, looking, caught by the beauty of this strange migration. Shadith heard the scrape of a foot behind her, looked around to see Marrin standing there, his face filled with wonder as he stared up at the Eolt.

The Goës shook himself free from his astonishment. "What are they doing? This against us? Where are they going?"

"If I had to guess, I'd say they're going to attack the ... what do they call it ... the Kushayt."

"Yes." Marrin's voice vibrated with conviction. "And they're going to die at it. So much glory lost. ..." He turned to the Goës. "You've got to do something. You've got to help them."

The Goës contemplated him a moment. "We'll discuss this inside." He turned his head. "Thofor, inform me immediately of any alteration in their progress."

Koraka laced his long fingers together, stared at them a moment, then lifted his head and smiled wearily at Marrin, his threat teeth hidden. "If you mean, Aide, that we should provide weapons to the locals, you should think again."

"Of course I don't mean that." Marrin leaned forward in his chair, his dark eyes intense. "Send guards with them. Send me, if there's no one else you can spare. A flier and the strongest firepower you have. At least it would be something."

Koraka's ears came forward. "You, Aide? Aren't you forbidden armed assault by University bylaws or something like that?"

"I don't consider this assault, but self-defense. When the Chave put a price on my head, they gave me that right."

"Yes, that's an argument that has a good chance of floating. Now explain to me why a pacific Scholar from University would be a help rather than a hindrance."

"I was fifth male heir to the Baron Ineca of Picabral and I survived past puberty."

"Ah. Succinct and convincing. Also rather astonishing, considering your present circumstances. Very well. I don't see any problem with supplying your needs. A matter of public service, as it were. If the ottodoc certifies you. You came out of there in a very short time. As to guards, I don't think I'm able to spare any. I'm expecting an attack from the Chave any day now. Rude and crude as they are, we're considerably outnumbered and outmuscled by that lot. I wouldn't want to face them outside these walls. Or inside, as the case may be."

"Pinched nerve and ruptured disk. Few more this and thats. Didn't take much fixing."

"I'll still require a formal analysis, a thorough workup. I'm sure you understand why."

Shadith sat looking at her hands. There wasn't really any point in picking at her deficiencies. If this business had taught her anything it was that if she wanted to be fully alive, to feel passionately about anything, she was going to have to spend a lot of time walking the edge. Might as well get a start at it. "I'll be going along also," she said. "You'll need me, Marrin, I have credibility with the Eolt. They're strong and dangerous, though I admit I find what I know to be true hard to believe when I look at them."

"Dangerous?" The Goës frowned. "How?"

"Stings. Capable of killing a man. Probably other defenses, but no one spoke of those."

"Interesting."

"They understand quite well their vulnerability so I doubt you'll have any problems." She stood. "I'll take your offer of a bath and a nap, Goës Koraka. And you, Marrin, you get to have your body cells assayed. Shall we say leave in three hours?"

## 5

The Eolt sang as they swept across the land toward the Bakuhl Sea, great crashing chords of sound that filled the sky and had a practical purpose as well since the air sucked in and expelled drove them even faster toward the killing field of Melitoëh. They flew high and swift, like golden leucocytes in the air veins of the world, swelling with the sunlight. A thousand and a thousand Eolt in the Béluchar way of saying many beyond counting, filling the sky to the horizon and beyond.

When the flikit rose from the Enclave to join the flight, Eolt began converging on it, like birds mobbing an intruder—until Shadith stood. Hands clutching the top of the windshield, she sang, her voice soaring, yet tiny against the great organ beats of the Eolt. It was enough. They knew her and went back to their single-minded surge toward the water.

Shadith fell back into her seat, reached for the water bottle, sucked greedily at the nipple.

Marrin shivered. "Spooky." He slapped the accelerod in all the way, and the small dark flikit leaped ahead, racing to catch up with the Eolt, then pass the front ranks of the throng.

## 6

Ceam stretched out on the limb, managed to focus the ocular without falling off. He scanned the mesuch fort, looking for anything that would give him a clue about the seethe of activity inside. After the firing of Dordan-that-was and the crippling of the airwagons, Tech and Drudge had been called behind the walls. The crawlers sat empty and dead in the mountains; the Keteng prison was abandoned. *Maybe Ilaörn had pulled off the coup after all. No way of telling. Except. . . .*

Three of the guards came trotting along the wall and positioned themselves behind slotted shields beside the gate. A small section of the Gate swung open and four male Drudges stumped out, one in an improvised harness linked to a crude sledge which bumped along behind him. Two guards came with them, clanking in armor, heads enclosed in glass, heavy dark weapons cradled in their arms with the tenderness of men cuddling their first borns.

One of the guards grunted something, Ceam couldn't make out the word, but the Drudge in the harness dropped to a squat and the other three stood hipshot and shoulders rounded while the guard moved to a large kerre, burned through the trunk with his cutter.

Ceam folded the ocular, eased it down inside his shirt, lay very still, watching the mesuch.

The second guard prowled about, head turning nervously, weapon in his hand. When he heard a rustle as some bitty nose twitcher scurried through the leaves, he spun round, dropped into a crouch and sent a burning beam cutting through the brush. There was a smell of roasted meat and burned hair. He went over, kicked the charred carcass and cursed it, then went back to his prowling.

The cut was so quick and clean, the tree shivered a little, but didn't fall over until one of the Drudges slammed his fist into it. The guard cut the tree in chunks and the Drudges stacked the chunks on the sledge until they had a tall pile of green, sappy wood.

The other Drudges attached lines to the sledge and with the first leaning into his harness, they dragged the piled wood back to the road and into the mesuch fort.

With a grin that threatened his ears, Ceam wriggled backward along the limb, went dropping down the tree and ran toward the Fen, the bearer of the best news he could imagine. If the mesuch had to use wood for heat and cooking and muscle to drag the sledge, Ilaörn had done the job. He'd killed the fort.

"Cursed clear day." Marrin started into a wide circle round the Kushayt. "Well, I suppose they'd know we're here anyway, the flikit screams at scanners."

Shadith shifted the viewfield of the binocs along the top of the eight-sided wall. "Marrin, at least thirty guards on patrol down there and they're all armored. Visors shut. What's going on?"

He looked nervously around. The first Eolt were arriving, moving into a pattern much like his, rising and falling to find the proper windstreams, their membranes pulsing as they fed air through their speaking sphincters and milled in a thickening circle about the kushayt. "Don't know, but the slaughter is fixing to start, so I'm going down. Shadow, set the stunner on widecast, we won't get the armored Chave this pass, but the others. . . ."

"Tail on fire, Marrin, remember their reflexes. Let's go."

Fast as he could take it, Marrin sent the flikit into a stuttering, twisting pass over the Kushayt, recalling the running tactics he'd learned as a boy to get him away from the near lethal teasing of his older relatives. The moves were ground into his bones and nerves.

As soon as the Chave saw him coming at them, they started shooting; pellets from the heavy duty projectors whined past or grazed the flanks of the flikit, exploding the instant they touched.

Screech of tortured metal. Fingernails on slateboard tearing.

Blams. Ears ringing.

Beams from heavy-duty cutters swept past, easier to avoid, but more lethal if they touched. As the flikit tumbled wildly after an explosion from one of the pellets, half the rear end went to a beam that missed the main lifter by a hair.

Flare. Searing. Heat.

Whine of laboring lifters.

Jolting, torsion, thrown against crashwebs.

"Marrin! Get us out of here. It's not working. Out!"

He didn't bother to answer, just sent the flikit in a wavery sweep toward the trees.

Deafening blast.

Flikit cartwheeling down and down.

Roar of emergency rockets, a gasp of steadier flight, then the flikit was plowing into the trees, crashing, bouncing.

Final jolting stop.

Silence almost painful.

The flikit was upside down and in a steep tilt, the nose crumpled against the trunk of the large tree whose branches were supporting it. Shadith was hanging head down and, due to the tilt, higher than Marrin. She fumbled for the catch on the crash web, swore when her fingers touched hot, twisted composite, swore again when she heard Marrin's catch open with that crisp bright click of finely machined parts.

Marrin chuckled. "Stuck?" He was clinging to the loosened web so he wouldn't fall out of the wreck before he was ready to leave it.

"Definitely. You'll have to cut me loose." She sighed as she watched him swing his body so he could get a foothold on the side of the flikit and reach the storage bins. She started wriggling around to see if she could find a way to get out of the web without waiting for Marrin and his cutter, but adding her movements to his made the limbs the flikit rested on creak alarmingly and the flikit itself began to wobble so she stopped that.

"Hah. Got it."

She heard the creak as he started pulling a bin door open.

"Pissssgattt!"

The flikit rocked wildly as he swung back into sight,

pushed off again. She heard the clatter and rattle as the bin emptied itself, and the cutters, ropes, mealpacs and other objects hit the limbs below, then the ground.

The quality of the light was starting to change, going a deep amber. The main force of the Eolt had arrived.

Marrin got the second bin open and started throwing things out of it in what sounded like a barely controlled panic. When he was finished, the flikit rocked again as he swung back. He grabbed the web, pushed a cutter through it, then swung away, dropping from limb to limb, using them to slow him a little, but not much. As she pushed the web away from her to get a shot at cutting it, she could hear the pound of his feet as he ran off.

She chuckled. "Not one of your conventional heroes, him."

By the time she'd cut herself loose and got to the ground, he was not only out of sight, but out of hearing.

## 8

Ceam whistled a warning to the band following him, flung himself behind a small bushy silver dudur and watched the airwagon go careening over the mesuch fort. Whoever they were in there, the Chave didn't like them, that was sure.

Heruit crept up beside him. "What'n ... what's that?"

"I figure it has to be the mesuch from Banikoëh, you know, ones Ilaörn told about."

"Not doing too good, are they."

"Better them than us."

"You said it. We were figuring it was going to be easy. I dunno."

"He's getting out ... aaaahhhhh ... right. Ouch. Hit him in the tailfeathers." Ceam winced as he listened to the prolonged crashing, the sudden silence. "Figure we ought to go see?"

Heruit didn't answer. He'd gotten to his feet and was staring at the sky.

"Ihoi! Get down before the mesuch spot you." Ceam looked up, got to his feet. "Chel Dé!"

The sky was so thick with Eolt the air itself turned gold. And still they kept coming, swirling in an immense silent vortex about the mesuch fort, out beyond the reach of the mesuch weapons, round and round, the eyes you never saw only felt fixed hard upon the killing folk. Golden anger. Golden hatred colder than a killing frost.

Sound of feet running.

Ceam wrested his gaze from the spectacle to stare at the man—a stranger with light brown skin and hair like a cabhi's fleece and a way of moving that said he was very fit and strong. He carried a pellet gun, heavy and ugly with a round drum fixed before the stock.

The man glanced at Ceam as he trotted past but said nothing, made no gesture. He was frowning, an intensity about the way he looked at the mesuch fort that convinced Ceam this was the one in the airwagon. What he couldn't manage in the air he was going to try on the ground.

He dropped to one knee suddenly, settled the gun against his shoulder, went very still, moved his forefinger to tap a dark spot rimmed in shiny metal.

The pellet gun made an odd spitting sound. A hair later there was a loud blam! and one of the armored mesuch tilted over. Before the last quiver of the sound had faded, he was on his feet again and trotting off to disappear in the shadows under the trees.

A few moments later Ceam heard another blam!, then a third. As the mesuch on the walls started shooting toward the sound, blowing trees apart or slicing them up with cutter beams, he grabbed Heruit who was still watching the Eolt, tugging him deeper into the trees. "Mesuch shooting at each other," he said. "Them in the fort, they're getting nervous. Anything that moves they're going to bang away at."

Heruit rubbed at his eyes. "Maybe you know what you're talking about."

"You didn't see him?"

"Who?"

"The mesuch out of the flier."

"I was watching Them. Thousands of them, Ceam. Maybe all the Eolt there are."

"Cha oy, I know. And madder than wet cats. And they're going to get killed. Fire in the sky, Heruit. You want to watch? Me, I'd rather not see it."

## 9

Standing behind one of the largest of the kerre trees in the strip of woodland, Shadith watched the two Fior walk off, glanced out at the sky again and the circling Eolt and sighed. *Fire in the sky. Gods, I want it to stop ... they won't listen to me any more now than they did before.*

She jumped, caught one of the broad low limbs and pulled herself onto it, then climbed higher into the tree until she was nearly level with the top of the wall. She straddled the limb, looked through the flutter of leaves, saw an armored Chav flicker in and out of view as he ran past the firing slots.

From the shouts and the direction of fire, they were a lot more worried about Marrin and his rifle than they were about the gathering of the Eolt. She frowned as she tried to figure what she could do to expand that worry. If her ability to move small objects had a greater range.... She shook her head. Trouble with that was she had to be almost in armreach. The Chave were too far away. She could use the mindride to gather an army of vermin, there were plenty of small lives lying low here in the woodland strip. But she couldn't see any way it would be worth trying.

*Maybe a cutter might. . . .*

The tree shuddered as a deep, powerful HUM shook the air around her. The vibration was bearable at first, then the intensity increased as the sound grew louder. The Eolt were singing. Thousands and thousands of Eolt were singing a single note, the sound focused somehow on the Kushayt, battering at the stone walls, vibrating cracks into them.

The HUM shaking her so badly she could barely control her hands, her eyes blurring, her body shivering with it, she managed to scramble from the tree and stumble blindly.

She broke from the wooded strip into an open, cultivated area, nearly impaling herself on a torn-up wire fence and falling on her face into some kind of tuber plant.

When she got to her feet, she found herself standing in the middle of a group of silent Keteng and Fior, drowning in a pool of hostility. A stocky gray-haired Fior woman stepped forward, a middle-aged Denchok just behind her.

"Who are you?" The Fior had to shout to break through the increasing volume of the HUM.

"I am Shadith, a Harper," she shouted back. "I came with the Eolt from Chuta Meredel."

"Ah!"

As the chill around her began to bleed off, the young Fior she'd seen before pushed past the woman. "Did Danor reach the Vale?"

"Oh yes. He rode with me and Ard Maorgan to a Klobach of the Meruu. It was his grief that convinced them." She waved at the throng of Eolt.

"Ahhhhhh."

The SOUND built and built, then broke off suddenly. Wave on wave the Eolt dived at the Kushayt.

And died. Fire in the sky.

Despite the fire, some Eolt reached the walls. Pairs of them seized Chave guards and carried them high. And let them fall to crack open on the earth. Those Chave that survived this were taken up again, carried out over the Bakhul Sea and dropped to drown there.

Wave on wave, the Eolt dived and died.

One by one the Chave guards died.

Until the walls and watchtowers were free of them, the few left retreating into the buildings where the Eolt couldn't reach them.

And the fire died from the sky.

The small army of Fior and Keteng waiting in the tuber field shouted their triumph, swarmed through the woods and over the walls. They died also as they pried the last of the Chave from their holes, one, two, six or seven at a time, but by sundown there were no more Chave alive on Béluchad.

## 10

"... so the attack is over now, the Kushayt cleaned out."

Marrin was sitting in the wrack of branches and leaves at the base of the tree where the flikit was still balanced precariously overhead, talking into the com. He looked up when he saw Shadith coming through the trees, nodded somberly and continued with his report. "How many dead? Maybe in the thousands for the Eolt, as to the others...."

Shadith said, "Fifty-nine."

"Shadow says fifty-nine Keteng and Fior dead from the cleanup."

Shadith dug into the branches and lifted the harpcase she'd hidden there, slung the strap over her shoulder. Then stopped, appalled at what she heard coming over the com.

". . . too bad. All those deaths really weren't necessary."

Marrin's face paled. "What! What do you mean, Goës Koraka?"

Shadith came to kneel beside him, her hand on his shoulder.

The small voice spoke again, calm and musing in a way that brought the hairs up on her spine. She closed her fingers tighter, felt Marrin wince, took her hand away.

"I tried to get hold of you, but I couldn't get an answer. We got a call here about an hour and a half ago. From the Chave docking station. It was the Highborn Genree ni Jilet in a panic. The docking station's kephalos was going insane, the argrav was turning lethal, they didn't know when or where it would dip to nothing or max out on them, crushing whoever happened to be standing in the wrong place. And the life support systems were shutting down. He wanted us to come get him and the others." The Goës's voice vibrated with malicious glee. "He didn't want to tell me why all this was happening, but I wasn't about to put my people in harm's way so he had to convince me it wasn't a trap." He started talking faster, the words pouring out of him as he relished the telling of his enemy's humiliation.

"The Ykkuval made a pet out of one of the locals, one of those harp players like the one we dealt with. Thought he was tame and harmless. Well, the harmless pet picked the moment when the Ykkuval was linked to the kephalos to shove a poison dart in his neck and toss some sort of spores to contaminate the circuits. Even the fuel cells were corrupted. Everything went blam. The techs cleaned the kephalos up and got it running again, Genree took over and had the Security chief shot for negligence. Then things started breaking down again, so he and the other highborn took off to the Docking Station where they could be comfortable, forgetting, I suppose, if they ever knew it, that it was Chave policy to keep the station slaved to the downside kephalos.

"They're down here now, not liking it much, but alive. All the locals had to do was starve the Chave out, they wouldn't last long with no power and not much food. It's too bad we missed connections. You're hard on flikits, Aide." He was almost giggling now, he was enjoying this so much. "I'll send another for you and the Harper. I hope you don't mind if I insist my pilot do the flying."

## 11

In the blaze from Béluchad's starfield the ceremony for the dead began.

Marrin sat on the crumbling Kushayt wall with a Ridaar remote flaking the scene, while Shadith moved into the middle of the white ceramic landing pad, stood with head back, her harp at her feet, the case transformed, her sleeves ripped off, and her arms held out from her body.

Singing in muted mode the Eolt swarmed overhead, dipping to brush her with their speaking tentacles, sending shudders of pain/joy through her body at the touch, sharing with her infinitesimal bits of Eolt energy.

She settled herself on the transformed case, took up the harp and touched the strings, searching for the song that would gather the grief and say it for all of them. There were no Ards here, bonded in sioll; she was all they had.

This great death by fire became for her the death of her homeworld which was also a death by fire when Shayalin's sun went nova. It was real for her for the first time in the twenty millennia since she'd got word her home was gone. Her eyes filled with tears and she wept, grief for Shayalin mingled with grief for the death of the Eolt. For them and for herself, she played the Death Song the Weavers of Shayalin made for their own.

The Eolt sang, blending their great voices around her small one.

The Fior and Keteng knelt beside the bundles of their dead and listened to the Requiem.

And Marrin recorded it, his face grim with anger, grief and regret.

## 12

Shadith stood on the beach watching the starlit shapes of the Eolt drifting away, north south east west riding the winds to the places they'd come from. She started at a touch on her shoulder, looked around. Marrin.

"It's time to go," he said. "The flikit's here."

# Epilogue

Harpcase on the platform beside her, Shadith stood looking out over the mirrored city, watching wearily the glory that was sunset on Helvetia. Light in crimson and gold ran like water along the slippery surfaces, flickered erratically off shattered diamanté walls, was thrown in fire spears mirror to mirror, mirror on mirror on the walls of the costliest city in known space, mirror mirror everywhere, spears of gold, spears of blood, going here, going there as the mirrors changed their inclination. Gradually muting as the sky turned purple then darkened further to indigo.

"From a battle that didn't need to happen to a fizzle in court."

Aslan turned from the city, dropped a hand on Shadith's arm. "Not really, Shadow. Helvetia set their grip on Chandava Minerals where it'll hurt the most. Blood money to Yaraka Pharmaceuticals. Endangerment recompense to University for the Endowment. And Chandava is barred from University for ten years. Those aren't small things." She smiled. "Something you don't know. An hour ago the Regent's Rep got me to a privacy alcove and gave me some messages. First, you get your stock. Two shares, not one. And the Regents are putting a commendation on your record. And Burya Moy says get your tail back home, he's seen the flake of the *Eolt Requiem* and he wants you working on a polished version soonest."

Shadith watched the colors start to glow in the

Darklands. University pulled at her for a moment, but only a moment, because she'd been happy there. No more. Béluchad had taught her that. Music was as necessary as breathing, but it wasn't enough to fill her life. "No," she said. "When I get back from Quale's place, I'm going to work for Digby. It's all arranged." She listened. "That's my shuttle. Thanks, Aslan. You did me a favor when you brought me to Béluchad. Greet Maorgan for me when you go back, tell him I may drop by again one day to hear the songs he's made."

She worked the strap of the harpcase over her shoulder and walked away without looking back.